God's

'Kidogo picked up a [...] shoulder, a trick she ha[...] danger to you?'

'By the Tusks of Tembo Jay! Can't you tell I love having you with me?' He reached out his trunk-tip and touched the centre of the smaller elephant's forehead in token of love and reassurance. Together we are much safer – and it's fun having you around.'

That was typical of Rafiki, Kidogo thought. He was a real friend to have. But who was this *Tembo Jay* and what was so special about his tusks? There was still so much she had to learn. They moved off again, pulling up various small plants and bushes and enjoying the differing flavours of their foliage.

Ahead of them was a tall kopje. Kidogo liked kopjes. Sometimes she would just stand and look at the way the huge rocks were balanced on top of one another and how the trees grew out from the cracks between the rocks. She was trying to remember the word that Rafiki had taught her which meant that something looked *exactly right*. The word 'elegant' came up from memory but so did 'grotesque' which meant nothing like elegant. Yet both seemed appropriate. Could the kopje be both elegant and grotesque?

Rafiki held his trunk to the side to prevent Kidogo from walking past him. 'Tembas ahead,' he said quietly.

Also by Michael Tod

The Silver Tide
The Second Wave
The Golden Flight

Now available as a single volume –

The Dorset Squirrels

Dolphinsong
A Curlew's Cry (Poetry)

GOD'S ELEPHANTS

Michael Tod

Cadno Books

First published in Great Britain by Cadno Books in 2006
Cadno Books
P.O. Box 34
Abergavenny
NP8 1YN
e-mail: michaeltod@cadnobooks.co.uk
website: www.cadnobooks.co.uk

Cover illustration: Alison Edgson

Printed by Cox & Wyman Ltd, Reading, Berkshire

ISBN 1-898225-06-0
978-1898225-06-5

To Daphne Sheldrick,
whose work with orphaned elephants
in Kenya has saved the lives of many
of these wonderful creatures.

Acknowledgements

Many people contribute to the writing of a book such as *God's Elephants*. The unsung heroes are the editors who never seem to get a mention. Whilst writing this book I submitted it to several people for editorial comment and advice. Most notable were my wife Jo, my son Stuart, John Inns, friends and fellow writers Catherine Merriman, Barbara Anne Knight, Michael Meredith, Trish Sharpe and, on a professional basis, Helen Wire.

I would also like to pay tribute to the guides and companions on my several research visits to Africa whose skill and friendship made these expeditions so memorable.

CHAPTER ONE

High on the slopes of Kilimanjaro, late on a bitterly cold day, two elephants were following a barely discernible track that wound between tumbled black rocks. The giant heather plants and the strange, cabbage-headed groundsel trees were crisp with a frosting of ice. The wind, moaning through crevices in the rocky ridges, carried the threat of snow to come.

The smaller of the two, a young tuskless female known as Temba Kidogo, was struggling to keep up with the huge old elephant she was shadowing. She had never been so cold in her life but Tembo M'zee strode on, his trunk swinging to left and right as he sought out ancient scents and memories. His sudden snort and long sigh told Kidogo that the old one had found the object of his search. Ahead, just visible in the fading light, a huge skeleton lay at the foot of a rock wall. Rank grass grew between the arching ribs, and the massive bones of the legs were green and grey with a coating of moss and lichens although the tusks of the dead one were clean and white.

The rising wind sang an eerie tune through the cavities in the hollow skull and Kidogo shivered, not just with the cold. She had seen many skeletons of dead elephants on the plains to the north but the ivories had been hacked out of the skulls of those. The presence of the tusks here made their find even more frightening, though she could not have explained why.

She hung back, turning her rear to the wind as Tembo M'zee, ignoring her completely, knelt by the bones as if

1

asking for some kind of forgiveness, running the tip of his trunk slowly and reverently along each massive tusk.

Whispers of snow were on the wind now, forming white ridges along the mossy bones and dusting the backs of the two living animals. Moving carefully so as not to be noticed by the still kneeling M'zee, Kidogo sidled towards a huge boulder that might offer some shelter. She pulled her ears in tight against her body and tucked the end of her trunk into her mouth to stop it from freezing. She watched as M'zee, now almost completely white with snow, got to his feet, wrapped his trunk tenderly around one of the dead elephant's tusks and, with a slight twist and jerk, withdrew it from the skull. He turned his head and signalled to Kidogo to come and take the tusk from him. Shaking with both cold and fear, she left the shelter of the rock, stepped forward and wrapped her trunk around the tusk as M'zee released it from his grip. Having no tusks herself, and having never before touched one that was not part of a living, breathing elephant, she was surprised by how heavy it was. She laid it gently on the ground, found a place to hold it so the weight was more evenly balanced and lifted the tusk again.

M'zee pulled the other one from the skull, stepped back and rested it upright against a rock before tearing up a few giant heather plants to lay gently across the snow-covered ribcage of the skeleton. Then, without a word to the shivering Kidogo, he picked up the second tusk and moved away uphill. The youngster followed, wondering why they were going on *up* the mountainside rather than heading back down to the shelter of the forest. She knew it was not for her to ask – she was just a Shadow. The tip of her trunk, now exposed to the bitter wind as she struggled to maintain a grip on the cold, heavy tusk, was going numb. Half-blinded by the stinging snowflakes and unable to see the hazards of the path beneath the snow, she stumbled and fell on her knees, almost dropping her burden. When she recovered and looked up, she had lost sight of M'zee's back and tail and as she rounded a bend a surge of panic hit her. The valley ahead was just a wasteland of snow and rocks. Where was M'zee?

'Here, Kidogo.' His voice answered her unspoken question. 'In here.'

She turned her head to the right. The old elephant was standing in a cave in the rocks, sheltered from the driving snow.

'Come,' he said.

And she backed in beside him, her ears, trunk and feet numb with the cold. What am I doing here? Kidogo wondered silently.

Only a few moons before she had been standing, well fed and comfortable, at the entrance of the Tsavo Camp looking out into the bush as she waited for her friend, Tembo Rafiki, to return.

3

CHAPTER TWO

Dusk was falling as Temba Kidogo had stood under the baobab tree at the entrance to the elephant rehabilitation camp in Kenya's Tsavo Park. Behind her she could hear the murmur of human talk and the occasional muted trumping of young tembos who, like her, had been brought to the camp from the elephant orphanage on the outskirts of Nairobi. None of those in the camp were yet confident enough to leave for an independent life in the bush.

She knew that at sometime *she* would have to leave, but there was no pressure from the human keepers for this to happen before she was ready and she also knew that, even when she did leave, she would be welcomed back at any time. She had heard the humans talk of one temba who had left but had come back years later with her new baby, just to show it to the people who had looked after and loved her for so long.

She moved nearer to the grey trunk of the baobab. Tembo-trees, as the elephants called them, had always represented a kind of security to her. Perhaps it was just their huge bulk and greyness that reminded Kidogo of her dead mother. She rubbed her side against the smooth bark, knowing that *she* was not yet ready to leave the camp and the caring humans who had looked after her for so long. Even though she had seen some seventeen years pass she was still smaller than all the other elephants of her age and she had no tusks. This lack of ivories was of ever-present concern to her. Other elephants who were even younger than her had tusks. Why didn't she have any? For the tenth time that day she felt her cheeks with the tip of her trunk hoping to detect the hard, round bump that might herald the emergence of an ivory bud. Left cheek first, then the right. As usual – nothing! Only the soft wrinkles of her skin and the bristly hairs around her mouth. She snorted her disappointment.

This was not the first evening she had lingered under the baobab tree until long after it had got dark. It had been several moons since her life-long friend, Tembo Rafiki, had walked out of the camp – and not come back.

As daylight faded she could see the glow from the humans' fire lighting up the underside of the flat-topped acacia trees and she could smell the comforting scent of wood smoke drifting past her. That scent had always been a part of her life and, since she had come to this camp, so too were the various and intriguing scents of the food that the humans ate.

A night-bird called with a wavering voice that was answered by another further away, and she knew that Rafiki was *not* coming back that day. She turned and walked across the hard-packed soil to where the other youngsters were settling themselves to doze and sleep as the equatorial moon, lying on its back, moved steadily across the speckled blackness above their heads. She looked up and wondered, not for the first time, why the sparks in the sky that the humans called *stars* didn't twist about and die like the ones that flew up from their fires. But such questions were unimportant – Rafiki had *not* come back.

She hadn't slept much when a dawn-dove in the nearest tree started its wake-the-world calling. '*De daadaa, de daadaa,*' it cooed. She flicked her trunk in irritation, picked up a dry stick and tossed it in the direction of the tree but the bird carried on calling, '*De daadaa, de daadaa.*'

Kidogo left the other dozing youngsters and walked to the round water tank, where she drank deeply, squirting many trunkfuls of cool water into the back of her mouth. She stamped in the sloshy mud around the tank but mud was no fun on one's own so she drifted towards the camp entrance, just in case Rafiki might be coming back with the dawn. She waited there by the tembo-tree for a while then daringly went a little way outside to meet him. There was no more of a reason why he should come back today than on the other hundred or so days she had waited there for him but she knew he *would* be coming back someday. He wouldn't just leave her there – he was her friend!

She walked further and the bushland around her didn't seem as hostile as she had always feared. A little further and the camp was out of sight – but still no sign of Rafiki. He wouldn't have just walked away forever. He was her friend! He must be waiting for her to come to him – perhaps he was playing one of his old games and hiding from her. She looked back towards the camp, saw the smoke from the cooking fire rising above the trees but still walked on, trunk raised, testing each breeze for the scent of her friend, half convinced that it *was* all one of his games and feeling comfortable and safe now that she was so sure he was near.

Treading delicately along a dirt path through the trees, she entered a clearing and disturbed a family of warthogs rooting around in the dry grass. She stood still and watched as they dashed away, the two fully grown ones followed by their piglets, all with their tails sticking straight up in the air. Yellow and gold antelopes flickered between the distant trees and, from much further away, she could hear the neighing and nickering of a herd of zebras. She walked on, looking from side to side and scenting for her hidden friend, only partially aware that, although it was light, the sun had not appeared over the horizon as usual and that the dark-

6

grey bank of clouds to the east was rising higher and higher and coming nearer. Such things were unimportant now that she was so close to where Rafiki must be hiding. Any moment now he would rush out at her, ears wide and trunk up in a mock charge, calling out false challenges before grinning and twisting his trunk around hers in a gesture of everlasting friendship.

Kidogo was not prepared for what did happen next. Walking quietly round a patch of dense bush she almost stumbled over a family of lions tearing at the body of a zebra they had killed in the night. She glimpsed a patch of white skin striped with black before the lions raised their heads and roared at her to keep away.

In panic, she half-turned and crashed into the bush, forcing her way through hooked thorns that tore at her skin. As she ran she called to Rafiki to save her but he did not call back and in that instant she knew he was *not* nearby and that she was alone – terribly, terribly alone.

When she had fought her way out of the thorn thicket and run a sufficient distance to dare to look behind her, she realised she had not been chased at all and felt foolish for having behaved so stupidly. Lions with a fresh kill would surely not chase an elephant! Even so, she turned to face the way she had come and watched the bush for any crouching tawny-brown figures as she recovered her breath.

It was then that the storm broke. Storms had often passed over the camp at Tsavo, and the humans usually retreated to shelter in the entrances of their tents and huts to watch the flashes of lightning. Even the thunder did not seem to bother them and their unconcern was shared by the elephants who always enjoyed the cool rain falling on their backs and dripping on them from the trees.

But now, alone and still fearing the lions, Kidogo panicked again. Each flash of lightning and crash of thunder sent her running in a different direction, ears wide and trunk high, squealing for help from her absent friend.

'Rafiki – RAFIKI – **RAFIKI**,' she called, only to be drowned out by an even louder clap of thunder and the slashing and roaring of the rain. How far she ran or in what direction she did not know, but when the rain stopped as suddenly as it had started she knew she was lost.

As the clouds passed on westwards, the sun came out in an eye-hurting glare of light and all around her wisps of vapour rose from the sodden ground. Thousands of winged ants poured out of holes at the base of a tall column of hard earth to her right and spiralled into the sky while birds of many colours, sizes and shapes flew in from all directions for their feast. Some pecked at the emerging mass while others fluttered up and snatched their meals from the air.

Kidogo looked about her helplessly, and seeing even the birds as some kind of threat she wailed, 'Rafikiiiii . . .' But, even as she called she knew, deep down inside, that he was probably far away and that she *was* on her own. The storm-puddles, which only a few moons before would have been irresistible places for stamping and splashing in, seemed to hold a secret menace and every bush seemed to conceal a lion bigger than herself.

The sun was at its full height before Kidogo's fears calmed but even then the slightest unexplained sound brought on a thumping in her chest. Never having been so far out into the bush in her life, she had little idea of how to find her way back to the camp. Whichever way she looked she couldn't see the familiar outline of the hill behind the camp. She tried following her own scent but it had been washed away by the storm. She tried testing the wind for wood smoke from the humans' fires but there was no trace of that – just the warm, damp, after-rain earth smell she normally loved. She circled

8

around, hoping to find her own tracks but the storm had washed them away too.

Terrified of having to spend a night alone in the bush, she set off in a direction she hoped would bring her back to the safety of the camp. After a while, she changed her mind and took another direction, then another. At one point she scented a waterhole, the scent subtly different from the steaming, rain-moist soil all about her. Her friend Rafiki loved waterholes – if he was anywhere nearby, that would be where she would find him. Trunk out, she moved upwind to find the pool.

Zebras and gazelles were drinking at the water's edge. They looked up briefly then ignored her – elephants were no threat to them. No Rafiki! She moved slowly around the pool, under the flat-topped thorn trees, until she found a thicket of dense thorny scrub and backed into that, its tangled mass making it almost impossible for lions, imaginary or real, to creep up on her from behind. She stood watching the pool and waiting. It would be some time before it got dark. She dared not think what she would do then if Rafiki did not come. But somehow, some sense deep within her told her that he was near.

The grass around her feet was long and green. She suddenly felt hungry, curled her trunk around a tuft and pulled it up by the roots. Something in the grass wriggled, and she tossed it away and snorted.

An answering snort came from across the shallow pool in front of her. Kidogo froze, then slowly raised her trunk to the air-scenting position and looked across the muddy water. She could neither see nor smell any other creature, yet she was sure that the sound she had heard was made by another elephant like herself. Kidogo called softly, speaking in the babytalk used by elephants who had grown up being cared

9

for by humans. She knew none of the Tembotalk used by wild elephants.

A voice from across the pool answered, also in babytalk. 'Who there?' it asked and she was *almost* sure it was Rafiki's voice.

She replied, 'Me am Temba Kidogo. Who you?'

The answer was a shrill trump of delight and Rafiki broke out of the bush on the far side of the pool and splashed towards her through the shallow water, causing the zebras and the gazelles to whirl away into the scrub.

Kidogo squealed and ran forward to greet him. They met in mid-pool, bumping into each other and falling backwards onto their haunches in the water. Waves spread outwards and a pair of plovers ran back from the shoreline, complaining loudly. Still sitting, the young elephants entwined trunks in greeting, both speaking at once.

'Me scared – am glad – meet now,' Kidogo said, as Rafiki asked, 'You lone?'

'Me lone,' Kidogo confirmed, then realising that she was not checking for danger, drew back and looked around quickly.

Rafiki reassured her, using Tembotalk. 'There is no danger. I have been here several days and this is a safe place.'

Although the words were unfamiliar to her, Kidogo read the message in the sounds and the trunk and ear movements and understood. She relaxed, took a trunkful of brown water and squirted it at Rafiki who swung his trunk sideways, spraying mud and water all down Kidogo's side. He squirted more water at her and the two rolled and splashed together as they had done as babies at the orphanage in far-off Nairobi so many years before.

Eventually, covered from head to tail in slurpy mud, the two waded out and stood side by side under the trees where the warm breeze dried the mud on their skins into a hard sun- and insect-resisting casing.

Rafiki spoke at last. 'Must learn you Tembotalk. Then meet you other elephants. Babytalk not with them.'

For almost three moons they wandered through the bush together as Rafiki taught his companion the language of the wild elephants. Kidogo learned rapidly. Although the language was complex and subtle it seemed to come naturally to her. The combination of throat and trunk sounds with body stances and trunk gestures enabled her to convey the most varied range of thoughts and ideas. Once she had mastered these Rafiki taught her the names for all the other creatures of the bush, the trees and the plants and for the senses of smell, touch, sight, taste and sound. She learned the words to describe the weather, and how she *felt* about things. After knowing only babytalk, Kidogo was excited by her ability to tell her friend about the things that interested her. They talked about the times they remembered from the past. They talked about the various pale-skinned and dark-skinned humans who had been at the orphanage and the camp and compared their experiences of them. Both elephants had learned to understand what they had heard the humans discussing between themselves in mantalk but had been unable to join in any of the conversations or convey the fact that they understood them. Humans could make such a wide range of sounds and words with just their mouths. Now, knowing Tembotalk, Rafiki and Kidogo conversed almost continuously – even when feeding.

They practised singing low~sound, with which elephants can communicate over long distances and which is heard as much with the feet as with the ears.

'Humans can't hear low~sound,' Rafiki told Kidogo. 'Maybe it's because their ears are so small and they wear

11

shoes on their feet. Anyway low~sound goes like this. He stood still and concentrated.

Kidogo could feel a vibration in the air and a sort of tremor in the ground. At first she could not detect any words – just a pattern of senses.

Dum de dum de ~ **dum** de dum de
Dum de dum de ~ **dum** de dum de.

Then she could detect Rafiki's voice within the sensations.

'Let the words come ~ do not seek them.
Only tembos ~ sing in low sound.'

She tried to produce the same feelings from within her head, and after a while the sounds came easily. Her first success was when she sang:

'You Rafiki ~ me Kidogo.
We good friends are ~ always will be.'

After this they practised at least once a day, taking turns to compose and to listen and soon it became almost as simple for them to converse in low~sound as with their other forms of speech.

One day, as they were resting under a tall tree on the edge of a riverbank, Kidogo asked Rafiki how he had learned low~sound and the language of the wild elephants.

'You know me – always wanting to find out things! What's beyond that hill? Why do humans do that? What's inside a termite mound? What's this? Why is that? Well – when I left the camp I tried to meet as many other tembos as I could and find out what *they* knew. I tried to join up with families of females but they mostly ignored me. What I didn't know then, because we had always lived with humans, was that families of wild tembos encourage the young males to leave when they are about fourteen years old. I say *encourage,* but the Tembella – that's what they call the eldest female who leads the family – is quite brutal. When *she* decides that a young tembull is ready to fend for himself she pushes him out of the family herself – even if he's her own son!'

Kidogo thought about this. There must be a good reason for such behaviour but she couldn't think what it might be.

'So *who* taught you?'

'I joined up with other young tembulls. They call themselves *jostlers* because they mostly go about in groups – but they all seem to have an obsession with size. They have this idea that the biggest and strongest is the *best* tembo and they spend much of their time shoving and jostling one another. It seemed stupid to me so I always let them think they were better than me and, after that, we got along fine. I talked a lot with them and I learned the language but they didn't really know much else and didn't seem interested in what I had done. Mostly the jostlers wanted to talk about themselves or about certain females with whom they wanted to joyn. I had hoped to make friends with an older tembull but *they* just ignored me.'

Kidogo wanted to ask Rafiki why he had gone away without her but put off doing so until she was sure that she could get the question right.

Her chance came one morning as the dawn-doves were calling their **Dee-daadaa, dee-daadaa's** in the thorn trees and the friends were walking through the bush together, each young elephant sweeping up trunkfuls of long grass and pushing the green bundles into their mouths. Kidogo chewed a mouthful and swallowed it before she spoke.

'Why did you leave without me?' she asked. 'I missed you so much, Rafiki. The other elephants didn't seem to want to bother with me because I was smaller than them – even though I was just as old as they were. And because I

13

had no tusks. I missed you so much,' she said again.

Rafiki finished his mouthful before answering. 'You *are* small,' he said. 'And you don't have any tusks – but that wasn't why I went away on my own. I needed to get out and learn how real wild elephants do things and you were so— well, *scared* of everything. So nervous all the time. I didn't think that I could protect you properly – and that would have been dangerous for us both.'

Kidogo picked up a stick and scratched her right shoulder, a trick she had seen Rafiki do. 'Am I *still* a danger to you?'

'By the Tusks of Tembo Jay! Can't you tell I love having you with me?' He reached out his trunk-tip and touched the centre of the smaller elephant's forehead in a token of love and reassurance. 'I wish *I* could see as well as *you* can. Everything beyond that bush is blurred to me. The eyes of most tembos are like mine. *Together* we are much safer – and it's fun having you around.'

That was typical of Rafiki, Kidogo thought. He was a real friend to have. But who was this *Tembo Jay* and what was so special about his tusks? There was still so much she had to learn. They moved off again, pulling up various small plants and bushes and enjoying the differing flavours of their foliage.

Ahead of them was a tall kopje. Kidogo liked kopjes. Sometimes she would just stand and look at the way the huge rocks were balanced on top of one another and how the trees grew out from the cracks between the rocks. She was trying to remember the word that Rafiki had taught her which meant that something looked *exactly right*. The word 'elegant' came up from memory but so did 'grotesque' which meant nothing like elegant. Yet both seemed appropriate. Could the kopje be both elegant and grotesque?

Rafiki held his trunk out to the side to prevent Kidogo

from walking past him. 'Tembas ahead,' he said quietly.

They had seen other elephants during their wanderings together but had not gone near them. At first, Rafiki had been reluctant to approach the family groups.

'They think because I'm a male all I'll want to do is joyn with their daughters. One day they'll probably be right. I expect they wonder what *you* are doing – females are always part of a family.'

Sometimes they had seen older males following the herds, trickles of sticky liquid oozing from either side of their foreheads. Those huge males had all seemed to be oblivious of anything but a desire to be near one of the females, even though the females were apparently trying to ignore all of them.

'It's the mustdo madness,' Rafiki had told her. 'It'll happen to me when I get older. All males get it – I don't know if it's a good thing or a bad thing!'

The family that Rafiki had scented was moving slowly across the open ground in front of them. Knowing now that Rafiki's eyesight was less sharp than her own, Kidogo described them.

'There's a big female in the front,' she said. 'Then one, two, three . . . six . . . ten other females, with five babies. All the older ones have tusks,' she added, envy in her voice. 'They've seen us. They've stopped and are looking this way. I'd like to talk to them.'

Rafiki sang out an ancient greeting to the females, using low~sound.

'Love, live long and ~ find sweet-water.'

The leader raised her trunk and sang back.

'May Mana bless ~ and keep you safe,
Tembo Jay and ~ goodness guide you.'

The other females acknowledged Rafiki and Kidogo with a slight raising of their trunks and the older calves edged forward trying to get a closer look at the strangers before being summoned back into line by their mothers or aunts with a slap of a trunk or a nudge with a tusk.

The Tembella walked up to Kidogo and asked sharply, 'Why are you alone with a male?'

'He's my friend,' Kidogo answered, wondering at the disapproving tone in the Tembella's voice.

'How long have you been like that?' the Tembella asked.

'Rafiki has *always* been my friend.'

'I meant – how long have you been alone with a male?'

Rafiki stepped forward to intervene but the Tembella waved him away. 'You. You stay over there.' She pointed to the kopje.

Such was the authority in her voice, Rafiki obeyed meekly and walked away to stand in the shade of a giant fig tree growing out of a crevice in the rocks.

Without him by her side Kidogo felt very uncomfortable. The female was so much larger than she was and had a fine pair of tusks. Unconsciously she felt her own barren cheeks. The Tembella reached out her trunk and sniffed behind Kidogo's ears, first one, then the other.

'You are kin of ours,' she said. 'Distant – but definitely our kin. You may join *us*.'

Kidogo looked towards Rafiki who stood, trunk hanging loose, under the spreading branches of the fig, then across at the females and the babies. She wanted to run over and fondle the ears and the tiny trunks of the little ones and had a great urge to belong to a large group. She would feel so safe amongst so many.

'Can my friend join too?' she asked.

The Tembella snorted.

'Of course not – he is far too old! Tembos of that age are nothing but trouble.'

'But he's my friend,' protested Kidogo.

'At your age, your friends should be within the family,' the Tembella said scathingly.

Kidogo realised that it had been an honour to be invited to join but she was not going to leave Rafiki. They needed each other more than she needed a family.

'I thank you for your kindness,' she said formally. 'But I choose to stay with my friend.'

The Tembella dismissed her with a wave of her trunk. 'So be it. May Tembo Jay guide you.' Then, as though having second thoughts, she reached out her trunk and touched Kidogo's forehead. 'Fare well,' she said, then turned and ambled back to the rest of her family.

Kidogo watched them move away into the trees. Rafiki came and stood beside her but did not speak.

'Did you hear what was said?' she asked.

'Most of it,' he replied and, like the Tembella had done, he touched her forehead with his trunk.

After watching the last of the family disappear, he stepped forward and sniffed at a pile of newly-dropped dung. 'They're well fed and have drunk recently. They were not in a hurry, so it's likely that where they have come from is safe.'

The mention of 'safe' made Kidogo look round nervously. *Should* she have gone with the others? Being with Rafiki had allowed her to be more relaxed recently but she was still acutely aware that danger for elephants in ones and twos might be lurking anywhere. At her feet dung beetles were tearing half-digested fibres from the steaming pile and forming them into round balls. She snuffled at one of the beetles, which raised its antlered head ready to defend the ball it had just made, before starting to roll it away into the grass at the side of the path. Kidogo thought, I have only to place a foot thoughtlessly and that beetle would be dead. No creature was *really* safe.

'We'll follow the tembas' tracks back to the last place they drank, and rest up there,' Rafiki announced.

The tembas' foot-scent was fading as they walked and when they reached the water it was in the bed of a river that had ceased to flow with the arrival of the dry season. The riverbed was now a series of muddy pools in which storks and herons waded, stabbing at the fish trapped there. Crocodiles lay on the banks of one pool they passed, mouths gaping in the sun. Birds pecked around the teeth of the huge reptiles, somehow knowing that the scaly beasts would not snap their mouths shut while they were busy there.

'Stay clear of those water-biters,' Rafiki warned Kidogo. 'They'll grab your trunk when you drink and bite it off. See those teeth!'

Kidogo looked at the resting monsters, saw their cold and hungry eyes watching her, shivered and hurried on. Water-biters weren't like any other animals she had seen. All the others she could think of had *some* warmth about them – but not these. She would never go near a place where such fearsome creatures might be lurking.

Far from the pool, the two friends stopped and rested in a grove of acacia trees on a high ridge where even Kidogo felt that no water-biters would ever find them.

CHAPTER THREE

Temba Kidogo slept little that night. The moon was full and the bush was alive with the calls of night creatures. A lion grunted not far away and a skulk of hyenas laughed and quarrelled amongst themselves over towards the riverbed. When she did sleep, Kidogo dreamed of water-biters snapping at her trunk and wondered if an elephant could live with the end of its trunk missing. Thinking how sensitive every part of her own trunk was, the pain would be cruel and the tembo must surely starve, unable to feed itself. Rafiki seemed to have no such fears and dozed for most of the night, shifting his weight occasionally to rest one of his legs at a time. Near dawn he even lay down and snored while Kidogo watched nervously, twitching and staring in the direction of every unexpected sound.

Watching him lying there, Kidogo thought about Tembo Jay. Who was he and why had Rafiki used the words, 'By the Tusks of Tembo Jay'?

The leader of the family they had met had also mentioned the name in her response to Rafiki's greeting. *'Tembo Jay and ~ goodness guide you',* the Tembella had said. She would ask Rafiki when he woke. Then she also remembered the leader saying, *'May Mana bless ~ and keep you safe'.* Who was *Mana*? There was so much to learn. She would ask about Tembo Jay first. If Tembo Jay had tusks he must be an elephant like herself. Mana, whoever or whatever it was, could wait.

When her friend did open his eyes and heave himself to his feet, Kidogo thought it best not to ask questions immediately. It sometimes took Rafiki quite a while to be ready to talk. He would first pass water, then dung, accompanied by great gusts of wind, then he would walk round in circles several times. Kidogo followed him about as he did all of these before she said a word.

They started to browse on some half-grown thorn trees. The flavour of the foliage was exquisite but long sharp thorns protected each tiny cluster of leaves. Both elephants were cautiously folding the foliage into their mouths while trying to keep their tongues away from the hard spines until they had ground them to harmless fibres with their teeth. Kidogo swallowed her mouthful and asked her friend, 'Who is Tembo Jay?'

'Who *was* Tembo Jay,' Rafiki corrected her. 'He died – well actually he was killed – about two thousand years ago. I don't know much about him but he must have been a very special elephant to be remembered after all that time.'

'Yesterday you said, *By the Tusks of Tembo Jay*. What did *that* mean,' Kidogo asked.

'It's just something that elephants say, when it's important, or if you are a bit cross. Did I say it yesterday?'

'Yes. When I asked if I was still a danger to you, you said, *By the Tusks of Tembo Jay* that you loved having me with you. Do you really?'

'By the Tusks of Tembo Jay—' Rafiki stopped and they both chuckled. 'There you are,' he said. 'It's something you say without really thinking. But Tembo Jay's tusks must have been very special to be talked about after all this time.'

Kidogo looked at Rafiki's tusks. She was sure they were longer and perhaps even thicker than when they had met at the waterhole. Then, when she thought her friend wasn't looking, she felt her own cheeks but there were still no

20

bumps on either side and certainly no smooth ivory buds. Why not, oh why not?

Rafiki *had* noticed her actions and came and put his trunk-tip to Kidogo's forehead. 'It bothers you that you are tuskless,' he said. It was a statement, not a question, and Kidogo fondled her friend's trunk with her own, then stroked his tusks.

'It has always bothered me. I suppose it's silly really. I've seen many elephants without tusks – mostly ones who are scared all the time – like me. Confident elephants like you always seem to have tusks. Perhaps it's *because* you have tusks that you are so confident.'

'It could work the other way,' Rafiki said. 'It may be that being scared all the time stops them growing. I don't really know. I don't know much about Tembo Jay either.'

'Who would know?'

Rafiki swung his trunk slowly from side to side. He was thinking.

'This is really important to you, isn't it? And *I'd* like to know too! I've been told that there is a very knowledgeable old tembull down at Amboseli. He lives near the swamp there. We could go and ask him. His name is Tembo M'zee. He should know – if he's as wise as they say.'

Kidogo knew that *M'zee* meant The Wise One. 'Could we go?' she asked. 'How far is it to Amboseli?'

Rafiki pointed with his trunk to what looked like a thin curved cloud in the sky to the south.

'That's water on the top of the Holy Mountain. I was once told it is so cold up there that the water gets hard and turns white – which I'd be really interested to see. You'd think that water is always just water. Amboseli Swamp is on this side of that mountain. Tembo M'zee lives there. It'll take us five days – three if we hurry.'

21

Tembo M'zee was feeling his age. In the sixty years of his life he had seen many changes and sired many calves. Now his legs often seemed extra tired and he was even more inclined to sleep through the heat of the day. He especially enjoyed wading deep into the swamp so that the cool water and mud half supported his weight. There he would suck up a thin slurry from around the roots of the reeds and spray it over his back to keep his skin cool. If he could find a dense mass of vegetation on which to rest his huge tusks he could be even more comfortable. In this restful state he would dream away the hot afternoons remembering the excitements of a full life and the many females he had joyned with when he was in his glorious prime. It would not be long now before he stepped-over. His last teeth were beginning to break up and soon he would not be able to eat enough to stay alive. He was not afraid of this happening – it came to all tembos, in fact to all living creatures, in time.

One thing *was* bothering him. He was sure the ice cap on Holy Mountain was getting smaller year by year and that this in some way affected him, though how, he never could work out. In the late evenings and early mornings when the head of the mountain was clear of clouds, he would look at the white streak high above him. *Was* it smaller than it used to be? He thought it was – but could not be sure.

CHAPTER FOUR

De/ne could smell porcupine. Had anyone asked him what a porcupine smelled like he would have grinned and replied, 'Another porcupine.'

Most of the civilised world would have called De/ne a Bushman, although it is now considered more politically correct to use the term 'one of the San People'. If anyone had asked *him*, De/ne would have referred to himself as 'one of the First People', his race having lived throughout most of Africa until dispossessed by dark-skinned people spreading south and pale-skinned people moving northwards with their cattle and sheep from what Mr Fotheringay had always called 'The Cape'. De/ne knew this but would not boast of his ancestry to others, although he was proud to have two granddaughters who had recently matured into beautiful young women.

In the leather bag he carried slung over his shoulder was a supply of dried meat, berries and shrivelled edible tubers but he was tempted by the thought of porcupine roasted over the embers of a fire.

The sun was low on the horizon, so the scent must be coming from a burrow as the creatures did not normally emerge until nightfall. He walked slowly upwind, reading the tracks in the dusty pathway until he could see the opening just beyond a mound of excavated sand. He crouched beside a bush and waited, his bag, his bow and the quiver of arrows on the ground by his side, his spear held ready in his right hand.

Hardly moving his head he scanned the foliage of the bush until he could see Mantis, crouched on a twig and watching him with its all-knowing eyes while holding its front legs together in a way that reminded him of his granddaughters' English father praying to his God – the one who lived in the sky above their heads and who was, in De/ne's mind, not a very nice God at all. De/ne preferred Mantis who was always near when you needed him.

'Roast porcupine,' he murmured, knowing he would shortly be eating the delicious meat. Had anyone asked him what porcupine tasted like, he would have grinned and replied, 'Another porcupine.'

The first porcupine to leave the burrow De/ne killed with a clean thrust of his spear, and after thanking it and its family, still in the burrow, for giving him its life he carried the body of the young male well downwind. Here, in an open place where there was no danger of it spreading, he lit a fire with his fire-sticks, and while the wood burned down to a bed of glowing embers he plucked out the black-and-white spines and skinned the animal, using the red-handled knife with the many blades that Mr Fotheringay had given him on his deathbed.

De/ne lay back with a full belly and looked up at the stars, each one the soul of a dead person. He had his own ideas as to which of the stars was his daughter and which was his wife but wondered if his daughter's English husband, the late Mr Fotheringay, had become a star or whether he was in that invisible place he had called *Heaven*, where he would be living with his God who looked like an Englishman with a white beard.

De/ne moved closer to the fire to keep warm as the air grew colder. Tomorrow he would continue his quest to find worthy husbands for his granddaughters.

Kidogo and Rafiki had not expected to see so many humans at Amboseli. The people here always stayed in their vehicles, which were everywhere, but they didn't bother the two friends, who had been accustomed to them during most of their lives. Kidogo spotted the vast bulk of a heavily-tusked tembull half-submerged in the swamp and they waded towards him, the cool mud sucking at their feet.

Rafiki sang a courteous greeting in low~sound to the old one.

'Love, live long and ~ find sweet-water,'

And the tembull responded.

'May Mana bless ~ and keep you safe.'

'How are you both named?' the old one then asked.

Kidogo sensed a warmth in his voice and was glad. Some of the older tembulls they had met had been morose and irritable.

'We are Tembo Rafiki and Temba Kidogo,' Rafiki called back.

'So, *Friendly* and *Little* ones, what is it you want of me?'

Kidogo waited for Rafiki to reply then, when he didn't, she said, 'We would like to learn about Tembo Jay, Great One.'

'M'zee will do, little Kidogo. I need no fancy titles – my tusks speak for me. As for the blesséd Tembo Jay, what do you want to know?'

'Everything you can tell us,' Kidogo replied, feeling a sudden itching on her left cheek. Could it be a tusk starting to grow? Oh joy if it was. She touched the spot and felt a bug wriggle under her trunk-tip. It must have crawled up from the swamp. She brushed it away, disappointed.

'Make yourselves comfortable,' the old one said, reaching deep into the mud and spraying an extra layer over his back.

Kidogo and Rafiki waded nearer until they were almost within trunk-reach and stopped to spray their backs as the old one had done. The mud was delightfully slurpy and cool. A flight of ibis flew over and a kingfisher perched on a sloping papyrus stem watching, with its head tilted, and looking as though it too was waiting to hear what M'zee had to tell.

'Tembo Jay . . . ahh . . . *Tembo Jay.*' M'zee spoke slowly, as if he had to gather his thoughts. 'Just so. Just so. Well, once, long ago, long, long ago, elephants were not the gentle, kind and caring creatures we are now. The biggest tembulls were always fighting one another and were arrogant and greedy. They stayed in the deepest shade or the coolest pools and forced other elephants to gather food and bring it to them. They bullied the smaller ones and thought only of their own comfort and prestige.'

'What is prestige?' Kidogo asked.

'It is nothing now, when all elephants are of equal worth to Mana, but *then* it meant who was the strongest or the most feared.'

Kidogo thought of asking who Mana was but did not want to interrupt again, and M'zee resumed his story.

'Well. Just so. Just so. The big tembulls were called 'Yellow Tusks' by the others, but never when they could be overheard, for the Yellow Tusks had short tempers and would readily kill any tembo who upset them. It was a bad time – but it had been that way for so long it was accepted that was how it *had* to be. In those days, when young tembulls reached a certain size, they challenged the older ones to fight to the death and, if they won by killing the older one, they became a Yellow Tusk in his place. It was a bad time. Ahh. A bad, bad time. The females, Mana bless them, tried to stay out of the way of the Yellow Tusks except when they carried fodder to them. But they were often *forced* to joyn with the Yellow Tusks and bear their calves. Joyning should only ever be an act of great pleasure. It was a bad, bad time,' he said again.

'Were *you* there?' Kidogo asked.

M'zee snorted in amusement. 'Mana forbid!' he said. 'This all happened some two thousand years ago! There have been a hundred or more generations of gentle elephants since then.' He sprayed his back again and the two youngsters copied him. The mud was cool and refreshing. Rafiki plucked a few reeds and chewed them as he listened.

'Ahh. Tembo Jay,' M'zee said, his voice full of respect. 'Well now. Tembo Jay was just an ordinary elephant when he was small – but he had the most remarkable tusks. Later, by the time he was killed, they were the biggest known on any elephant, ever. They were so long they crossed one another at the tip. Just so.' He raised his trunk and showed in the air how they had crossed.

'But of course, when he was young, his tusks didn't do that and Tembo Jay wasn't like the other tembulls either. He didn't bully the smaller ones or demand to joyn with the females. He just went round quietly saying that Life did not have to be that way. He taught the other elephants that Love was the most important thing and that care and compassion were better than greed and arrogance. Of course, the Yellow Tusks didn't like what he was teaching. If Tembo Jay's ideas were to catch on then *they* would have to leave the shade and forage for themselves and not have their selfish rights over the females.

'So, whenever Tembo Jay came near them, they challenged him to fights but he always turned his back and walked away with the Yellow Tusks jeering after him. But he just sang his Song – the words of which have been forgotten now – and more and more elephants heard his Song and knew that what he taught was a better way of living. The Yellow Tusks hated him and arranged for Tembo Jay to be killed in a terrible and painful way, as an example to the others.' He paused and looked thoughtful.

27

'*How* was he killed?' Kidogo asked.

M'zee was silent for a long time, then said, 'Well! It's not important how he *died*. It's how he *lived* that's important!'

Having decided he had said enough for one day, Tembo M'zee snorted a that's-all-for-now snort and closed his eyes. If the youngsters wanted to know more, they would come back. It was best for them to learn a little at a time. When he had mentioned Mana both had looked puzzled. Could it be that they didn't know about Mana either? Where had they grown up? Had their Tembella never told them what every young elephant should know? If they hadn't known about Tembo Jay, nor about Mana, was it possible that they didn't know the true meaning of Love, either? He would call after them to come back the next day.

He looked up and saw the two youngsters splashing ashore. Many of the wheeled vehicles full of humans had stopped and M'zee knew he and the youngsters were being watched. They were probably uneasy at having to walk past so many vehicles so he didn't call out to them. Then he thought he *would* call but in low~sound. He knew the humans couldn't sense that. Then he decided not to do that either. The two young elephants would almost certainly come back sometime anyway. He lowered his head and drifted off into a dream.

In his dream he was a bird. A bird flying over Holy Mountain which towered above where he knew he was in *reality*, half-submerged in the swamp of Amboseli. Flying was strange but exciting. The great bulk of his body was far below, down in the reeds and the mud but *he* was up here, floating weightless on the wind, like one of the long-legged storks that paced around the swamp, or even one of the eaters-of-dead-flesh whose real name was never spoken aloud by the elephants. The air around the mountain felt crisp and cold and his vision was clearer than it had ever been. Perhaps all birds saw things this clearly.

He floated up past the forests and past great open slopes covered with strange, oddly shaped plants that he had seen only once before. Somewhere below him, amongst the dark rocks and the strange plants, lay the remains of Tembo Steadfast and he once more felt the savage pang of guilt at having killed his friend, even though that had been so long ago.

Up and up he soared, through the thin mists he guessed were the clouds which so often hid the top of Holy Mountain. He caught glimpses of steep slopes of fine loose stones, then, as he passed over the edge of the hard-water, he rose above the swirling mists into brilliant sunlight, which made him blink his eyes. Higher still and he could see into a vast hollow in the top of the mountain. There were walls of ice around the sides of the hollow but, far down at its centre a small cone was giving out little puffs of smoke. M'zee sensed that the whole mountain was alive – but sleeping.

He drew his wings closer to his body and dropped down past the columns and sheets of ice which formed one of the walls. Level with him now was a cave and inside it he could see two huge tusks lying with their points crossed just as he had described Tembo Jay's tusks to the two youngsters. Love radiated from the tusks and engulfed him—

M'zee woke with a snort. The two white egrets perched on his back rose up into the air, flew in a small circle, dropped down and settled again. The vehicles had gone, taking all the humans away, and he couldn't see the two young elephants anywhere either. The clouds had cleared from Holy Mountain and the setting sun was turning the snow red on the summit. Even though his body was deep in the cool water and mud of the swamp, M'zee realised with awe that somehow he had just seen the tusks of the long-dead Tembo Jay!

29

CHAPTER FIVE

M'wangi Kamathi sat on the low rocky ridge watching the setting sun colour the mountain top as he smoked the thin cigarette he had just made with the last of his tobacco. As he did so he stroked the barrel of the AK47 he had been given by the smartly-dressed big man in the black Mercedes behind the Uhuru Stadium in Nairobi. The gun, ugly and functional as it was, would be his passport to riches. The big man had told him that if he shot a tusk-bearing elephant and brought the ivory to him, he would give him more money than he could earn working in the city for ten years. Then he, M'wangi from Kiambu, could get his eldest son into a good school and the boy would grow up to be a big man in the Government and be driven around in a black Mercedes. His son would then make sure his father and the rest of his family would never again go hungry. The big man had made it sound so easy.

Two months of walking through the bush without seeing a single elephant, let alone one with tusks, had toughened him up both mentally and physically. M'wangi had not realised how soft he had become since he'd gone to live in the city but he had not forgotten the lessons he had learned as a boy. He knew how to make fire by twirling the end of one stick into a notch in another and, using an old, dry birds-nest to catch the glowing embers, he could blow them into a flame. He knew he must keep the fire small to avoid it being seen and he knew how to make posho porridge with the maize meal he carried in a small canvas bag. He knew how to vary his diet with nestlings taken from the weaverbirds' nests that hung in clusters from riverbank trees, and he had sometimes been able to spear fish in a drying-out pool.

Now, at last, he had seen fresh elephant droppings. He counted the bullets the big man had given him, regretting that there had not been enough for him to practise firing the gun. He aimed at an imaginary elephant's head and mimed pulling the trigger.

When two real elephants came into view his hand was not so steady.

Kidogo walked nervously past the vehicles full of humans. There were *so many* of them and she did not recognise any of the faces peering at her from the windows. She and Rafiki knew that humans called the vehicles *four-by-fours* but neither of them understood the name. Some of these were striped to look like the zebras they had so often seen on the plains – others were a drab dust colour.

Rafiki seemed less concerned than she was and said, 'Here we are safe – the humans do not allow elephants to be killed at Amboseli. Soon the *four-by-fours* will leave – none stay after dusk.'

He was right. As the sun dropped towards the western hills the vehicles turned away from the swamp and moved out of sight. The acrid stench from their low down dung-holes hung in the air long after they had gone.

They were walking across rocky ground which was ribbed with small ridges. Tall termite mounds were all about them. Some, higher than a man, had ventilation holes near their tops, others abandoned and dead, had weathered down to low mounds of hard-packed soil on which no plants grew. The vegetation here was sparse and the two elephants were finding little to satisfy their appetite. Although Kidogo was uneasy, Rafiki walked ahead, swinging his trunk carelessly.

Kidogo stopped and sniffed the air. She had caught a slight human scent. Not the sickly-sweet smell of soap-clean bodies but the harsh scent of human sweat mixed with smoke. She sang out to Rafiki in low~sound.

'Take care my friend ~ I scent—'

Her warning was cut short by a crackle of shots. She stopped and stepped backwards, trembling. She could see Rafiki on his knees making whimpering sounds and a human behind a bush, struggling with a gun. The man had shot her friend! Enraged, she rushed at the man, seized him in her trunk as he started to run and threw him high into the air, the gun flying from his hand. The man screamed as he fell, then lay writhing in the dust, whimpering like Rafiki. Kidogo trumped angrily, strode to where the man lay and knelt on his chest, feeling the bones crack and collapse under her weight. Soon the man's arms and legs stopped moving and dark blood trickled out of the corner of his mouth. Kidogo got up, kicked at the body with her foot, turned and went over to where Rafiki, who had struggled to get up, was standing now, feeling along his left tusk with his trunk. The end of the tusk was shattered, leaving a jagged, broken end. Otherwise he seemed unhurt.

'Where – where is the human?' Rafiki asked, his voice shaking.

'Over there – dead,' Kidogo replied casually. 'That'll teach him to shoot at tembos.'

Then the enormity of what she had done hit her like a falling tree. Had it been an act of courage or blind rage? She suspected it was the latter and felt horrified at what she had done. Life – any life – should be more precious than that.

Rafiki walked slowly over to the body and sniffed it.

'Thank you,' he said to Kidogo. 'But now the humans will name you a *rogue* and try to kill you.' He searched among the bushes until he found the gun, picked it up cautiously and smashed it again and again against a rock.

'Come,' he said. 'Follow me. We must leave this place. Now!'

After talking with Rafiki and Kidogo and dreaming of finding the tusks of Tembo Jay, Tembo M'zee had heaved himself out of the swamp. Where were those youngsters now? He had enjoyed teaching them. Their bright-eyed interest had excited him in an almost forgotten way. He regretted letting them just drift away. Supposing they *didn't* come back?

He was standing indecisively in the short reeds on the shoreline when he thought he heard distant shots. Humans rarely fired guns around Amboseli. He must be mistaken – it might just have been the clacking sound of a dung-beetle flying past his ear. Even so, he was concerned and felt he should investigate.

He set off cautiously in the direction he had seen the two young elephants take when they had left the swamp, crossed the vehicle track and slipped quietly into the bushland on the far side.

After climbing several ridges he heard the quarrelling of hyenas and could smell the scent of a recently dead carcase. Mixed with the death-smell was the scent of an unwashed human's clothing and an especially rank and unpleasant smoke smell. He followed up the scents and drove three hyenas away from a gnawed-at human corpse. He sniffed it disdainfully. There was a pile of elephant droppings close by, still tinged with the odour of fear and, searching further into the bush, he found the mangled gun. On the ground were splinters of ivory but no indication that any elephant had been otherwise injured.

Relieved at this, he picked up the man's corpse and carried it further into the bush, then as darkness was falling

33

he covered the body with rocks to keep the hyenas from gnawing it further or dragging the skull or other bones to where humans might find them.

When he was satisfied with this, he returned to pick up the fragments of ivory one by one and drop them into a hole in the top of the nearest termite mound. Finally, he took up the mangled gun and carried it through the darkness to the swamp where he tossed it into one of the deeper pools. Far behind him he could hear the frustrated hyenas complaining to the moon that their meal had been taken from them, and when he raised his head he could see the summit of Holy Mountain gleaming in the moonlight. A night-bird called across the swamp, its call eerie and forlorn. The old elephant's trunk started to twitch uncontrollably and his body shuddered again and again. Something big was about to happen and he, M'zee of the Swamp, was to be a part of it, though how he knew this he would have been unable to say. Only Mana would know that.

Kidogo and Rafiki walked all night, hurrying northeast away from Amboseli and its cool, lush swamplands. The rolling, bush-covered ridges became steep hills and in the starlight they could see the bulky shapes of elands grazing between the scattered trees. Then the land sloped down and became more and more inhospitable and barren as they walked. At one place they blundered onto an ancient lava-flow where the ground was split into dark crevasses that could easily trap an elephant's foot. As the sun rose lizards crept out of cracks and lay on the rocks to warm themselves. A pair of tiny antelopes leaped delicately from one jagged rock to another, the early light silhouetting the dainty creatures against the eastern sky as they watched the elephants trying to find a way through the sharp-edged, black rocks.

It was Kidogo who eventually said they must go back and

seek a way *around* the maze of cracked rocks and distorted trees. Rafiki seemed in a kind of daze, repeatedly feeling his broken tusk and his left cheek with his trunk-tip. They turned and picked their way back, their feet sore, to skirt round the lava-flow, pushing their way through dense bushes that scratched at their skins, and only finding a more used path when the sun was well above the horizon.

Kidogo was in the lead as she walked along a dusty track with Rafiki stumbling behind her. She knew her friend was in pain and needed to rest but the trees here were sparse and would offer little shade. Although they had drunk deeply before leaving the swamp and could go for at least two more days before water became critical, it would be better if they could rest up near some pool, however muddy. They were in a part of the country where neither of them had been before and Kidogo searched her mind in the hope of summoning up some deep ancestral memory that could guide her. A giant tree appeared and vanished in an instant – had she really seen it? She looked around – nothing but scraggy thorns and leafless bushes. Behind her, Rafiki was trying to suppress a whimper of pain. They couldn't stay *here!*

'Follow me,' she called to him and strode on. Anywhere would be better than this barren place, where they would die of thirst within a few days, and she didn't know if he would be able to travel if the pain got worse.

Rafiki followed her meekly.

The path led to the top of a ridge and Kidogo stood between two towering rocks, searching the distant skyline. Far ahead she could see a clump of trees, dark in the parched, tawny-coloured landscape. By their bulk she knew them to be tembo-trees and that the huge trunks would provide cover as well as shade for them. She pointed out the baobabs to Rafiki, and led him down the path and through the bushland towards them. Strangely, as they neared the grove, the vegetation around them appeared to be green and fresh, so unlike that through which they had been passing. There was a scent of recent rain, although this was not the rainy season, and in the branches of the acacia trees above them small yellow birds were weaving intricate grass nests. Doves fluttered and coo'd in the bright green foliage.

Kidogo was only half aware of this. A great tiredness was overwhelming her as thoughts of the day before were running through her head. I *killed* a man, she was thinking. The humans will call me a *rogue*. They will try and kill *me*. But I was only trying to protect my friend. They can't kill me for that. Surely the humans would understand? Wouldn't they show compassion? But she knew, from listening to her keepers talk that, as well as killing elephants, men even killed one another. It was a pity there had never been a human Tembo Jay to teach *them* a better way of living!

She stumbled and felt Rafiki touch her back with his trunk. She must keep going for his sake.

Between the bushland and the huge-trunked trees was a swathe of open ground and above the tops of the tall grasses rippling in the breeze, she could see the shapes of three elephants standing under the grotesque branches of the baobabs. Immensely relieved, she stopped and sang a greeting in low~sound.

'Love, live long, and ~ find sweet-water.'

A female's voice called back softly.

'Here the waters ~ are always sweet.

Come. Welcome to ~ the Sacred Grove.'

Trunk raised, and with Rafiki close behind her, Kidogo moved towards the voice. The tembo-trees were growing amongst rocks that formed a circle around a large pool of clear water that bubbled and gurgled where springs forced their way up from deep underground. Standing close to the largest of the tembo-trees were the three elephants, all females. The middle one was very old, her skin wrinkled and baggy and her trunk hanging slack. Two younger but fully mature tembas stood, one either side of her, looking towards the youngsters. The old one's tusks, much longer than those of the other two, were slender and elegant, unlike the thick, heavy ones of the tembull in the swamp, old Tembo M'zee. The ancient temba's eyes were closed as though she was asleep. A heap of freshly pulled, sweetly-scented grass was nearby.

The old one moved her trunk, her eyes still closed, and spoke to her companions, the words coming slowly. 'Thank you, my sisters. You may go and drink. I will speak with our visitors.'

The Sisters stepped gracefully down a well-worn track to the water and drank.

The old female spoke. 'We have waited a long time for you to come.'

Rafiki moved forward to stand by Kidogo's side and they stood silently, waiting for her to speak again. She seemed to be gathering her strength before doing so. Her eyelids opened to reveal blank white eyeballs beneath them as she raised her trunk and reached it out towards the visitors, drawing in a deep rasping breath. 'A young male and a young female – as was told to me. Which of you has the broken tusk?'

Rafiki glanced at Kidogo. 'It is I, Ancient One,' he said. 'I am named Tembo Rafiki and this is my friend, Temba Kidogo.'

'I am Tembella Grace,' the old one introduced herself, her trunk still scenting the air in the direction of the visitors. 'My sisters are named Temba Comfort and Temba Kindness. We have awaited your arrival for a long time.'

Kidogo wondered how she could have known that they

were coming, when they had not known it themselves.

As if she could read her thoughts, Tembella Grace said, 'These trees are far more ancient and more wise than I. *They* told me of two youngsters who would come to seek sanctuary here – one with a broken tusk – but who must be taught what they don't know before being sent on to fulfil their destiny.'

Reading Kidogo's thoughts again, she said, 'Yes. Mana will tell things to the great-bodied trees that we shorter-lived ones can never hear.' She turned her head towards the youngster. 'Compared to these trees even I, who have seen more than a hundred years pass and will soon *step-over*, am short-lived.'

Kidogo found the presence of the blind old female curiously comforting and she felt much less tired. The Sisters had returned and were examining Rafiki's smashed tusk.

'When the pain is less you should rub the end on a rough rock to smooth away the jagged spikes,' one said. 'Otherwise it will catch on every twig and branch when you are feeding.'

The other disagreed. 'It will go bad in here,' she said, touching Rafiki's cheek tenderly. 'It will hurt most awfully, then the tusk will drop out and the hole in your face will heal.'

Tembella Grace reached out her trunk and felt along the whole length of the shattered tusk and then Rafiki's cheek. She lowered her trunk and pushed the pile of grass towards the youngsters.

'You must both eat,' was all she said, as her eyelids dropped shut.

Having eaten the grass, which tasted fresh and delicious, the five stood together in the shade under the baobab trees, the youngsters waiting for one of the others to speak or move. Occasionally a large, soft, mauve flower would drop from a tree onto one of their backs. Rafiki stood with his eyes closed, trembling occasionally. Kidogo was thirsty. Eventually, she asked, 'May we drink from the pool?'

Tembella Grace signalled her assent, and the Sisters led Kidogo and Rafiki down to the clear waters where they waded in before drinking. The youngsters followed them and Kidogo stood up to her belly, took up a trunkful of water and sloshed it down her throat. It was cool and sweet. She did it again and again, as did Rafiki. While the youngsters drank, the Sisters sprayed water onto them to wash away the dried mud and dust from their travels. To Kidogo it all seemed magical and exciting but Rafiki began to shiver and Temba Kindness nudged him towards the bank. He clambered out and went to lie down in the shade of one of the trees. Kidogo followed him out of the water and stood beside him.

'He needs to sleep,' Temba Comfort said. 'The hurt is deeper than we can see.'

Rafiki lay on his side through the rest of that day but woke and struggled to his feet in the early evening. Kidogo had walked a little way out from the shade and gathered a bundle of grass for him. She had been intrigued to find that the area where the grass and bushes grew strong and green, reached out only a few hundred paces all around the grove, while beyond this the bush-land was parched and dry. She had wondered why and was still puzzling over this when she looked over to where the old females had been standing. They had moved out onto a promontory above the pool and, as she watched, she saw the Sisters and Tembella Grace entwine their trunks and raise them together. They stood like that for a while, all three with closed eyes.

Soon, with the night creeping up on them, a gentle rumble of thunder sounded overhead and rain started to fall, pattering on the leaves of the trees and soaking the surrounding bushes. Night-insects started to chirrup and sing. After a while, the rain ceased and, by the light of the half moon above the trees, Kidogo could see that the three females had left the promontory and were now standing side by side where they had stood for most of the day. Had *they* made the rain come? She asked Rafiki if it was possible but got no reply. He had eaten a small amount of the grass and was now dozing on his feet, swaying slightly from side to side.

In the morning Rafiki was feeling a little better and he walked out and grazed with Kidogo and the two Sisters in the surrounding grassland. The females were kind and gentle to the youngsters and to each other, but said little. Both Sisters carried a bundle of fodder back to Tembella Grace who thanked them and waited while they chewed mouthfuls of the most tender grasses and leaves, forming a wad of the chewed foliage before taking it from their mouth and placing it reverentially in hers.

For the rest of the day the youngsters bathed in the pool or rested in the shade, Rafiki sometimes groaning or whimpering when the pain in his cheek became almost unbearable. Kidogo could do little to help him except to reach out a comforting trunk when it seemed his pain was at its worst. Later, he slept fitfully, awakening as the shadows of the baobabs lengthened. Kidogo nudged him as the elder ones again walked out onto the promontory and entwined their trunks. Shortly afterwards the rain started. 'What do you make of that?' she whispered to Rafiki.

'These are very special elephants,' her friend replied. 'If tembos everywhere could do that, this whole land would be green all year round!'

Rafiki woke as the sun rose, its rays striking the smooth, grey trunks of the huge tembo-trees. The pain in his cheek had lessened but he yearned for the touch of cool water there. He stood up, saw that Kidogo was awake and signalled that he was going down to the pool. She shook herself and followed.

He waded in, feeling the water taking much of the weight off his legs as he found a deeper place. Further on, he closed his mouth, raised his trunk high and waded on until his head was under the surface, the water cool and comforting on the hot skin of his cheek. He opened his eyes and saw shoals of small fish swimming around him. Some came forward fearlessly and nibbled at his skin while larger ones, more cautious, observed him from a distance. For the first time since the bullets had shattered his tusk, the pain subsided to a dull ache. Turning his almost weightless body he could see Kidogo coming towards him through the clear waters. He called to her in low~sound, which seemed to work as well underwater as on land.

Feeling better ~ pain is less now.

And Kidogo, who had followed him into the deeper water, sang back to him.

May this heal you ~ give you comfort.

They spent most of that day, either together in the deeper water or dozing under the trees, while Tembella Grace and the Sisters Comfort and Kindness stood patiently, seemingly at peace with themselves and the world. In the evening, when the youngsters had returned from browsing, Tembella Grace signalled to them to come onto the promontory and take part in the rainmaking.

The five stood in a circle facing inwards and entwined their trunks together. 'We call this *linquing*,' Temba Kindness told the youngsters. 'Now shut your eyes and think of rain. Nothing else – just rain – wet and cool – bringing life to the land.'

Soon Kidogo could sense that the tembo-trees behind them and all five elephants were joined in some way that caused the hairs at the tip of her trunk to bristle and tingle. She heard the gentle rumble of thunder overhead and rain started to fall, gently at first, then more heavily, splashing down on their backs and the rocks around them until Tembella Grace withdrew her trunk from the others and the rain stopped.

Kidogo took a deep breath. The scent of the rain on the leaves, the grass, the bare earth and the warm rocks was the most wonderful of all the scents she knew.

CHAPTER SIX

The next day, after the youngsters had spent a long time together in the deep water and had come out to warm up, Temba Kindness walked over to them.

'Tembella Grace believes you are ready now,' she said. 'Come with me.'

Wondering what was meant by *ready now*, they followed her to where Tembella Grace stood with her eyes closed. 'Mana has chosen you for a special role in his plans,' she announced. 'A very special role.'

Kidogo hesitated. There was that name again. But who was Mana? Should she ask – or would it all become clear soon? She had heard the word spoken several times now, always in the respectful voice elephants used when speaking of older or wiser elephants. But she did not like to interrupt.

Grace seemed to sense what the young one was thinking. 'Could it be a Truth that you *don't know* about Mana?'

'It is a Truth,' Kidogo replied. 'Is he a Wise One?'

'I am sure Mana is wise, far wiser than any elephant – but he is not an elephant and I am not even sure Mana is a *he*. In fact, no tembo has yet been able to say who or what Mana actually is. But *I* think of Mana as a *he*, a sort of invisible being who cares for us all. And that's not just caring for tembos! I believe that Mana cares for all living creatures – even humans.'

'When I was at Nairobi living with the humans I heard them speak about such a one – but not often. *They* thought he was a *he* and they called him *God*.'

'I am pleased to hear of that,' Tembella Grace said and was silent, as though digesting what she had just heard.

Eventually Kidogo said, 'I prefer the name *Mana*.'

Grace was silent again, until Kidogo asked, 'Where does one find Mana? The humans spoke to one another of a place in the sky which they called *Heaven* where their *God* lived.'

'In the days before Tembo Jay . . .' She paused. 'You *do know* about Tembo Jay?'

The two youngsters signalled 'Yes,' with their trunks, but when Kidogo remembered that the old one could not see their response, she spoke aloud, 'Yes, we do.'

Tembella Grace continued. 'In the days when the Yellow Tusks dominated tembokind, they told the other tembos that Mana lived on the top of Holy Mountain. They said that, if the other tembos didn't do what the Yellow Tusks told them to do, Mana would make the mountain burn and melt. They frightened them by saying that they would all be burned to death by flaming rocks rolling down the mountainside.'

Kidogo could see how frightening this would have been. Elephants fear fire more than anything, although having lived with humans, small fires held no fear for her.

Tembella Grace was drawing pictures in the air with her trunk. Flaming rocks tumbled and rolled, engulfing all in their path. Rafiki stepped backwards.

The Tembella lowered her trunk. 'Tembo Jay taught that this was *not* true and that the Yellow Tusks were lying. He is said to have sung a wonderful song although the actual words have been lost over the years. He taught that Mana was everywhere and we could all linque with him if we wanted to. Tembo Jay showed how this was done. That is why the Yellow Tusks hated him so much.'

'If Mana is everywhere, why can't I see him?'

'Can you *see* the wind that blows, or *see* the warmth of the sun?'

44

Kidogo had to admit that she couldn't but, after a pause to think, she said, 'I can see the *effect* of the wind, when grass bends over, trees shake and dust flies up into my eyes. And I can *feel* the sun warm on my back.'

'Exactly. You can see the *effect* of what Mana does for us and feel the warmth of his Love and, if you listen carefully, you can sometimes hear Mana talk to you – but always in a very quiet voice.'

Kidogo recalled overhearing two humans in Nairobi. One of them had said almost exactly the same thing. 'Humans call that a *conscience*,' she said.

'Now, that *is* a new thing for me to know. I didn't think humans had such things.'

It was still and quiet under the baobabs. No birds called and there was no breeze to rustle the leaves. Even the bubbling of the springs in the pool seemed muted and far away. Kindness and Comfort stood patiently watching the old one, ready to help her in any way. In the silence Kidogo noticed how white the ivories of the females were and that none of their tusks had been worn at the tips like those of the other elephants they had met.

A flower fell from a branch above them and Grace shifted her body slightly and spoke. 'I was taught about Mana by an old tembull many, many years ago, when I was about your age. He thought that Mana was somehow the intelligent parts of all creatures thinking together – outside of their bodies.'

'How could that be?' Kidogo asked. Rafiki was feeling the end of his tusk as though his thoughts were elsewhere and Kidogo was concerned for him. Usually, her friend wanted to know all he could find out about everything.

'My teacher didn't know, but we – my sisters and I – know that we elephants can linque *our* ideas through low~sound even when we are far apart, and we have heard that humans can linque *their* ideas through the wires that they hang on poles. The trees whisper to us that humans can even communicate without wires and over huge distances, though how they can do it – if they can – we do not know.'

'Humans *can* do this.' There was excitement in Kidogo's voice. 'That I learned in Nairobi. They do it with things they call *phones,* and *mobiles* and *televisions* and something they called a *radio*, though all of these were just names that I learned from hearing them talk. I do not know how any of these things work for them.'

'Exactly so! If humans can communicate with all those things, Mana, who must be greater than all humans, should be able to do much more than they can and make things better than they would be otherwise.'

Kidogo digested this along with the bellyful of grass and foliage she had eaten earlier. Rafiki appeared to be asleep standing up. She stepped closer to Tembella Grace so that her voice was less likely to wake him. 'How would Mana *know* what had to be done?' she asked quietly.

'I asked my teacher that,' Tembella Grace replied, she too keeping her voice low. 'He thought that Mana must use the eyes and ears of all his creatures to see what needs doing – then use a part of their brains, all sort of linqued together, to work out a plan. If that is true and Mana exists in all our brains linqued up, then we are all a part of Mana and Mana is in all of us. This is an idea that I like – but it is a big idea and my teacher may have got it wrong. What I *do* know is that Mana makes plans that involve us.'

'How do you know when Mana has a plan?'

'If you are a part of his plan, he will tell you what your role is – if you are listening! As I said earlier – Mana always speaks in a small voice. You expect a roar and you hear a whisper.' Tembella Grace touched Kidogo's trunk with her own. 'I believe that *you* are a part of a Mana-plan now and he has given to *me* the task of preparing you for it.'

Kidogo felt apprehensive. She was small for her age and had no tusks. Why should this Mana choose *her* for his plan – whatever it was? She said, 'I have not heard Mana speak to me – even in a small voice – so I *can't* be a part of his plan.'

Tembella Grace was silent again, then said, '*I* have heard him speak. He needs *you*. It is an honour to be chosen.'

'What do I have to do?' asked Kidogo, feeling even more apprehensive. 'What is this plan?'

'I have not been told that. It may be that Mana does not fully know himself yet – or he is being like a wise leader. A *really* wise leader does not tell the whole of a plan to those who must follow it. If a leader tells everything and the plan has to be changed, the leader will appear not to be so wise after all. We will know when Mana is ready.'

'Why would Mana choose me? I am small and tuskless. Any other tembo would be better than me.'

'It may be *because* you are small and have no tusks. It may be because you are willing to learn. It may be because you have lived with humans and understand their talk. Only Mana knows. In the meantime I must ensure that you learn as much as I can teach you.'

Rubbing his cheek with his trunk, Rafiki wandered away from the group and down to the water, where he sprayed the left side of his face. Kidogo wanted to follow him but felt she had to stay.

'I must sleep now,' Tembella Grace said. 'My sisters will tell you more. Come to me.'

As Kidogo stepped forward the old female raised her trunk and searched around until she found the centre of the young one's forehead, which she then caressed. Her trunk-tip felt dry and cool and immensely comforting and although Kidogo felt inadequate, she was thrilled by what she had been told. Then Temba Kindness led the younger one by the trunk to the shade of a baobab far enough away from Tembella Grace not to disturb her rest. Temba Comfort followed behind, and as they walked Kidogo could see Rafiki standing in the water apparently not interested in what they were doing.

The Sisters stood either side of Kidogo and they all looked out over the pool as Rafiki waded out to the deepest part. Temba Comfort spoke, her voice gentle and low. 'We believe that you know more about the lives of humans than you do about the lives of elephants.'

'That *is* a Truth. I have lived amongst humans for most of my life – but I killed one before we came here,' she said. 'He was trying to kill Rafiki,' she added in mitigation, expecting the Sisters to be shocked but they showed no emotion.

'Humans kill many tembos,' Kindness said. 'Though why Mana allows this I fail to understand.'

'Surely Mana could stop them,' Kidogo said. 'If Mana is the same as the humans' God, then he is all mighty and can do anything and stop anything.'

'How do you know the humans' god is all mighty?' Comfort asked.

'They say *All Mighty God* when they speak of him.'

'That sounds like Yellow Tusk talk. If you say something often enough and loud enough, others will accept it as a Truth. We do *not* believe that Mana is all mighty – otherwise he would not need *us* to work his plans for him.'

Kidogo was thinking about this when Kindness asked, 'Is there anything you want to know about tembos?'

Kidogo remembered the Tembella who had suggested that she join her family when they met near the kopje. 'Human females and males live all together,' she said. 'Why don't elephants?'

It was Comfort who answered. 'Females have to do the real – the serious things – the important things – in life.

They have to bear the babies and teach the youngsters all they need to know. They have to show them how to behave properly, how to find water in the dry times and how to remember the way to where food might be found when they are hungry. Females stay together to protect the others in the family. The oldest and wisest always leads and when she *steps over* the next eldest takes charge.'

Kidogo guessed that *when she steps over* meant when she died or was killed. *Steps over* sounded nicer.

Temba Kindness spoke next. 'Males have a different role. We need them to joyn with the females or no more babies would be born. Mostly that is all the males do.'

'That's not really true,' Comfort said. 'Sometimes Mana needs their size and strength for his plans. When the world was younger and there were enough elephants to linque together and call down a lot of rain, it was the males who pushed down many of the trees when the greedy forests were trying to cover *all* the lands. Then the whole country was green and no animal went hungry. I would have liked to have lived then.'

'In those days,' Comfort added, 'males sometimes had great tasks given to them. They would choose a *Shadow* from the younger ones and he would have to go wherever the older one went. If it became necessary, the Shadow had to give his life to protect the older one. Even so, young tembulls vied with each other for the honour.'

Kidogo looked down to check that Rafiki was still in the pool and asked a question that had been puzzling her for some time.

'You say that females do the important things – especially caring for babies and youngsters. But *you* live here with just Tembella Grace. How is this important?'

Comfort glanced at Kindness. 'A normal female life is not for all of us. Some choose to serve Mana in other ways.

49

Temba Kindness and I believe that it is our place to look after one so wise as she is, until it is her time to step-over. Had we not done so she would not have been here when *you* came.'

Rafiki had left the water and was coming up the path towards them. 'I'm hungry,' he said. 'Shall we go and find food?'

The next day Rafiki seemed stronger and in less pain, and he stayed with Kidogo when she stood with the three older ones for instruction. The talk of the humans' God had raised another question in her mind. It was good to be able to discuss such things with other elephants who were interested and knew so much more than she did.

'I recall one of the humans saying that their God was everywhere, not just here on the land but even out beyond the stars and had been there since before the beginning of time. *Could* that be a Truth?' she asked.

Comfort and Kindness waited for Tembella Grace to speak. The old one was obviously giving the question much thought. Eventually she said, 'If that *is* a Truth then their God can't be the same as Mana. If Mana was *that* big and *that* old he could not have an interest in you and me – and he clearly does. My teacher believed that each of the stars was like the sun, only farther away and that each may be the mother of many worlds like ours. If *that* is a Truth then I would expect each of these worlds to have their own Mana.'

She was silent again, and Kidogo tried to absorb the greatness of the thought. She looked at Rafiki but he was not listening. Having not been involved the day before, perhaps he was not able to follow what was being said. She thought about the different ideas involving God and Mana.

'Could it be that *both* are right?' she asked. 'If Mana is the intelligent parts of all creatures of one world – linqued up outside of their bodies to make one intelligence – could it be that *all* the Manas of *all* the worlds can linque up in the same way to make one *God*?'

Tembella Grace reached out, found and caressed the centre of Kidogo's forehead. 'That is a Big thought and maybe a Great one. I am beginning to see why Mana chose you, even though you are small and have no tusks. You have given *me* much to think about. Leave me to consider these ideas. My sisters will tell you anything more you may wish to know.'

Rafiki wandered away down to the pool as Kidogo stood with the females in the same place as they had the previous day. She was secretly pleased he was out of word-reach. She wanted to know more about the life of male elephants.

'What is *joyning*?' she asked.

Comfort said, 'It is a necessary thing for starting babies. As the seeds of plants must be put into the ground for them to grow – so must the seeds of elephants be planted in the bodies of females. It is the males who do this.'

'How is it done?' Kidogo asked.

It was Kindness who replied. 'There is a place under our bellies where the seeds go in and the babies come out. A male stands with his feet on a female's back and plants the seeds in there with their joyner. The males make a great thing of this – but that is *all* they have to do.'

Kidogo tried to think of it happening to her but found she could not imagine how it would feel. 'Have either of you joyned with males?' she asked.

The Sisters answered in unison, 'No.' And Tembo Comfort added, 'We chose not to have babies. We chose to serve Tembella Grace and, through her, to serve Mana.'

Somehow this admission, and Rafiki's absence, seemed to lower the formal barriers between the three and the discussion became more general with the Sisters asking as many questions about the ways of humans as Kidogo asked

51

them about the ways of tembos. When Rafiki did eventually come up out of the pool, they were standing side by side in companionable silence and the four of them wandered out into the bushland to feed. After a while the Sisters returned to Tembella Grace with trunkfuls of tender grasses, and again they chewed it into pulpy wads before placing them in her mouth. Kidogo could see Respect and Love showing in their every movement.

The next day's instruction started as before except that Rafiki went straight down to the pool.

Tembella Grace greeted Kidogo warmly, then said, 'Yesterday you offered a Great Thought which I am still considering. What can we tell *you* today?'

'Would you tell me all about *Love*?' Kidogo asked.

Tembella Grace chuckled, the sounds coming from deep in her throat. 'You want me to tell you *all* about Love. I have not that long before it will be my time to step-over. But I will try.' She raised her trunk and sniffed long and hard.

'I love the scents that tell me much about what is going on around me. I used to love the sights I saw before my eyes failed me. I love the sounds my ears hear of the songs of the birds and the wind in the trees. I love to feel the warmth of the sun and the coolness of the rain on my back. I love to have my friends beside me and I love the care they so willingly give to me. But these are *little* loves. It would be more of a Truth to call them Joys.'

Tembella Grace paused to rest, and Kidogo tried to experience each of these Joys in turn. Each was a wonderful experience. Why had she not been so aware of them before? Was it because she had always been so afraid, that there had been no room for Joys? She looked down at Rafiki standing up to his belly in the water. Was he experiencing the Joy of it – or was the pain in his face driving his Joy away?

Tembella Grace was speaking again. 'Somehow, when we can drive Fear from our minds, we can take these Joys and turn them into Love. This is the *Great* Love that grows within us and through us and flows out to support others. I believe that it is this Great Love that powers Mana in the way that humans use forces, unknown to us, to power *their* world. It is the Great Love that my sisters give that powers me beyond my normal years. And here is a secret that is known only to a few.' She lowered her voice. 'We tembos can store this Love in our tusks. Only we, of all creatures, can do this as we have *such* a capacity to turn Joy into Love. In our ivories we hold the Love we have stored in the whole of our lives – and it stays in our ivories even after we have stepped-over.'

Kidogo felt her barren cheeks and wondered, if ever she did have enough Love to store, where *she* would keep it.

Tembella Grace had evidently sensed her concern and said, 'Be not concerned, Kidogo – trust in Mana – he will provide.'

Kidogo thought she now knew why humans killed elephants to take their tusks. They must have so little Love in their lives that they needed the stored Love of the elephants to survive. They must need it very badly! But surely all the forces they controlled should be enough for them! Why did they have to kill elephants to take *their* Love too? Maybe their *God* needed the elephants' Love to power him, if humans couldn't produce enough Love of their own.

Tembella Grace was speaking again. 'Love can't really be described – it must be experienced. Open your eyes, open your heart, relish the Joys and Love will come to you. You will know when it happens. Now, is there anything else I can tell you?'

Kidogo raised her trunk slowly. 'What happens when we step-over?'

'That, Blesséd One, is a mystery that Mana keeps to himself. I believe that even the cleverest of humans and the wisest of tembos, don't know the answer to *that* question.'

The old one stood serenely still as though in deep thought, then turned her head towards Kidogo and said, 'You must resume your journey now. Return to the swamp below Holy Mountain, where Tembo M'zee will be waiting for you.'

Tembella Grace reached her trunk deep down into her throat and drew on the reserve of water that all elephants carry. She touched the centre of Kidogo's forehead and the dampness she left there was even more comforting than the dry touches of previous days.

'May Tembo Jay guide you, and Mana keep you safe. We shall not meet again.' Tears trickled from the corners of the old one's blind eyes. Kidogo felt stronger than she ever had, and she touched Tembella Grace's forehead in return.

'Thank you,' she said, her eyes moist. 'Thank you for your teaching – and for your Love.' She turned away and called to Rafiki to come up out of the pool.

Temba Kindness and Temba Comfort walked on either side of Kidogo and waited with her as Rafiki came up out of the pool to join them. Kindness looked at his inflamed cheek and said, '*You* must stay. You are not well enough to travel.'

Rafiki ignored her. 'Are we leaving?' he asked Kidogo.

'I am to go back to the swamp,' she replied.

'Then I come too.'

'You are not well enough to travel,' Kindness told him again.

'Where she goes, I go,' he said firmly. 'She is my friend – and she needs me.'

Kindness did not argue. 'Come back when you need us,' she said.

'We will be waiting for you,' Comfort added as the two

54

youngsters turned towards Holy Mountain and the Swamp of Amboseli. 'Fare well to you both.'

When they reached the two rocks from where they had first seen the Sacred Grove, Rafiki turned and looked back. He touched Kidogo's back and said, 'Turn around and tell me what you see – or don't see.'

Kidogo turned. There appeared to be only scrub and thorn trees where the ancient tembo-trees should have been. It was then they heard the low~sound vibrating all about them.

> *'Here the Sacred ~ Grove is waiting*
> *Peace and healing ~ here in plenty*
> *Bear in mind what ~ we have taught you*
> *Joy and Love be ~ ever with you.*
>
> *You are chosen ~ for a duty*
> *Often painful ~ never easy*
> *Testing for a ~ tuskless youngster*
> *Mana needs you ~ do not fail him.'*

'That must mean you,' Rafiki said. 'You're the tuskless one.'

Without even thinking what she was doing, Kidogo felt her cheeks – still no sign of tusks starting to grow.

The return route was imprinted on their memories and they walked confidently along the tracks through the bush with Rafiki giving only an occasional groan when a clumsily placed foot jarred his loosening tusk.

CHAPTER SEVEN

Old M'zee had been dozing in the swamp when the voice spoke to him. It was a quiet voice and almost inaudible but the message was clear.

'You are to choose a Shadow for yourself, go to the top of Holy Mountain and find the tusks of Tembo Jay.'

By the time M'zee was fully awake, the voice had gone. He knew it must have been Mana's voice he had heard and he wanted to know more. How? Why? When? But he knew that Mana never answered such questions. He felt honoured to have been chosen but was apprehensive about his abilities. He looked up at the mountain, which was unusually free of clouds for that time of the day. Tembo Jay's tusks were up there – legends were clear about that – and he had seen them in his dream but he was old and his joints were often stiff, especially in the evenings. Just that morning a large piece of tooth had broken away and he had nearly swallowed it. All too soon he would have no teeth left and the slow starvation would begin. Why hadn't Mana chosen a young, fit elephant to work his will? Still – it was not for him to question the choice.

'*Choose a Shadow*' the voice had said. Not many old tembulls bothered with *Shadows* now. They were often more trouble than they were worth but, with such a task ahead of him, he could see it was a good idea. He thought immediately of the two youngsters who had come to ask him about Tembo Jay. That young male, Rafiki – he would make a good Shadow for him. But where was he now? And that young female with the bright eyes – was she still with him?

Somehow the word had got around amongst the tembulls and the jostlers of Amboseli that a great and exciting expedition was being planned – a journey of adventure to be led by the Tembull of the Swamp, old M'zee. None knew what the expedition was about or where it was to go but many young males eagerly made their way through the woodlands and across the plains to the swamp in the hope of being allowed to take part. There was even talk of one of them being chosen as a S*hadow* to the old one. That would be something!

In the way of tembulls everywhere, they jostled and shoved one another on the shoreline, each trying to show M'zee that *he* was the strongest and fittest and should be the one to be chosen. Tusks were much displayed and frequently clashed together in false battles. Old M'zee stood up to his belly in the water, mud and reeds, slowly chewing on swamp vegetation as he watched the contenders brashly showing off their skills. Where *were* those bright youngsters who had visited him? Maybe the shots he had heard had injured them both and they had died in the bush, but he thought not. He shut his eyes, raised his trunk and tried to linque his thoughts to those of Mana but the trumping from the melee of tembulls on the shoreline distracted him. How had *they* heard of his quest? Had Mana spoken to *them* in a dream too?

M'zee called one over to join him. The tembull, the largest of the contenders, raised his trunk, gave a little trump of jubilation and waded into the swamp. As he approached, M'zee could see the stain of mustdo on either side of his head. Not a good sign for a reliable companion in what he was expecting to be a challenging journey. 'How are you named?' he asked.

'They call me Tembo Lusty.'

'Well, Tembo Lusty, tell me what all the excitement is about. Why do you, and those with you, show off to me as they might to a female in *joyneed*?'

'Word is in the wind that you are to lead a quest where there would be a chance for recognition.'

M'zee pretended not to understand. 'What is this *recognition*?'

Lusty tried to answer. 'Life can be very dull. We all want the chance of an adventure. The chance to do something special. The chance to be noticed. The chance to impress – to be *recognised*!' He raised his trunk. 'Didn't *you* want that when *you* were my age?'

'That was a long time ago,' M'zee replied without answering the question but, remembering his youth, he knew exactly what Tembo Lusty meant. Only now he felt as if he would cheerfully give one or even both of his tusks if he could spend the rest of his life here, quietly munching reeds in the swamp.

'It is true about the quest,' he said. 'I am going to choose several young and fit tembulls to come with me. One is to be my Shadow.' He was watching Tembo Lusty as he said this and saw Lusty feel the girth of his left tusk with his trunk.

'I would relish that honour,' Lusty said. 'I would stay near to you always and protect you with my life.'

Something in his voice made M'zee unsure of this. He was certainly not going to choose the first of the tembulls he had spoken to. He took a trunkful of reeds and pushed them into his mouth while Tembo Lusty, standing up to his belly in the swamp, waited for a reply.

A family of females were strolling along the shoreline, attracted by the antics of the young males. The breeze was from their direction and M'zee could tell that one of them was in joyneed. Even at his age the exquisite scent moved him. What effect would it have on Tembo Lusty? He did not have to wait long. As the first tantalising odours reached the young tembull he raised his trunk, brought his ears forward and turned his body to face upwind, the water and mud around him splashing and squelching as he moved. He surged forward, calling over his shoulder, 'I'll be back.'

M'zee thought of calling after him but Tembo Lusty would not have heard. M'zee watched him go, remembering just how it felt when the mustdo was on one. He sighed and gathered a mouthful of reeds before calling another tembull to join him.

He talked with them all, one at a time, as the afternoon progressed. While he did so he watched Tembo Lusty pursuing the joyneed female and being rejected at his every move. A larger, fully mature tembull had appeared and had jostled Lusty aside. The female readily accepted the huge newcomer who joyned with her to rapturous trumping and squeals from the other females. Tembo Lusty walked back to the other tembulls on the swamp edge, his trunk hanging dejectedly.

When the joyning was complete the successful tembull turned away from the female and waded out towards M'zee in the swamp. Even while he was engaged with the female, M'zee had recognised him as Tembo Notail from the Forest Edge.

Notail sang out to him.

'Love, live long, and ~ find sweet-water.'

M'zee raised his trunk in acknowledgement of the greeting. 'What brings *you* down here?' he asked Notail. 'Apart from them.' He pointed with his trunk at the females who were now moving away from the swamp edge.

'Does there need to be anything else?' Notail replied. 'It's all we males are good for. It's the tembas who do all the work. Carry the babies, give birth, suckle them, teach them manners – all the hard stuff!'

M'zee thought for a minute. 'I've been given a quest and I think it's going to be a difficult one. Are you game to join me?' He expected Notail to ask more about it but he replied, 'Not for me – I'm past that kind of thing. It's the peaceful life for me. Eat, sleep and joyn. That's me.'

M'zee snorted his disappointment. It would have been good to have another mature tembull to share the challenges that he knew would lie ahead. However, if that was Notail's attitude he'd be better off without him. He half-shut his eyes and pretended to doze as Notail ambled away through the swamp. The two white egrets that had been sitting on M'zee's back flew across to perch on Notail's head, fluttering off now and then to snatch at insects disturbed by his passage through the reeds. It would be so easy to pretend he had not heard the message from Mana.

'You are to choose a Shadow for yourself, go to the top of Holy Mountain and find the tusks of Tembo Jay.'

Perhaps he hadn't really heard it. Perhaps it was just a meaningless dream and he could just forget it. The temptation was as big as a storm cloud, but he *knew* he couldn't. Maybe Notail would have ignored a message like that. 'Eat, sleep and joyn' – indeed! M'zee did not like to think that tembulls with that attitude were fathering the next generation. Where *were* those bright-eyed youngsters who had been curious to know about Tembo Jay? It would be really good to have *them* along on the quest. Both of them!

The Bushman, De/ne, sat under an acacia tree looking out over the valley, which Mr Fotheringay would have said was about two miles across but the measuring system used by the First People was based on travelling times and was far more complex.

Down the centre of the valley a winding ribbon of dark green trees marked the presence of a watercourse but De/ne was too far away to tell if it had any running or standing water in it. Many river channels like that one could vary from being sandy beds in the dry season to raging torrents of angry water when heavy rains in the hills rushed down to fill the lake he could just see far to the north. He would soon need to top up his water supply in the two ostrich-egg shells he carried in his bag. He was not too concerned, as he knew how to find water in the crevices of tree trunks or, if he had to, even how to use a hollow reed to suck it up out of the driest of streambeds.

Scattered across the open grassland, herds of cattle were grazing, tended by young boys carrying sticks, and in a place where no trees grew De/ne could see the mud-covered huts forming a Maasai manyatta. People were coming and going through several of the openings in the thorn fence surrounding the village. They were mostly women, some of whom carried babies, while other slightly older children played in the dust.

De/ne was relieved that there was no sign of any warriors, the Moran, men between the ages of thirteen and thirty whose sole duty was to guard the village and the cattle. In the past, there had always been enmity, if not open warfare between the First People and the Maasai. The First People resented losing their traditional hunting grounds to the Maasai, while in their turn the herdsmen accused the Bushmen of killing their livestock and had ruthlessly hunted them almost to extinction.

De/ne sat in the shade gnawing the last of the meat from the porcupine's leg-bone wondering how far he would have to travel to find two worthy men who would be willing to come and marry his granddaughters to save his own family line at the *Place of Peace* from becoming extinct. No Maasai men would do – they cared more for their cows than for their womenfolk and would insist on bringing many cattle to the Place of Peace. Definitely no Maasai!

Sensing a movement behind him he turned his head slowly and swore in Bushmantaal. Six Moran were outlined against the skyline and appeared to be studying tracks in the dust where he had walked down to this spot an hour before. He tipped his body forward and wriggled away through the sparse grass under the tree, trying to avoid the long sharp thorns on the many twigs and branches that had fallen from the tree over the years. Some, hidden under tufts of grass, scratched and pierced his skin, drawing blood.

By the time he was clear of the thorns he could tell from the shouts of the Moran, that they were following his tracks – and getting nearer. He abandoned his spear, his bow and his quiver of arrows, tucked the skin bag tight up under his left arm, leaped to his feet and ran downhill towards the trees on the riverbank. Cows lowed as he ran between them and the herd boys threw their sticks at him and shouted encouragement to the pursuing Moran.

De/ne was smaller than any of the warriors – a tall Bushman would hardly come up to nipple-height on a Maasai – but in a sprint he could outrun any of them. He knew, though, that the Moran could lope along at their own pace for a whole day if they choose to and could wear him down like wild dogs following an antelope. Although initially faster, he would inevitably slow down and get caught, and probably killed. He made for the riverside trees, hoping to outwit the Moran by using the water in some way but when he reached the streambed it was virtually dry and running in the sand left clear footprints and was far more tiring than running on the hard-packed earth at the top of the bank.

The Maasai, who had cast off their cloaks and any footwear they had been wearing, were running naked along the bank watching him through the trees, ready to surge down whenever he tired or stumbled. Rounding a bend De/ne saw the log-like body and gaping mouth of a crocodile lying across his path. Leaping over it before it gathered its wits enough to lash out at him with its tail, he ran on.

The Maasai were now jogging easily along the bank, waiting for him to tire.

De/ne reached a long pool and ran to the side that put it between him and the warriors before he scrambled up the steep earth bank and onto the open grassland beyond. The Moran had seen the crocodile and were hesitant about splashing through the pool. They split into two groups of three, one group going round each end of the pool. In the few precious moments this gained him he looked around and saw an ancient thorn tree.

He paused and leaned forward, as though out of breath, to allow the Moran to regroup on his side of the riverbed. Then, when they were all together, he ran as though to pass downhill from the tree before turning sharply back above it.

His ruse worked. The warriors, barefoot as he was, were now close behind and sure of their quarry. They ran under the tree to cut him off and found themselves running over hard thorns as long as a man's little finger.

They didn't cry out. A Maasai warrior is taught at an early age to bear pain in silence but they couldn't run – at least until they had pulled the thorns out of their feet and got clear of the tree.

De/ne ran on, breathing more easily, until he was among the rocks leading up to the ridge. Here he could move without leaving tracks and, using all the trickery he knew, he leaped from rock to rock on the far side of the ridge until he was sure that not even a *Bushman* tracker could have followed his trail.

Eventually, he sat on a rock, opened his skin bag, took out the one ostrich eggshell that had survived intact, pulled out the grass stopper and drank deeply, his eyes searching the nearby bushes for the mantis he knew he would see there. When he did, he said a simple 'Thank you.'

He decided not to return to collect his spear, bow and quiver of arrows. The Moran, who would be angry at having been tricked might be waiting in ambush.

Temba Kidogo and Tembo Rafiki, on their way back to Amboseli, stopped to rest under a tree at the edge of the lava-flow and Rafiki began to rub the end of his shattered tusk against a rock as Temba Comfort had suggested. The scraping and rasping irritated Kidogo but she tried to ignore it. She had seen how the jagged end snagged on vegetation when her friend foraged. Maybe it was better to have no tusk at all than to have a shattered one . . . but no, it wasn't better!

When they had started on their return to Amboseli, she had been refreshed by her stay at the Sacred Grove. While there she had felt protected from dangers but now the old fears were returning, especially as her friend seemed to have lost most of his old cheerful self-confidence and was content to follow wherever she led.

Rafiki trumped in frustration when the rubbing seemed only to make the pain worse. Three giraffes, who had been watching them from a distance, lolloped away through the bushes, their heads swaying backwards and forwards as they ran.

'Funny looking animals those. Why do you think they have such long necks?' Kidogo asked. In the past a comment like that would have set Rafiki on a quest to find out but today he wasn't even trying to listen.

The friends moved on when the heat of the day had passed

its fiercest, Kidogo thinking wistfully of the cool waters and the shade of the tembo-trees at the Sacred Grove. She would have liked to stay there for the rest of her life, but Tembella Grace had said they *must* return to M'zee at the swamp. And the old female always spoke in a way that made one know that whatever she said, had to be done.

Nearing the swamp, Kidogo wondered about the man she had killed. Had other humans found the body and named her as a *rogue* and even now be seeking her out to be shot as a man-killer? She looked about fearfully. The safe feeling she had acquired at the Sacred Grove had totally left her.

The sun had dipped below the western hills and the clouds hiding Holy Mountain glowed golden above the forests as the two youngsters neared the swamp of Amboseli where Kidogo could see other elephants feeding at the swamp-edge. There was a family of females far to their left, while ahead of them many young tembulls were foraging in a desultory way. Occasionally, a bout of jostling and shoving would break out, the smaller of the contestants always giving way to the larger, and she could see old M'zee on the shore looking up at the cloud-covered mountain.

Kidogo, standing next to Rafiki, waited for her friend to make the next move but his mind seemed to be elsewhere.

'Rafiki . . .?'

'It's my tusk. It's hurting badly again.'

Kidogo reached out a comforting trunk. 'Do you want to rest or shall we go down to M'zee.'

'Rest I think. It looks too busy down there. I'll be better by sun-up.'

CHAPTER EIGHT

M'zee was again looking up at Holy Mountain, the summit clear of cloud in the early morning light, and thinking of the quest he had been given.

'You are to choose a Shadow for yourself, go to the top of Holy Mountain and find the tusks of Tembo Jay.'

It was too big for him, he was too old, too tired. But, when he saw that Kidogo and Rafiki had returned, the task seemed less daunting. He would choose Rafiki to be his Shadow. He called to them joyfully.

Love, live long, and ~ find sweet water.'

Kidogo and Rafiki both raised their trunks in response. M'zee expected Rafiki to give an appropriate low~sound reply but it was the young female, Kidogo who responded.

'Tembella Grace ~ sent us to you.

We had to come ~ and here we are.'

M'zee gave a little trump of surprise as they walked up to him. 'Tembella Grace. Tembella Grace! So she still lives. Well! By the tusks of Tembo Jay, she must be a hundred years old by now. Tembella Grace. How is she?'

Kidogo replied. 'Very *old*. Very calm – even though she can no longer see. She is cared for by two other females at the Sacred Grove.'

'So you've been to the Sacred Grove. Well! Tembella Grace can't see, you say. She could always see more than any other elephant I've ever known. And not just with her eyes. Well! If I didn't have other, very, very special things to do I'd go to the Sacred Grove and see her myself. She is my

66

mother, my own Tembella, you know.'

He stood still for a moment, then looked around. The tembulls who had gathered the day before had formed a circle around him and the two youngsters, and were listening to what he was saying.

M'zee thought before speaking again. So his mother was still alive but blind – how he wanted to go and see her – but he had a quest to fulfil. He had to choose a Shadow for himself and go up the mountain, however much he doubted his ability. Once more he looked up at the summit, not yet covered by clouds although they were beginning to form around the forested lower slopes. None of the tembulls he had already spoken to had impressed him, so it would have to be Tembo Rafiki – the bright young tembull who had made a favourable impression on him when they had last met. He stepped back to look at the youngster. The end of his left tusk had been shattered and he seemed subdued. It was the female, Temba Kidogo, who was now taking the lead. M'zee reached out and touched Rafiki's cheek with the tip of his trunk. The skin behind the damaged tusk was much warmer than it should have been. Trouble was coming – the youngster might even lose his tusk.

What should he do? He had been directed to choose a Shadow but the only tembull he was prepared to choose was sick and because of that could not be relied on to give the quest his whole attention. He looked around the circle of elephants again. Not one of them had come up to his expectations and hopes. Then he saw that the odd little tuskless female, Temba Kidogo, had the brightest eyes and the most attentive attitude. A *female* Shadow? Why not? The choice was his. So be it. He felt unexpectedly at ease with his decision.

'Temba Kidogo,' he said formally. 'I choose you to be my Shadow. Do you accept?'

Kidogo looked startled. 'Me?' she spluttered. 'I'm a female – Shadows are always males. Temba Kindness told me that at the Sacred Grove.'

Several of the jostlers sniggered behind their trunks.

M'zee laid his heavy trunk over the youngster's shoulder. 'It is my choice, and I have chosen *you*. But I must warn you what it means if you accept. You'll have to stay close to me in whatever I do. If you think *my* life is in danger, you must be prepared to give *yours* to save mine. If I ask you to do something, however strange it may seem, you must do it at once, without question. It means that, whatever you think *my* needs are, you must put these ahead of *your own*.'

Kidogo was overwhelmed by all of this and, stunned by what might be expected of her, said nothing. She didn't even have tusks. Why had M'zee chosen her? Surely one of these strong young tembulls with tusks could do the job better?

As if he had read her thoughts, M'zee said, 'Any of the tembulls here could have been chosen. I could have chosen Tembo Rafiki – but he has just suffered a shattered tusk. I could have chosen Tembo Lusty – but he is easily diverted. I could have chosen any one of these jostlers – but I have chosen you, Kidogo. I cannot say, even to myself, why I made this choice.'

Temba Kidogo was aware of the weight of M'zee's trunk on her back. It was warm and comforting. She wanted to accept but felt inadequate.

M'zee spoke again, as if instructing the other tembulls. 'It is not for nothing that Shadows serve. I have obligations too. I must protect my Shadow as a temba protects her young and as a Tembella protects her family. I must teach my Shadow what I have learned in my life so that she may become wise in her turn. I must not ask her to do things because I am too lazy or too arrogant to do them for myself. That would make me no better than the Yellow Tusks of old.

He lifted his trunk from Kidogo's back and held it up in query as he asked, 'Do you accept, Temba Kidogo?'

Kidogo looked at Rafiki who was nodding his head vigorously.

'I accept,' she said. 'But—'

'There can be no *buts,*' M'zee cut her short.

Kidogo looked again at Rafiki who was still nodding. 'I accept,' she said.

With Kidogo standing at his side, M'zee rumbled for attention. 'My Shadow, Temba Kidogo, and I are going to set off today on a journey to the top of Holy Mountain. There we will undertake a difficult task that I have been commanded by Mana to perform. All those of you who want a chance of recognition may join us. It will not be easy and it will almost certainly be dangerous. It may be that none of us will return. Any tembo who comes must do whatever I, or my Shadow, ask of them. Who will join us?'

Rafiki stepped forward, followed by all the other tembulls with Tembo Lusty just a little behind the rest.

'Good,' said M'zee and, with Kidogo at his side and Rafiki just behind him, he turned towards the mountain, which was now wholly covered in cloud.

CHAPTER NINE

The Bushman De/ne had reached the road leading from
Arusha to the Ngorongoro Crater. The road had a hard black
surface made from some material unknown to him and every
few minutes a *gharri* would pass along it, some going one
way and some the other. Mr Fotheringay had taught him the
word gharri when he had described to him how people in the
'civilised' world travelled about. De/ne sat inconspicuously
watching the road from a patch of dry reeds by an almost
empty pool, which he could see was not a natural one but
had somehow been scraped out to catch and hold water.

In each of the gharries was at least one person but usually
with several others. De/ne watched them pass for several
hours, trying to work out what made the *gharries* move.
Failing in this, he followed the road for several miles,
keeping just back in the scrubland where he would not be
seen. He crouched down and hid when he saw a lone Maasai
man herding cattle and goats near to the road. A *gharri*
stopped close to the Maasai man and two pale-skinned
people, a man and a woman, got out. The man held a small
box up to his face while looking in the direction of the
Maasai man. Mr Fotheringay had told him about cameras
and this person must be – he struggled to recall the word –
photographing the Maasai man and his cattle. Then the
white man took some pieces of paper out of a pocket in his
trousers. De/ne suspected the paper was the 'money' that Mr
Fotheringay had also told him about. He'd warned him that
the 'love of money was the root of all evil' in the world. He

crept closer, unafraid of the Maasai man who was elderly, his time as a warrior long behind him.

De/ne enjoyed wriggling through the grass without being seen. The woman and man were arguing in English, the language Mr Fotheringay had taught De/ne to speak and understand.

'Ah think we should give him ten dollars, Honey,' the woman said. 'We got some nice pictures of him with the cows an' all.'

The white man snorted. 'That's a whole month's wages for one of these guys. I'll give him a dollar. We don't want to be upsetting the local economy!'

De/ne decided to show himself and stood up, wearing only his soft leather loincloth and a small pointed cap. His bag was tucked under his arm and he held a long stick in his hand. The Maasai man glowered but De/ne ignored him and walked closer to the pale-skinned couple.

'Hey, look here! A Bushman! This must be our lucky day – these guys are real rare,' the man said, holding up his camera again.

De/ne pretended he didn't understand what was being said.

'Ain't he tiny?' the woman said. 'Get a shot of him by the tall guy with the cows.'

As though it had been his own idea, De/ne moved closer to the Maasai man and the man's camera clicked and clicked.

'How much should we give *him*, Honey,' the woman said.

'If they're as rare as they say they are, he must be good for ten dollars,' the man said and held out a note. De/ne took it solemnly, thanked the man in perfect English, turned and slipped away into the bush before the Maasai man could hit him with his herding stick.

That evening Lars Petersen, a local guide, ushered his latest group of climbers into the brightly-lit departure lounge of

71

Kilimanjaro Airport, bracing himself for the emotional farewells that always followed a successful climb. All the women would kiss him, some would hug him as well to show their thanks, and the more emotional of the men would embrace him before shaking his hand vigorously. The tall Canadian man and the female estate agent from London were swapping e-mail addresses, and Lars noticed that the Canadian had carried her pack from the minibus, in addition to his own.

Lars Petersen's climbers always called him *The Viking*, which he found amusing most of the time. With his height, his blond hair, blue eyes and beard, he knew he looked the part, and having the trade name THE VIKING boldly emblazoned in machine-sewn letters on his Bergen backpack made it inevitable that the name would be transferred to him during each expedition.

When all the guests had passed through the airport controls he waited in the empty lounge, looking out past his reflection into the blackness until the KLM jumbo had taxied to the end of the runway and taken off for the long flight to Europe.

Driving the mini-bus back the forty or so kilometres west towards the town of Arusha, he mentally calculated how much this last party would have raised for the elephant-protection charity which had organised the trip. If each of the fourteen climbers had raised an average of £3,000 in sponsorship money, that would be fourteen times three thousand. That made—

He swerved to avoid a jackal caught in his headlights as it crossed the road. The jackal paused on the roadside, then slipped away into the darkness.

That made . . . £42,000! Wrong! It had been a *minimum* of £3,000 each climber had to raise, and he knew one of them had been sponsored for at least £10,000, so that would be £52,000. Wrong again! He must take £3,000 away from that. What the hell? A lot of money would soon be available for their 'Save the Elephants' campaign.

Nearing the town, Lars turned off the main road for the Riverside Hotel, parked, strode into the bar and ordered a glass of beer and a sandwich. He took the beer out into the garden and walked across the lawns to be away from the glare of the lights. The summit of Kilimanjaro was just visible, the ice and snow gleaming in the moonlight. *Was* the ice-cap really shrinking? *Was* global warming melting it away as the Earth's temperature inexorably rose? It was hard to be sure. In the few years since he had made his first climb, the snowline varied daily but the locals, who had lived within sight of the mountain for decades, were convinced that the underlying ice was in retreat. He hoped not. Kili would not be the same if the summit were just ash and scree. Much of its magic would have gone, and Africa would be the poorer for it. Cicadas chirruped in the trees over towards the river whose small waterfalls sounded cool and pleasant in the warm night. He drank from the glass, took another look at the mountain and turned back to collect his sandwich.

Apart from himself and the barman, there was no one in the bar or the restaurant. He sat on a tall stool and ran his finger up the side of the glass, drawing a line in the condensation. An owl called, and the barman grimaced. Africans regarded owls as birds that foretold strange happenings. Lars gave him a sympathetic smile. Having lived in Africa all his life he knew one could never just dismiss these old beliefs. He rubbed his bearded chin. I'll shave this off tomorrow, he vowed, as he did after every trip, but he knew he wouldn't. After a shower it would stop itching and besides, without his beard he wouldn't feel like himself.

This last trip had been his twentieth that year, leading a different party each time. Now, with Christmas coming, he was going to take a three-week break. Should he head out west to explore the Serengeti again? Perhaps a trip to Lake Victoria and some fishing? Or perhaps he would drive up to Nairobi and spend Christmas with Ryan Kavanagh? He would decide in the morning. He ate the sandwich, finished his beer and walked across the hard-packed murram yard to his room, undressed and took his long-anticipated shower, scrubbing away the sweat and grime accumulated on the mountain.

As he lay on his bed, listening to the tinkle and burble of the river on the far side of the lawn, the owl called again.

Perhaps he would fly down to Cape Town where he had lived since his now-dead parents had moved there from Oslo when he had been a little boy. It had been in South Africa that he'd developed his love of climbing while learning new routes on the sheer sides of Table Mountain. But he wouldn't go there. Reports continued to highlight violence in the post-Apartheid era and he hated violence in all its forms. The reports were probably exaggerated but life there *would* have changed, and he was not sure he would like it in the new Rainbow Nation. Most of his boyhood friends had gone to live in England or Australia, but he had chosen Tanzania. How *they* must be missing Africa – with all its faults and frustrations! He tried to get to sleep by thinking how lucky he was to still be able to live on the continent he loved so deeply, but . . .

The lack of close female company was the one disadvantage of the life he was now living. There was always at least one woman who tried to seduce him on every trip. This time it had been Jenny, the estate agent from London, who had eventually transferred her affections to the Canadian. As their guide on the mountain, he knew that any favouritism shown, for whatever reason, to *any* member of the party would be resented by the others and consequently destroy the team spirit he worked so hard to engender. It would have to be someone who was not one of his climbing guests, but . . .

There had been Lisa, who had been in Africa working with a charity, but she had gone back to England and, however much he cared for her, his recent trip to the UK had put any idea of living *there* totally out of his thoughts.

He had met a few very attractive local women but AIDS was so rampant throughout Africa that any form of liaison here was out of the question. Yet at twenty-eight he was in what was quaintly called *the prime of his life*, and he knew that being a guide on the mountain could only be an interlude. He must be acceptable or he wouldn't have the recurring problem with the female climbers. But . . .

Eventually he slept, occasionally half-waking when a blood-hungry insect whined outside his mosquito-net.

Towards dawn Lars dreamed he had become a bird and was flying over the forested slopes of Kilimanjaro. Flying was strange but exciting. He was aware that his *body* was far below, down in the wooden hotel room with the corrugated iron roof – but *he* was up here, floating on the wind, apparently weightless, like a stork or one of those supreme gliders, a vulture. The air around the mountain felt as crisp and cold as always and his vision was clearer than it had ever been. Perhaps all birds saw things this clearly.

He glided up past the forests and over the moorlands that were covered with the giant heather and lobelia plants that grew taller than a man and which his climbing groups always found so intriguing. Up and up he soared, carried on invisible currents of air, up through the clouds that so often hid the top of the mountain. He caught glimpses of the ash slopes, then he was gliding over the snowline, above the swirling mists and into brilliant sunlight that made him blink. Higher still and he could see into the crater itself. There were the familiar ice-walls around the sides but, far down in the centre, a small cone was giving out little puffs of smoke. Not for the first time, he sensed that the whole mountain was alive but sleeping.

He drew his wings in closer to his body and dropped down past the sheets and columns of ice forming one of the walls. He dropped past a cave entrance, spread his wings to check his fall and circled round to pass the entrance again. Inside, he could clearly see two huge elephant tusks lying with their points crossed. A quiet voice was saying, '*Climb the mountain and get these tusks out of the crater.*' He circled again and mentally marked the place by an oddly shaped rock on the crater rim above the cave as the dream faded and vanished.

When he awoke, he tugged the lower edge of the mosquito net out from under the mattress, swung his legs out of the bed and walked barefoot across the room to open the door. The sun was just rising, turning the distant snowcap a glorious red.

Lars took another shower, turning the water from hot to cold and back to hot before finishing with cold. Feeling refreshed, he dressed and strolled casually across the tree-shaded yard. He replayed the dream in his head as he breakfasted on the veranda of the hotel, enjoying the fresh papaya and slices of pineapple while bulbuls fluttered down to the table and pecked at the crumbs of toast. There were a few other guests but they were all engrossed in their own worlds, those new to Africa exclaiming loudly about everything bright and colourful they were seeing.

He loved this old-fashioned hotel, redolent of colonial days with its flame-trees and jacarandas, neatly mown lawns and swept earth paths. Beyond the gardens he could glimpse African women picking the flowers the hotel grew for the European market. They'd be flown out that night. Exotic flowers he could understand, but his friend Ryan, who lived in Nairobi, had told him that even vegetables were grown in Kenya and flown to Europe. The world was crazy!

Sipping his coffee, Lars realised he could recall the whole of his dream. Mostly dreams slipped away as one woke up, leaving just a few tantalising scenes which quickly faded and were forgotten.

After a second cup of coffee he went to the office and sent an e-mail to Nairobi.

> To: Ryan@computertraining.co.ke
> Ryan. I am going to climb Kili – getting to the top on Christmas Day. Can't tell you more about why, as I am not too sure myself. You've always said you'd like to be on the mountain without all the other people and we are likely to be the only ones there then. I would love to have you along as did so enjoy your company (if not all your jokes) when we did Mt Kenya last year. We could be going down into the crater so bring along a rope and your ice axe. Crampons could be useful too. Hope you can come. Waiting your reply. Lars P.

By the time he had swum twenty lengths of the unheated pool, towelled himself dry in the crisp morning air and walked back to the hotel office, a reply had come.

> Hi Lars. Be with you teatime on 23rd. Your trip sounds just what I need. Will bring gear as suggested. Did I tell you the one about the Irishman who . . . ? Ryan.

On the other side of the mountain, the first day's upward trek had been uneventful for the elephants. Tembo M'zee led, followed by Kidogo and Rafiki who walked side by side whenever the track was wide enough. Twenty young tembulls followed in a disorganised group, shoving, nudging and jostling one another in a light-hearted way when in open country but forming naturally into single file when passing through rocky areas or woodland. Tembo Lusty took up the position of last in line, keeping some small distance behind as though not really wanting to be involved.

Tembo M'zee was thinking about his choice of a Shadow. Had he done right to choose a female? Especially one who was under-size for her age and had no tusks? He had another minor cause for concern. When he had laid his trunk on Kidogo's back at the time of choosing, he had read a kin-scent. Only then had he realised she was a descendant of his, probably a granddaughter. His marker scent within hers had been *too* faint for her to be a daughter and, with her being so young, that would have been unlikely anyway. But did it matter? The Blesséd Tembo Jay had taught that one should never favour one's own descendants over other elephants – but he had *not* done that. At the time of choosing, he had been unaware of any kinship, and anyway she had seemed the most worthy. He *had* chosen her and, now he did know of their kinship, he was secretly pleased. So be it. He pushed the knowledge down into deep memory.

At the lower edge of the forest, the group crossed a well-worn elephant track littered with fresh droppings. M'zee sniffed at these and detected the recent scent of a female in joyneed and remembered how such a scent would have once affected him and sighed. As he walked on he kept glancing back to see what effect it would have on Tembo Lusty. To M'zee's surprise, Lusty sniffed once and carried on, apparently unconcerned.

M'zee did not hurry the elephants. He encouraged them to browse as they walked, and when they got into the forest

78

proper the pushing and shoving among the youngsters died down to an occasional good-natured nudge. In the late afternoon, M'zee called a halt in a clearing and the elephants spread out through the tall trees to feed. Large black-and-white monkeys with long tails leaped through the branches above their heads and forest birds called mournful warnings to one another. Darkness came early and the elephants returned to the clearing, where they gathered in small groups to sleep.

At first light, Kidogo saw that Tembo Lusty was not in the clearing. M'zee had also noticed and called into the forest, facing downhill, first in tembotalk, then in low~sound, knowing that this would travel further. But there was no reply to either. M'zee snorted his feelings and turned uphill. The other tembos shook the night from their minds and fell into line behind him.

That day's climb seemed easier, the mood more relaxed and less competitive. Kidogo found, like the other elephants, that she was breathing harder, as though the air itself was getting thin. The pace slowed perceptibly but M'zee made no attempt to speed them up – whatever had to be done on the mountain did not need to be done in a hurry. Sometimes the path was narrow and the elephants walked in single file, at other times the winding track passed through forest glades lit by sunbeams striking through the trees, although Kidogo hardly noticed the beauty of it all. She was concerned about Rafiki, who was breathing even more loudly than she was and frequently rubbing his left cheek with his trunk. Once, Kidogo tried to touch it but Rafiki pushed her away.

'I'm all right,' he told her brusquely.

There was occasional dung-evidence of forest elephants but they neither saw nor heard any nearby. The tembos who lived in the forest were known to be more wary than those on the plains below.

When the light woke her the following morning, Kidogo saw there were fewer tembulls in the clearing, several having slipped away in the night, as Lusty had done. M'zee did not call after them but shrugged his shoulders, reached up with his trunk and pulled down some fresh soft foliage from above his head and chewed on it slowly. Kidogo and Rafiki did the same and the remaining tembulls spread out to forage in silence.

They climbed for three more days. Each day the air seemed thinner and colder and their breathing more difficult. Each morning when Kidogo counted the group there were fewer elephants than the previous day. She watched M'zee do *his* count and expected him to show concern or disappointment.

'They have failed the testing of Mana,' was all the old one would say and those remaining climbed on, mostly in silence as talking made them even more breathless and the climbing more difficult.

By the time they reached the top of the forest, where the trees were hung with streamers of dank, grey moss, the party consisted of only three, M'zee, Kidogo and Rafiki. Since M'zee seemed unconcerned about it, Kidogo did not comment, and Rafiki remained withdrawn and silent.

They paused in a rocky gully at the edge of the heath-land, the shoulder-high heathers and other grotesque plants looking gaunt and frightening in the mist that swirled about them. On either side of the gully, strangely weathered and distorted rocks gleamed as moisture ran down their sides and dripped into the mosses below.

Kidogo was now very concerned for Rafiki whom she had heard groaning and whimpering throughout the night. She had tried to comfort her friend but once again he had told her brusquely, 'I'm all right,' although she could see that his left cheek was swollen and was obviously causing him a lot of pain. M'zee had also noticed it. The old one reached out and touched the swelling lightly. Rafiki winced.

'You will have to turn back,' M'zee told him. 'Travel as fast as you can and go to the Sacred Grove. Tell Tembella Grace where you left us – though I expect she knows more about our quest than we do.'

Kidogo looked from M'zee to Rafiki and back. If Rafiki had to make that journey, *she* should be at the side of her sick friend to care for him. Yet she had promised to stay with M'zee as his Shadow and that promise was clearly something no elephant could walk away from and still be able to hold up their trunk.

M'zee understood. 'It is not an easy choice, Kidogo,' he said. 'But your friend is not in danger. If he can stay alert he will make it to the Sacred Grove. Mana may have another role for one as worthy as he.'

Rafiki looked relieved and said, 'You stay with M'zee, Kidogo.' Talking was obviously causing him pain and his voice was low. 'That is your promised duty. I'll be all right!' He turned back the way they had come, giving just a feeble wave of his trunk as he disappeared amongst the trees.

Kidogo called after him in low~sound.
'May Mana bless ~ and keep you safe,
Tembo Jay and ~ goodness guide you.'

M'zee, standing beside Kidogo as they watched Rafiki stumble down beyond the tree-line, put his trunk on Kidogo's back and called out to the young tembo.
'Your friend and I ~ will be all right,
Tembella Grace ~ will care for you.'

So, it was to be just the two of them. Himself, an aging, tired old elephant whose last teeth were crumbling away and the young female, his granddaughter, tuskless and small for her age. Mana had an odd way of choosing those he needed to work his will. The old tembull looked around at the oddly-shaped rocks on either side of them. He had been here before, many years ago, and he had seen these rocks again in his *flying* dream. How had he forgotten that terrible time? Was his memory beginning to fail him as well as his body? The rocks *were* familiar – it had been near here that his friend Tembo Steadfast had died and M'zee knew there was something he must do now that he was so near.

He forced his aching joints into action and lumbered up a side valley, with Kidogo following close behind. It began to snow, lightly at first, then more heavily as they climbed higher and the wind rose. But, once he had started to move, the aches eased and he was soon striding up the valley, ignoring the snow, his trunk swinging to left and right as he sought out ancient scents and memories. He rounded a large rock, its stark blackness streaked by the driving snow. Ahead, just visible in the fading light, a huge skeleton lay at the foot of a rock wall.

He found himself going down on his knees and saying, 'Steadfast, my friend, forgive me – forgive me.' But the only answer was the low moaning of the wind through the bare bones of the ribs. M'zee ran his trunk along each of Steadfast's tusks, relieved that they had not been found and carried away by humans. The tusks were loose in their sockets and moved at his touch. Although they were not the tusks of Tembo Jay which he had been sent to find, he knew it was up to him to preserve and protect them too. He stood, eased one of the tusks from its socket and signalled to Kidogo to take it from him. He then drew out the other tusk and stood it out of the way against the black rock. He started to uproot heather plants and lay them over the skeleton then, realising the young female, his Shadow, would be as cold or colder than he was, he abandoned this task, wrapped his trunk tightly around the second of Tembo Steadfast's tusks and set off uphill through the ever-thickening swirls of snow. He had remembered the cave in which he had hidden after Steadfast had died. They could shelter there.

CHAPTER TEN

Kidogo backed into the cave beside M'zee. The tusk the old one had been carrying was on the ground beside him, and Kidogo laid hers alongside it. The two great ivories lying between them were a perfect match, nesting together for the whole of their length. Cold as she was Kidogo had to admire their symmetry, but she was also aware of something else. There was a warmth, a kind of special feeling emanating from them.

The cave was deep enough for the two elephants to stand side by side out of the wind, although they could still hear it blustering about the entrance. Only occasional searching fingers of cold reached Kidogo, causing her to shiver briefly, but she could feel the snow on her back melting to water and trickling down her skin. The tip of her trunk, numb a short time before and now resting on her tongue, was returning painfully to its normal sensitive self. She felt safe here in the darkening cave with M'zee beside her.

When her trunk-tip was warm again and the daylight had gone altogether, she felt around in the darkness. The cave wall was cold but dry and long-dead leaves on the floor rustled when her trunk touched them. The massive bulk of old M'zee was now radiating body-warmth and, when her body rubbed against his as she moved, she could feel his internal digestive rumblings through the thickness of his wrinkled skin.

Cave-scents were beginning to emerge. The crisp leaves around her feet were pungent with age and decay and a lingering feline scent told her that a leopard had visited the cave at some time. Reaching up, dusty cobwebs tickled and stuck to her trunk. She snorted, pulled it back and wiped the sticky threads against her leg, wondering if any of the tiny eight-legged creatures she hated and feared so irrationally were even now crawling over her body. She shuddered in the darkness and curled her trunk up so that it didn't touch the ground.

Later, she dared to reach down and touch one of the tusks, both of which were beginning to glow as with some faint internal moonlight. She flicked her trunk back in surprise – M'zee's trunk was doing the same.

'This was the venerable Steadfast. Quite a life!' M'zee rumbled gently.

Kidogo did not know what he meant, but there was a kindness in the old elephant's voice that encouraged a response. 'I'm sorry . . .' she said, not sure what it was she was sorry for.

'He had quite a life, many adventures, many joynings, many descendants, much wisdom and compassion. A truly venerable tembull.'

'How do you know?' Kidogo asked, her voice sounding slightly tremulous in the void of the cave.

'I knew him in life – but were you not reading Steadfast's tusks?' the old one asked.

'Reading?'

'Yes. Reading the tusks. Do you not know how? I thought all of tembokind could do that.'

The tembotalk word and the concept of *reading* were new to Kidogo, although she remembered that humans had a similar ability. They read things in what they called *books*. Perhaps reading was another of the elephant ways she had not yet learned. But being able to understand the language spoken by humans had not been of great use to her when

Rafiki had been teaching her tembotalk. Learning *that* language with its rumblings, snorts, whispers and trunk signals had been a curious mixture of effort, frustration and joy.

'I'm sorry,' she said again, although she knew that most of her apology would be invisible in the darkness. 'I lived with humans for my first sixteen years.'

'That I did not know,' the old one replied.

Kidogo thought it courteous to explain. 'When I lived with them I learned to understand the two languages they use but of course I couldn't speak back to them in either. I once heard a human tell others that I was found near my dead mother when I was a baby and taken to a place they called an *orphanage* near to a city of people called *Nairobi*. I have some memories of that place and can recall how the people there were kind and cared for me until I was older. It was there I met Tembo Rafiki. Then, when we were older, they took the two of us to a place in the bush-land that they called *Tsavo* where I lived until I was in my seventeenth year. But Rafiki wanted to be a real elephant, so he left and I followed after him. The humans were always very kind to me – but I think now that we *both* wanted to be real elephants.'

'I understand,' old M'zee rumbled in the darkness. 'But humans can be different – not all are kind. Many can be worse than hyenas, killing us to steal our tusks, not even for the meat that makes our bodies. They carry away just our ivories and leave our meat and bones for the vultures and the hyenas to squabble over. But what they do with our ivories we tembos have never learned.'

There was a silence in the cave. Kidogo thought she did know but was too tired to say, and visions were rising up out of her deeper memory. Dreadful visions from a darker part – pictures of her mother with the vultures tearing at her lifeless body. She wanted to lose the frightening images that were crowding her mind.

She tried to think of something else. 'What is *reading*?' she asked.

She felt M'zee take her trunk-tip in his own and draw it down to one of the tusks on the ground between them.

'What can you see?' he asked.

'Nothing,' Kidogo replied, feeling a little foolish. 'There is just darkness here, although the tusks seem as if they are holding moonlight.'

'No – not seeing with your eyes – seeing in your mind.' The voice was kind and patient. 'Relax your body, clear your mind, open your thoughts – as when you commune with Mana.'

Three moons earlier Kidogo had not even heard the name *Mana* and, even after her talks with Tembella Grace and the Sisters at the Sacred Pool, she was not really sure that she fully understood who or what Mana was. There was still so much she didn't know.

M'zee's trunk guided the tip of hers backwards and forwards along the length of the nearest tusk. Although the bones of the skeleton outside had been covered in moss and lichen and had been encrusted with snow, the tusk here in the cave felt smooth and even warm. She tried doing what M'zee had suggested, relaxing her body, clearing her mind and opening her thoughts as she touched the ivory. Hazy pictures began to form in her head, appearing and disappearing as her trunk moved. She stopped in one place and a picture emerged from the haze. She recognised the scene.

It was in the swamp at Amboseli where the humans' roadway crossed from one side to the other. She could see hippos in the water looking towards her and, up to her belly in the reeds on one side, was a nubile female elephant making welcoming signals with her trunk. Kidogo felt a strange urge to go to her but, as she moved her trunk to the left, the scene changed.

She studied the new picture, one of a newly born baby elephant and she felt proud – as if it had been her own. She lifted her trunk and placed it further along the tusk.

Now a huge Tembull was coming towards her, his trunk raised in a challenge. A female, not the one she had just seen, was watching the challenge in excited anticipation of its outcome.

'What do you see?' M'zee asked.

Kidogo told him as she pulled back her trunk and the pictures faded.

'Not difficult then? You must be a natural reader. Try again.'

Kidogo explored the pictures in the tusk, the night slipping away as she did so. She found the order in which they lay, some near to the surface, some deep within and harder to read but of greater intensity and significance. Far into the night she found a series of scenes that explained how the tusks she was reading had got where they had found them, high on the mountainside. Sometimes, she felt M'zee's trunk against hers in the darkness as the old elephant read with her the experiences and the emotions hidden deep within the tusk. Kidogo could feel tremors of excitement as they read the final scenes together. When she was reading from one tusk she was just an observer at the scene but if she read the other one she felt as if she were Tembo Steadfast himself. Then she was no longer a small, tuskless female but a massive tembull – full of life and power and driven by an irresistible urge to joyn with the female who was standing impassively nearby. It was *his* right and *his* duty to do so!

But, making insulting challenges to him was his rival, Tembo M'zee. M'zee seemed to no longer be the friend he had been for so many years – but just another obstacle to delay the joyning. That stupid M'zee creature couldn't seriously believe that *he* had a claim to the temba. She was his – his – Tembo Steadfast's. He signalled back his contempt but M'zee would not yield. He, Tembo Steadfast, would show him who had the greatest right. M'zee may have tusks of the same size, maybe even a tiny bit larger, but the temba was his – his! He had seen her first – he had scented her joyneed before M'zee had. He trumped his right as loudly as he could – but the fool would not back off. He charged, head down, his forehead slamming into M'zee's and their tusks clashing so that it hurt the very roots. If it hurt him, it would also have hurt M'zee. Soon the fool would recognise who was the greatest and turn away.

Around them red dust was being thrown up by their feet, dust that swirled through the air and was caught by an invisible wind which spun it into twists and spirals around their wrestling bodies. Each tembull pushed and shoved at the other. Both were breathing with deep, racking breaths and suddenly he, Tembo Steadfast, knew that M'zee *was* the strongest after all and it was time to concede. He suddenly felt weary and drained of energy – perhaps the temba was not worth all this effort – other females would come into joyneed when M'zee was elsewhere. Steadfast raised his trunk to signal submission but M'zee ignored this and made a last savage sideways thrust with his left tusk which penetrated Steadfast's ribs and he dropped to his knees. M'zee stepped back and withdrew his tusk, red with blood, from the wound, then circled and readied himself to make yet another charge. Had he not seen the signal of submission? Steadfast made it again, lurched to his feet and stumbled off through the scrubland. Looking back once he saw that M'zee had claimed the female – as was his right.

The passion of his mustdo was replaced by the pain of his wound but even this was overshadowed by the feeling of having been betrayed by his friend. Tembo Steadfast wanted to be alone and headed for the slopes of Holy Mountain. As he walked he reached back and felt the wound with his trunk. It was deep and sticky with blood that bubbled as he breathed, and flies were clustering around it. No tembo could survive a wound like that. He headed upwards through the forest, just wanting to be away from the place where his friend had betrayed him, a so-called friend who had ignored the ancient rules of a challenge. This hurt him far, far more than the wound. If he had to die, he wanted to die as far away as was possible from M'zee – the unworthy. M'zee – the cheat.

He climbed as fast as the wound allowed him to, growing weaker all the time. On the second day, he sensed M'zee following him. He drew on his last reserves of strength to stay ahead and out of sight, although he knew if he *was* being followed it would be only a matter of time before M'zee caught up with him. His blood-scent trail would be easy to read.

As Kidogo, trembling with anger, read on, her trunk-tip close to the roots of the tusk, she recognised the place where they had found the skeleton the previous day. She saw, as through the eyes of the dying Steadfast, M'zee coming up the path towards him where he leaned against a huge rock, the last strength draining out of his body.

The pictures faded away and she heard M'zee saying into the darkness, 'I killed my friend. I killed my friend. I killed my friend.'

Kidogo, once more herself, moved closer, reached up with her trunk to touch the old elephant's forehead and they stood silently close together until a slow dawn broke and the sun, rising out of a pink haze far to the east, lit the cave entrance. M'zee shook himself and stepped outside. The snow was melting in the early sunlight, each drop of water on the plants catching the light and sparkling as it fell. The valley leading up the mountainside glowed golden in the horizontal rays as a tiny brown bird fluttered up onto the rock above the cave entrance and sang joyously.

M'zee sniffed at the cool air, touched Kidogo's trunk with his own, then reached back into the cave to fondle the end of one of Steadfast's tusks. He shook himself and sniffed the air again. 'We must feed,' he said. 'And it will be good to know what the mountain is like farther up. A wise tembo likes to know the dangers and the potential of his surroundings.'

Leaving the tusks in the cave, the elephants wandered up the valley, passing more grotesquely shaped formations of rock, many of which were still white with snow on the sides that were out of the direct rays of the sun. In the shadowed areas, the icy ground scrunched under their feet. As they walked side by side, they tore up tussocks of grass and stuffed them into their mouths but Kidogo found much of the grass to be coarse and bitter so tried the woody stems of the heather plants that grew as tall as their shoulders and found they were sweeter. M'zee soon gave up trying to eat.

They rounded a shoulder of the mountain and the summit cone came into view. Kidogo looked up and gasped.

She was familiar with the faint outline of the ice-cap as seen from the plains far below but from down there the line of permanent snow in the sky had seemed remote and unreal. Now, with a closer view of it, the sight was breathtaking – but it was more than that. The scene was sharp, clear and frightening. She shuddered and turned away. The snow on the mountaintop drew up the deep memories of the stinking, white vulture-droppings that had streaked the skin of her dead mother's body while she had stood helplessly by and watched the hook-beaked birds tearing at the flesh. Overcome by the remembered horror, she sank to her knees, trembling. M'zee turned and reached out a comforting trunk but she hardly noticed.

M'zee had been preoccupied by other thoughts. He had been relieved that the snow was melting and the wind had stopped. The young temba by his side would be missing her friend but the youngster should be far down the mountain by now, on his way to the Sacred Grove. He was going to lose that damaged tusk for sure.

Even though M'zee still knew they must *sometime* climb to the summit for the tusks of Tembo Jay, they need not start today – they both needed a rest and he needed some food. He was not troubled by thoughts that any humans might ever find Steadfast's tusks in the cave. He had detected no human scent since way down in the forest and, since the skeleton had lain undisturbed for many, many years, humans could never have come to this part of the mountain. He was happier to think of those huge and beautiful ivories, with their hidden memories, resting in the cave out of the snow and the rain. Otherwise they would eventually have sunk into the moss and the soil as the skeleton disintegrated and all knowledge of Steadfast's life would been lost for ever. If humans had ever found them, they would have taken the tusks for sure. They seemed to have an insatiable lust for ivories.

His granddaughter, who had been feeding at his side, suddenly dropped to her knees. He reached out and touched her shoulder – the experience of reading Steadfast's experiences must have drained her more than he had thought. They would go back down to the cave – and he would have to find some softer vegetation to eat, although where he would find this so high on the mountain, he didn't know.

De/ne the Bushman had discovered that virtually all other people, black-skinned or white, wore shirts and trousers, either long or short. None wore a comfortable skin loin-cloth like his, and he'd realised that to have any chance of finding worthy husbands for his granddaughters he would only be taken seriously if he dressed as these other people did. He knew the ten-dollar note in his skin bag would enable him to buy some things but he had no idea what it was really worth. If standing and looking at a camera for a few seconds was worth ten dollars, then it surely couldn't buy much.

Mr Fotheringay had warned De/ne about the thieves and robbers he would be likely to meet if he ever went out of the Place of Peace to 'civilisation'. De/ne especially remembered the story of the man in the black book 'who fell among thieves' and hoped that, if it happened to him, there would be a 'Good Samaritan' around to help him.

He spent several days observing different aspects of civilisation from the cover of rocks and bushes near to villages and the black road, and came to the conclusion that it was not as bad as Mr Fotheringay had told him. He observed people going into shops and coming out carrying things that they did not have when they went in and noted one where people went in wearing old and ragged clothes and came out in smart new ones. Would his ten-dollar paper buy him a shirt and some short trousers?

He left his stick in the bushes and boldly walked into the shop. 'I would like to have a shirt and some trousers like those,' he said in English to the man who was clearly in charge, pointing at some shorts laid out on a table and ignoring the stares of the other people in the shop. 'How much money do I give to you for those?'

'How much have you got?' the shopkeeper asked.

'I have a paper for ten dollars,' De/ne replied.

'In that case, they cost ten dollars.'

De/ne felt uncomfortable when the other people laughed, and he wanted more than anything to be back in the Place of Peace where he knew exactly what was what. He laid the note on the table and the man took it and studied it closely before folding the shorts casually, dropping a small T-shirt on top of them and pushing the pile in De/ne's direction.

He had planned to put on his new clothes inside the shop but the other people were laughing more openly now and he hurried out and back to the bush where he had left his stick.

CHAPTER ELEVEN

Ryan Kavanagh's Land Rover swung into the yard of the Riverside Hotel and stopped with a spurt of murram dust from under each wheel. Ryan got out and walked around the building to the bar under the thatched verandah. The barman raised one hand in greeting and was reaching for a bottle of beer with his other hand even as Lars turned to welcome his friend.

'Good run down?' Lars asked.

'Much as usual. Time it was all tarmacked. T'anks for the invite – I'll be glad to be forgetting about computers for a few days!'

'Have you eaten?'

'Had a bite at the Namanga Lodge.' He hoisted himself up onto a bar-stool and helped himself to a handful of peanuts before sipping the beer. 'Tell me what it is you've got planned for us, then.'

Ryan, short, dark and clean-shaven was the very opposite in appearance to his friend, the tall bearded Scandinavian, although they were both dressed in khaki safari suits. The two men sat together, drank beer and planned the climb. They would leave the Riverside before dawn the next morning, drive down to Marangu and breakfast at the hotel there. They would give themselves only a day and a night to reach the summit instead of the leisurely three or even four days that Lars would normally allow for his groups. Both he and Ryan were acclimatised to altitude, were young and strong, and would be unencumbered by porters and less-fit trekkers.

Ryan wanted to know more about the object of the trip but Lars was reluctant to tell him. His *flying* dream was fading and the chance of actually finding tusks in an ice-cave in the crater now seemed quite stupid and unreal. He waffled a bit about having the mountain to themselves and enjoying some ice-work but he was sure Ryan suspected some other motive. Ryan knew his friend better than to push the point. They were going to enjoy the trip, whatever.

While driving to the Marangu Hotel in Ryan's Land Rover, they decided to skip a formal breakfast and snack on the way as they had a long walk to do that day. Usually, Lars would have started from The Riverside Hotel at mid-morning and enjoyed sharing with his guests the sights, sounds and smells of Africa as he drove them in the minibus. The guests, especially those from America and Canada, were always intrigued by the rawness of everything – the brightness of the forested places, the starkness of the bare-earth plains littered with half-finished and seemingly abandoned concrete buildings and, initially, by the incongruously smooth tarmac road that had been paid for by the World Bank. When the tarmac finished abruptly, they bounced about in their seats as Lars steered the minibus from side to side to avoid the worst of the potholes in the murram road. The guests would comment excitedly at each little village with its tiny dukas selling everything from meat to medicines. The women's brilliantly-coloured clothes, contrasting with the men's drab khaki shirts and trousers, were the stuff of many of the *National Geographic* pictures with which they had grown up. Banana plantations and papaya trees added to their feeling of really being in Africa.

Today, Ryan just drove hard along the almost deserted road with Lars dozing in the passenger seat. As they approached the park gates, Lars prepared himself to argue with the wardens for Ryan's four-by-four to be allowed through – he knew them all well enough but the gates, although closed, were unattended and unlocked. He supposed the wardens must be staying at home for their Christmas break.

Lars opened the gates for Ryan to drive through, then closed them again.

They parked near the Mandara huts, put on their boots, checked their gear and set off up through the final belt of moss-draped trees before breaking out onto the moorland zone.

Although it was now mid-morning the main peak of Kilimanjaro, the crater rim known as Kibo, was clearly visible, but Mawenzi, the mountain's rugged secondary peak, up to their right-hand side, was hidden in an ever-changing mass of gleaming mist and clouds. It was often the other way around and could reverse in minutes, with Mawenzi clear and Kibo hidden. Often, neither was visible and sometimes dark clouds, lit from within by flashes of lightning, hid *both* summits.

The two men stopped and looked in silence at Kibo's snow-covered rim. This view never failed to move Lars, and it was one his climbing groups always found totally entrancing. It was the first sight of the summit seemingly within reach, but when he was leading his guest climbers, their awe was quickly followed by the sobering thought that they still had some three thousand metres to climb. Lars usually converted the figure into a round *ten thousand feet* for the sake of the Americans and Brits in his party but now he found it a welcome relief to be able just to stand and look. On this trip he would *not* have to explain everything and be asked to name each new plant and bird they saw. Suddenly, he felt overwhelmed with joy. The feeling was so intense it almost hurt. This had been happening to him more and more lately and it was not always a grand view that brought on the joyous feeling. Sometimes it was just the sight of a brightly-coloured flower or the graceful movement of an antelope. Even an overheard snatch of African laughter or song had the same effect. Life was good!

He and Ryan ate a cereal bar each and drank from a chilly stream at midday and were about to take up their packs and move on when Ryan pointed out a movement on the ridge ahead of them. A shining black ball was coming over the skyline – then another, and another. The black balls were quickly revealed to be tightly filled plastic bin-bags carried on the heads of men.

'Follow me,' hissed Lars, grabbing his Bergen by the shoulder-straps and scuttling down the streambed, ducking down to keep out of sight.

Round a bend, where the bag-carriers could not readily see them, he stopped and crouched down. 'They must have been having a litter-sweep. God knows the mountain needed one. Sorry about the panic – I just didn't want them to see us up here without a permit.'

'They'll be seeing the Land Rover anyway,' Ryan reminded him.

'They will, but they won't connect it with me.'

'They will when we come down off the mountain, if there's anyone at the gate.'

'Oh well! We'll cross that one then.'

A malachite sunbird with a scarlet tuft on its head flitted from a cabbage-headed groundsel tree to perch on the spire of a giant lobelia. Lars felt that surge of joy again.

When he was sure all the bag-carriers had passed and they were climbing back up to the track, he realised that a man in a warden's uniform was standing there, watching them and holding the hand of a small boy who had a full bag balanced on his head. The bag the man must have been carrying was on the ground at his side.

'Good afternoon, Mr Petersen,' the man said gravely, although his eyes were smiling. 'I did not expect to see *you* here today.'

Lars held out his hand. 'Hello, Aaron. Cleaning up the mountain at last then? You know it's not *my* guests who leave the taka-taka?' He turned to Ryan. 'This is my friend, Ryan. He's from Nairobi.'

The barefooted boy watched wide-eyed as the two men shook hands, then he too was introduced. 'Gentleman. This is my grandson, Jeremiah.'

The boy shyly held out his hand to Lars, then to Ryan, the shiny black bag unwavering on his head. Lars once more felt the wave of joy. Such a meeting seemed so easy here on the mountain. The difference in the colour of their skins utterly immaterial. Then, suddenly, it wasn't. It was people like him, people from Europe and America who had littered these people's mountain with the rubbish they just couldn't be bothered to carry away with them.

'I'm sorry about this,' he said, pointing to the bag still balanced on the boy's head.

'*You* do not have to be, Mr Petersen. As you said – it is not *your* guests who leave the taka-taka.' He was looking at the ropes and crampons strapped to their packs. 'You are going to climb on the ice?'

'That's the plan,' Lars replied.

'God be with you.' Aaron picked up his bag with one hand and took the boy's hand with the other. They walked off down the track side by side, neither looking back.

'He won't make any trouble for us,' Lars said confidently.

Lars and Ryan passed the empty Horombo huts, refilled their water bottles at the next stream and walked up onto the bleak saddle between the peaks, where Kibo once more came into view. Both men were breathing deeply.

Very late in the afternoon they reached the highest group of huts, which were also unoccupied. In front of the huts were rows of neatly tied, black bin-bags.

'They didn't take all of them then,' said Ryan needlessly.

'They must be coming back for this lot,' Lars replied equally needlessly.

Inside one of the huts, Lars lit their tiny gas stove while Ryan made up a two-man pack of dehydrated soup. They ate this and half a loaf of bread between them in the silent hut, and followed the scanty meal with mugs of hot tea before unrolling their sleeping bags and wriggling into them, half-dressed. Within a short time it was dark but sleep does not come easily at that altitude.

'Now, are you going to be telling me what all this is really about?' Ryan's voice spoke from the darkness.

Lars did not answer directly. 'Do you believe in God?' he asked.

'That depends on what you're calling God. I don't believe in the old-man-up-in-the-clouds kind of God. I don't believe in the going-to-church-and-praying-every-Sunday kind of God. I find it hard to believe in a benign, loving and almighty God who allows dreadful things to happen, like wars and children being murdered. I get sick in the guts when the Protestants fight the Catholics and the Muslims are killing the Jews and the Jews are bombing the Muslims – all in the name of God, or religion, which is much the same thing. But, when we came over the ridge and saw Kibo ahead, I felt an awe and respect for something much, much bigger than you or me. Even so, I suppose the answer has to be *no* – not really.'

Lars was silent.

After a minute, Ryan said, 'Why did you ask me that, then?'

'It all sounds a bit silly now but the night before I e-mailed you, I had a dream. At the time it seemed like a message, saying I had to do something.'

'Something to do with us being here, now?'

'The *real* reason for my asking you, in fact.'

'Tell me about it, then.' Ryan's voice was gentle.

'I'd just seen my last party onto the plane and gone back to the Riverside to decide what to do for the next couple of weeks. The last thing on my mind was coming back up here. It's a novelty to you but I've done it, up and back, up and back, more times than I can remember. That night I dreamed I was flying over Kili – flying like a bird – not in a plane. I flew down into the crater and saw two huge elephant tusks in a cave in the ice-wall. I have an absolutely clear picture of them in my mind – every detail – even the way the tips crossed over one another. In my head a tiny voice was saying, *"Climb the mountain and get these tusks out of the crater"*. Like I said, it all sounds a bit silly now.'

'So tomorrow we go and look for this cave, right? It should give us some good practice on the ice. Maybe we'll find your jumbo's tusks. If we do, I may have to believe in a God. Good-night to you, now.'

'Good-night, Ryan. Thanks for not laughing at me.'

The hut was silent again, then Ryan spoke. 'Did you hear the story about the climber in the Alps? Climbing solo on an overhang, he was. Bloody fool, but it's only a story. Everything went pear-shaped and he ended up dangling on the end of a rope with a two-hundred-metre drop below him and no way to climb back up. Now – he knew he couldn't hold on much longer so he tipped his head back and called, "Is there anybody up there?" And a deep voice answered, "I am God. I have been watching you. You must trust in me. Let go of the rope and I will take you in my hands and bring you down to safety." The climber looked up, couldn't see anyone – looked down at the rocks far below, looked up again and called, "Is there *anybody else* up there?"'

There was no response from the other bunk.

'Lars? I hope I haven't offended you, now.'

'Of course not, you silly goat. *I* told *you* that story last year. Good-night.'

'A good-night to you, my friend.'

The tiny alarm clock woke them at 2 a.m., its insistent beeping silenced by Lars' fumbling hand. He stretched, wriggled out of his sleeping bag, dressed and made tea for them both. Then, as Ryan pulled on his trousers and boots, he made soup and poured it into a Thermos flask. They repacked their gear and stepped out of the hut into the moonlight. The ash slope and the summit snow were easier to walk on when frozen hard at night.

When the two elephants, trundling back downhill, neared the cave where they had left Tembo Steadfast's tusks, M'zee sensed that Kidogo seemed less frightened and tense than she had been higher up the mountain. They passed water and dropped dung clear of the entrance before M'zee checked that the ivories had remained undisturbed. He moved them so that one lay along each wall of the cave, then went into the cave tail-first, signalling to Kidogo to back in beside him. The two elephants, one huge and the other small only by comparison, stood side by side. M'zee could hear Kidogo's belly rumbling quietly as she digested her food. He had not eaten himself that day, the grass had been too coarse and his teeth were too few and painful for him to be able to grind up the stems of the heather plants. Why had Mana chosen a decrepit old elephant like him for such a testing task?

Kidogo was feeling secure and almost content. The old elephant by her side was huge and wise and it was an honour to be his Shadow. She thought of Rafiki, who by now would be almost out of the forest. It would be so much faster for him going downhill than up and he would soon be back at the Sacred Grove where Tembella Grace and the two Sisters would look after him. She wondered if she would try reading the tusks again and was about to reach down and touch the nearest when she realised she felt very tired. Reading was interesting and exciting but exhausting, and the day had been a hard one for her with the air seeming to be so thin. She wondered briefly why M'zee's belly was silent, then remembered that she had not actually seen him swallowing food all day. Why had he not eaten? He was dozing now, it must be just as hard for him so high up a mountain, perhaps even harder as he had so much more weight to carry than she did – especially those great tusks of his. They must be very heavy. She was lucky not to have any. No, she wasn't!

The two elephants dozed through the rest of the night, sometimes resting their bodies against the walls of the cave. Occasionally, Kidogo would swing her trunk across to touch the tusk that lay at her feet, just wanting to feel the smooth ivory and sense the great love and wisdom it seemed to radiate.

CHAPTER TWELVE

Lars and Ryan had carried all their gear with them rather than leave some of it at the hut, in case they wanted to descend by another route or spend more nights in one or other of the shelters around the mountain. Lars knew the route to the crater rim intimately and they climbed the frozen ash-slopes in the moonlight without the need for a torch.

'*Is* this retreating?' Ryan asked as they stepped onto the first area of snow.

'People who've lived around here a long time think so. It's sometimes lower than this after a storm but they say that the *permanent* snowline is higher each year.'

They had timed their climb to arrive at the crater rim as the sun rose over the horizon far to the east, turning the snow all about them a rosy red colour. This was one experience of which Lars never tired. His heart lifted with joy and he turned to Ryan, holding out his hand. The two friends shook hands and embraced spontaneously, laughing together as they did so.

'Happy Christmas,' said Lars, producing a bar of chocolate from his pocket.

'So it is, now. Christmas Day, I mean. I'd quite forgotten. Happy Christmas to you too.'

'Not everyone would like to get up at two o'clock on Christmas morning – but they don't know what they're missing.' As Lars turned back to watch the sunrise, Ryan asked, 'What do we do now?'

'We find the cave with the crossed tusks, then you'll have to believe in God!'

'How sure are you about this, then?'

'Follow me.'

Lars turned to walk along the path around the rim, glancing frequently down into the enormous crater with its ash-pit and sheer cliffs, some of which were sheathed in ice.

The sun rose higher as they walked until a wisp of cloud suddenly blotted it out. The cloud twisted and vanished only to be replaced by another which lasted longer before it too disappeared just as suddenly. The next cloud was denser and closed in around them, making the rocks on either side of the path take on a kind of menace.

One rock, larger than the rest, loomed out of the cloud. 'We're here,' Lars said, working his shoulders out of his Bergen and leaning the pack against the foot of the rock.

'Where?' Ryan asked.

'Above the cave. This is the rock I saw in my dream.'

Ryan watched his friend go to the edge of the rim and look over.

'Ice all the way down,' Lars called back.

They drank the hot soup from the Thermos flask, ate another bar of chocolate each, then strapped on their crampons, uncoiled the ropes and put two slings around convenient projections on the rock. 'Do you mind if I go down first?' Lars asked, clipping a shining figure-of-eight onto his harness.

'You're in charge,' Ryan replied. 'I'm just here to see that you don't fall down and die on your own, chasing dead jumbos round the mountain.'

Lars grinned, threw one rope over the cliff edge and clipped the safety rope to his harness and Ryan paid out the rope as his friend walked backwards down the ice-wall. He listened as the scratch and clink of the crampons grew fainter. After a while he knew Lars had stopped.

'Are you OK?' he called down.

'There is a cave here. Pay out more rope – I'm going in.'

Ryan waited, letting the rope slip a little at time over his shoulder as Lars jerked for more.

After what seemed like a long time, Lars called up. Ryan could hear the excitement in his voice. 'Lower the packs down – then come on down yourself.'

'Did you find your tusks now?'

'Come down and see!'

Ryan tied their two packs to the end of a rope, lowered them to Lars then swapped the ropes over and abseiled down as his friend paid out the safety line. Ryan went down slowly, enjoying once more the strange sensation of walking backwards with his body horizontal. The crisp bite of the spikes on his crampons into the ice was also supremely satisfying. At the cave entrance he checked and swung himself in, unclipped the ropes and looked around.

The cave was formed within the rock rather than being just a cavity in the ice and there was ample room to stand up. The entrance was surrounded by columns of ice, and light penetrated only a short distance into the cave while the far end of it receded into darkness and he had the impression that it had been formed by volcanic activity a long time before. Within the area lit from the entrance, two huge elephant tusks lay on the floor, their tips crossed one over the other, just as Lars had told him to expect. Lars himself was standing between the tusks, spreading his hands in a gesture of welcome. 'What was it you said last night? If we find the jumbo tusks you'd have to believe in God?'

'I said, *maybe* I'd have to. I'm not convinced yet. Even so, I'm impressed. I've never seen tusks this size before! How did they get here?'

'I've no idea.' Lars undid the top of his Bergen, found his

torch and walked towards the far end of the cave, shining the beam across the floor and around the walls. 'Come and see this,' he called, his voice echoing slightly.

Ryan had taken out his own torch and followed Lars, shining the beam down onto the floor so that he could avoid the small ridges and hollows as he walked.

'Look here. Look at this!' Lars was shining his torch on one of the side-walls. The smooth stone was covered in simple drawings of humans and elephants in shades of brown, red and black with the elephants' tusks showing either yellow or white. He swung the torch from left to right and back again. There were dozens of elephants and more of the human figures.

'I've seen pictures like this before – in South Africa and Botswana,' Lars said. 'Bushman art. Well, it's more correct to call them San people now, but they painted pictures like these on cave walls all over Africa. Some are thought to be thousands of years old.'

Ryan stepped forward to examine one of the scenes more closely, and Lars said, 'Look. All the men here are shown with erect penises – that's typical Bushman – the men are actually like that all the time. The women are usually shown with protruding buttocks – but all of *these* are men.'

He went to the extreme left-hand painting. It showed only elephants, all of which had faded yellow tusks except for one with large white tusks that crossed each other at the ends. The next picture was less distinct as a mineral stain had obliterated most of it but it seemed to show the white-tusked elephant lying dead on the ground with others grouped around it as if in mourning. These all had white tusks, though none were as large as those on the dead one.

The two men shone their torches onto the next picture, the first in which human figures appeared. Two large, white-tusked elephants were carrying what appeared to be the dead elephant's tusks up a steep slope followed by a line of Bushmen in single file. Some carried bows and arrows, some spears, while the last four clearly had coils of rope over their shoulders.

'I think we're seeing how these tusks got here,' said Lars, swinging the beam of his torch onto the next picture that covered the rock forming the back of the cave.

This showed elephants in silhouette at the top of an ice-wall, and men lowering a tusk down it with a rope. The men were no longer naked but appeared to be wearing cloaks made from animal skins.

The only picture on the right-hand wall was almost obliterated by water stains but a fire was just visible with men and elephants near it. In the background was the unmistakeable outline of Kilimanjaro with its two peaks, Kibo and Mawenzi, both clearly recognisable.

'Not God then – Bushmen and elephants!' said Ryan.

'I never claimed God *put* the tusks here. All I believe is that somehow God showed me this cave and the tusks in a dream and wanted me to come up here.'

Ryan moved sideways, then leaped back when his foot touched something soft and yielding. He shone his torch down before stepping forward and kneeling by a mass of fibres. He poked it cautiously then picked up a section of twisted rope that fell apart between his fingers. 'How long do you think this has been here?' he asked.

'God knows,' said Lars wryly.

The fibres were dry and smelled musty. Ryan dusted off his hands and asked, 'What do we do now?'

'I've been waiting for you to ask me that. The voice in my dream said I was to climb the mountain and get these tusks out of the crater. I suppose we should work out how to do that.'

A flash from outside lit up the cave. Lars went cautiously to the entrance and peered out. Dark, swirling clouds swept past, the wind making eerie noises in the columns of the ice-wall outside. Suddenly the clouds cleared, torn away by the wind as flash after flash of lightning leaped around the crater rim and thunder growled and rumbled in the great hollow.

The two men watched from the shelter of the entrance, stepping back when showers of ice particles fell past the opening.

'Quite a storm,' said Lars. 'I've only seen one other like this up here before. Had to get my party down to the huts pretty quick. They were all mightily fed up with not getting right to the top though. One silly bugger wanted to carry on regardless. There's one in most parties!'

He stepped back, hit his ankle against the pointed end of one of the tusks, swore quietly, rubbed his ankle and said, 'Time to eat, I think. Help me move these out of our way.'

With Lars at one end and Ryan at the other they half-dragged, half-carried the tusks to the back of the cave, laying them one on either side of the heap of rotted ropes.

M'zee and Kidogo had left their cave much farther down the mountain at about the time Lars and Ryan had reached the snowline.

Before leaving, M'zee moved Steadfast's tusks to the back of the cave and arranged them to lie snugly side by side, then covered them with layers of uprooted giant heather plants that he'd dragged in from outside. Only then did he start to walk back up the valley they had explored the day before. Kidogo browsed as she climbed, now knowing which stems and leaves were sweet on her tongue and which were sharp and bitter and to be avoided. After a while she noted that M'zee was not making any attempt to eat.

Walking slowly, with frequent rests to catch their breath, they came once more to where the oddly shaped plants were replaced by small rocks and ground-hugging mosses and lichens, but the view that had so upset Kidogo the day before was hidden by clouds. The two plodded steadily upwards across the stony ground until they reached the ash-slope and found that walking uphill was very tiring with the loose ash slipping under their feet. They had made little progress when they heard the first rumble of thunder above them.

M'zee raised his trunk and stopped. Another rumble, then a crash nearby and for a moment the cloud around them glowed.

'Down,' was all M'zee said, and the two elephants turned and hurried downhill pursued by the storm, giant hailstones bouncing off their backs until they reached the shelter of the cave. They backed in and stood breathing heavily, steam rising from their skin.

'Mana does not mean us to climb to the top of Holy Mountain today,' M'zee wheezed to the shivering youngster.

Later, when Kidogo had stopped shaking and the storm had eased, M'zee said, 'I am sure that Tembo Steadfast would not mind if you ate some of the heather I brought in to cover his tusks.'

It was the chance Kidogo had been waiting for. She said, a little hesitantly, 'There is enough here for us both. Will you eat too, M'zee?'

M'zee didn't speak for a minute, then said, 'It's too coarse for me. My teeth can't grind it up. I'll just have to wait to eat until we get back down to a swamp where the feed is soft. But you go ahead.'

Kidogo ate a little but was thinking of what M'zee had said. She knew that elephant's teeth ground down and were replaced six times in a full lifetime by new teeth moving forward to replace the worn ones. Temba Comfort had told her that, when she had asked her why she and Temba Kindness chewed up food and passed it to Tembella Grace.

'She lost her last teeth nearly forty years ago.' Comfort had replied. 'She would have stepped-over in hunger long ago if we had not been doing that. It's just a little thing that we do for her.'

Kidogo had been very moved. For forty years the two Sisters had been chewing food and passing the wads across to the ancient one to keep her alive. They must have a great love for her, she had thought. Nearly forty years! That was more than twice as long as she herself had lived!

The clouds did not clear and the thunder rumbled around the summit for the rest of the day. Night came early and once more M'zee reverently placed Tembo Steadfast's tusks along the sides of the cave. As the two elephants stood together, facing outwards, Kidogo was feeling the tusk lying nearest to her, too concerned about M'zee to try and read the pictures but thinking how much she would like to have even small tusks of her own. Forlornly, she felt her cheeks hoping in vain that tiny buds might even now be trying to break through.

M'zee must have felt or sensed what she was doing, and spoke softly in the darkness. 'I believe you yearn for tusks, my Shadow.'

Kidogo did not answer. It was true, she did, but there was *no* chance of her growing any now. Other elephants of her age either had strong tusks or none at all. She had never seen newly growing tusks on any elephant other than very young ones. Then she thought of Rafiki whose precious tusk had been shattered by a bullet. Had he made it to the Sacred Grove? Would they ever meet again? She knew she was privileged to be a Shadow to the venerable M'zee but at that moment she would rather be splashing with her friend in a sun-warmed waterhole, water-biters or no water-biters.

M'zee did not ask again. It was Kidogo who eventually

broke the silence with a question that had puzzled her for a long time. 'What are tusks made of?' she asked.

The old one must have been dozing. He snorted himself awake and repeated the question. 'What are tusks made of? Well. Just so. Well. They *feel* like the stuff teeth are made of, but teeth are rough and tusks are smooth. I asked my old Tembella that question when I was much younger than you. She said they were made of Love. I didn't know if I should believe her then, and I still don't know. She told me that was why the tusks of Tembo Jay were taken to the top of Holy Mountain. Then all the Love stored in his great tusks could flow down over the elephants of this land forever. If you let yourself think about it, you can feel the Love stored in the tusks of Tembo Steadfast here in this cave. A Love that has forgiven me for what I did to him all those years ago.'

He was quiet again and Kidogo realised that the old one must be very tired as well as hungry. She would not trouble him with more questions that night.

When the storm finally rumbled to an end, Ryan chipped some ice from the cave entrance and melted it in a pan over his stove to make tea. Both men knew they would have to spend the night in the cave but neither was bothered by this. Compared with some bivouacs they had shared on glaciers in the past, this was almost cosy.

Lars was first to remark on how warm it felt in the cave. He ran his hand along one of the tusks and was sure it was radiating a very faint warmth. He suggested Ryan do the same, and asked him what he'd felt.

'Sure, I can't describe it,' he replied. 'It's sort of warm but more like when you're in a room with old friends and a few bottles of Guinness. I like it here. I could stay in this cave forever.' He laughed and added, 'Your parties can bring me food when they come up. I shall be the wise old man of the mountains.'

After drinking the tea and eating biscuits, sardines and chocolate as the last of the daylight faded outside, they flattened out the rotted fibres of the ancient ropes to make a soft bed between the two huge tusks, and unrolled their sleeping bags, working mostly in the dark to save their torch batteries. Half into his sleeping bag, Lars switched his torch on, sat up and surveyed the Bushman paintings in sequence. He focused on the one showing how the ropes had been secured to the tusks, then switched off the torch and lay down, wriggling his body to shape the loose fibres.

'I've slept on harder beds than this,' he said into the darkness.

Ryan grunted. ''Tis probably the best bed on the whole of Kilimanjaro. Made of old rope it is. Money for old rope! Actually, old rope for no money . . .'

Lars gave him a kick. 'Go to sleep!'

Although now snug and comfortable, Lars lay awake knowing he had to work out how to get the tusks out of the cave and up onto the crater rim. He slid his hand out of the sleeping bag and reached out to touch the one nearest him. It was smooth – and warm! It must have some inner warmth – but he could not think how that could be. It must be the strange warmth which had prevented the cave from filling with snow and freezing solid. He touched it again and realised he had always loved the *feel* of ivory. His aunt had had a fan made of thin blades of ivory. As a boy, he had enjoyed opening and closing it on the rare occasions when she had taken it out of the glass cabinet to show him. Then there had been ivory keys on pianos and ivory billiard balls but they were made from something else now. How long had these tusks been here?

In the night, Ryan woke thinking he could smell burning sulphur. The scent was very faint and he suspected it must be coming from the fumaroles Lars had earlier told him still existed down in the crater below the cave entrance. It was a distinctive smell that took his thoughts back to experiments in the chemistry lab at his old school in Dublin. He could remember how the fumes had caught the back of his throat and he had been led outside, coughing violently. Now they were so faint they didn't really bother him, but the memory tickled his throat more than the fumes and he coughed several times before going back to sleep.

Lars heard Ryan have his coughing fit but said nothing. He had been lying awake remembering the time when he'd left his family home in Cape Town and taken a summer job at the hotel called Bushmans Kloof in the Cederberg Mountains, three hundred kilometres to the north. It was a luxurious place with a clientele of mostly overseas visitors who enjoyed the sensation of being out in the real African veldt but with gourmet meals, attentive servants, convenient swimming pools and the chance to see for themselves some of the many examples of Bushman rock art in the caves and shelters all around the hotel complex.

He had enjoyed his summer as a guide, driving the visitors around the huge estate and walking them from the safari vehicle to the Bushmen's sites, pointing out the springbok, the gemsbok, the imported herd of elands and the various birds. He had encouraged the tourists to try to be the first to see the smaller creatures, the elephant shrews and occasional snakes, and was always pleased by their reactions to the enigmatic paintings when they reached the rock shelters.

Now he was in a cave on Africa's highest mountain near to some unique paintings that had not been seen for hundreds, if not thousands, of years. But he had been given a job to do! If he believed in the message in his dream – how could he not believe it now? – he had to find a way to get the two tusks out of the cave.

'*Climb the mountain and get these tusks out of the crater*,' the quiet voice had said. Everything else had been true. The cave *was* just where he had dreamed it to be. The two tusks *had* been there – lying with their tips crossed, exactly as in the dream. So now he *had* to get them out of the crater somehow. His not to question why, his just to do and— He hoped it would not come to that!

Ryan was snoring. Lars sat up and shone the torch on the rock paintings, trying to see how the Bushmen's ropes had been fastened to the smooth ivory. With the tusks being tapered it would be difficult to secure the ropes so that they wouldn't slip. The paintings were not very detailed but he could see how the fibre ropes had been tied in such a way as to use the taper of the tusks and their weight to tighten the knots, but it would take more than Ryan and himself to pull them up.

He turned off the torch and lay back down. He would need a lot of people to haul up the tusks and there was no one else on the mountain. Then he remembered the guides and porters who had been carrying off the rubbish, the taka-taka. There had been more bags at the Kibo huts – they must be coming back for these. Now, if he and Ryan were able to get the tusks back to the cave mouth – which they could – secure the ropes to the tusks – he would find a way to do this – and leave the ropes fixed to the rock on the crater rim – which was easy – all he and Ryan would have to do was to go down and wait at the huts until the guides and porters came back and persuade them to make the final climb to the crater rim with him and haul up the tusks. Problem solved!

He turned over and wriggled his hips to make a hollow in the soft fibres of the rotted ropes. Fine dust must have been disturbed for it tickled in his nostrils as he went to sleep and he felt himself to be an unseen observer sitting on a fallen tree-trunk watching the activity in a Bushman camp. Although what he could see was hazy, he knew just where it was located by the relative angle of Kilimanjaro's two peaks etched against the sky. The camp must be near to the north end of the swamp in what was now the Amboseli National Park – only this was a greener Amboseli, with many more trees. He checked the snowline and it was notably lower than it was now. He knew, from the training he had undertaken to be a guide in Tanzania, that there had been no Bushmen in that area for at least a hundred years.

Through the haze he could see more animals than when he had last visited the Park, and elephants, including many with magnificent tusks, were browsing fearlessly close to the cluster of grass-covered shelters. Naked children played around the fires and bare-breasted women, wearing leather aprons, sat cracking nuts, leisurely placing them one by one in a hollow on a rock and tapping the nutshell with a heavy stone. Five men in soft leather loincloths carried the severed neck of a giraffe into the camp and handed it over to the women. The whole ambience was of peace and calm and he felt he wanted to stay there for the rest of his life.

Feeling uncomfortably hot he wriggled his arms out of the sleeping bag and one hand touched the unfamiliar smoothness of the tusk at his side. Immediately, the haze cleared and the scene became so intense that he became a part of it himself. He looked down and found he was wearing a loincloth like the other men. He touched it and it felt as if it was made from chamois leather. The skin on his arms and legs was an apricot colour and on his feet were thin leather soles much like the rubber flip-flops he used to wear on the beaches at the Cape when he was a child.

He stood up and walked across to the men who had just come into the camp. They greeted him in a language full of clicks and throaty noises, which he was surprised to find he understood perfectly. He was even more surprised to find he could speak it himself as he asked about the hunt. A small boy came and stood at his side, reaching up to hold his hand.

Behind the hunters a huge bull elephant was approaching. Lars called out a warning and made as if to step backwards. His hand again touched the tusk by his side and the picture faded.

Lars woke when the blackness at the cave entrance was beginning to lighten. He got out of the sleeping bag and put on the clothes he had taken off the previous evening then, trying not to waken Ryan, he carried the stove to the entrance and boiled water to make tea. When he came back carrying two mugs, Ryan was dressing.

Nodding his thanks for the tea, Ryan asked, 'So. What have you got lined up for us today?'

'My dream said that I must get the tusks out of the crater and I've been thinking about how to do it.'

'And . . .?'

'We can't do it on our own.'

'So . . .?'

'So we need some help. You remember those rubbish bags at the huts. The wardens must be coming back up for those. Yesterday was Christmas Day so they wouldn't have come then, and probably won't come today. If we were to get the tusks ready to haul up the cliff we could then go down to the huts and wait there until they do come. We've got enough food for a few days.'

'OK – so far. But how do we get the wardens to come up here and haul the tusks up the ice-face? And do they carry them down the mountain as well?'

'We'd have to pay them of course. Enough to make them *want* to do it.'

'They'd get into trouble with their boss. He sent them up to bring down the taka-taka.'

'I'm sure I could fix that. It'll make one hell of a story for the Park. Hemingway made a whole book out of a dead leopard being found on the crater rim – and he never even climbed Kili. Think of the publicity value of finding two enormous and ancient elephant tusks that had been hidden by Bushmen in a cave inside the crater. I could write a book about it that would have Ernest H rolling around in his grave with envy.'

'So . . .?'

'So we get the tusks back to the entrance. Tie them, one to each rope, leave them here, and we jumar up the ropes to the rim. Then we go down to the hut and wait. Simple!'

'Suppose the wardens *don't* come.'

'They will. They can't have collected all that rubbish just to leave it there in bags. Anyway, here's a Plan B. If the wardens don't come, trekkers will. The mountain is only closed over Christmas. Soon it'll be swarming with climbers. They'll want to help – and for free. They could dine out on that story for years!'

Ryan was not easily convinced. 'How do you fix the ropes to the tusks? They're smooth and tapered. The ropes'll slip off.'

'Oh thou of little faith! Look . . .' Lars shone the torch onto the picture of the Bushmen lowering the tusks down the cliff. 'See how they did it. We could fix them in the same way. *And* I've got a roll of gaffer-tape in my bag – if we use some of that the ropes can't slip.'

The sun, which had lightened the sky outside the cave in the ice-wall, also shone into the cave where the two elephants had spent the night. Temba Kidogo moved restlessly as she waited for M'zee to open his eyes. Eventually, he sighed and using the tip of his trunk he pushed his eyelids apart, reached back into the water reserve deep in his throat and sprayed a little into each eye, blinking hard as he did so. Kidogo turned her head away while he did this, pretending to study a beetle climbing up the cave wall. She thought he might be embarrassed if he knew she was watching him.

Conscious now of M'zee's rapid ageing, she started to worry again as to whether she was up to supporting him on their task. Any movement of trunk or legs so far up the mountain took more energy than lower down and she could see, by his ribs, that the lack of food was beginning to tell.

Remembering how the Sisters had fed Tembella Grace she wandered casually out of the cave and started to browse on the coarse stems and foliage of the giant heather plants, grinding each trunkful to a soft paste. When she had a mouthful of finely ground pulp she walked back to the cave, took the wad out of her mouth and offered it to M'zee. He stared at it, not understanding what she had done.

'It's for you,' she said, a little shyly. 'My teeth are stronger than yours and these heather stems are very hard.'

The old one reached out and touched the centre of her forehead with his trunk-tip before taking the wad from her and placing it in his mouth.

'That was good,' he said after swallowing it. 'I chose my Shadow well.'

'I'll get more,' Kidogo said. 'It's a long time since you ate well and we will both need to be strong when we climb the rest of the mountain.'

M'zee again touched her forehead, his trunk lingering there slightly longer than before.

She went browsing again, alternating between feeding herself and chewing up heather stems for M'zee. He took each food-wad she brought to him and swallowed it grate-fully. Every time she returned he would shake himself awake

118

and reach out an eager trunk for her offering and each time she left, he would thank her with a touch to her forehead.

With the tenth present of food, he was fully awake and looking much brighter. She could see that he had once more moved Steadfast's tusks to the back of the cave and covered them with foliage. He took the last food-wad from her, swallowed it, touched her forehead and said gently, 'Thank you, my Shadow. It is time for us to leave.'

M'Zee led the way up the track to the scree, where he rested for a while before continuing upwards towards the snowline with Kidogo following, both elephants breathing hard.

As he walked, M'zee was feeling stronger than he had for several days. He had known he needed food but his last vestiges of teeth were useless for eating anything but the softest of swamp vegetation and there was none of that up here. It had not occurred to him that his Shadow might do what she had done – truly he had chosen well. He savoured the last remnants, feeling around in his mouth with his tongue. The food-wads she had brought him had tasted sweeter than any he could remember. It was more than the taste of the food itself – it had been prepared and given with Love and Care. It was a long time since any tembo had shown Love and Care for him. Respect – yes, but Love and Care – not for many years. He climbed energetically with Kidogo close behind, their breath forming little clouds of mist in the cold air of the mountain.

In their cave, Lars and Ryan had dragged the tusks to the entrance and secured the ends of their climbing ropes to them. They fixed the ropes as the Bushmen had done but with the added security of generous amounts of the silver-coloured gaffer-tape. When this had been done they brewed another mug of tea. There was no hurry to start the climb up to the crater rim – it was Boxing Day and they didn't expect the litter-carrying party to reach the Kibo huts until the following day at the earliest.

While they drank their tea, Lars told Ryan about the Bushman vision he had experienced in the night. He did not call it a dream as dreams so often fade and vanish when one wakes and, like the one where he was flying and saw the tusks in the cave, this was still clear in his mind. The earlier flying one must have been a vision too. After all, what he had seen in his sleep had subsequently proved to be fact. He touched the smooth ivory of one of the great tusks just to reassure himself.

They talked about the tragedy of the virtual extinction of the Bushmen all over Africa, the lands used by the hunter-gatherers being always taken from them by stronger, more numerous cattle-herding tribes and eventually by farmers of European descent.

'My grandfather had an interesting theory,' said Ryan. 'He came from the Burren in the far west of Ireland. That's a vast area of limestone rock all cracked by fissures and full of caves. Now, to make any sense of what he said, you have to imagine Ireland and, indeed, the whole of Britain and most of Europe covered in dense bush and forests with plentiful wild animals. It must once have been like Africa used to be – only colder. No one disputes that there were cavemen living there, only they are always depicted as heavily-built men with shaggy hair, receding foreheads and low intelligence. Yet *someone* painted animals in the caves in Europe in those times and, if you look at pictures of these paintings, they are almost *exactly* like the Bushmen rock paintings. My grandfather believed that there were *Bushmen* inhabiting Europe, including Britain and Ireland, in those days. Remember that Britain and Ireland were part of the mainland, until the seas rose and made them into islands.'

He unwrapped a chocolate wafer-bar, broke it in half and passed a piece to Lars who was now sitting on one of the tusks.

'It's quite possible that there were both Neanderthal types *and* Bushman types living side by side when the Celts came from the east and ousted them,' Ryan continued. 'The Celts would have killed out the Neanderthals *and* the Bushmen. They would both have been seen as a dangerous nuisance to them, just as the Bushmen were seen to be a dangerous nuisance by the herdsmen and farmers in Africa. Now here's the bit I like, although if it's true, it's terribly sad. My grandfather believed that the Bushmen of Europe lingered on in Ireland until just a couple of centuries ago – living in the deepest woods and the least frequented parts – such as the Burren.'

He paused and Lars said, 'The Little People!'

'Exactly so. Think of what you've heard of the Little People in Irish legends. Small brown-skinned men and women – sometimes they were even called *Brownies*. People who could disappear when you got close and who avoided contact with other people but who could sometimes be seen by children. Little people with a wicked sense of humour but a strong sense of gratitude, leaving a dead rabbit or some mushrooms on your doorstep if you left out a bowl of milk or cream for them.

'Then there are the stories of the Little People dancing around a campfire in the forest, singing pagan songs and chanting. How the priests must have hated them – children of the devil to be sure – and encouraged their extermination. Saddest of all to me were the stories of babies being abducted and brought up amongst the Little People as their own. Now, is that not the way the older survivors of a dying race might behave when their own young men and women have been caught and surreptitiously killed?' Ryan paused for a response.

121

Lars said, 'If they lived in caves, they would be like the Trolls in my family's old country. In their legends and folk-law, the Trolls would sing and dance in the forests and *they* were believed to abduct babies. It fits horribly well. Your grandfather could have been right! Did he tell this idea to anyone else?'

'I don't think he did so. In those days, anything that the priests would call *ungodly* was not spoken of. It's different now, but my grandpa's dead and I'd forgotten about it until I saw those pictures and you told me what you dreamt in the night. To think what people did to the Bushmen here in Africa might have been done all across Europe by our ancestors, is horrifying. Worst of all, there's no way for us or anyone to make amends.'

They sat silently in the cave entrance, until Lars stood up. 'Time for us to finish clearing up here – don't pack your jumars though.'

A little later, standing with his Bergen on his back, he said, 'Bad climbing practice I know, but I'm going up my rope without a safety line, my rope's a new one and I'm happy about the belay at the top. How about you?'

Ryan agreed, and they decided to go up side by side, each clipping their Jumar ascenders onto their ropes and attaching the slings before starting the climb. The sun, that had been bright on the far side of the crater earlier, was now hidden by thick mist and they worked their way up the ropes in a silence broken only by their grunting at the effort and the clicking of the ratchets in the Jumars. Both men had some difficulty in getting over the crater rim where the ropes were tight over the rocks, especially as fresh snow had fallen sometime in the night and frozen into a hard crust. Safely over the rim, they unclipped the jumars, took off their backpacks, scraped the snow off the top of a convenient boulder and sat down to recover their breath.

Lars turned in surprise at the sound of crunching snow to his left and saw a huge shape emerging from the mist. Behind this was another, smaller than the first but, seen through the mist, it too was enormous. Elephants – two elephants – up here! He nudged Ryan and whispered, 'Keep sitting down and look to your left.'

He felt Ryan turn and his body stiffen. The elephants had stopped and were scenting the air with their trunks.

'Holy Mother of God,' Ryan gasped. 'What should we be doing now?'

Lars whispered back, 'Just sit still and see what happens.'

Kidogo had seen past M'zee's side and had also scented the presence of men on the crater rim. What were *they* doing up here? In fact, what was *she* doing up here? It must all be part of Mana's plan. She knew, from living among humans, that most people were afraid of elephants if they encountered them unexpectedly. These two men were probably scared that they might be attacked and even killed. She wondered what M'zee would do now and stepped forward to stand beside him, the humans just visible through the thin vapours.

M'zee made no move but just stood still, looking at the dim forms through the mist.

'I think we should show them we are not going to harm them,' Kidogo rumbled to M'zee. 'They must be part of Mana's plan too.'

'Just so. Just so,' M'zee rumbled back. 'You know humans better than I do. How can we do that?'

'Stay here – I'm smaller than you.'

She moved forward, her ears back against her body, holding out her trunk with the tip near the ground and waving it slowly from side to side in an obvious gesture of friendship.

'Do you see that then?' Ryan said. ''Tis wanting to be our friend, I'm sure.'

'Careful now,' said Lars, but Ryan had stood up and was walking towards the elephant, holding out both his hands, palms upwards. The elephant waited until he was quite near, then slowly reached out her trunk and sniffed at his hands.

'There you are now,' he said, turning towards Lars. 'I told you it was wanting to be friends.'

Lars shook his head. It was all too much. Here he was on the top of Kilimanjaro, having spent the night in an cave with the largest tusks he'd ever seen – and now he was watching his friend patting the trunk of a wild elephant on the crater rim. He stood up but did not join Ryan. Someone had to act responsibly. Even so, his mind was exploring new possibilities. Something big was going on – he had been sure of that for some time – and he was a part of it, willing or otherwise.

He knew that in many parts of Asia elephants were used to move big loads of timber. Could these two somehow be used to haul up the tusks from the cave? Ryan was walking towards him, a huge grin on his face and with the end of the smaller elephant's trunk resting on his open palm. The bigger one was still standing almost out of sight in the mist, its ears back and trunk dangling, not in any way threatening them.

Ryan led the elephant up to Lars and said, 'Meet my new friend, Miss Jumbo.' The elephant held out her trunk towards Lars and he touched it, feeling a little foolish. It was like shaking hands – but this was the creature's nose! The skin was surprisingly soft and he noticed several coarse hairs around the moist opening at the end. 'Hello,' he said, feeling even more foolish.

The elephant blew softly into his hand, then left them standing together and walked cautiously to the edge of the crater where it peered over into the swirling mist. It reached down to touch the ropes from the cave, out of sight far below.

'Do you think we could get *them* to haul up the tusks for us?' Lars asked Ryan, not now feeling any need to lower his voice.

The elephant turned back from the crater edge and walked towards them, its trunk movements and eye contact showing very clearly that it had understood what he had said. She touched Ryan then Lars on the forehead before turning and ambling into the mist towards the other elephant.

M'zee raised his trunk in query as Kidogo approached. 'They *are* a part of Mana's plan,' she said. 'The tusks are in a cave over the side of the cliff and they have ropes going down to them. *Ropes* are like thin creepers,' she explained. 'Humans use them to lift and pull things. They want us to pull the tusks up to the top of the cliff with the ropes.'

M'zee shook his head as he remembered the words of his dream. '*You are to choose a Shadow for yourself, go to the top of Holy Mountain and find the tusks of Tembo Jay.*'

That was what the voice had said and he had done the first two things requested – but there had been nothing in the dream to say that humans were to be involved – but then there was nothing to say that they weren't. Did it matter if it had been them who had actually *found* the tusks? Clearly not! If Mana had inspired him to come up here, he had probably inspired the humans too. They had not harmed Kidogo – it was unlikely they would try and harm him.

'Where are these *ropes*?' he asked.

'They are wrapped around a rock and go over the edge of the cliff. I am sure that they go down to the cave and are fixed in some way to the tusks. The humans will show us what they want us to do.'

M'zee followed her to where Lars and Ryan stood. Both men were looking a little apprehensive as he approached and

125

they could see how enormous he was.

'They're coming back,' Ryan said. 'They've come to help, I'm sure.' He went over to where the belaying slings were looped over the projecting rock, lifted the two slings securing the first rope and held them out to the smaller elephant. He was wary of approaching the great bull standing behind her. The smaller one took the slings and, following his signs, looped them over one of the bull's tusks.

The bull, working out what was required of him, started to walk downhill, accompanied by the smaller one.

Ryan went with them, calling back to Lars, 'Shout when you want us to stop.'

Standing on the crater rim, Lars watched as the rope tightened and it was obvious that the tusk was being drawn out of the cave and up the ice-wall. He was glad he had taken so much trouble in securing the rope to the tusk. Had he used the guides and porters, as he had planned, he would have gone down himself and guided the tusks up but the elephants had given him no such chance. All he could do now was hold the other rope out of the way while the one being pulled by the elephants slid over the ice-lip on the rim, cutting a deep groove. He hoped that the edge of the underlying rock was not sharp, which might cause the rope to fray and break and let the huge tusk fall down into the crater. Soon however, the root of the tusk appeared and the tusk itself slid gently over the rim.

'Hold hard,' he called into the mist as he eased it carefully onto the flat ground. The pulling stopped.

Lars was drawing back the slack rope and coiling it as Ryan and the elephants reappeared out of the mist. Ryan took the slings holding the second rope from the rock and looped them over the bull's tusks himself, while the smaller one watched.

The second tusk came up as easily as the first and, while

Ryan and the elephants stood by, all breathing loudly, Lars cut away the gaffer tape and untied the knots.

'What now?' Ryan asked, but before Lars could answer, the biggest of the elephants reached out, lifted one of the tusks and held it for the smaller one to take. She fumbled awkwardly until she found the point where it would balance, then she stepped clear, carrying it. The huge male reached out his trunk, touched first Lars then Ryan on the forehead, picked up the other tusk and followed the smaller elephant down into the mist.

As the two men stood looking after them, there was rumble and a hissing sound from the crater behind them and the ground trembled slightly.

'Mother of God!' Ryan swore again. 'The mountain's erupting on us.'

Grabbing their packs but abandoning their other gear, the two men ran down the snow-covered slope towards the huts. Behind them the mist flickered and glowed red and orange.

Kidogo felt the ground moving beneath her. She could hear the crunch of M'zee's feet in the frozen snow behind her as she hurried on down the mountainside. The tusk was much heavier than Steadfast's had been but at least she was going downhill. The ground shook again and she stumbled and fell, letting go of the tusk and, to her dismay, it slid down the snow slope and out of sight. Not daring to look round at M'zee, she ran after it, following the groove it had made in the frozen crust. Behind her the sky pulsed in surges of orange and red and the air was full of a strange scent that caught in her throat.

The tusk had come to rest where the snow no longer covered the ash-slope. It appeared to be unharmed. Kidogo picked it up, again aware of how much heavier it was than even Steadfast's huge tusk had been. She turned as M'zee lumbered out of the mist, outlined dark against the glowing sky.

'Hold that tight and follow me,' he panted as he passed.

She ran, thinking of what the Yellow Tusks had told the other tembos so long ago. If they didn't do what the Yellow Tusks told them to do, *Mana would make the mountain burn and melt and they would all be burned to death by flaming rocks rolling down the mountainside.*

She ran faster, wondering what they had done to upset Mana. Surely they had only done what Mana had directed M'zee to do?

The old elephant was waiting for her at the forest edge, the tusk lying at his feet. 'That was well done,' he said, touching her forehead.

CHAPTER THIRTEEN

When Tembo Rafiki left Kidogo and M'zee at the top of the forest, he had felt the blessings they'd called after him as he trundled alone down through the trees. He wanted to be out of the forest and into open country as quickly as he could but when he tried to run the damaged tusk wobbled horribly in its socket, causing him unbearable pain.

He stopped until it eased, then went on more slowly. Going downhill was much easier than climbing and even when it got dark he tried to continue, following the faint scent his party had left on the way up. But after he'd caught his shattered tusk in the undergrowth, then bumped it against a tree trunk, he stopped in the next glade and waited impatiently for dawn.

He reached Amboseli when the sun was at its height, and passed small groups of the shame-faced tembulls and jostlers who were browsing by the swamp. There was none of the usual shoving and pushing going on, and Tembo Lusty called out to him to ask where M'zee was.

Rafiki did not reply but hurried on, eager to reach the Sacred Grove and its refreshing waters.

It took him another two days and nights of agony before he came to where he could see the tembo-trees through the gap in the rocks. He felt as if he was coming home and sang out in low~sound.

'I have come back ~ and need your help.
My tusk is bad ~ the pain is great.'

Rafiki waited for a reply, agonising spasms shaking his

whole body, and his cheek feeling as if it was on fire.

'Come to us now ~ the waters wait.

Your pain will soon ~ be past and gone.'

The message itself, sung with care and compassion, seemed to ease the pain and Rafiki hurried on, eager to reach the fresh green which he remembered surrounded the baobab trees but, when he reached the trees, the earth all around was parched and dry.

He saw the two Sisters standing in the shade but did not stop. He rushed past them and down the track into the water, wading out until it was above his head. He stood in this deep place, feeling almost weightless, holding his trunk above the surface and breathing through it as the healing waters washed away much of the pain.

Eventually, he waded out and climbed the bank to where the Sisters stood watching him. Temba Kindness touched his forehead in greeting and asked, 'Where is the Blesséd One?'

Rafiki told them what had happened up on the mountain before he'd been forced to turn back at the top of the forest, then he looked around and asked, 'Tembella Grace . . .?'

Temba Kindness lifted her trunk and replied, 'She stepped-over the day after you and the Blesséd One left us. She said her job here was done.'

Rafiki looked at where the ancient one had always stood. There was a pile of branches obviously covering a body, the twigs and leaves dry and brown. He could understand why the foliage *there* was dead but he was used to seeing the surrounding grass and bush fresh and green from the frequent rains.

He started to ask, 'Rain? Why—?'

Kindness interrupted him. 'We just couldn't linque for rain as we used to do. Maybe our Love was not enough with only the two of us. Now, let me look at your tusk.'

Although the pain was far less, Rafiki winced when she

130

touched his cheek, then wrapped her trunk carefully around his tusk. Standing behind him, Temba Comfort smacked her trunk across his rump and as he swung round in surprise his damaged tusk remained in Kindness's trunk. He stood there shaking at the suddenness of it and the agonising pain as she walked down to the pool, waded across and dropped the tusk into the water near the far bank. Meanwhile, Temba Comfort was looking into the hole where the tusk had been.

Rafiki was aware of a sickly scent of decay now mingling with the stench of rotting flesh that came from the body of Tembella Grace whenever the breeze blew from that direction. Temba Kindness left his tusk in the pool, waded back and was now filling her trunk with water. But she didn't squirt it into her mouth as she did when drinking, instead she came up the bank and stood facing him. Quite suddenly, and again without warning, she put the end of her trunk close to the hole where his tusk had been and blew a jet of water into it. Rafiki trumped in shock and pain as water, blood and pus ran down his cheek.

'It is necessary to do this,' Temba Kindness said and reached her trunk back into her throat to draw on the reserve of water there. This time Rafiki braced himself before she squirted it into the cavity. 'I may have to do this each day,' she warned him.

He was already feeling better. Whether it was because the weight of his tusk was no longer pressing on the bone, because of the cleansing of the wound, or because of the Love he felt was being given to him, he didn't know. He thanked the Sisters and went down to the pool himself, wading across to look at his tusk where it lay in the water. Small fish were nibbling at the remnants of skin and flesh around the root. He was intrigued to see from a different angle something which had been a part of him for so long. The tusk seemed bigger.

He took a trunkful of water and squirted it into the cavity in his cheek. It hurt – but he was sure it was good to clean out the hole. He waded to a deeper part of the pool where his cheek was half under the surface and, when he flushed it there, the pain was more bearable. He squirted water into the cavity again and again until the water coming out was no longer red. When he did eventually climb out of the pool, totally exhausted, he lay down beneath one of the tembo-trees and slept, while the Sisters stood guard on either side of him.

While Rafiki was finding relief from his pain, Lars and Ryan were running down the snow-covered mountainside drag-ging their packs, not even stopping to hoist them onto their backs until they were well down the ash-slope. When they did finally stop, both men bent over double, desperately gasping for breath as they turned to look back up towards the crater rim. Apart from a faint orange glow in the mist there was nothing to indicate that anything unusual had happened. Then the ground moved under their feet. They both lurched sideways and fell to the ground, terrified.

The solidity of the ground – terra firma – was the marker by which all their actions and senses were set. When that very *terra firma* moved, completely outside of their control, if only for a few seconds, it seemed as if the whole world was crumbling and nothing would ever be right again.

But the shuddering did stop.

Lars helped Ryan to his feet, lifted his friend's pack and guided his arms into the straps before shouldering his own Bergen. His mind was racing with thoughts of a documentary he'd once seen showing the pyroclastic flow from Mount Saint Helens in America when it erupted in 1980. 'We've got to get off the mountain,' he said urgently. 'Are you OK, Ryan?'

'Me? I'm all right. But what about those jumbos? I hope they're not hurt, now.'

'Never mind them. We've got to get going!' The documentary had shown a mass of super-heated gases racing down the side of the volcano, engulfing and destroying everything in its path. 'Come on!'

They passed the Kibo huts with the neatly stacked black bags outside and, still half-running, headed on down towards the saddle between the two peaks. Looking back once before turning down the track towards the Horombo huts, they saw the cloud had cleared from the summit and a plume of white-and-grey smoke now streamed out to the northeast. There was no other sign of an imminent eruption, and the ground was steady underfoot. As the immediate danger seemed to have passed, they slowed and walked down to the huts, feeling totally exhausted. Here they ate a little and rested for an hour or so before plodding down to the Mandara huts, where they met a group of wardens who were going up to the ridge to observe the after-effects of the eruption.

'I think it'd be best not to mention the elephants – or the tusks,' Lars cautioned Ryan.

'No one would believe us anyway,' said Ryan, nodding his agreement. 'I'm knackered. Shall we be sleeping here, or going on down?'

'I reckon I can make it back to the Riverside. What I need most is a shower, a real meal and a couple of lightly boiled aspirins!'

M'zee had led Kidogo down into the shelter of the forest, feeling very tired and concerned. They were now on the south side of the mountain – an area completely unknown to him. In their panic they had not run back the way they had come and, if they found a cave on this side, it would be

133

purely by chance. Neither of them was in a fit condition to go up and over the flat ground between the two peaks and he felt it was best to be well away from the fiery summit. They halted in a glade as darkness fell, thankful to lay down the heavy tusks.

Later in the night, M'zee was not surprised to find Kidogo standing so close to him that her body was in contact with his. After a few minutes, he rested his trunk over her shoulders and left it there until her shaking stopped. He was trying to forget the empty feeling in his belly. The huge tusks of Tembo Jay, lying at their feet, glowed with a faint white light just as Steadfast's had done when they had carried them into the safety of the cave on the other side of the mountain.

The message in his dream had said, *'You are to choose a Shadow for yourself, go to the top of Holy Mountain and find the tusks of Tembo Jay.'* He'd done that, and now all he could do was wait to be told what was expected of him next.

With the dawn, Kidogo woke knowing she would have to find food for them both, and leaving M'zee's side she wandered around the glade, gathering fodder and chewing it to pulp as she had done the day before. She took several food-wads and left them at the feet of the old one as he slept on. Only then did she forage for herself, walking a little way out of the glade but frequently looking over her shoulder to be sure she could find her way back. There were no droppings or other signs that forest elephants had been here recently, even though there was plentiful feed and a clear stream from which she drank.

When she returned to the glade, M'zee was finishing the last of the food-wads and he thanked her graciously.

'There is a stream not far away for when you are thirsty,' she told him.

'Thank you, my Shadow,' he said. 'I chose well when I chose you, Kidogo. We might be wise to go farther down the mountain to await what Mana will require of us next.'

Kidogo was not sure the old one was fit to travel and knew she could not carry the great tusk of Tembo Jay for long, but she agreed to his suggestion.

Both drank deeply from the stream before M'zee took up one of the tusks and Kidogo the other and, with the old one leading, they turned downhill to follow the watercourse through the trees.

It rained during the morning but by midday the sun was visible through the canopy of leaves far above their heads and they rested in a clearing where the sunbeams reached the forest floor and warmed their backs.

M'zee's ears came forward when they unmistakeably heard tembotalk in the forest.

'Up here,' a tembo's voice was saying. '*We* can go uphill faster than *they* can.'

Three youngsters broke out of the forest into the clearing where M'zee and Kidogo were standing. Each of the newcomers had a fine pair of tusks and each was carrying a stem of green bananas in his trunk. As they came nearer they shoved and shouldered each other in the way of excited young males.

Kidogo could tell by the size of their tusks that the three were much her age although they were considerably taller and heavier than she was. How she envied them their tusks. An almost forgotten jealousy tore at her guts like an anteater attacking a termite mound.

'Hold hard,' the first of the jostlers said, putting down his bananas. 'We have strangers in *our* woods!'

Kidogo cringed. M'zee was obviously big enough for them to recognise him as an elder – if not a Wise One. This

135

was no way to speak in his presence. The youngster had not even waited for a greeting from the tembull who was so clearly their senior.

M'zee seemed to swell up and he swung his trunk in irritation. 'Step forward and name yourself,' he commanded, a power in his voice that Kidogo had not heard before. The three jostlers lined up side by side but made no forward move.

'Name yourselves.' M'zee spoke again, his voice low and challenging.

The youngster on the left took a step forward and spoke in an insulting tone. 'My friend here is Tembo One Eye. We call him that because, as you can see, he has only one. To his right is Tembo Two Eyes. I am Tembo Three Eyes. I have two eyes in my head and one under my tail so I can see if I am being followed.' He winked at the other jostlers who smirked at his daring.

M'zee spoke coldly, his ears still held wide. 'An eye under your tail? I thought that was where your *mouth* was. Is this how you greet travellers on this side of Holy Mountain?'

Before Tembo Three Eyes could reply, a sound like a branch breaking came from the forest below them and blood spurted from a small hole in M'zee's left ear.

He spun round, bellowed, 'Follow me!' grabbed Tembo Jay's tusk and headed off up the hill into the forest. Close behind him came Three Eyes, followed by Kidogo. Then came One Eye with Two Eyes trailing behind.

When they were safely well above the humans, M'zee signalled a halt. He looked at Three Eyes, close behind him and Two Eyes who was only just catching up, still carrying his stem of bananas. M'zee spoke savagely to Three Eyes. 'I think *you* should be called Tembo *Fearful* because you are the first to run away – leaving your friends to follow. If you have an eye under your tail – as you claim – you should

136

have been the *last* in the line – protecting them!'

One Eye came up the hill, panting hard. Tembo Three Eyes lowered his trunk in apology and moved backwards to stand downhill from the others, watching the forest. M'zee was looking at Kidogo who felt uncomfortable but could not think why; she had only done what M'zee had ordered and followed him. Then she realised she had not carried the tusk that had been entrusted to her. In her haste she had left it in the clearing. Ashamed of herself, she lifted her tail and dropped dung then felt even more ashamed. M'zee said nothing.

'I will go back for it,' Kidogo said, her voice a little unsteady.

'It won't be there,' M'zee replied, flicking his ear to disturb the flies that were already clustering round the bullet wound. 'The humans will have lifted it and carried it away. They always take any tusks they can get.'

The others were all looking downhill, waiting. Two Eyes was putting down his bananas where they were not too obvious to M'zee. His movement had not gone unnoticed.

'So you, Tembo Two Eyes, prefer to carry *food* rather than take up the tusk of the greatest tembo who has ever lived. Have you no shame?'

'What is shame?' asked Two Eyes.

'Did you not learn that from your family? Didn't your Tembella teach you that?'

'We have no family. We have no Tembella. We three were the only ones to escape when all the others of our family were killed by the humans so they could grow food for themselves where we used to live. We were very young then.'

M'zee was silent for a while then asked more gently, 'So how have you lived since then?'

Tembo One Eye spoke now. 'We live any way we can. Bananas are good food but they only grow where the humans live. We like their mealies too. We go in the night and take what we need.'

'Humans *kill* tembos for doing that. How is it *you* are here and alive?'

Three Eyes spoke. 'We only go to their growing places in the dark, we quietly take the foods when they sleep and slip away before they wake. They chase us in the morning but we hide up in the forest and they never find us.'

'They did today!' Kidogo ventured when M'zee didn't respond. She was afraid the humans would still be hunting for them.

'That was different. One human saw us and called the others who came after us with their things that kill. We only stopped because we met you.'

'They call those things *guns*,' said Kidogo.

'There is good food up here on the mountain,' said M'zee, 'and plenty on the plains. You do not *have* to take food from the humans.'

'They took ours,' One Eye responded sullenly.

'Don't the humans wait for you with their guns?' M'zee asked.

'We never go back to the same place the following night. We go to different villages, and we let many nights pass before we go back to the same one.'

M'zee remained silent for a while before he spoke again. 'We must get Tembo Jay's tusk back before the humans take it far away. Can my plans include you three?'

Although it had been worded as a question Kidogo knew it would have taken a braver tembo than any of these three to refuse M'zee. They each indicated their willingness by raising their trunk, though clearly they did so with some reluctance.

'This is my plan,' M'zee said. Kidogo had forgotten her shame at having left the tusk behind and was impressed with the way M'zee had taken total charge. He no longer seemed to be the increasingly-tired old tembo she had been getting used to supporting. Now he was vibrant and energetic, striding about the clearing. He showed Kidogo where to hide the tusk he had been carrying, pushing it deep into the leaf-litter under some bushes.

The moon was high when five elephants, one vastly bigger than the others, reached the humans' banana and maize plantations that surrounded their village on the edge of the forest. A dog came forward sniffing the air, then barked furiously. M'zee reached over the dog's head, caught it by the tail and lifted it, whining, into the air, then lowered it again. As soon as its feet were back on the earth it started to bark even more loudly. Still holding its tail with his trunk, M'zee stepped forward, put his foot on the dog and pressed down slowly until the barks turned to breathless wheezes. He lifted his foot and flipped the terrified dog into the bushes. In the ensuing silence they could hear it scampering away towards the village. No other dog barked that night.

The tembos waited, ghostlike in the moonlight. No sound came from the direction of the village. Then, on a word from M'zee, the three young males moved into the banana plantations, Tembo One Eye to the left, Two Eyes and Three Eyes to the right. M'zee paced forward, swinging his trunk, following the scent of the humans who had carried away Tembo Jay's precious tusk. He felt invincible – like in his younger days when the mustdo madness was on him – only then his quest had been to joyn with a female, now it was to recover the sacred tusk.

With his Shadow close behind him, M'zee walked silently along the dusty paths through the sleeping village. The scent of wood smoke filled the air from the cooking fires, the ashes of which still glowed in the darkness, while from some of the smaller slat-sided huts came the muted bleatings of goats and the low cluckings of chickens curious about the giants they could glimpse passing by in the moonlight. Human snores came from several of the larger huts. These villagers had evidently learned that the elephants who raided their crops never returned to the same place on two consecutive nights.

M'zee raised his trunk and stopped as he came close to a hut that stood a little apart from the others. A man was slumped on a stool in front of the door, dozing with a *gun* across his knees. They're not expecting *us*, Kidogo thought. A guard means they must fear the ivory might be taken by other humans.

M'zee stepped towards the dozing figure, his feet making no sound in the dry dust, snaked out his trunk and wrapped it around the lower part of the man's head so that he couldn't call out. As he struggled, the *gun* dropped to the ground and M'zee stepped on it, firmly and deliberately.

Kidogo could see the man's fear-filled eyes staring white in the moonlight as M'zee held him by the head. The Wise One rumbled to her quietly, 'Lift the top of *this* hut, my Shadow. Tembo Jay's tusk is in there.'

Kidogo felt cautiously around the edge of the overhanging roof. It was made of flattened water containers, fixed firmly onto cut branches with the spikes that humans called *nails*. The metal plates grated harshly against each other as she lifted the whole roof, heaving and twisting until she could move the structure sideways and reach inside the hut. The tusk, standing on its root-end in a corner, seemed to welcome her probing trunk. She lifted it out and, with difficulty, held it up for M'zee to see in the moonlight.

Subdued voices were coming from the nearby huts – some of the sleeping humans must have been wakened by the sound of the roof being lifted, and she wondered if unseen *guns* were being pointed at them. She looked towards M'zee. He had manipulated the man until he was sitting on the ground, his eyes still wide with terror, but making no sound other than a faint whimpering. M'zee released his trunk, lifted his foot and tapped the terrified man twice on the top of his head, then stepped back and prodded him gently in the ribs with a tusk. The whimpering stopped but started again when M'zee raised his trunk and trumped loudly.

His signal was answered by the three young males in the plantations, each trying to give the impression that he was just one of many tembos surrounding the village. Showers of stones, uprooted bushes and clumps of turf came flying over the huts, rattling onto the metal roofs and thudding on the paths.

M'zee took Tembo Jay's tusk from Kidogo and walked briskly back through the village then, at the forest edge, he called to the jostlers, 'Join us now, One, Two and Three Eyes. You have done well.'

A dog barked once from behind them but was swiftly silenced. Human fear seeped out of the huts and spread into the forest, silencing the calls of the night birds. No other sounds were heard as Kidogo and the jostlers followed M'zee up through the forest, the jostlers each carrying a stem of bananas. Dawn was breaking as they reached the clearing where the other tusk had been hidden and, in the half-light, Kidogo retrieved it from under the bushes. Two Eyes broke off a section of his banana stem and offered it to her.

'Leave that,' M'zee ordered, his voice hard. 'Tembos who take the crops of humans will end up having their lives taken by humans.'

Three Eyes held up his stem. 'Do we just leave these here to rot then?'

141

'You have a choice. If you eat the bananas you stay here in the forest, taking from humans until they prove to be too clever for you. Then you die! If you wish, you can join us – but the bananas stay.'

The jostlers glanced at one another and dropped the stems. Kidogo looked longingly at the fat green clusters. It was a long time since she had tasted their succulent sweetness.

M'zee picked up one of Tembo Jay's tusks and headed back up the mountain. Kidogo went to lift the other but Tembo One Eye shouldered her aside, took it up with his trunk and followed M'zee. Even though she could see that One Eye's tusks were almost as slim as a female's and were much nearer together than a male's ivories usually were, Kidogo felt small and inadequate again and looked back over her shoulder. Two Eyes and Three Eyes were walking sombrely behind her, Three Eyes guiltily swallowing the last of his banana stem. Kidogo pretended not to have noticed.

Tembo Three Eyes knew the little female had seen that he had disobeyed the order to leave the bananas behind. He didn't care. Leaving them would be a waste and they had worked hard down at the village just to get back the tusk of some stupid dead tembo. They would *all* be dead soon and the humans could have his, or any other tembo's tusks, for all he cared. He swung his trunk nonchalantly as he followed the others. Who did that M'zee think he was anyway?

CHAPTER FOURTEEN

M'zee was desperately tired and, although he was sure they would not be pursued by the humans, he forced himself to climb ever higher. He had seen that Tembo One Eye had taken the burden of carrying the tusk from his Shadow, and he was glad – Temba Kidogo really was too small for such a load and he knew her strength had already been tested to the utmost.

They reached the glade near the stream where they had rested only two nights before and here he called a halt and encouraged the others to find food. M'zee saw the young males watching Kidogo as she brought him food-wads, and was sure that no male Shadow would have done *that* for him.

In the night M'zee thought of the mountaintop far above them and wondered if the fire that had driven them down was still burning there. He had not felt the ground moving since then, so it may have died – but he couldn't be sure. Should he wait for Mana to tell him what to do next – or was it up to him to take the tusks of Tembo Jay to a safer place? He hoped Mana would not need him too soon – the way he was feeling now, he would have to rest before he could do *anything* more.

What should he do about the three young males? Although they had seemed unpromising when they had first met and had led the humans to him, they hadn't let him down on the expedition to recover the sacred tusk. They could be valuable as carriers once he was fit enough to move on – but he knew how easily jostlers get bored. An idea was forming in his mind. He had been reluctant to leave the tusks of his friend

Steadfast in the cave on the other side of the mountain. Now, if those three were to go and fetch those, there would be five elephants and four free tusks. That would relieve his Shadow from having to carry and he needed all her energy to forage for him until he could reach a swamp with soft vegetation – and that could be many moons away.

Three Eyes was waiting for his fellows to wake up so that they could leave this old windbag and the silly young female who hung on his every word. He could still taste the flavour of bananas in his mind and he wanted more, regardless of the risks. But in the early light, the big old bull woke the others and called them together. 'I was mightily impressed with the way you all behaved last night,' he said, looking particularly at Three Eyes. 'Do you think you are up to another daring adventure?'

One Eye and Two Eyes looked quite eager but Three Eyes glowered at him. What was the old fool going to ask them to do now? He just wanted more bananas!

Without waiting for an answer, the old tembull continued. 'Over the mountain is a cave and in that cave are two free tusks from a tembo who stepped-over many years ago.'

Why can't he just say *'died'* or *'was killed'*, Three Eyes thought, rebelliously. All these fancy words were just stale dung.

M'zee was looking straight at him and saying, 'Tembo Three Eyes, I sense you are intelligent and have the qualities that would make a fine leader. Will *you* take charge of an expedition to bring the tusks of Tembo Steadfast to this glade?'

The young female and his two fellows were all watching him. If he refused, he would be stating that he was not intelligent, nor up to the task being offered.

'Of course I can,' he replied. 'I can live without bananas for a couple of days.'

Tembo Three Eyes was cold and hungry. The *couple of days* he had spoken of so casually had long since passed and he felt certain they were no nearer to finding the cave that had been described to him by the old fool in the forest. He was tempted to forget it all and head back downhill to find bananas but he was not sure if there were any on the north side of the mountain, and his fellow jostlers still seemed to want to continue the search. One more day – he'd give it just one more day!

They had been able to follow the scent trail of M'zee and Kidogo up to the snowline but had not gone higher as there were choking fumes in the air. These caught in their throats like the smoke did when humans burned black rings and for several days afterwards they could scent nothing else. He had led the others around the mountain below the snowline hoping to find tembo footprints in the ash but had not found any. Now they were exploring the little valleys trying to find the one that fitted the description given to him by the young female and the old bull.

'Hey,' Two Eyes was calling. 'Hey. Over here!'

Three Eyes ambled over, with One Eye close behind him.

Two Eyes was sniffing at some fairly old tembo dung, scattered by a rodent or a bird. Three Eyes sniffed it. It was from the tuskless female, he was sure of that and, scouting around, they found traces of elephant footprints in a muddy place. Following these downhill the jostlers discovered the cave and Three Eyes entered cautiously. The scents of the old bull and the young temba were strong and there were no other recent scents to alarm him. At the back he found the tusks where M'zee had hidden them under the heather branches.

'Here they are,' he called to the others at the entrance. 'I *knew* we would find them!' He ignored the snorts from the others, picked up a tusk and carried it outside. Two Eyes retrieved the other and they set off back up the valley with Three Eyes leading.

Ryan joined Lars at breakfast on the day following their retreat from the mountain. He sat down and poured a cup of coffee for himself. 'What now?' he asked.

'The manager says Kili is closed to climbers indefinitely, so that's me without a job. What are your plans?'

'Back to Nairobi and the goddamned computers, I suppose.'

'I thought you liked them.'

'I did once, but they're taking over and everyone is forgetting how things *should* be done. If you're not into computers, you just fall farther and farther behind in the scramble. Especially here in Africa.'

'Scramble?'

'The scramble to have more material things. More than the next person – more than your share.'

'Hasn't life always been like that? *Especially* here in Africa. The strongest person becomes chief, his friends and family get all the goodies until he gets displaced, then it's the turn of the next strongest.'

'Add to that, western consumerism and blatant corruption . . .'

'Is it better anywhere else?' Lars refilled his coffee cup.

Ryan tipped a few toast crumbs from his plate onto the floor and watched the bulbuls fly down and peck at them.

'I was thinking, up in that cave. Maybe the elephants have got it right. Living from day to day. No possessions, and they seem to care a lot for each other. Even those tusks in the cave seemed to be full of love in some odd way.'

A waiter walked by and the bulbuls flew up and perched on a beam.

'I wonder where those tusks are now. Can you believe what

146

happened? It did happen, didn't it? Or was it me having one of my crazy dreams?'

'It happened – but I'm not too sure that we should tell anyone. Despite what the conservationists are trying to do, ivory is still traded and if people hear about them they'll be trying to get those tusks.'

Lars looked up towards the summit of Kilimanjaro. The snowcap was emerging from a collar of cloud, looking just the same as it always had, except for a plume of smoke streaming away on the wind. Somewhere up in the forest, two elephants, a huge old male and a much smaller, tuskless female, were doing something with two huge tusks. Were they carrying them to some place, just guarding them, or maybe hiding them again, out of the covetous sight of greedy men?

'Back to what we were talking about just now. I think I might start a safari operation. I've got the minibus, I know the country, speak the language, know about the wildlife – I've even got a guide's licence. Kili's going to be out for a bit but there are more and more tourists coming to see the Serengeti and Ngorongoro. I'd need an agent – but there are a few of those in Arusha.'

'And you'll be wanting a partner, now,' said Ryan. 'Someone with a Land Rover to carry the heavy gear. Someone you get on with who also speaks the language and is looking for a change of job.' He grinned expectantly at Lars.

His friend laughed. 'Are you serious? . . . That'd be great. Petersen and Kavanagh. P & K Safaris . . . No, that sounds like chewing gum. K & P Safaris . . . No, that sounds like peanuts! We'll think of something.' He laughed again and held out his hand. 'I'm on, if you are. We'll make a great team.'

Ryan took his hand. 'I'll need a couple of weeks to wrap things up in Nairobi, then I'll come down and we can get under way.'

While the three jostlers were searching for the cave where Tembo Steadfast's tusks were hidden, Kidogo was looking after M'zee as best she could. The hole in the old one's ear was healing cleanly but the raid on the village to recover the tusk had used up much of his strength. She spent a large amount of time foraging and bringing food-wads to him, all of which he took and ate immediately. He had moved to stand beside the stream, always within reach of the tusks of Tembo Jay, which were now leaning against a fallen tree. M'zee drank often and only moved away from the stream to pass water and drop dung. At night Kidogo stood by his side and he encouraged her to read *these* tusks.

As when she had been reading Steadfast's tusks, she felt she had become a male but did not experience the savage lust of mustdo, nor the desire to fight for females. Living Tembo Jay's early life through the pictures in the tusk, she relished the kindness and Love that was all about him and felt wonderfully safe in the company of a large family led by a temba of great wisdom, known to all as Tembella Gentleness. Kidogo was surprised to see how many other families were always foraging nearby – often in the scenes she was reading, there were elephants as far as she could see and the grass and foliage was always green and fresh. She saw the elephants linquing trunks, as Tembella Grace had done with the Sisters at the Sacred Pool, and calling down rain whenever it was needed.

As she read scenes later in Tembo Jay's life, she found an anger growing in her at the sight of the many huge tembos who stood about in the shade and bullied others into fetching them food. Tembella Gentleness always insisted these tembulls be left alone and that they should all move to another part of the country, but Tembo Jay tried to tell the idle ones that what they were doing was wrong.

They mocked him. 'Come and join us,' they called.

'You've got big tusks. You can make the lesser ones fetch you food – *and* you can joyn with any temba you fancy. There are enough of them for all of us.'

Kidogo, as Tembo Jay, felt tempted, but only for a moment. The weight of his tusks felt good – they were bigger than any of those who called out to him. She lifted her trunk, stopped reading and became herself again. What would she give to have tusks like that – to have any tusks at all?

The envy passed. She lowered her trunk to the tusk and was again Tembo Jay, faced with the temptation of an easy life, eternally in the blesséd shade. It was so, so tempting – but the temptation had to be fought! It would be so much easier just to stroll across and join them than to do what he knew he must do. The desire for the easy life passed and he replied, 'What you are doing is *wrong*.'

The largest of the Tembulls called to him, 'Come and fight me then. I'm in the mood for a scrap.'

Tembo Jay turned away. His beloved mother, Tembella Gentleness, had taught him it was never right to fight.'

Kidogo lifted her trunk from the tusk to wipe a tear from her eye. Enough reading for one night.

Far away, in the city of New York, Walt Schwiner threw the newspaper down onto his desk, took a deep pull from his cigar and pressed the buzzer to summon his PA. That was what she liked him to call her – but he still secretly thought of her as his secretary.

He pointed to the item about the eruption of the volcano, Kilimanjaro, in Tanzania and said, 'Will you ring the travel agent, Honey, and see if this makes any difference to my trip?'

She picked up the paper, looked briefly at the item, said, 'Sure, Mr Schwiner,' and walked out.

CHAPTER FIFTEEN

Two Eyes and One Eye took turns at carrying one of Steadfast's tusks around the mountain, but Three Eyes hung onto the other. It was the first time he had ever had to do anything except for himself, and he kept thinking of what that wise old elephant had said to him. How did it go? *'Tembo Three Eyes, I sense you are intelligent and have the qualities that would make a fine leader. Will you take charge of an expedition to bring the tusks of Tembo Steadfast to this glade?'*

Well, here he was, carrying one of the tusks and on his way to the glade, with the other tusk being carried close behind him by his fellow jostlers. . . . *intelligent and have the qualities that would make a fine leader.* . . . Yes, yes, *yes*!

Three Eyes had thought they might reach the glade before nightfall and he urged the others on, but they were making quite slow progress carrying the tusks and, when they came off the ash-slope and into the forest, One Eye and Two Eyes insisted on feeding. They ate hungrily until it was dark, then stood together, Steadfast's tusks on the ground between them.

'I wonder why the old one wants these tusks carried about the mountain?' Two Eyes asked. 'It doesn't make sense to me.'

'It's not as if he hasn't any of his own,' One Eye agreed. 'His tusks are just as big as these.'

'But not as big as the ones those two were carrying. They were enormous!'

'I'll have tusks as big as that one da—' Three Eyes started to say but Two Eyes jostled him from one side and One Eye shoved at him from the other.

Later, unable to sleep, One Eye idly caressed the smooth ivory of Steadfast's tusk but snatched it away as a younger M'zee came charging towards him. One Eye blew noisily through his trunk as if it had touched hot ashes.

'Go to sleep,' grumbled Three Eyes in the darkness.

Temba Kidogo was again foraging to make food-wads for M'zee. She was pleased that he ate these so readily and could already see the effect the food was having on him. His ribs were no longer so visible, he did not shiver so much in the nights and his eyes, which had been looking quite dull, were beginning to twinkle like she remembered them doing down in the swamp on the other side of the mountain. Sometimes he would stroll around the glade, swinging his legs easily, before returning to stand near the stream. He did not seem to be worried that the three jostlers had not returned. She had expected them to come back, with or without Tembo Steadfast's tusks, in just a few days.

She had not tried to read the tusks of Tembo Jay again. M'zee had noticed this and asked her why.

'It was so painful, so humiliating,' she replied. 'When one feels so involved – when one *is* that Tembo – it all hurts too much to bear.'

'Just so. Just so,' Tembo M'zee had replied. 'Try reading the other tusk. You have always read the left one.'

'How is it different?' she asked.

'Try it tonight and *you* tell *me*,' was all he would say.

Kidogo had not realised there was any difference in reading the left or the right tusk so, as darkness filled the glade and the forest birds called their last mournful notes, she stood close to M'zee and reached her trunk out to touch

Tembo Jay's right tusk. She ran her trunk along it slowly, reading many of the same scenes she had read in the left one, only now she was not so involved. It seemed as if she were observing the scenes from some way off. It was much easier reading and sometimes one could see the event more clearly from that distance. Seeing it only from the point of view of the tembo whose tusk it was, had frequently obscured the whole picture.

She read on until she reached the scene where Tembo Jay walked away from the mocking Yellow Tusks towards where other tembos were standing amongst the trees. Halfway there, he turned and ran back, trumping furiously. He ran among the Yellow Tusks, scattering the piles of fresh fodder that had been placed there for these idle ones to eat. Kidogo trembled for him. There was no way the Yellow Tusks could allow *that* behaviour to go unchallenged. She was right. As Tembo Jay stood panting, the Yellow Tusks advanced towards him in a row then, as those at each end of the line walked faster, they closed a silent circle around him. There was a lot of dust above their heads and the picture faded. She was glad that she had not been reading the left tusk.

Kidogo was remembering that reading as she foraged. M'zee seemed unconcerned about any possibility of the humans coming up this far but she kept her ears and trunk alert for any sounds or scents that might spell danger. Each day she had to go farther from the glade to find enough nourishing food to grind up with her strong young teeth to make food-wads for the old one. Today, she was farther away than she had ever been, alert as usual, when she sensed low~sound coming from a long distance along the mountainside. She held her ears wide and touched the ground lightly with the toes of her right forefoot.

'I am Lonely ~ I am Lonely
Singing in this ~ empty forest
Here upon this ~ Holy Mountain.
Are there tembos ~ who can hear me?'
The song came again.
'I am Lonely ~ I am Lonely
Singing in this ~ empty forest
Here upon this ~ Holy Mountain.
Are there tembos ~ who can hear me?'
Kidogo sang back in response.
'I can hear you ~ I can hear you,
Singing in this ~ quiet forest
Come and join us ~ come and join us
Here upon this ~ Holy Mountain.'
As before, when Kidogo had sung in low~sound, the words seemed to have come from deep within her – they were not her conscious thoughts. A reply came.
'I have heard you ~ I am coming
Not alone soon ~ thanks to Mana.'
Kidogo waited, chewing slowly on the food-wad, grinding down the harder twigs into a soft and palatable pulp. When she could hear footsteps approaching and the rustle of leaves as a tembo pushed through the undergrowth, she took the food-wad from her mouth, placed it on the ground and sang the ancient greeting.
'Love, live long and ~ find sweet-water.'
The traditional response came at once.
'May Mana bless ~ and keep you safe,
Tembo Jay and ~ goodness guide you.'
A tembo stepped out of the bushes. By his bulk Kidogo judged him to be of about twenty-five years, but his tusks were underdeveloped and he looked travel-worn and tired. She reached out her trunk in greeting. 'I am Temba Kidogo,' she said. 'I am Shadow to Tembo M'zee who is resting in

the glade behind me.'

The stranger touched her trunk and said, 'I am Lonely – Tembo Lonely. I had another name long ago but I have forgotten what it was.'

For a tembo to forget its own name something terrible must have happened to it, thought Kidogo, but she said, 'Come and meet M'zee.'

She picked up the food-wad and led the way back to where M'zee was waiting for her. 'I heard you singing,' he said as Kidogo introduced Lonely. 'Welcome to our glade.'

Kidogo stood back as they greeted one another. Lonely was looking at the tusks of Tembo Jay leaning against the fallen tree. His eyes were wide. 'Whose tusks are *those*?' he asked.

M'zee glanced at Kidogo and said slowly, '*Those* are the tusks of Tembo Jay.'

Tembo Lonely looked from M'zee to Kidogo, then at the tusks, took two steps towards them and went down on his knees. He stayed there with his eyes closed for some time, then got to his feet.

'There is a story to tell me here,' he said. 'And I, Tembo Lonely have a story to tell to you.'

As he said this, there was a sound of crashing branches from the far end of the glade. M'zee, Kidogo and Lonely turned and saw the three jostlers come out from under the trees and trot towards them. Tembos Three Eyes and Two Eyes were each triumphantly holding up one of Steadfast's tusks as if they were as light as hollow logs, while One Eye trotted alongside waving a small, leafy branch for no apparent reason.

They stopped and Three Eyes and Two Eyes laid the tusks they had been carrying at M'zee's feet and stepped back. One Eye went to lay his branch besides them, thought better of it, whisked it about once or twice then, looking rather foolish, started to eat it.

M'zee stepped forward, ran his trunk lightly along both of the tusks on the ground, then touched each of the jostlers on the forehead.

'Well done,' he said. 'That was well done.'

The youngsters glowed with pride. 'It was nothing,' Three Eyes said, as if they did such things every day. 'Anytime you—'

He stopped as he noticed Tembo Lonely standing a little way behind M'zee. 'Who's this?' he asked, pointing rudely with his trunk.

M'zee ignored the rudeness. The jostlers had much to learn but they had clearly made a start.

'This is Tembo Lonely,' he said as the newcomer stepped forward and greeted each of the jostlers gravely.

'I have come a long way and I have a story to tell to you,' he said.

'Let's hear it then,' said Three Eyes.

M'zee reached out and flipped the youngster lightly across his left ear. 'Not so fast! Our friend has come a long way. He told you that. He will wish to feed and drink. Later, when he is ready, he may choose to tell us his story. Now, will you put the tusks of Tembo Steadfast with those of Tembo Jay before you feed yourselves?'

Kidogo noticed that Three Eyes handled Steadfast's tusk quite casually but One Eye was much more careful, picking it up almost as if it was alive and standing it gently next to Tembo Jay's. She wondered if the jostlers had been reading the tusks in the night. Could *they* read? Only a short time ago *she* had not known that any tembos could. Maybe, like her, these three had never learned.

She picked up the now cold food-wad and gave it unobtrusively to M'zee who took it gratefully. Lonely and the jostlers were pushing into the forest to feed.

'We will have to move on soon,' M'zee told her. 'The

155

food here is almost gone. I am much stronger – thanks to my Shadow's care. *You* must go and find food for yourself now.'

M'zee pondered his next move. If Tembo Lonely were to join them that would make four strong carriers for four free tusks and neither he nor his Shadow would have to carry any. He was too old and too weak now to carry tusks for a long distance and, with Kidogo having to forage for them both, she would not have time nor energy to carry anyway. It was *good* that Tembo Lonely had come – Mana must still be helping them but he had not heard his voice yet about where they were to go, and he would soon need to know. M'zee reached deep into his memory, trying to recall just how one spoke *to* Mana – it had been a long time since his family had linqued trunks and asked for guidance. Just how did one linque trunks? The memory would not come and he knew that this was a sure sign of growing old. *How* did one do it? If only he could read his own tusks, he could go back to when he had done it last – so long ago. It would be interesting to be able to read one's own tusks – especially the right one. To see oneself as other tembos saw one. That would be a path to true wisdom – but in his heart he was glad he couldn't. Tusks could only be read when the bearer had stepped-over and set them free.

He walked slowly around the glade, stopping by the four tusks leaning against the fallen tree. Tembo Jay would know about linquing, if any tembo did! He cleared his mind and reached out to touch the smooth ivory.

In the first light of dawn, Kidogo saw that Tembo One Eye was standing next to the tusks, cautiously touching each in turn. She moved silently across to him, careful to approach from the side where he could see her coming, so as not to startle him. He touched her forehead in greeting.

'Were you reading the tusks?' she asked.

'What is *reading*?' he asked and she recalled having asked M'zee the same question not long before. How much she had learned since then!

'Would you like to see what is hidden in these tusks?' she asked.

'Then there *is* something there! I sensed it when I touched a tusk up on the mountain,' he answered.

Kidogo took his trunk-tip in hers as M'zee had done with her in the cave, and drew it down to Tembo Steadfast's right tusk.

'Now, relax your body, clear your mind, open your thoughts. What can you see?'

'I can see a tembo standing in a swamp – just as if he was over there.' He waved his trunk to show he meant *across the glade*. 'He's gone now!'

'Put your trunk back where it was,' Kidogo directed him patiently.

'He's there again.'

'Now move your trunk very slightly.'

With a little more guidance from Kidogo, One Eye soon learned to read and was wanting to try the other tusks but Kidogo was reluctant. 'One tusk at a time – there is a whole lifetime of stories in these,' she told him and stepped back, bumping into Three Eyes who had come to stand behind her, watching and listening.

Two Eyes and Lonely were also close behind her, while M'zee stood back studying the whole scene approvingly.

'Can *I* have a go?' Three Eyes asked eagerly.

Soon the three jostlers and Lonely were all exploring the four tusks, each mumbling to themselves as they discovered ideas and feelings quite new to them.

Eventually, M'zee intervened. 'The stories will be in there forever,' he said. 'Those who travel with my Shadow and I will have much time for reading later on our journey. We leave today. Who will join us?'

The trunks of the four readers rose together.

'Where are we going?' Three Eyes asked. 'Will there be any bananas when we get there?'

M'zee glowered at him. 'You disappoint me. You must forget bananas – they are fodder for humans, not tembos. Humans have to spend most of their lives digging in the ground and growing food to eat. *We* are the lucky ones – our food grows all around us. As to where we are going – I don't know yet. We will linque trunks and ask Mana.'

Kidogo was not sure if the three jostlers and perhaps even Tembo Lonely knew any more about linquing than she did, or even if they knew about Mana – but she said nothing. She stepped forward and twisted her trunk around M'zee's as she had done with Tembella Grace and the Sisters at the Sacred Pool, then she called on the others to join them. They stepped forward, each raising his trunk cautiously.

With the six elephants in a tight circle, their trunks entwined, Kidogo could feel the heady sensation of them all merging into one, together with the trees of the forest around them. Even the birds and the four great tusks nearby, seemed to be a part of the . . . the . . . She searched for a word in tembotalk but couldn't find one, so she ran through the words she could recall from her time living with humans. The *group*? No, it was more than that. The *company*? No, that didn't fit either. The *party*? No. The *pack*? No. The *crew*? No. The *team*? That was closer. The *oneness*? She had never heard humans use that word, but it somehow seemed right.

M'zee was talking quietly, as though to any of the tembos there. 'We have linqued to ask for guidance. I know the time has come to move on with our precious burdens – but we don't know which way to go.'

He was silent and a voice, even quieter than his, seemed to reply, saying quite clearly, '*Follow the tired sun.*'

'Who said that?' asked Three Eyes, pulling his trunk away from the others. Kidogo felt the *oneness* dissolve but M'zee did not seem to mind. 'Mana,' he replied and walked away to pass dung for the first time in several days.

Kidogo knew now that the jostlers *were* ignorant of the meaning of Mana. At some time she would have to tell them. Now she could see that M'zee was preparing to leave. *Follow the tired sun,* the voice of Mana had said. That could only mean going west – the sun always went from the east to the west and, when it was tired, went down to sleep below the horizon so, if one had to follow it, one had to go towards the west. That way would take them around the side of Holy Mountain above the human villages but below the ash-slopes and the snow. She wondered how Rafiki would ever find them when he was well enough – how she missed him – but now she had to make sure that everything was done in the way M'zee directed.

Soon, with Three Eyes carrying one of Tembo Jay's tusks and One Eye the other, and with Tembo Steadfast's ivories carried by Two Eyes and Lonely, they left the glade. Tembo M'zee set an easy pace and Kidogo was able to gather food and make wads for M'zee as they walked.

When they found a broad path leading almost due west, the travelling became much easier. The elephants walked one behind the other with no jostling or even talking. Kidogo found it easiest to be the last in the line, as the others often matched the pace set by M'zee and swung their legs in time with his while she, being so much smaller, had to move her legs faster. Even so, the pace was easy for all of them. The togetherness of it brought back the word *oneness* but oneness was not quite right here. *Team* was though.

Standing amongst the tembo-trees at the Sacred Grove, far to the northeast of Holy Mountain, Rafiki was trying to get used to holding his head level as the weight of his remaining tusk dragged that side down, making his neck ache. He had spent a lot of time in the water as he was recovering and while the hole in his cheek closed up but now he was impatient to set off and find Kidogo again. That morning the Sisters had succeeded in withdrawing Tembella Grace's elegant tusks from her carcase and had spent most of the afternoon washing them in the pool and polishing them with wet sand. He had stood in the shade watching until he saw them climb the path from the pool, each reverently carrying a tusk. He met them under the first of the baobabs and asked, 'What do we do now?'

Sister Kindness put down the tusk and said, 'Now Grace's tusks are free my Sister and I believe, if you will join us, we may find the strength and the Love to form a linque with Mana and ask for guidance.'

They went out onto the promontory where they had linqued for rain so many times, laid the tusks on the ground and entwined their trunks. Once more the tembos, the free tusks and the trees became as one.

Rafiki said nothing, feeling that it was up to one of the Sisters to ask the question but, without a word being said, he heard a voice, seemingly from nowhere – but from everywhere – say, '*Follow the tired sun.*'

The Sisters picked up one of Tembella Grace's tusks each and, without a word to him or a backwards look at the pool, set off through the parched bush towards where the sun was setting over the hills far to the west.

Rafiki started to follow but then turned back, drank his fill from the sweet waters and hurried after them.

Lars had spoken to several safari agents in the town of Arusha, hoping to find work for his fledgling business but the publicity generated by the minor eruption of Kilimanjaro had caused many tourists to cancel their planned visits. He was concerned, not so much for himself but for Ryan who had insisted on giving up his job in Nairobi and was, that afternoon, driving his Land Rover down to Tanzania with what he called 'all his worldly goods'. He was to join Lars at the Riverside Hotel until they had secured some contracts.

There was one more agent to try. Lars parked the minibus under a blue-flowered jacaranda tree across the road from Mr Burns' office, locked it and stepped out of the shade. He waved away the touts who clustered round him trying to sell crudely printed maps and guide books. A few sharp words in Swahili quickly convinced them that he was not a tourist. One of the touts recognised him and called out a friendly, 'Jambo, Sir. Jambo, Mr Petersen.'

It was hot in the street and he was glad to get into the office where he paused until his eyes adjusted to the shade. One of the two women there was busy at a computer screen. The other, the receptionist, rose from her chair and after he had given his name she offered to get him a cold drink. He had finished it before he was invited to enter the inner office where a tanned white man sat behind a desk.

Mr Burns did not rise but indicated that Lars should sit on one of the other two chairs. 'Lars Petersen,' he said. 'You stay out at the Riverside – a guide on Kilimanjaro, yes?'

'I was,' Lars replied, 'but, as you know, Kili's closed at present. I'm looking for some other job as a guide for the time being.'

'Do you know the area around Olsandura?'

Lars had heard of Olsandura, up beyond Maasailand, but he had thought it was a hunting area. 'No,' he admitted, 'but I could do a reconnaissance run up there.' He would need Ryan's Land Rover – but that would be here by nightfall. 'When are the clients due?'

'Client – singular. A couple of weeks yet. An American sportsman – wants to kill himself an elephant. Can't think why – but it pays the bills.'

'Not my bills,' said Lars, thinking of the two elephants on the mountain. 'Not *my* bills!' He stood up, turned and left the office feeling sick to think that in the third millennium there were still people who could kill a great animal in the name of sport.

Stepping out into the street he passed a young man going in. He had met him once at a meeting of Arusha-based guides. His name was Moses something – a townified Maasai, probably educated by missionaries.

Moses Jackson was not his real name. When he had appeared at the mission tired and hungry, and claiming to be an orphan, not too many questions had been asked about his background. *God-sent* was the term the missionaries used. He had spoken only Maasai and appeared to be about fourteen. However, he proved to be an apt pupil, quick at learning English, Swahili, drawing, and Bible studies.

The superintendent Mr Washington Jackson had been happy to lend his name to the lad and treated him almost as an adopted son. Although the boy was often morose and inclined to spend a lot of his time staring vacantly out of windows, Mr Jackson was proud of the many drawings young Moses had produced. Lifelike drawings of elephants, giraffe and antelope were pinned to his office walls but, when the boy was on his own he would draw cows, cows and more cows.

'Good Morning, Moses,' the agent greeted him civilly as he was shown into his office, 'I hope *you* won't let sentiment stop you from earning an honest buck. Actually – a lot of bucks.'

'It sounds to me as if you have an American client, Mr Burns. A very rich one!'

'They don't come much richer! His name is Walter Schwiner and he wants to get himself an elephant – one with big tusks. Seems he is in some kind of hunting club where you have to shoot certain big game to qualify for the highest ranking. He's got his grizzly bear, his moose, his mountain sheep and, last year in South Africa, he killed one of their lions – which was probably doped. All he wants now is an elephant.'

Moses thought of the magnificent tuskers that had wandered past the herds he was guarding when he was a boy. The elephants seemed to know that the Maasai had no interest in killing wild animals – cattle were their whole lives and provided all the food they needed. Now he was sure he was going to be asked to guide a hunting trip to kill one of these gentle giants.

Mr Burns must have seen the look on Moses' face but knew from bar-gossip that the fellow was heavily in debt and also that he had some secret that was only ever hinted at.

'The pay is going to be *very* good,' he said. 'And, if you get a big one with fine tusks, Mr Schwiner is likely to give you a tip that can pay off a lot of debts and keep some nasty people from your back door.'

'When and where?'

'Two weeks time. Are you free then?'

'Yes – but where?'

'There's a suitable bull been seen up in the hunting area above Olsandura. I've fixed the permit.'

It was just as Moses had feared. Olsandura was the one place he did not want to go but – as Mr Burns had surmised – he *was* in fear of opening his back door at night.

'Will Mr Schwiner be bringing his own rifle?'

Tembo M'zee called frequent halts, alternating the carrying time with equal periods for them all to forage. Mana had not indicated that there was any rush to *follow the tired sun* and well-fed tembos would be better able to deal with anything unexpected on their journey. During these halts Kidogo brought him the welcome and tasty food-wads and he knew she was gathering and eating food herself as she walked, as she did not have to carry a tusk. He was pleased at their progress. It was not too uncomfortable walking on a good path under the trees and, although they were well above the areas cultivated by humans, they were not so high that breathing was difficult, nor was it too cold. Yes, he was pleased – especially when they found another pleasant glade near a waterfall at the end of the day.

When they had laid down the free tusks in a neat row and drunk from the pool at the foot of the fall, Kidogo asked M'zee, 'Can we read the tusks tonight?'

'If we spread them out in the glade we can all read whichever one we choose before we sleep.'

Lonely chose the left tusk of Tembo Jay but first knelt before it, oblivious of the sideways glances of the others. He was thrilled to be able to read the life of this great, if long-dead, teacher and hoped to be able to learn how Tembo Jay had been able to get and hold the attention of other tembos when he was trying to tell them things of huge importance. He too knew things of great importance but had never been able to get other tembos to listen to him. They had all been too obsessed with minor things, such as where to find the next meal or the direction of the nearest waterhole.

Whenever he had tried to tell what he had learned, their eyes had gone dull and they had wandered away before he had hardly started his story. No wonder he was known as 'Lonely'.

He stood and ran his trunk slowly along Tembo Jay's left tusk, passing over the experiences of babyhood and the jostling times until he came to when he, as Tembo Jay, first became aware of the gross unfairness of the Yellow Tusks' habit of bullying the other elephants. The anger built within him as it had in Lonely himself when the flying knock-us-down machines came in that far-off land from which he had fled.

He read on, living Tembo Jay's life and learning how to control his emotions and wait until the time was ripe for action. He lived through the emotions of *let-it-be* and the temptations of *mustdo* and *come-and-join-us* and it was far into the night when he withdrew his trunk from the tusk and found the other tembos sleeping around him.

The elephants progressed this way for three days. On the fourth, M'zee woke to the call of the dawn-doves. The warmer air of the morning told him that the path they had followed on the previous day must have been leading them downhill as they had circled the shoulder of Holy Mountain, *following the sun*.

He was pleased with the progress of his 'team'. His shadow, Temba Kidogo, had used that word to describe them and it seemed to fit perfectly. *Team* seemed to imply more togetherness than a *herd*, a term he had never liked unless there were very many tembos together, and a *family* was clearly not appropriate in their case.

Each tembo had settled into a place in his team. As leader he was always in front, testing the air for danger, listening for unusual sounds and deciding which route to take whenever there was a choice. He had noticed that the other tembos were no longer carrying the same tusks as they had when they first set off together. Behind M'zee now came Tembo Three Eyes, who watched and imitated whatever he did and who always carried Tembo Steadfast's left tusk. Behind Three Eyes came Tembo One Eye with Steadfast's other tusk – then Two Eyes with Tembo Jay's enormous right tusk. Behind him, Lonely carried Tembo Jay's left tusk in such a way that he seemed to be able to read parts of it with his trunk-tip as they walked. Temba Kidogo seemed to be wherever she was needed – sometimes at the rear, gathering fodder and chewing it to make food-wads for him, but also helping the other tembos when there were difficult streambeds to cross or holding up one end of a free tusk when the ground was slippery. At night she would sleep within trunk-touch at his side.

Unless they had had an especially tiring day they all spent some time reading from one or the other of the four free tusks and it was clear that what they were learning was having a good influence on their behaviour. Yes – he was proud of his team.

Kidogo was foraging, chewing up food-wads to take to M'zee, when she heard a rustling in the bushes and stood, trunk outstretched and ears wide, ready to turn and flee if she suspected danger. There were traces of human scent about but it was several days old and overlaid with the smell of antelope-dung, fear and pain. She moved forward cautiously until she could see a bushbuck held by a taut wire around its neck. The other end of the wire was twisted around a heavy log. She stepped forward, hoping to be able to release the wire and free the antelope but as she did so the buck fell on its side making choking noises and, before she could work out how to break or untwist the wire she saw the deep glow of Life in the animal's eyes turn dull and fade away. She was too late.

Knowing there was nothing she could do, she covered the slack, soiled body with a few branches and returned to the other tembos and told them what she had seen.

'We must move on,' she said and they all agreed.

One evening, M'zee and his team stopped early when they reached a place where the foraging was particularly good. They all ate their fill and were watching the sun set far to the west when M'zee recalled that, when Lonely had first joined them, he had said he had a tale to tell them. Lonely had been with them for many days now but had kept whatever it was to himself. M'zee called to him. 'Tembo who is known as Lonely, do you still have a story to tell us or has it gone like the memory of your real name?'

'I do have a story to tell,' Tembo Lonely replied. 'Like most stories worth telling, it has within it a mixture of good times and bad times but also within it there is much that I feel is important for others to know.'

'Will you tell it now?' rumbled M'zee. 'It will be a change from reading what happened in the long-past days.'

'Some of it is *long-past* for me as it concerns the time when I was a jostler like our friends here.' Lonely waved his trunk towards the three young males.

'Just so. Just so,' M'zee said. 'Tell us your story, Lonely. We are all ears.'

Lonely stepped back and turned to face them.

'I was born,' he began, 'in a place far to the south of here. When I was small all the tembos lived in safety as the humans protected us and came to stare at us and the other animals who lived in that place. We were happy and, as we were safe, the tembas had babies and the families grew ever larger in numbers. But the area where we lived was surrounded by a fence, which we could not pass through, so soon there was not enough food for all of us within the fence.

I had just been ousted from my family but had not yet found a group of jostlers to join, so I hung around making a nuisance of myself as young tembulls do. It was then that we heard the first of the flying knock-us-down machines. Of course we had seen the humans' flying machines before but

167

they had always stayed away from us. Now the word went about that they would fly low and make us panic, then one by one we would be stung by something that came from the machines and our legs would fail us and we would fall over. There we would lie, unable to move, until the humans came with their lorries and cut our throats so that the blood would run out and we'd died. They would then take our bodies away on the lorries.'

Lonely was trembling as he said this. He lowered his trunk and said, 'Those were terrible times and it is a terrible story. Do you want me to go on?'

M'zee replied, 'It is best to know the truth, even if it is terrible. We can all learn by hearing truths. Go on.'

'When my family heard the *tunk, tunk, tunk* of the flying knock-us-down machines we all ran away, trumping and screaming in fear. We tried to hide but the fence was in the way and we knew if we tried to push it down something hidden in the wires would hurt us. We had just turned back from the fence when the stinging-things came out of the machine and knocked all my family down. There they lay, helpless and unable to move, until the humans came with their knives. I had been lucky. I had been stung near the fence and I pushed into some thick bush before my knees gave way, and the humans did not look for me there. When I *could* stand up again all my family had been killed and carried away.

'I had to escape. I walked along the wires trying to find a way through – but there were no gaps. I touched the wires many times but each time my trunk was hit by whatever was hidden in the wires and the pain was savage – but I kept trying. Finally, I noticed that when my *tusk* touched the upper wire I felt no pain. I touched it again with my tusk. Still no pain. So – carefully – I lifted my trunk high out of the way, hooked my tusks under the wire and walked backwards. Suddenly the wire broke and I could step over the lower one and run off to safety in the bushland beyond.'

Kidogo had been listening intently. No wonder this tembo was called 'Lonely' if all his family had been killed at one time while he lay, unable to move, in the bush just out of sight. She sucked a tear from her eye with her trunk-tip and noticed that she was not alone in doing so.

Lonely walked away to the edge of the clearing and passed water and dung before coming back to continue his story. He stood as if waiting to be asked to go on.

M'zee made the 'Please do,' movement with his trunk.

'I just wanted to get as far away as I could,' Lonely said. 'I walked for many days, sometimes through bushland, some-times through plantations and sometimes through dark, fearsome forests. If I saw humans I hid, moving on when it was dark but not knowing, or caring very much, in which direction I was going as long as it was *away* from the flying knock-us-down machines. Then I came to the *sea*.' He paused.

Kidogo had heard humans at the orphanage speak of the *sea* – but not often. From the way they had spoken she had pictured a large pool filled with water that was not sweet and on which they could ride in things they called *boats*. She was sure the others were unlikely to have any idea how it looked and asked, 'What was this sea like?'

Lonely lifted his trunk and swept it around, taking in not just the clearing, but the whole of the land beyond, now coloured yellow-red by the last rays of the sun. 'It was a pool of water so big it was beyond description. I stood with my feet on soft sand and I could not see the other side. Behind me were tall trees with huge nuts on them but these were far above my head and out of reach. Later, I learned how to bump the trees and make the nuts fall but at first I just wanted to be *in* the sea. I waded in and it was wonderful. In a strange way I felt as if I had come *home*.

'As I waded, I tried to drink but the water was salty and I

spat it back and waded further. Soon my body lifted and I had to control my breath to keep my eyes above the water. Then I found I could close my mouth and raise my trunk to breathe and I floated there as the aches and pains from my journey were taken away. It was the first time for many moons that I felt safe and experienced Joy in Life.

'When I finally raised my head I could see I was far from the tall trees and had to move my legs in the water in such a way that I came nearer to them and, after a long time of doing this I could walk out of the water and up the beach. I found some of the nuts lying under the trees which I opened by standing on them. They were delicious and I ate all I could find before sleeping under the trees in a warm, sweet breeze that came in from over the sea. The breeze rustled the leaves on the strange branches far above my head and I thought I would stay there forever, living on the nuts and floating in the gentle sea. But next morning, when I was thirsty, I could not find sweet water. There I was, faced with more water than I could ever have imagined, and I was thirsty!

'I walked along the sand, occasionally tasting the water but it was always salty. Disappointed, I turned back inland and walked on, keeping the sea just in sight to my right. I came to a small, sandy streambed just before the ground started to rise and I dug in the sand and waited for the sweet-water to seep in and fill the hole. Later, when I had drunk enough, I walked to the top of the higher ground and then onto where a cliff fell sheer into the sea. The sun was going down behind me and I could see what looked like a massive log floating some way out. Every now and then a shower of water-spray would rise out of this log and, as I watched, I was sure I could hear a singing in low~sound.'

Lonely stopped. The other tembos were all wide-eared, wanting him to continue with his story but he said, 'I will tell more tomorrow – if any tembo is interested.'

CHAPTER SIXTEEN

Walt Schwiner walked across the hot concrete apron of Kilimanjaro Airport and into the Reception Area. Even with the comforts of the First Class cabin the flight had been long and boring and he had seen both the in-flight movies before. He was irritated by having to wait at passport control and he got even more cross at the delays in waiting for his baggage to be opened and his hunting rifle examined before his Firearm Importation Certificate was approved and endorsed with a huge rubber stamp.

All the other passengers had left the foyer before he was finally allowed through to where a tall black man was waiting for him. The man stepped forward – he must be his driver. Schwiner ignored the man's outstretched hand and snapped, 'Get my baggage, will you! I'll bring this.' He tapped the rifle as the other man turned towards the luggage trolley where the porter waited in vain, hoping for a tip.

Moses took an instant dislike to this arrogant man who clearly had not recognised him as his guide. He said nothing as he held open the Land Cruiser door before loading the bags into the rear compartment. As he drove out of the airport and turned towards Arusha, the man – his client – lit a cigar. Moses pressed the button to lower the driver's window. This was not going to be an easy safari.

At the hotel, Moses supervised the unloading of the bags and saw his client into the reception area. 'What time would you like me to pick you up, Mr Schwiner?' he asked. 'I would suggest nine o'clock and I can then drive you to Mr Burns' office. Everything will be ready by then.'

Mr Burns stood up when the receptionist showed Moses and Mr Schwiner into his office. His client was short, red-faced and well-groomed, if a little overweight.

'Good morning, Moses,' Mr Burns said. 'And a good morning to you, Mr Schwiner. Was the flight comfortable? And the hotel? Everything is ready for you. Moses here will see that everything goes smoothly for you.'

Mr Schwiner ignored the questions and looked around the office. 'When do I meet my guide?' he asked.

Moses was scowling behind the client's back and Mr Burns guessed at the situation. 'Would you mind just waiting outside for a moment, Moses?' he said. 'And close the door, please.'

'Please sit down, Mr Schwiner. There seems to be bit of a misunderstanding. *Moses* is to be your guide.'

'But I thought—'

'If you were expecting a tall, tanned white hunter in a safari suit, looking like Gregory Peck in *The Snows of Kilimanjaro*, I have to tell you that it's not like that now.'

'But when I was in South Africa—'

'It's not like that even there now. Africa's moved on. I can assure you that Moses is a qualified guide. He will look after you well.'

Mr Schwiner grunted. This was not what he had hoped for – but all he wanted to do now was to get his jumbo and be able to boast about it when he got home. 'What do I call the guy?' he asked.

'*Moses* will do. He's a Maasai and has probably got another name that nobody but another Maasai can pronounce. They're a very proud people. Whatever you do, don't call any of the Africans '*boy*' or you might find a scorpion in your bed. *Bwana* and *boy* are two words we don't use any more. Now, is there anything else you need to know?'

Moses sat in the outer office where the two women were pretending to work – but were actually watching him.

One asked, 'Would you like a cup of coffee, Mr Jackson?'

Moses had been trying to blank the recent humiliations from his mind by thinking about which of the women he fancied most. Which of the two would he ask out when he returned with a triumphant Mr Schwiner and the biggest tusks anyone had ever seen? But he knew nothing could ever come of it. Even if one of the girls had accepted, it would be no use. It would only end up as frustrating and as humiliating as it always had been. He blamed the other Mr Jackson for this. That stupid, interfering, well-meaning but stupid, stupid missionary, Mr Washington Jackson.

He accepted the coffee and drank it slowly, waiting for Mr Burns and his client to come out of the office. Even though the door was shut, he was sure he could hear laughter and smell the reek of one of Walt Schwiner's stinking cigars. He knew it was just his imagination but, even with the sugar he had spooned in, the coffee seemed to taste as bitter as the cocoa had the night after he had told Mr Jackson why he needed to go back to Maasailand, just before his seventeenth birthday.

After Walt Schwiner had left with Moses, Mr Burns sat at his desk and wondered if Moses was the right man for the job. He had not used him before and the American was not going to be an easy client. Did it matter, the way business was going? He was sure he would soon be able to pick up a number of four-by-fours cheaply when the tour operators went bust through lack of work. Then he could lead a convoy of these down to Botswana and sell them to the safari companies there for a handsome profit. So – if the Maasai did foul-up and spoil Mr Burns' reputation in Tanzania, it may not really matter.

Lars was seriously concerned about the future of the newly formed *Rylar Safaris*. The newspaper and television reporters, who had flown into Kilimanjaro Airport from all over the world to cover the eruption of Africa's most famous volcano, had filed their stories from the International Hotel in Arusha and flown out again to cover other assignments elsewhere. Reading their reports in the American and European press had misled potential clients into believing the whole of East Africa was being deluged with molten lava and rocked by frequent, severe earthquakes.

It was true that there were still minor earth tremors on many days and smoke still trailed away from the summit of the mountain but the exaggerated stories had frightened away most of the tourists.

Ryan was less concerned than Lars. 'They'll be back,' he said cheerfully. 'The Riverside has dropped our rates and neither of us are short of the readies. We should take advantage and check out some of the safari lodges. When we tell them we're guides and why we're coming, they'll probably put us up for free.'

It seemed better than moping around at the hotel so they had taken the new tarmac road and driven the one hundred and twenty kilometres west to Lake Manyara and the Ngorongoro Crater.

Both had done the journey before but now tried to see it as if *they* were tourists. They waved at the Maasai herdsmen dressed in their red-and-blue toga-like cloaks, each of whom raised a hand in a dignified salute; and they smiled sympathetically at some teenage Maasai boys with their white painted faces and wearing the black shukas that indicated they had just suffered the emorata – the circumcision ceremony – and were now on their way to manhood and warrior status. Though the fact that the boys were loitering near the road hoping to be given dollars for having their photographs taken by passing tourists, did somewhat cheapen the experience.

The road zigzagged up the two thousand steep feet of the western side of the Rift Valley in one of the few places where the escarpment was not an almost sheer cliff. On the southern bends they caught glimpses of Lake Manyara between the huge baobab trees before they reached the fertile plateau leading to the enormous Ngorongoro crater. Here, they parked the Land Rover and looked down into the caldera. Far below them they could see herds of zebra and buffalo, a few scattered elephants and what was possibly a rhino but it was too far away for them to be sure. The rim of the salt lake in the crater was pink with flamingos.

'There are no words for this,' Ryan said. 'This is the Africa I love. Isn't that view just stunning?'

In the evening Lars and Ryan sat on the veranda of the bar from where they could look out over the crater, drinking cold beer and playing chess.

'Checkmate,' said Ryan, moving his queen halfway across the board in a move Lars had not foreseen. 'Another beer?'

'Not for me, thanks. I've had more than enough. That's why you beat me.'

Ryan came back from the bar carrying a bottle, the condensation already forming on the outside. 'Do you ever hear from Lisa?' he asked.

'Not since she went back to England and got married,' Lars

replied with just a touch of wistfulness in his voice. 'Did you leave a girl in Nairobi?'

'Hundreds of them,' Ryan replied, then added, 'No one special, though.' He was silent for a minute as Lars put the chessmen back in the carved wooden box, then said, unexpectedly, 'I was married once.'

'I didn't know that,' said Lars. 'What happened?'

Ryan adopted his stage-Irish voice. ''Twas incompatibility, it was, it was! In come Pat – and he had more ability.'

Lars smiled. His friend usually had a joke to cover up his real feelings.

'No. We *were* incompatible – really. *I* liked to get up at dawn when the world was fresh and new, and all *she* wanted to do was lie in bed till the crack of noon. Then, at about nine in the evening, there she was trying to drag me out to some dance or other and me so knackered, I could hardly stand up.'

'Larks and owls,' said Lars, and when Ryan looked puzzled, he added, 'The whole world is divided into larks and owls. You and me, we're both *larks*. Your wife was, is, was clearly an *owl*. My Uncle George reckoned he'd made a lifetime's study of it and that in ninety-five per cent of cases, larks married owls. It seemed illogical, but he reckoned that it was nature's way of ensuring the survival of the human race.'

A waiter hovered at his elbow.

'Perhaps I *will* have another beer. Yes.' He turned, 'Beeri baridi. Sante.

'Uncle George's idea was that we were all subconsciously programmed to choose a mate opposite to us. A man *lark* chooses a woman *owl* and vice versa. That way there was always someone alert in the cave through the night to stop the hyenas taking away the children. Those parents who had made the wrong choice of mate, never had any offspring that grew up and bred. Hence the gene-pool was full of genes for choosing opposites. It all hangs together.'

'It wasn't just that. My wife and I were incompatible in other ways.'

'Everybody is. You just have to *make* it work – it's not always easy.'

'Now – is it nature or nurture that makes us different?'

'If you listened to my Uncle George you'd believe it was both. He had some lovely ideas.' Lars pushed the chessboard back into the centre of the table.

'*This* was one of his. I want you to imagine there are twelve squares instead of eight on each side of that board – making one hundred and forty-four squares altogether. Down this side we label the lines according to the signs of the Zodiac and along this side we label them according to the Chinese years – the Year of the Ox, the Year of the Monkey, et cetera. Yes?'

'If you say so.'

'Now. Imagine you're God. You can't spend all your time deciding what character every baby that's born would have, so you set up a matrix like this. If you're born in *this* month of *this* year, you have the characteristics of a crab and a monkey. In *this* year and *this* month, you would be as proud as a lion and as stubborn as an ox.'

'So everyone is a mixture of two types of character then. So every one-hundred and forty-fourth person gets the same mix.'

'Uncle George took it further than that. Did you ever hear the rhyme that starts: *Monday's child is full of grace; Tuesday's child is fair of face* . . .? Or it might have been the other way round – it doesn't matter. The point is, that would make a *three-dimensional* matrix, so your character depends on, not just the month and year you were born, but the day of the week as well. That gives nearly a *thousand* different combinations.'

177

'If we're all larks or owls as well, it's a wonder *anyone* is compatible with anyone else. What was your Uncle George? A graceful lark, monkey, crab or a good-looking owl, ox, lion?'

'At the time I thought he was just a boring old fart. I'm off to bed!'

After Tembo Lonely had finished telling the first part of his story, none of the tembos did any reading. Each was preoccupied with thoughts concerning what they had heard.

Kidogo tried hard to imagine a sea so big that the other side could not be seen from where one stood. She remembered the shape and taste of the big nuts that Lonely had described, as she had once been given one by a human who had called it a *coconut*. The flying knock-us-down machines that made the *tunk, tunk, tunk* noise would have been what the humans called *helicopters*. She had never liked those machines and had always instinctively hidden whenever that penetrating sound reached her, whatever she had been doing. But what was the log that floated in the sea and sprayed water into the air? Perhaps Lonely would tell them when they rested next day.

Although the air was clear and bright and the forest paths good, the team only covered a short distance the following morning. The forest had started to thin out before the sun was high and they could glimpse plantations of bananas and mealies through the trees ahead of them.

'We'll stay here among the trees until nightfall,' M'zee declared, and the tembos laid down the tusks they were carrying and started to browse. Kidogo knew M'zee was watching to see that Three Eyes did not sidle down towards the banana plantations, but the jostler foraged on the upper side of the glade. When they had all fed, and M'zee had eaten the food-wads she had prepared for him, she looked at the old one who knew her thoughts and he nodded.

'Tembo Lonely, it would please us to hear more of your story,' she said.

Lonely moved to where he could face the others and said, 'Last evening I told you of seeing what I thought was a log floating in the sea and of hearing singing in low~sound. When I heard this I turned on the cliff-top to see where the tembo was who sang to me – but none was there and now the low~sound came from behind me. I turned again, spread my ears, lifted my trunk and toe-touched the ground. There was no doubt – the singing came from what I had thought was a log in the sea – but it wasn't a log! I listened carefully and this is what I heard.

"I have seen you ~ *on the cliff-top.*
Can you see me ~ *in the water?"*

'I sang back to it.

"I can see you ~ *in the water,*
I can hear you ~ *singing to me."*

'I was excited – but the sea was making noises of its own at the bottom of the cliff and it was sometimes difficult to hear clearly. I thought it must be another tembo in the sea and so I sang a suggestion that it come round to the sandy place where we could meet. The creature in the sea sang back that it was not a tembo but an animal even bigger than we are, who called himself a *whale* and who always lived in water like a fish does.

'Of course I wanted to know what a *whale* looked like, as all I could see was the top of its back. Somehow, it seemed to know this and leaped straight up out of the water three times, falling back into the sea, making a great splash each time. It was huge. I could tell that even from where I stood, and it had a flat tail as fishes do. It called to me.

"Come and join me ~ *in the water,*

179

I would like to ~ know about you."

'Well, as you will remember, the day before, I had learned to *swim*, although I didn't have a word for it then, so I walked back to the sandy edge of the sea and waded in. The whale was waiting for me where the water was deep enough. I'd always thought tembos were big, especially old tembulls like M'zee, but when I swam close to the whale I found that he was many, many times larger than I was. 'He greeted me in low~sound.

"Welcome to you ~ *from the dry land,*
May Mana bless ~ and keep you safe."

'I was intrigued to learn that a whale should know about Mana, and I sang back to it.

Love, live long and ~ find sweet-water,
Tembo Jay and ~ goodness guide you.

'And that was the start of it. The whale and I became great friends and conversed easily in low~sound. He could not understand tembotalk, which was not surprising to me as he had no trunk to make the subtler gestures, but he knew so much – not just about life in the sea – but also much of what happened on the land.

'I would swim out each day until I was near him and then float about, breathing with my trunk out of the water. Low~sound works even better in the water than on the land, though on one day the sea was lifting me up and down and soon I had to wade to the shore, feeling ill. By the way, I was living by bumping the trees with my head until the coconuts fell – but that day I did not even want to look at one – I just wanted to lie down and die.'

Lonely paused, recalling that painful memory.

Kidogo looked around at the other tembos in the glade. Each was leaning forward, ears wide, to catch Lonely's every word. Not even M'zee was watching in the direction of the plantations. Humans might be creeping up on them,

180

and no tembo would know until it was too late. She stepped back, walked to edge of the glade, passed water then returned and positioned herself so that she could watch for danger without alarming the others or breaking into the flow of Lonely's story.

He had waited until she rejoined them before he continued.

'I asked the whale what his name was, and he replied that whales don't have names. When I asked him what he called himself, he told me,

*"I am just **me** ~ I need no name."*

'So I asked him what other whales called him, and he told me,

*"They call me, **you** ~ as I call them."*

'I wanted to find out more but, as I was composing my question, the dolphins arrived.'

Ears widened and trunks were raised quizzically.

'What are *dolphins*?'

Lonely looked at the listening tembos. He had never before had such an attentive audience.

'Dolphins,' he said making a joyful movement with his trunk. 'Dolphins are like little whales but they swim even faster than you can think. They leap out of the water and dive deeply and all the time they talk to one another in such a fast language they must have wonderful brains to follow what the others are saying.

'They dived under my legs and leaped over my back, chattering all the time – then they were gone. But the sea behind them was awash with the Love they trailed as they swam. It was a wonderful experience!'

Kidogo, still watching the forest in the direction of the plantations asked, 'How big were these dolphins? Were they as big as a human?'

'Bigger than that. Probably the size of a zebra but shaped

more like a fish. And they seemed to be happy as they swam. I only saw them for a short time but I will remember them as long as I live. They were so full of Joy and Love!

'The whale asked me how humans were treating tembos – as humans with boats were still killing many whales. I had to tell him that the humans were killing us to steal our ivory and to take our land to grow their food. Then he told me of an ancient prophecy that whales know.'

Lonely paused and said, 'I'll be back,' and walked about the glade, exercising his legs. The other tembos followed his example, passing water and dung as they walked. Soon they were back facing him.

'The prophecy the whale told me said that,
"When the stone mount ~ breathes fire and smoke,
Mana will ask ~ a Gift of Love.
***Tembos** give this ~ though it hurts them.*
Only the Love ~ of Tembo Jay
Can save the world ~ from human greed."

'Of course, I didn't know then which mountain he meant, though now I believe it must be the Holy Mountain on which we stand. The whale knew nothing more about what the *Gift of Love* was to be – nor how it would hurt the tembos who had to make it. He didn't know either how the whales had learned of this prophecy or even who Tembo Jay was – but he was sure it had come from Mana to encourage the whales at a time when so many were being killed.

'This gave me a chance to ask what he knew about Mana – and he sang me a song so beautiful I learned it all.'

'Sing us the song,' urged Tembo One Eye, speaking for the first time in days. 'Please, sing us the song.'

Lonely turned to him. 'It is too sacred to sing so close to where humans are living. Also it is best heard from a distance, and at night. When the time is right I will sing the song for you all.'

As darkness fell, the elephants prepared to pass through the plantations. Kidogo was pleased that M'zee did not find it necessary to warn the jostlers to leave the human food plants alone. The tembos were to follow the old one in single file and to make no noises and drop no dung. If they had to say anything, they were to use low~sound, which they were all sure humans couldn't hear. The moon was high when they left the forest carrying the four free tusks. As usual, M'zee was in the lead and Kidogo at the tail-end of the line.

The humans were in or near their huts and the tembos could see their cooking fires and smell the smoke and the food-scents in the air but none appeared to notice the elephants passing between the banana plants and the tall mealie stems nearby. Kidogo was concerned to see that even in the moonlight their footprints showed clearly in the dust of the path, and she began to worry that the humans might notice the prints in the morning and follow them. She considered dragging a branch behind her to brush them away but that would leave a trail almost as noticeable as the footprints themselves.

When they had passed through the plantations and come to some rocky uncultivated ground, M'zee called a halt. Kidogo went to him and confided her fears.

'I should have thought of that,' he said. 'But if I had, I don't know what we could have done about it. Nor do I know now.'

'Have you ever made rain come?' she asked him.

'I know tembos *used* to be able to do that,' he said, 'but I never learned how.'

'It's easy,' Kidogo told him. 'I learned from Tembella Grace and the Sisters at the Sacred Pool.'

'Ah, Tembella Grace! If anyone would know – she would. But why do you ask?'

'If enough rain were to fall now, our footprints would all

be washed away and we know that humans can't scent things like we can, so they would never know we had passed.'

M'zee touched her forehead. 'Truly, I chose well,' he said. 'Show us how it is to be done.'

Kidogo guided the tembos into a tight circle like the one they'd formed when they'd heard the voice of Mana telling them to *follow the tired sun,* and asked them to linque their trunks.

'Now shut your eyes and think of rain. Nothing else – just rain – wet and cool – rain – bringing life to the land.'

They stood like this for a short time, then Kidogo noticed the moon had hidden itself behind clouds which she was sure had not been there before they linqued. Soon, they heard the patter of small raindrops on the dry soil around them and felt the coolness of the drops on their backs and ears.'

'Think harder,' Kidogo urged. 'Think of enough rain to wash away our footsteps.'

The rain fell more heavily, rivulets running down the sides of each tembo, and forming puddles around their feet.

'Think harder – harder!' she urged. Lightning flashed and rain drummed on their backs until it almost hurt.

Finally, she whispered, 'Enough,' and they unlinqued their trunks and stepped backwards, each surprised at how exhausted they felt. It was no easy thing, this rainmaking!

They moved down onto wooded lower-ground, well away from the plantations, where they were less likely to be seen by any wandering human, and rested here throughout the next day, browsing intermittently and savouring the after-rain scents and sounds of the bushland.

Lonely sought out Kidogo as she prepared food-wads for M'zee, who stood alone a short distance away, his trunk hanging down.

'This rainmaking,' Lonely asked. 'Where did you learn that?'

She told him about the Sacred Grove, Tembella Grace and the Sisters. 'I think *any* tembo can call for a *little* rain,' she said. 'The more tembos there are, and the harder they try, the more rain will come. But I think it is a gift from Mana that must not be used lightly.'

Lonely pulled down a branch from a small tree and pushed it into his mouth. 'Even so soon after the rain, food tastes fresher and sharper,' he said. 'It is a good skill to have.'

'When will you sing the whale's song for us,' she asked him.

'Tonight – if M'zee agrees – before we walk on. I could go up among those rocks and you could all listen down here.'

Kidogo saw how the position of the rocks and the hollow of the land would hold and intensify the low~sound.

'I will ask him when I take him these,' she said, touching the pile of food-wads she had prepared.

The elephants waited in the early darkness while Tembo Lonely chose his singing place among the rocks. The moon had not yet risen and the tusks of Tembo Jay and Steadfast glowed softly where they lay on the ground. All the tembos in the hollow were alert, ears wide, trunks raised and feet placed ready to catch every nuance. A night bird was calling but this, and the chirping of the insects, ceased even before the first wave of Lonely's song reached them.

In the dim and ~ distant ages
This our planet ~ was quite lifeless.
Came a time when ~ it was ready
Ready like a ~ flower, open,
Craving for a ~ speck of pollen.

185

Floating in from ~ where we know not
Came a drift of ~ cosmic pollen
Carrying the ~ sacred Life-force
To this silent ~ waiting planet.

Like the flower ~ gaining pollen
Earth responded ~ to this Life-force.
Simple plants and ~ simple creatures
Flourished here in ~ great abundance
Making from this ~ sterile body
Something more than ~ rocks and water.

As time passed these ~ plants and creatures
Grew more complex ~ found their places
Leading to a ~ wondrous richness
Making up the ~ world around us.
On the way a ~ million, million
Plants and creatures ~ formed and flourished
Failed and perished ~ died and vanished.

Others, fitter ~ stronger, better
For the role that ~ needed playing
Took their places ~ in this complex
Web of inter~active life-forms.

At some point, a ~ mystic union
Of these plants and ~ other creatures,
With the earth and ~ rocks and water
Formed a being ~ whales call Gaia
Mother-being ~ of our planet.

Gaia, like a ~ mother whale,
Knew the Joy of ~ Procreation
*Knew **her** role, to ~ care and nourish.*

But another ~ force was needed
With intelligence ~ and forethought
*Powered by Love ~ she named **him**, 'Mana'.*

Gaia chose from ~ all her creatures
Four to serve our ~ planet's interests
Four to give it ~ thought and focus
Four to save it ~ from destruction
*Four were given ~ **souls** and **duties**.*

*From the oceans ~ she chose **whales***
Great in body ~ great in wisdom
With a brain that ~ could develop
Play a part in ~ forming Mana.

*As a balance ~ she chose **dolphins***
Smaller, joyful ~ fond of playing
Loving freedom ~ kind and caring
Dolphins would be ~ good for Mana.

*Greatest on the ~ land were **tembos***
Like the whales ~ great in wisdom
Storing in their ~ tusks the Loving
Mana needed ~ for his workings.

*Lastly, Gaia ~ chose the **humans***
Smaller, joyful ~ fond of playing
Loving freedom ~ kind and caring –
Humans would be ~ good for Mana.

Whales, dolphins ~ tembos, humans
All were granted ~ 'beings' greater
Than their bodies, ~ blood and brains were.
*Call these 'beings' ~ **souls** or **spirits**,*
Hallowing the ~ chosen foursome.

All the myriad ~ other life-forms
Fill the needs of ~ whales and dolphins,
Feed the tembos ~ and the humans
So they can devote ~ their lives to
Service for the ~ good of Mana.

Linque the spirits ~ of the Foursome
Linque the Whales ~ and the Dolphins
With the Tembos ~ and the Humans
Linque these spirits ~ round the planet
Blend with Love ~ and we have **Mana**

Think of Gaia *~ as **our mother***
Caring for the ~ plants and creatures
Think of Mana *~ as **our father***
Planning for our ~ planet's future
Seeing what needs ~ doing. Only -
With no hands or ~ trunks or flippers
He needs US *to ~ do what's needed.*

His the vision ~ ours the labour
Without Mana *~ we are nothing*
Without us he's ~ nothing either
Mana *needs us ~ we need* **Mana.**

We need food to ~ fill our bellies,
Give us strength to ~ live and flourish,
Make more whales ~ dolphins, tembos
Make more humans ~ Each are needed
To ensure that ~ Mana *lives on.*

Our role is ~ serving Mana
Seeking Joy in ~ all around us
Seeking Joy and ~ with it forming
Love, to power the ~ work of Mana

It's from Joy that ~Love emerges
Transmuted by ~ our souls and spirits
Joy – to Love. Our ~ gift to Mana.

He needs Love ~ as we need fishes,
Meat or plants to ~ fill our bellies.
It is Joy that we must cherish
Forming Love to ~ nourish Mana.

If we choose to ~ take what's offered,
Giving nothing ~ being greedy,
Never giving Love to Mana,
Thinking that our ~ selfish comforts
Justify our ~ whole existence –
We will grow away ~ from Mana.

Then our lives will ~ be so empty
We won't ever ~ linque with Mana.
Arrogance and ~ fear will fill us
Fear of loss and ~ Fear of dying.

Love and Fear can't ~ live together
In the hearts and ~ souls of whales
In the hearts and ~ souls of dolphins
In the hearts and ~ souls of tembos
In the hearts and ~ souls of humans.

Real Love and ~ real caring
Take away these ~ Fears forever.

Listen to the ~ voice within you
That is Mana ~ speaking softly
Saying what you ~ should be doing
Sometimes hard and ~ sometimes easy
Don't ignore that ~ voice within you
Or Mana's plans ~ can't reach fruition.

Mana needs the ~ Love we give him,
Formed from Joy and ~ care for others
For Love is the ~ magic power
The force that linques ~ us all together

Here's the wonder ~ here's the beauty
Here's the honour ~ here's the duty
We can all be ~ part of Mana
We will all be ~ part of Mana
If we share the Love within us
Love that Mana ~ needs to function
For the future of our planet.

For the future of our planet.

For the future of our planet.

The song died away but it was some time before the insects started to chirrup again and the night-birds to call. The tembos stood silently in the hollow waiting for Lonely to come and join them.

When Kidogo heard the sound of his body pushing through the bushes, she stepped forward to greet him. 'That was wonderful,' she said. 'There is much in that song I would like to talk to you about.'

The other tembos had gathered round, each with questions to ask but it was M'zee who spoke first. 'Did this whale tell you what happens to us when we *step-over*,' he asked. 'It was not in the song.'

'The whale called stepping over, *to swim across,* but I am sure it means the same thing. One day I asked him that question and he was about to tell me when the dolphins came again. But now they were not so joyful. They were twittering in voices that warned of danger and the whale and I lifted our heads and saw a boat coming towards us. It was

190

much bigger than even the whale and he dived and swam away without a goodbye or farewell, so I swam to the shore as the boat passed behind me. I turned once and saw that it had a flapping cloth on a pole at the back end of it.

'Humans call that a *flag*,' Kidogo said. 'There are many different ones.'

'This one was white with a picture of the sun on it. I waited on the sands for many days but the whale never came back.'

CHAPTER SEVENTEEN

Lars drove the Land Rover down the steep track and onto the floor of the Ngorongoro crater before most of the other tourist vehicles had left the hotels on the crater rim. He drove slowly in the crisp morning air, looking to right and left and reporting what he saw to Ryan.

'Buffalo at eleven o'clock; bull elephant at one o'clock,' he said, using the method popular with guides in Africa. 'Look over there – three o'clock. It's an aardvark. You don't see many of those in the daylight.'

The long-snouted anteater was shuffling away from them and suddenly disappeared. 'Gone to ground,' Ryan said. 'Pity that. They make very safe pets.'

Lars suspected a joke was coming and asked in a formal voice, 'Go on then, tell me why.'

'Aardvark never hurt anyone,' Ryan replied, and Lars groaned.

They drove on for a short way before Lars asked, 'Did you know aardvarks used to be called zimmers?'

'I did not,' replied Ryan. 'When was it changed?'

'When the zimmers discovered that Noah was taking the animals onto the ark in alphabetical order.'

It was Ryan's turn to groan.

They stopped near the soda lake. 'That may be a rhino over there,' Lars said.

Ryan asked, 'No binoculars?'

'I gave them up at the same time as I put away my camera.'

'Now, there's a story here – I can tell.'

'Not much of one.' Lars drank from his water bottle. 'I went to London last year to meet some of my relatives who'd gone there from South Africa. I couldn't believe it – there were cameras *everywhere*. On every wall, in every shop – even in the taxis and filling stations! There are cameras on the streets to check your speed and cameras to charge you for taking your car into London. Even when you get out of the city, there are yellow boxes with cameras on posts and white police-vans filming you from lay-bys. I began to get paranoid. My uncle said, "You've nothing to fear if you behave yourself – they're there for our protection." But it got so as I couldn't scratch my backside, or look in a shop window, without wondering who was watching me – and why. Did you ever read that book, *Nineteen Eighty-four*, where Big Brother was always watching you? Well it was like that. I was planning to stay for a couple of weeks but I booked the earliest flight out.'

'Back to Africa?'

'Yes. And when I got back here, I realised that's what *we* do to the animals. Some lions kill a zebra and the poor sods are surrounded by a ring of four-by-fours, all full of tourists, gawping and clicking cameras. So far the lions have had the dignity to ignore it but, if one jumped into a vehicle and chewed up a couple of voyeurs, I'd be more inclined to applaud than condemn.'

'And the binoculars?'

'Same sort of thing. If you watch animals from a natural distance, it's giving the beasties the chance to walk away or hide if they want to. It's sort of unfair to look at them from a greater distance than they can see you.'

'I know what you're saying. But we could be doing with some binoculars now, though. That might be a rhino at three o'clock – or it might just be a termite mound. Let's see if we can get closer. But not too close!'

On the first day of the hunting safari, Moses had driven the leading vehicle, a new climate-controlled Land Cruiser, with Walt Schwiner beside him in the front passenger seat. In the rear was a mobile refrigerator filled with fresh produce and cans of beer and *Coca-Cola*. Behind, in an older Land Rover, came the three camp-staff with the heavy gear. They had left Arusha in the early afternoon and driven northwest towards Olsandura. Moses had called an early halt to camp as he was not familiar with the ways of his crew, and he expected his client to complain if everything didn't appear to run smoothly.

They camped under a vast flat-topped thorn tree, with views over a shallow valley studded with kopjes, right on the edge of Maasailand. Moses didn't expect to meet any Maasai, as the ground was parched and bare and he knew they would have taken their cattle farther north to be near the riverbeds and waterholes.

The camp was set up quickly while Walt Schwiner sat in a director's chair watching the men work, enjoying the view and smoking another of those small cigars his guide had come to loathe.

'Hey, Moses, when do we get to see the elephants?' he called.

Moses came over, trying to hide his dislike for the man. 'Two – maybe three days, Sir. There are not so many in Africa now as there used to be.' He wanted to add that only a hundred years before there had been six million and now there were believed to be only a tenth of that number, at most. But that would have been insulting to his client, even though it was people like him who had killed most of the elephants to steal their ivory.

Instead, Moses asked, 'Would you prefer coffee or tea, Sir? The kettle is nearly boiling.'

'Coffee will be fine. Will you bring me my rifle – I want to check it over?'

Walt sat, sipping at the coffee, with the rifle resting across the arms of his chair, as Moses supervised the setting up of the camp toilet-tent and the shower enclosure, both for the sole use of Walter Schwiner. Periodically, the American stroked his gun lovingly. Any moment now he will lift it up to his lips and kiss it, Moses thought, and wished there was more than one client. When there was only one the guide had to dine with him, and these people from overseas, especially the Americans, ate so much.

The moon was high and the crew had put up their own tents and eaten their evening meal when the American announced he was going to bed, and now they sat around the embers of the campfire talking in low voices. Moses got up and walked out into the darkness, stood there silently for a while, then came back, picked up a clean cooking pot and walked away again. The other men watched him go and he knew they would be making comments about the funny ways of the Maasai.

He walked into the bush for some distance, aware that the familiar night noises were absent and, when he was out of sight of the camp, knelt and placed the pot upside-down on the ground, hoping that it would act in the same way as a dry gourd had done when he was a boy. He lay down and put his ear to the upturned base. He had been right – an elephant *was* singing tonight.

He could only detect the familiar rhythm and was unable to sense the direction, but Moses was sure it was not very far away. His mind drifted to those childhood days – long, long days of standing guard to his father's herd of beautiful cows. He had known every one of them as well or better than he knew his Maasai friends. He could, even now, describe each animal's size, its colour, the shape of its horns, even its food preferences and the daintiness or otherwise of its walk. If any cow or calf wandered out of his sight he had known which ones and how many, instantly, just by glancing at the herd – he didn't need to count the ones who were still in sight.

And *how* he had envied his elder half-brother Sambeke and the others of his age group, who had been initiated as warriors and could carry spears and sleep with the unmarried girls.

When the elephant's singing faded and the insects and night-birds were calling again, he got up and walked slowly back to the camp, carrying the cooking pot.

'It's all right,' he said to the cook, 'I haven't peed in it,' but offered no other explanation.

Moses dressed and left his tent as dawn first showed itself with a hint of pink on the highest of the tiny clouds. He walked down the valley to the first of the kopjes, undressed completely, except for his sandals, folded his clothes neatly as he had been taught at the mission and left them on a rock at its base, where he could easily find them later. He searched for a short stick such as he had carried when he was a herd-boy and walked on, feeling the coolness of the dawn air caress his body. He had no fear of wild creatures. Lions in Maasailand kept well clear of humans, as did any leopards. Snakes and elephants didn't bother you if you left them alone and he was too far from any water for hippos or crocodiles to be a threat.

A dove started to call. '*De daa daa, De daa daa,*' it cooed. Tears came to his eyes and he wiped them away with the back of his hand. Maasai men don't cry! He walked on as it grew lighter, listening to the familiar sounds as Africa awoke. If he hadn't been such a coward as a boy, all this would still be his.

He walked on, heading for the tallest kopje that would

give him a view over the low ridge into the next valley where the elephant would be – if it were still there. How he knew this, he couldn't have said but seeing elephants frequently as a boy had given him a deep sense and feeling for their ways.

A long-necked gerenuk antelope, feeding with its front feet up on a branch, scampered away from the base of the kopje as he approached. The kopje, an unusually large one, was made of huge rounded boulders heaped on top of one another by long-past volcanic activity and earth movements. Fig trees grew in the crevices between the rocks with their long grey, exploring roots reaching down to seek new cracks to enter in their search for moisture. Small, brightly-coloured lizards were creeping out to warm themselves as a red sun lifted slowly over the horizon and an eagle, perched on a dead branch of the highest fig tree, squawked and launched itself heavily into the air when it saw the man approaching.

Moses undid his sandals, took them off and climbed the rocks, his bare toes gripping the weathered surface. Naked and now barefoot, he felt once more at one with the world. Using every nook and cranny for hand and footholds, he watched where he placed each hand as it was on rocks like these that a basking snake could be a danger, although he was sure it was too early in the day for them to be out.

Reaching the topmost rock he didn't climb up on top of it but sat on a ledge with his back against it to avoid appearing against the skyline. The stone under his buttocks was smooth and cool and he felt good, more alive than he had for years. Looking down between his knees he studied his *eniwatok*. The hospital to which Mr Jackson had taken him, half-drugged, had done a tidy job, not like some he had seen. His half-brother's *eni* was badly scarred from a botched operation, carried out in front of a group of men, each

197

willing him not to cry out – but the pain must have been dreadful to bear in silence, as tradition demanded.

Moses had known for years before he reached thirteen, when his turn would come, that it was something he would not be able to bear. When he had been given the ceremonial knife to sharpen before it was used on him, he had fled into the bush, dropped the dreaded knife down a hole in a termite mound and slipped away to the anonymity of the town and the welcome at the mission station. But what they had done so neatly at the hospital had *not* made him into a Maasai man. It needed to be done *without* anaesthetics to prove that he could, as a man – a Maasai man – stand any pain in silence. Mr Jackson would not have understood that – the stupid, interfering, well-meaning but stupid, stupid missionary man.

Moses raised his head when he heard what he was sure was the squeal of a young elephant from upwind and turned slowly towards the sound. Some distance away, in the next valley, which had a scattering of baobab trees, he could see several grey backs. He counted six – four of a similar size and one much smaller, but it was the sixth that held his attention – a huge bull – and he waited until it turned sideways on. Its tusks were enormous. Never before had he seen such tusks.

If he could get Mr Schwiner in range of *that* bull, the safari would be successfully completed and he could pay off most of his debts with the inevitable large tip. But this was not an official hunting area and he would have to ensure that the crew would not report him. But then, they too would be in line for handsome gratuities. He would have to spell out the situation to each one of them and he was sure they would keep their mouths shut for the kind of cash this man evidently had.

He slipped quietly down the rocks, strapped on his

sandals and hurried back to where he had left his clothes. As he put them on he was aware of the barrier the European clothes made between himself and the life of the bushland. He longed to be back where he could wear just the simple, loose shuka of the real Maasai. No wonder they had named the early Europeans *lloredaa enjekat* or 'fart smotherers', after the clothing they wore.

CHAPTER EIGHTEEN

Walt Schwiner was seated in his chair, smoking one of his favourite cigars when Moses arrived back at the camp. He walked round the American to get upwind before saying, 'Good morning, Sir. Did you sleep well?'

'Well enough, I guess. What time is breakfast?'

'The cook is making it now, Sir, but I have some news for you.'

Walt Schwiner grunted. 'Huh?'

'Last night I heard elephants not too far away and this morning I found them.' Now that Moses had the man's attention he paused for dramatic effect.

The American leaned forward, blowing out a stream of smoke, and asked, 'Any of them have decent tusks?'

'One did, Sir. Much longer than this even.' Moses stretched his arms wide. 'Much longer – and very thick around.'

Walt Schwiner was on his feet in an instant. 'I'll get my rifle.'

'One moment please, Sir. It is not as easy as that. Please sit down again while I explain.'

The American sat down reluctantly. 'What's the problem?'

'Well, Sir, if we were in the hunting area, there would be no problem. But here we are not allowed to shoot any animals, even though we have a licence for one elephant.'

'Who's to know? Are there any other people around? Any of *your* people?'

'All the Maasai are likely to be farther north with the cattle but sometimes the young men walk through the bush alone or with other warriors, just for the excitement – for the joy of it. I didn't see any though. It's the crew who might report us.' He made a gesture towards the other men standing around the fire out of earshot.

'What'll it take to keep them quiet?'

Moses named a figure, way above what he thought his client would accept and prepared himself to haggle on their behalf.

'Done deal – and you?'

'Whatever you think,' Moses replied. He would have been happy with the amount he had named for the men, so *his* would naturally be much more, certainly enough to pay off the most dangerous of his debts.

'Let's go get him!' Walt strode off to fetch his rifle and ammunition belt.

The elephants were in no hurry to leave that morning. Every one of them had spent most of the night awake, thinking of the whale's song that Tembo Lonely had sung so movingly the night before. Lonely himself seemed drained and listless, as though the song, or the memories it had invoked, were bearing heavily on him.

Kidogo had wandered a little way away from the others and was collecting food and chewing it into wads for M'zee. She was a little ashamed of herself for waking with a squeal after a disturbing dream in which humans had killed *all* the whales and *all* the elephants in the whole world. Now she was wondering about the prophecy the whale had told to Lonely, and what it meant. It had burned itself into her memory even though she had heard it only once.

'*When the stone mount ~ breathes fire and smoke,*
Mana will ask ~ a Gift of Love.
Tembos *give this ~ though it hurts them.*
Only the Love ~ of Tembo Jay
Can save the world ~ from human greed.'

Lonely had said he believed 'the mount' must mean Holy Mountain which they had so recently left to *follow the tired sun*. That mountain had been breathing fire and smoke. She looked back at the sky behind her. Above a bank of grey clouds that hid the lower slopes, the summit was visible with a trail of smoke streaming out to one side.

What could the *Gift of Love* be – and why would it *hurt* them? Giving and receiving Love had always been a pleasurable experience. Kidogo realised she had grown to love all the elephants who were travelling together, especially old M'zee who seemed to really appreciate the food-wads she brought him each day. Were those *Gifts of Love*? In a way they were, as she always took the trouble to select the tastiest plants to make them, and she chewed each one enough so he could swallow it easily. But Mana had no *body* so could not need anything like that.

She also loved Tembo Lonely who had experienced that wonderful episode with the whale and who had sung the whale's song so beautifully the night before. She even felt bonds of love with the three jostlers who were becoming less selfish, and more respectful towards M'zee. They no longer grumbled about carrying the tusks of Tembo Steadfast and Tembo Jay and each of them often spent time in the night reading one or other of them.

She wandered on, topping a small rise and looking down into a shallow valley with several kopjes rising above the trees. She was drawn towards the nearest and as she was approaching it she saw the footprints of a human in the dust. She put down the food-wads she had been carrying and snuffled at the footprints with her trunk. The scent told her they had been made earlier that morning. She picked up the food-wads and hurried down to warn the others.

Walt Schwiner watched Moses hold up, then drop, a few

wisps of dry grass to test for wind-direction and followed behind him as he circled round, keeping down-wind of the elephants. Walt carried his own rifle and was pleased to see that his guide also had one, which he carried in a competent way. Mr Burns had told him that Moses was an excellent shot and could be relied upon if things went wrong. The American could not see or hear anything of the quarry himself – but his guide seemed to know just what he was doing and where he was going. Walt crouched when he saw Moses go down on one knee and stayed still in response to an unmistakeable hand-signal. His heart was beating as rapidly as it had done when he was a boy stalking his first pronghorn on his uncle's ranch in Montana.

Moses crawled sideways to take cover behind a termite mound near a baobab tree and made a signal for Walt to join him. Walt moved forward in a half-crouch and dropped down beside the guide.

'Raise your head slowly and look over there.' Moses was pointing towards a gap in the bush two hundred feet away. Walt knelt up slowly, rifle in hand, and gasped. Five elephants were standing together in a glade near one of the huge trees, four of the beasts were nearly full-grown and each bore collectable trophy tusks, but the fifth, just ahead of the others, was massive and bore the most enormous tusks. Walt's hands started to tremble as they had when he'd got within shooting distance of that pronghorn, and again when he'd got near his grizzly in Alaska.

'Take your time,' Moses whispered. 'They don't know we're here.'

Walt steadied himself, decided on a heart shot, sighted on the exact spot – he'd rehearsed this many times with an elephant-shaped target – closed his eyes and squeezed the trigger. Closing his eyes at that crucial point was a bad habit he'd never been able to get out of. At that precise moment, one of the smaller elephants stepped forward alongside the bull.

Lonely was standing just behind and to the side of M'zee when he saw a cautious movement at the base of a termite mound. Humans were there – he was sure it was humans! He stepped forward to get a better view and, as his head was in line with M'zee's chest, the bullet smacked into his skull. He was dead before he'd even had time to hear the shot, and slumped to the ground as the other elephants wheeled and crashed into the bush in panic.

'What in hell happened?' Walt growled as he opened his eyes and saw an elephant slump to its knees and roll over on its side – but it wasn't the one he had shot at! He raised his rifle again and aimed at the back of his original target as it lumbered into the bush. Moses reached out his arm and pushed the barrel to one side.

'We do not want to have to deal with an injured bull here, Sir. We may decide to follow that one later. Stay back while I make sure that this one is completely dead.'

Moses walked forward carefully, safety catch off, and circled the body. '*Kufu sana,*' he called back. 'It is very dead. You may come and see.'

Walt joined him, furious at himself. If he had not seen the great bull he might well have been satisfied with this tusker, but it was a second-rater compared with the one he had aimed at. He wanted *that* one but knew his licence was for one male elephant only. The dead one's upper eye was still open, looking at him accusingly as he circled round it so he poked at the eye-lid with the barrel of his gun until it closed and he felt better.

Moses had walked away towards the baobab tree and stood with his back to Walt, presumably to urinate. Walt heard him whistle, then call, 'Come here, Sir, and look at this.'

He ambled over, his gun under his arm. On the ground in front of Moses were four tusks, laid side by side. One pair was about the same size as those on the bull he had missed – but the other pair were nearly a third as long again. He looked at his guide. 'Jeez! Where did these—?'

'I've no idea,' Moses said, awe in his voice. 'But they are magnificent.' He touched one of the nearest tusks with his foot. 'These are big – but *those* are even bigger than Ahmed's.'

'Who the hell is Ahmed?'

'He was an old bull elephant who lived on Mount Elgon in Kenya. President Kenyatta had him declared a National Treasure because of the size of his tusks, but these are definitely bigger than even Ahmed's.'

Walt forgot the elephant he had shot which lay behind him, flies gathering around the hole in the side of its head. He was wondering if there was any way he could claim *these* tusks as his trophy. They'd certainly open a few eyes back in Illinois.

'How do we get these out of here?' he asked.

'Sir?'

'Come on, Man. These are *ours*. We found them.'

'No, Sir. According to the game laws—'

'To hell with the game laws! These tusks are mine. How do we get them out? Can we get the vehicles up here?'

Moses' mind was working on a parallel track to Walt's, but for him these tusks could be the way out of all his financial problems. The American was obviously even richer than he had believed and would do anything, and pay whatever it took, to get the biggest pair of these tusks to America. He might even leave the other four for him to dispose of. If enough money was available, there was always a way to move ivory around the world, CITES ban or no CITES ban.

Even if an officially-stamped licence could not be bought, there was always that Arab he had heard of, down at Dar es Salaam. The one who had that fleet of dhows . . .

'We will go back to the camp, then drive up here for the tusks. Will you want to take the tusks from the elephant you shot, Sir?'

'In for a dime, in for a dollar,' the American replied. 'No point leaving them here. They can be *your* share.' Moses had hoped for a substantial amount of cash as well as some tusks for himself – but now was not the time to discuss that.

Walt stepped over the nearest pair of tusks and crouched down to touch one of the largest. He put his fingers on the smooth ivory, trying to guess how old it was. He felt suddenly calmer and was momentarily moved to believe he had cheated his guide. He lifted his fingers and was immediately sure he hadn't. The guy was only an African, after all – even those smaller tusks from the elephant he had just shot would mean real wealth to him.

As he stood up his heart started to dance about in his chest. He was not too worried, this had happened several times before, and he only needed to take the four tablets he always carried with him and sit quietly for a few hours.

The guide was talking to him. 'Are you ready, Sir? We will go back to the camp now.'

Walt felt in his pocket for the tablets but they were in his other jacket, left hanging in his tent.

'I'll stay here,' he said. 'You go and bring the other guys with the jeeps.'

'It is best that you come with me. The other elephants may come back.'

Walt knew he could not walk that distance with his heart doing stupid things but did not want to explain his disability to this man.

'I've got my rifle. I'm going to stay here and make sure no one comes and steals my ivory. Don't be long. And bring me the jacket that's hanging in my tent.'

Moses was unhappy about leaving Walt Schwiner behind but the man had been insistent. Supposing the elephants did come back – which he thought was unlikely – could the man defend himself? What if his gun jammed? The man was still his responsibility.

'I'll leave my rifle with you, Sir. Just in case.'

'What about you? While you're walking back.'

'I will be fine, Sir. Remember I have always lived here. I know—'

The American took the second rifle and dismissed Moses with a wave of his hand. Moses glanced back as he left the scene – Schwiner was feeling for his own pulse.

Once out of sight, Moses took off his European clothes and carried them folded on his arm as he walked through the bush, alert for any sign of the other elephants but he neither saw nor heard anything to cause him alarm. He dressed again as he neared the camp.

Walt Schwiner walked slowly around the dead elephant after Moses had left. As he had expected, his pulse was racing one moment, then stopping completely for a count of three or four, then racing again, before fading until he could hardly feel it at all.

'Don't worry about it,' the consultant had told him after putting him through a whole series of expensive tests before he had left for Africa. 'Take the tablets immediately it comes on, then rest until the arrhythmia stops.'

The sun was hot now but if he went into the shade of the baobab, he wouldn't be able to see if any elephants or even lions were approaching. A twig cracked behind him and he spun round but could see nothing unusual. That patch of grey had always been there – or had it? He raised his rifle, then lowered it again. 'Steady, Walter. Steady, son.' He could hear his father's voice.

Standing near the corpse whose belly was rapidly distending in the hot sun, Walter jumped violently when a long fart burst from the dead elephant's anus. He knew it would be at least two hours before Moses got to the camp, organised the packing up and came back with a vehicle. A whistling of air through feathers overhead told him that the first of the vultures had arrived. He sighted his rifle on the bird as it glided round to land on the flat top of a nearby thorn-tree and shot it dead before it had time to turn and study him. He ejected the cartridge and slid another into the breech as more vultures followed the first but he left these alone to conserve his ammunition. The carrion-eating birds sat in ranks on the surrounding treetops, waiting for him to go away – or die. Feeling his knees about to give way, he sat down on the upper one of Lonely's tusks and mopped his forehead with a khaki handkerchief.

Temba Kidogo, carrying food-wads for M'zee, was on her way back to join the other elephants when she'd heard the first shot. She put down the wads and lifted her trunk to test the air. The tiniest trace of gun-smoke reached her on an eddy of wind and she feared the worst. Some human had shot M'zee while she, his Shadow, had not been there to protect him. She recalled what he'd said when he asked her to be his Shadow. *'If you think my life is in danger, you must be prepared to give yours to save mine.'* She'd failed him when he had needed her most. If only she had been there, with her good vision, she was sure she would have seen the hunter coming.

But Lonely would have been with him – and the jostlers – they *all* had good eyes. Perhaps the hunter had missed his target, she knew from living with humans that they did sometimes miss. And the man she had killed near Amboseli had shot at Rafiki but had only hit his tusk. Perhaps M'zee was alive after all! She left the food-wads in a pile and walked on slowly, testing the air at every step. She found the fear-tainted dung from each of the three youngsters where they had fled into the bush. Then she was sure she recognised M'zee's scent and was about to follow it when she decided to see what had actually happened. She moved forward cautiously, using every scrap of cover.

What she saw made her very angry, and sad. Tembo Lonely was lying on his side – clearly dead – and a pale-skinned man, whom she'd not seen before, was sitting on one of his tusks holding a gun. At least the dead one was not Tembo M'zee, whom she had vowed to guard with her life. But Tembo Lonely *had* been killed by this man. Only the night before, Lonely had thrilled them all by singing the whale's song, and there were so many things in that song she had wanted to talk to him about. Kidogo wanted to kill this man for what he had done – but one more killing wouldn't bring Lonely back to life. Why did Mana let such terrible things happen?

The man with the gun turned and pointed it in her direction, and the fear he radiated filled the glade. Kidogo froze and waited until he had turned away before she stepped backwards slowly and went to find M'zee and the jostlers.

An eater-of-dead-flesh bird glided over her head and shortly after she heard another shot come from the direction of the glade. She hurried on. When she found the tembos they all raised their trunks in a thankful greeting, and M'zee touched her forehead three times.

Kidogo described what she had just seen. 'A man with a gun is sitting on Tembo Lonely's tusk but there was the scent of another man nearby.'

'He will have gone to fetch more men to cut out Lonely's tusks – and I am sure they will have found the other ivories,' M'zee said. He was ashamed of himself for running away. It hardly seemed any time since he had criticised Temba Kidogo and the three jostlers for leaving one of Tembo Jay's tusks behind when the men had shot at him in the forest. Now he had done the same. *Both* of Tembo Jay's tusks *and* Tembo Steadfast's were now in the possession of humans, and they were about to get Tembo Lonely's as well. He knew he must work something out – but he had not fed for a long time and there seemed to be locusts hopping around inside his head and a honey-badger gnawing its way through his guts. He just wanted to lie down and sleep.

Three Eyes stepped forward. 'I have a plan,' he said.

Kidogo and Tembo One Eye watched from the cover of dense bush as the Land Rover, with three men inside, drove carefully up the narrow track to the pass between the two valleys, heading towards where Lonely's body lay. Once the vehicle had passed out of sight, they followed its scent and wheel-tracks back to the humans' campsite. As Three Eyes had predicted when he had told them his plan, there was only one man left there, stirring something in a black iron cook-pot on the fire. The elephants ignored him when he ran away, climbed a tree and clung to a high branch. They wasted the camp thoroughly before tipping the Land Cruiser on its side so that One Eye could puncture the metal box on its underside several times with his tusks. A stinking liquid which Kidogo knew humans called *fuel*, poured from the holes and soaked into the ground. She pointed out the emergency radio set to One Eye and suggested he poke a tusk through that as well.

Before they left the campsite, One Eye walked slowly across to the tree where the man clung, put his forehead to the trunk and pushed the tree over. He then snuffled up a trunkful of dust and blew it all over the terrified man before walking away to catch up with Kidogo.

At the pass, they joined Three Eyes and Two Eyes who were waiting there, hidden amongst the rocks. A small tree they had pushed down lay across the track and would have to be moved before any returning vehicle could get by.

When the elephants heard the Land Rover coming, they froze until it stopped at the tree and four men got out. The pale-skinned one stood back to watch the other three drag the tree clear of the track.

'Now!' trumped Three Eyes, and the tembos rushed forward to separate the men from their vehicle, in which Three Eyes had been sure they would leave their guns. He was right.

The men scattered and ran off to hide themselves amongst the rocks, while the jostlers, working silently, pushed and pulled at the six tusks lashed to the roof-rack. Being tapered, they slid easily out of the bindings. Kidogo reached in through the open door, found the two guns, pulled them out and smashed each of them against the rocks, just as she'd seen Rafiki do when he had been shot at near Amboseli.

Walt Schwiner watched helplessly as his beloved rifle was trashed by an elephant. He vowed revenge, but there was nothing he could do now except watch from a distance as the elephants tipped the Land Rover on its side and proceeded to puncture its fuel tank and wreck its radio with their tusks. The scent of diesel drifted up to his hiding place. Sod you, he thought, as the four elephants each took one of the largest tusks and walked away, leaving the blood-covered tusks of the elephant he had shot lying by the track. You won't beat me – we'll come back with the Land Cruiser and get those, and when I've bought a new rifle in Arusha, I'll be back for the others.

'And yours too!' he shouted after the departing elephants.

Even though he had taken the tablets his heart was still racing wildly and erratically. He slumped down on the rock and tried to breathe slowly. That sometimes helped.

CHAPTER NINETEEN

Left on his own, Tembo M'zee had found the food-wads where Kidogo had told him they would be, and had eaten them gratefully. He was beginning to feel better, and a little stronger, but was glad *he* hadn't had to plan the recovery of the tusks. He had admired and approved Three Eyes' plan and was sure, together with his own bright young Shadow Kidogo, the youngsters would succeed. However, one thing was still worrying him – he didn't want to leave Tembo Lonely's tusks for the humans to take away and cut up, especially as he was certain Lonely had given his life to save M'zee himself. But now there were only five tembos, and six tusks to carry. He and Kidogo might each manage one of Lonely's – but that still left one of the strong young jostlers having to carry two of the heavier ones. They *could* take turns to do that but it would slow them down, and now that the humans had seen the size of the tusks of Tembo Jay and Steadfast, they would surely come after them.

Although he was waiting in the shade of a baobab tree there was no wind and M'zee flapped his ears steadily, trying to keep cool.

If Mana really was using them in some plan, then at least one more elephant was needed in what his Shadow called *the team*. As there were no other elephants near, he turned and pressed his forehead to the smooth bark of the baobab and tried to linque with Mana that way, concentrating hard.

'We do not have to know your full plans,' M'zee said. 'But I am getting older and less strong. More tembos are

213

needed to do your work – whatever it is.'

As he stepped back, hoping that his request had been heard, the leaves above his head rustled quietly. He looked up into the foliage but could see no birds or monkeys.

Walt Schwiner was not going to let himself be robbed so easily. When the elephants had gone down the track, carrying the four largest tusks, he waited until they were well out of sight, then joined Moses and the three camp-staff where the Land Rover lay on its side. Flies were buzzing around the pieces of raw flesh that still adhered to the tusks of the elephant he had shot but these tusks looked insignificant compared to the others he had seen and so briefly owned.

He waited for Moses to say what should be done next, but Moses appeared to be waiting for *him* to say something.

'Come on then. Whadda we do now? You're the goddamn guide!' he stormed.

'I am sorry, Sir, I was thinking. This vehicle here is badly damaged and I have thought that maybe you are not too well and don't want to walk back to the camp – it *is* very hot today! But if I leave you here while I go back for the Land Cruiser and, if the elephants come back for these tusks, you will not have a rifle. I am still thinking what is the best thing to do.'

'*You* seem to be happy walking through this goddamn bush on your own. Leave the two boys with me and go get the other jeep.' As he said this, he remembered, too late, that *boys* was a no-no word. 'We'll hide up there in the rocks until you get back.'

'That is a good plan, Sir. The *men* will be pleased to look after you until I come back.'

Moses gave his instructions, speaking in Swahili, and strode off towards the campsite. Walt picked up the mangled remains of his rifle and followed the two sullen men up the hillside. Moses was hardly out of sight when two other elephants, which Walt could swear he'd not seen before, appeared from a different direction altogether. From his hiding place he watched them stop where the tusks lay beside the Land Rover, and examine them by sniffing along their lengths with their trunks. He'd been led to believe elephants were no longer common – now it seemed the whole of Africa was crawling with the savage and vindictive brutes!

Boy pushed at the first tusk with his toe, then sniffed at the second, while Girl ambled around the Land Rover before reaching inside it with her trunk to sniff about.

'This has only just happened,' she said, and walked right around the vehicle again, her trunk just above the ground.

When she had made a second full circle she said, 'One man has left here and walked that way – and three more have gone up towards those rocks. Four elephants were here too – but they have gone *that* way.'

'Are we in danger?' Boy asked.

'I think not. I have found a broken gun, so the men cannot shoot at us. What should we do with these ivories?'

'I don't think we should leave them here for the humans to carry off. We will take them and follow those other elephants.'

The flies flew up and buzzed around their heads as they each picked up one of Tembo Lonely's tusks.

Hardly were the two elephants out of sight before Walt saw from his hiding place a party of six Maasai men walking through the bush in single file. Each was at least six feet tall and dressed in a simple red and blue checked cloak and each man carried a broad-bladed spear, a stick with a round knob at one end, and a short sword in a red leather scabbard.

The men clustered round the upturned Land Rover, peering in at the windows. One picked up the remains of Moses' gun while another circled round in much the same way as one of the elephants had done, evidently trying to work out what had happened.

One of the camp-staff, who Walt knew only as Joe, called from his hiding place to the Maasai, who signalled for him to come down. Walt decided to stay hidden until Joe, after talking to the Maasai, called up in English, 'You may come down now, Sir. These men will not harm us.'

Walt came down through the rocks, carrying his damaged rifle across his arms and said the one word of Swahili he knew, the greeting, '*Jambo*'.

A Maasai, who appeared to be their leader, replied in halting Swahili, none of which made any sense to Walt.

'Doesn't he speak English?' Walt asked Joe impatiently.

'No, Sir. But we both can speak to each other in Swahili. What did you want to say to him?'

Walt thought for a moment but there was really nothing he wanted to say or ask, although he was glad to have other humans nearby when there were so many elephants about. Then he thought to ask Joe, 'Could these men get the jeep upright?'

Joe translated and the Maasai gathered around their leader, each making suggestions as to how it could be done, before two of them went off through the bush, leaving the others to roll a large boulder over to where the Land Rover lay on its side. Walt heard the sound of chopping and shortly afterwards the two men came back dragging a small tree trunk. Using this as a lever and the rock as a fulcrum, and by piling smaller rocks under the side of the vehicle as they lifted it, within about twenty minutes the Land Rover passed the point of balance and dropped onto its four wheels, the last of the diesel oil flowing onto the ground from its punctured tanks.

Just then Moses reappeared, carrying a tool kit and accompanied by Sam, the cook. The Maasai watched as they approached, then one seemed to recognise Moses and, without a word, spat in his direction. Each of the other Maasai followed his action and, at a word from their leader, followed him silently away through the trees.

'What in hell was all that about?' Walt asked.

'Now is not the time to tell you,' Moses said in a subdued voice. 'I have to tell you that the elephants have been to the camp. It is all broken up and the Land Cruiser too has been damaged.' He looked round for the tusks.

'Where are—?'

'Some more goddamned jumbos came and took them,' Walter snapped angrily. All this was getting too unreal and he wished he had stayed in America. At least, back in God's own country, one knew that a grizzly was only a bear. He was beginning to believe that here, in goddamned Africa, the elephants were as clever and as cunning as he was himself. Then he suddenly realised the significance of what Moses had just told him about the other vehicle.

'How do we get out of here, then?'

'I have brought the tool kit. I will try to repair the Land Rover enough to get us back to Arusha.'

'What about the radio – can't you call up for help?'

'The elephants have put their tusks through that too, Sir.'

Walt shook his head and went to sit on a rock out of the sun, convinced there was no way the man could repair the punctured fuel tank. His heart was thudding unevenly again.

With the tools he had and no electrical power, Moses knew he could do nothing about mending the fuel tank. He checked the reserve cans and to his great relief one of them had survived the attack undamaged. It would contain enough diesel to get them back to a road and possibly even as far as

Arusha – if they were lucky. He got Sam and the other two camp-staff to help him push the Land Rover away from the fuel-soaked patch of soil, and felt annoyed that the client made no attempt to help. The man just sat on a rock, smoking one of his stinking cigars. If the Land Rover had run on petrol, they would have all been incinerated by now, he thought, as he slid under the vehicle to find the connection between the fuel pipe and the damaged tank, then called for a spanner to be passed to him.

An hour later, with the fuel pipe diverted into the spare fuel can, Moses started the engine and cautiously tried the gears one by one, before easing the vehicle gently forward, moving the steering wheel from side to side. The steering was a bit erratic but he was sure he could manage that. The handbrake no longer functioned but the footbrake seemed to be working.

Schwiner quickly got to his feet, as though he was afraid they would drive off and leave him stranded. Serve him right if I did, Moses thought – *he* was the one who had suggested breaking the game laws, and if there was one thing the mission school had taught him it was that God punished those who broke the law.

CHAPTER TWENTY

Lars and Ryan were enjoying what felt like a holiday but which they kept telling each other was a necessary trip to sample the various 'African experiences' being offered to visitors. They visited the Tarangire National Park and Lake Manyara, where they canoed, all the while watching the wildlife, especially the elephants, from a totally different viewpoint. Ryan wondered aloud how huge pelicans could glide for miles just above the water with no apparent movement of their outstretched wings.

They had floated over the veldt in a hot-air balloon at dawn and looked down on vast herds of wildebeest and zebra. The owners of the various lodges and campsites were glad to show them what they had to offer, as most of them had been short of visitors since the eruption of Kilimanjaro had discouraged people from visiting Tanzania. Most owners considered that, once the mountain was quiet again and tourism back to normal, it would be useful to have sympathetic safari operators, such as Lars and Ryan, guiding clients to *their* camps. That was, of course, if any of them were still in business by then.

Lars was not too happy about what was advertised as 'The Elephant Experience', but Ryan had been enthusiastic. The couple who ran the operation, Douglas and Jayne Somers, had both lived in Africa all their lives and, soon after they married they had 'acquired' two young elephants.

The Elephant Experience leaflets told how the elephants, who were known as Boy and Girl, had been captured in the wild when they were about five years old, held in a zoo for another five years and when that closed down they had been bought by Doug and Jayne. For the last ten years all four had lived together in a bush camp and lately Doug and Jayne had been giving tourists the opportunity 'to interact with habituated elephants in their natural surroundings', as their leaflet described it.

Lars was relieved and Ryan disappointed when, a few days before they were due to visit the elephants, they received a message to say their visit would have to be cancelled because the elephants had wandered off into the bush and disappeared, and even the most celebrated trackers had failed to find where they had gone. Instead, Lars and Ryan decided to visit the Olduvai Gorge and see where the remains of early man had been found, then go on into the vast Serengeti National Park and check out some of the lodges there.

M'zee, who had been waiting near the baobab tree, walked out to meet Kidogo and the three jostlers when they returned, triumphantly carrying the tusks of Tembo Jay and Steadfast.

'Well done,' he trumped before turning to Tembo Three Eyes and congratulating him on successfully leading such a daring expedition. Hardly had he finished doing this when he heard Kidogo singing the ancient greeting.

'Love, live long and ~ find sweet-water.'

M'zee turned to see two unknown tembos approaching, each carrying a tusk. He immediately recognised the ivories as Lonely's.

The two elephants did not sing back a response but stepped forward hesitantly and laid the tusks on the ground before him. The male one said, 'We found these where the men had left them, but did not think it right for them to be alone – so we carried them away. We followed the tracks of these other elephants. I am Boy and this is Girl.' M'zee thought Boy's speech was clumsy, especially with the trunk and ear movements, as if he rarely spoke tembotalk.

He bowed a 'thank you' to them for bringing the tusks and said, 'You are welcome to join us – but we must not linger here. I am known as Tembo M'zee. We will speak at length later. Now we must find water. Will you again carry the ivories of our friend?'

'We can guide you to water not far away,' Girl said. 'We had dug water holes and were waiting for them to fill in the night when we heard a tembo singing. Did you hear it too?'

'That was the song of our friend, Tembo Lonely, whose ivories you carry.'

Lars and Ryan were spinning along the road on their way back from the Serengeti, enjoying the smooth tarmac after the bumpy murram tracks in the park.

'The whole world must have been like that, once,' Ryan mused. 'Even England and Ireland. Animals just doing their own thing. How does that hymn go? . . . *Where only man is vile*?'

'Remind me why you left Ireland.'

'The bloody politicians sold us out to Europe. Ireland used to be a very special place. Laid back and still with our feet in the soil. It's a beautiful country – especially the west. Have you ever been there?

'No. I've been to England briefly – I told you about that – but not Ireland.'

'We used to pretend we hated England and the English, but it was a sort of love-hate relationship. We hated what England had done to Ireland in the past but, when English people came to Ireland on holiday, we treated them as honoured guests – and they were nice people, mostly. We looked at the way money had corrupted their country and thought it couldn't happen to us.'

'So?'

'So. Some greedy politicians in Dublin saw how much money the EU was giving to Portugal and the less well-off countries like that and wanted to get *their* snouts in the trough. They saw opportunities for themselves and to hell with Ireland and all that made it special. You wouldn't believe how much money came in – but it spoiled Ireland. Dublin's full of crime and drugs and all anyone wants to talk about now is money and the stock exchange – and how the value of their houses have gone up! And the *truth* is not the *truth* any more – it's what the politicians want it to be.'

'Isn't it like that everywhere?' Lars raised his hand to salute a Maasai standing by the road, his cows, goats and donkeys grazing the sparse grass behind him.

'Sadly, yes. But out here in the bush a lion is a lion and an elephant is an elephant. That's why I prefer it here.'

'Would you ever go back, Ryan?'

'I can't see it. It'd be like watching your own child taking drugs. Nothing you can do about it – and all the time, everything you loved about them would be disintegrating before your eyes. The whole world is worshipping the gods of *progress* and *growth*. What was wrong with *stability* and *contentment?*'

'Do you ever think about Ireland now?' Lars asked.

'Sure I do. I dream of a little cottage in County Galway with a patch of potatoes, a few sheep and a cow, and the sea near the door so as I can catch a fish or a lobster should I be fancying one.'

'But . . .?'

'If I found one, I couldn't buy it now. It'd be the second home for some rich banker from Dublin or Galway City and I'd be taxed to hell to pay for farm subsidies in Poland and the Czech Republic.'

'Africa it is then?'

'Africa it is!'

'No going back?'

'I can't see that happening.'

They passed an almost deserted shop selling African souvenirs and where the road curved gently to the left, they were waved down by a man holding up a jerry-can.

'Careful,' Ryan warned as Lars slowed.

Lars knew such actions could be part of a trap to rob tourists but he had recognised the Land Rover under the tree by the roadside and stopped.

The man put down the can and walked over. '*Jambo*, Sir,' he said.

'*Habari*?' Lars asked. 'What's new?'

'*Hapana nzuri*,' the man replied. Then he switched to English. 'It is not good. My party have been attacked by elephants and I am trying to get my client back to Arusha. If you could spare a can of fuel, I would be most grateful.'

Lars had by now recognised the man as the townified Maasai who, a couple of weeks before, had been going into Mr Burns' office as he had been leaving. His client must be the American who wanted to kill an elephant and, having so recently enjoyed watching these huge but peaceful creatures living apparently happy lives in the parks, he was inclined to refuse.

But 'safari etiquette' would not allow this and he got out and started to ease a can of fuel out from under their gear in the back of the Land Rover.

'Hi, guys.'

Lars turned and saw a white man wearing a soiled safari suit. 'Can you fellows run me into the city while this guy fixes this mess? I could use a hot shower and a decent meal.' The man paused, then added, 'I'll pay what it's worth.'

Lars wanted to hit him, but the Maasai, who had moved round to stand behind him, was making, 'Please do what he

223

wants,' signals.

'In this country,' Lars replied coldly, 'we help one another without charge. It is our custom. I'll make some space in the back.'

He gave one of his reserve fuel-cans to Moses, who thanked him, then got back into the driving seat. They were hardly over the first rise when the scent of cigar smoke reached the front of the cab. Ryan turned and asked, 'Would you mind not smoking. Neither my friend nor I care for the smell, especially in here.'

Lars heard the rear window being wound down and braked harshly, stopped and jumped out to run back to where he thought the cigar might have landed. Ryan joined him and, after a brief search, found it by the flicker of flame and the smoke rising from a patch of dried grass. They stamped out the fire before it had a chance to spread and together peed on the patch of black earth before returning to the Land Rover. Their passenger stood near it, looking sheepish.

'I'm sorry, guys, I should have known. I'm not really such a greenhorn.'

Lars and Ryan glared at him, got in and waited for the American to clamber awkwardly back into the rear seat. The rest of the long journey was made in a strained silence until they'd dropped off their passenger outside the International Hotel.

'To the Riverside Hotel, Driver,' Ryan said to Lars. 'I could use a hot shower and a decent meal. I'll pay what it's worth. Yes, Sir. Cigar, anyone?'

Tembo Boy, carrying one of Lonely's tusks, led the way to the watering place, followed by M'zee who carried Lonely's other tusk as it was lighter than those of Tembo Steadfast and Tembo Jay, and it felt like the right thing to do that day.

The three jostlers each carried one of the heavier tusks, as did Temba Girl who followed them, walking side by side with Kidogo. The tembas talked between themselves, Kidogo pleased to have some female company.

'Did you hear Tembo Lonely singing in the night?' Kidogo asked, even though Temba Girl had already told them she and Tembo Boy had heard the singing. But it seemed an appropriate way to open the conversation with this stranger who had joined them so opportunely.

'We did. I have never heard such a wonderful song, but then, as we have lived with humans for so much of our lives, Boy and I have not heard many tembo songs.'

'That was the song of a *whale*,' Kidogo told her, then had to say what a whale was, before telling her more of Lonely's story.

In turn, she learned how Girl and Boy had decided to leave their human friends after so many years together.

'They loved us and would do anything for us,' Temba Girl told Kidogo. 'And we loved them. They looked after us and often gave us what they called *pony nuts* to eat – which we always enjoyed.'

Three Eyes, who had been listening to them talk, asked over his shoulder, 'Did they give you mealies – and bananas?'

'Both of those, when they could get them – but mostly we fed ourselves in the bush.'

'So why did you leave?' Kidogo asked.

'One day I heard the humans, who called one another Doug and Jayne, talking about what they call *holydays*. We had lived with humans so long we understood their *English* language but were not able to speak it back to them.'

'I, too, lived with humans and understand both their *English* and their *Swahili* talk,' Kidogo said. 'But it is not possible for tembos to talk back – which is a great pity. But I do not remember hearing the word *holydays*.'

'It is when the humans, especially the pale-skinned ones, leave what they usually do and go to some other place *for a change*. This seems important to them – but I didn't learn what they do when they get there.'

Girl put down the tusk she was carrying, flexed her trunk and picked it up again. 'Jayne was saying to Doug that they never went on a *holyday* because Doug wouldn't *ever leave those damn elephants*. That was the first time I ever wondered if they really loved us as much as we loved them. But then I wondered if it was *right* for us to be together – tembos are tembos and humans are humans. Jayne was very upset that day and was saying to Doug – *I want babies of my own, our babies. I don't want to be a mother just to a couple of elephants all my life.* She was crying and tears were coming out of her eyes like they do out of ours when we are sad. Doug put his arms around her and said, *I do too – but what can we do with Boy and Girl – they need us. No one else would look after them properly.* I slipped quietly away then so they wouldn't know I had heard all that. I found Boy and told him what I'd heard.

'He understood and we talked about it many times. Finally, we decided that, because we loved Doug and Jayne so much, *we* had to leave *them* so that they could be totally human and have their own human babies to love. So, one night when there was no moon, we left. I was sad to go, knowing we would never see them again, so I picked one of the flowers that I knew were Jayne's favourites and left it by the door of the place where they were sleeping.'

Kidogo reached up her trunk as they walked and touched Girl's forehead to let her know that what she had done, had been the right thing to do. They walked on in silence until Three Eyes said, 'If they *really* loved you – they'd have come after you.'

'We thought of that,' Girl said. 'In the days before we left, when we didn't have to show ourselves off to tourists, Boy and I would play hiding and searching games in the bush. One of us would go away and try to conceal our tracks and then hide. The other would then come and follow. We learned all sorts of tricks – like walking over rocky ground where our tracks wouldn't show and walking through water to wash away our scent. We got very clever at it, so, when we left Jayne and Doug, we did the same. I am sure they *did* try to find us,' she added. 'I'm *sure* they did!'

They walked on, close behind the males. Kidogo looked at the temba by her side who was much larger than she was and, by the size of her tusks, fully mature.

'Did you not want babies yourself?' she asked Girl.

'Oh, yes. All tembas want babies. It was very difficult when Boy had his mustdo at the same time as I was in joyneed – but we are close kin . . .'

They had reached the bank of the dry riverbed. The males put down the tusks they were carrying and each raised his own trunk and put his ears forward to test for possible danger. Two giraffes were near the holes made the previous evening by Boy and Girl. One giraffe, head down, was spreading his forelegs awkwardly to enable him to reach the water, but they both lolloped away when the elephants arrived.

Once satisfied that there was no danger, the seven tembos went down to drink, soon exhausting the water that had collected and having to wait for more to seep out of the sand. The jostlers decided to dig new holes for themselves.

M'zee stood a little apart from the others, waiting for Kidogo to bring him the food-wads he could see she was gathering.

He had overheard most of what Tembo Girl had been saying to his Shadow and was puzzled. Mana had clearly heard him when he had linqued with the tree and asked for more tembos to carry the tusks. M'zee had been pleased, but not surprised, when these two had arrived, but . . . he had only asked *that* day and, from what he'd overheard, Boy and Girl had decided to leave their human friends to live in the bush several, even many, days before. Had Mana anticipated his request?

He took the food-wads Kidogo held out for him and swallowed them gratefully. He was part of something very important – but only Mana knew what.

At M'zee's suggestion, when the tembos had finished eating and each had drunk their fill, they took it in turns to stay awake and alert while the others slept.

Kidogo found it hard to sleep, even when it was not her turn to keep watch. The excitements of the day had almost driven thoughts of the whale's song from her mind. Now, in the quiet of the night she thought of the hyenas who would have found Lonely's body and shuddered. To blank out the thought, she tried to remember the whale's song. She could recall the beginning.

> *In the dim and ~ distant ages*
> *This our planet ~ was quite lifeless.*
> *Came a time when ~ it was ready*
> *Ready like a ~ flower, open,*
> *Craving for a ~ speck of pollen.*

Then it had continued,

> *Floating in from ~ where we know not*
> *Came a drift of ~ cosmic pollen*
> *Carrying the ~ sacred Life-force*
> *To this silent ~ waiting planet.*

And she could remember how the song had ended.

> Mana *needs the ~ Love we give him,*
> *Formed from Joy and ~ care for others*
> *For Love is the ~ magic power*
> *The force that linques ~ us all together*
>
> *Here's the wonder ~ here's the beauty*
> *Here's the honour ~ here's the duty*
> *We can all be ~ part of Mana*
> *We will all be ~ part of Mana*
> *If we share the Love within us*
> *Love that Mana ~ needs to function*
> *For the future of our planet.*
>> *For the future of our planet.*
>>> *For the future of our planet.*

Kidogo had loved the way those last thoughts had faded away towards the end. Had that been how the whale had ended the song, or was it just the way Lonely had sung it?

She tried hard to remember more but the song had been a long one, and she had heard it only once. Another part came back to her.

> **Whales, dolphins ~ tembos, humans**
> *All were granted ~ 'beings' greater*
> *Than their bodies, ~ blood and brains were.*
> *Call these 'beings' ~* **souls** *or* **spirits** . . .

She tried hard to remember how it continued, but couldn't. Perhaps some of the other tembos could recall it – but what if they couldn't? She was sure, from what Lonely had said, that the whale had been killed by the humans in the boat with the sun flag on it, so *he* would never be able to sing it again. Lonely himself had now stepped-over and taken his knowledge of the song with him. And *she* could only remember a small part of it. Kidogo felt small and inadequate again and shivered bleakly in the darkness.

Walt Schwiner booked into the International Hotel for an indefinite stay. The reception staff appeared not to notice his dishevelled appearance and were more interested in his platinum American Express card. 'That'll do nicely,' the receptionist had said and had been rewarded with a scowl.

Now, after a shower and shave, he was eating the meal he had ordered to be sent up to his room. He looked round and thought of the many similar rooms he had slept in all over America, Europe and Asia during his business life.

He had built a huge and enormously rich company, Schwiner Enterprises Inc., by combining all the various family businesses he had inherited, one by one, from his father and his Schwiner uncles. These ranged from logging, through mining and quarrying, to ranching and fishing although most of its vast income now came from oil and natural gas. These enterprises had themselves developed from the work of several early Schwiner pioneers who had exploited the rich resources that God had prepared for any American with the guts to go and get them. *Walt Schwiner* was not going to be beaten by a few dumb jumbos.

He pushed the plate away and walked to the window. Outside, on the other side of the road, children in ragged clothes were standing outside a food store but he didn't see them. He was imagining himself showing off tusks bigger than any of his Safari Club fellow members had ever seen in their lives. Bigger even than those in the New York Museum of Natural History. None of the members need ever know exactly how he had come by them – since he had come to Africa to shoot a jumbo, they would assume he had shot the elephant which had borne them. All he had to do was find those other goddamn elephants, shoot them all if necessary and get the giant tusks back to America.

He would need that Maasai guy to help – and *he* could be bought, Walt was sure of that. There was something about the man's manner that told him the guy needed money badly, and Walt was a good judge of desperation. And then there was the way his own people had treated him. . . . Yes, Moses was his man.

CHAPTER TWENTY-ONE

M'zee was taking his turn on guard near the water-pits in the riverbed, watching the dawn sky lighten, when he heard the sound of many tembos approaching through the bush on the riverbank behind him. They were walking without talking but, with so many moving in the near darkness, they inevitability made some noise and he could hear babies amongst them, who whimpered if they lost touch with their mother for even a moment.

M'zee snorted to alert the others.

Immediately, the sounds of movement died away and a tembo sang in low~sound.

'Who is it there ~ are you tembos?'

M'zee sang back in response.

'Love, live long and ~ find sweet-water.'

The tembos in the riverbed heard a huge sigh of relief from the bank above them, followed by the traditional response.

'May Mana bless ~ and keep you safe,
Tembo Jay and ~ goodness guide you.'

Kidogo squealed with delight. Even though the reply had been in low~sound, she recognised that it had been sung by Rafiki. She forgot her duty to be at M'zee's side, and scrambled up the riverbank to entwine trunks with her friend as hundreds of other tembos surged down to drink from the water-pits, or to dig out more for themselves as the sun rose over the eastern trees.

After his client had gone on with the two guides in their Land Rover, Moses had coaxed the damaged Land Rover back to Arusha and left it at a repair garage owned by a friend of his. On the way, he had told the other three men of the camp-crew how the American would make it well-worth it for them, if they just told anyone who asked, that their vehicles and camp had been damaged by rampaging elephants. And, as they had not yet reached the hunting area, they had not been able to shoot any.

'What's it worth?' Sam the cook had asked bluntly and, when Moses told him the figure he had agreed with Walt Schwiner, they all seemed satisfied.

Now, as the sun was setting he walked back through the dusty streets to his home, but stopped and looked along the alleyway before getting too close, and was glad that he had done so. Sitting on a low wall opposite his door was a huge Wachagga man who he knew was called 'The Collector.' The man was casually swinging a panga, the blade of which caught the last rays of the sun. Moses turned quickly and walked away down a side alley.

Walt Schwiner was wondering about the best way to contact Moses when the internal telephone rang.

'A Mr Moses Jackson is here to see you, Sir.'

'Give him a drink in the bar. I'll be down shortly.'

Walt thought Moses looked even more distressed than he had done when the Maasai men had spat at him. He was standing in a corner of the almost empty bar room, a glass of iced water in his hand. Walt ordered a whisky and rye, and went over to him.

'You got back OK? And the crew – they all understand? How much will that be altogether? US dollars or that *shillingi* stuff?'

Moses gave him a figure in dollars.

'I'll get that sorted in the morning. Now – I've got a little business proposition for you.'

Moses stayed at a friend's house that night and by midday had paid off the crew, bought a nearly-new Land Cruiser, complete with a winch on the front bumper and a range of camping gear from Mr Burns with money given to him by the American, and was once more on the road out of Arusha.

In the seat next to him sat Walt Schwiner, nursing a new rifle he'd bought that morning. A less expensive one for Moses and a case of ammunition for them both was packed with the rest of the gear in the back. When they turned off the main road to head north, the American spoke for the first time since leaving.

'I reckon you and I got off to a bad start,' he said. 'From now on I'm Walt. OK?'

'Is that *Walt* – or *Walt, Sir*?' Moses was smiling, as much with relief at being safely away from Arusha, as at the American's attempt to be friendly.

Schwiner gave a little cough, reached across and punched Moses lightly on the upper arm. 'Walt will do nicely.' He grinned. 'Buddies?'

Kidogo led Rafiki back to where M'zee stood, now surrounded by many elephants, most of whom she had never seen before. She recognised Tembo Lusty, and some of the other jostlers who had set out with them to climb the mountain but had turned back. They were in a group who stood some distance away down the riverbed, obviously embarrassed. Then she saw Temba Comfort and Temba Kindness standing at the top of the bank, each lovingly holding a tusk that could only be Tembella Grace's slender ivories. Kidogo looked enquiringly at M'zee who signalled a

'Yes', and once more she scrambled up the bank.

The Sisters laid down Grace's tusks and greeted her with trunk twinings and much touching of foreheads. Kidogo caressed the smooth ivories of the blind old Tembella but did not attempt to read them. That would come later – if the Sisters allowed it. Then she led them down to meet M'zee.

M'zee was talking to Rafiki, learning what had happened to the youngster since he had been forced to turn back at the top of the forest. It was clear his damaged tusk had come out and he was now well again. A young jostler stood close by, proudly holding the shattered tusk. Other tembos of all ages were gathered round, wide-eared, listening to a story they must have heard several times before.

'When I got to the Sacred Grove,' Rafiki was saying, 'I found that Tembella Grace had stepped-over, and Temba Kindness pulled out my damaged tusk. When my wound had healed and Tembella Grace's ivories had come free, we linqued trunks under the tembo-trees and asked Mana for guidance.

'*Follow the tired sun*,' was what we heard – just *Follow the tired sun*.' We thought it would be wrong to leave the tusks so we took them up and carried them with us.'

The jostler beside him held up the tusk with the shattered end, as if to confirm what Rafiki was saying.

'Whenever we met other tembos,' Rafiki continued, 'be they families, lone tembulls or groups of jostlers, they all wanted to know what we were doing and, when we told them that two of the ivories we carried were those of Tembella Grace, they all wanted to join us – as you see.'

Rafiki waved his trunk around to include all the tembos on the bank and in the riverbed. M'zee noticed that many of them were carrying or guarding other free tusks. None, though, began to compare in size with those of Tembo Jay, or even those of Tembo Steadfast. Some were the tusks of immature elephants but quite a number amongst them were larger ones. Many bore stains which indicated they had been buried in the ground for many years.

'And these other tusks?' M'zee started to ask.

'Each group we met knew where the tusks of dead tembos had been hidden away from humans,' Rafiki replied. 'They dug them up and carried them along. It must have been because they had seen what we were doing.'

He paused as Kidogo joined them, followed by Tembas Comfort and Kindness. M'zee reached out and respectfully caressed each of the tusks they carried. 'Tembella Grace was my mother,' he said. 'I have not seen her for many, many years.' He looked wistful. 'There was something I had always wanted to ask her before she stepped-over – but it is too late now,' he added.

Rafiki and Kidogo were together again, touching foreheads and twisting trunks. Kidogo gently felt the scar where Rafiki's left tusk had been. He touched her cheek and said quietly, 'No tusks yet, then?'

Kidogo felt her own cheek, something she had not done for a while. 'No,' she replied. 'We've just got one between the two of us.'

Tembo Lusty left the main herd and walked over to M'zee, holding his trunk in the 'Please forgive me,' attitude.

M'zee moistened his trunk-tip in his mouth and touched Lusty's forehead. 'Mustdo can be a burden sometimes,' he said, then grimaced. 'But not for me for many years. It's good to meet you again.'

'Where are we going?' Lusty asked.

'West. *Follow the tired sun*, our message said. Though to where and for why, only Mana knows.'

Lusty was looking at the tusks of Tembo Jay and Tembo Steadfast where they were being guarded by the Tembos

One Eye, Two Eyes and Three Eyes. He whistled through his trunk. 'Those are some tusks! May I?'

M'zee nodded his assent and Tembo Lusty walked across to caress Tembo Jay's smooth ivories. Almost immediately he went down on his knees and stayed there for some time, quite overcome, and oblivious to the other tembos standing around and watching him. When he finally rose he asked, 'Have the humans seen these?'

'A few. A hunter saw them when he killed Tembo Lonely.'

'When was that?'

'Only a few days ago,' M'zee replied, understanding immediately what Lusty was implying and blaming himself for not having hurried on. 'We should be moving off now.'

'Those humans will desire these ivories very much and they may come to look for you in one of their machines that fly. It might be better if we travel at night.'

M'zee pondered this and agreed. He turned to Rafiki and Kidogo and said, 'Put the word round that all tembos must drink their fill, then move under the trees and keep out of sight of any of the machines that fly. The tembos may eat as much as they wish but must not leave the cover of the trees. We will all walk westwards in the moonlight.'

CHAPTER TWENTY-TWO

De/ne had given up his quest to find two worthy husbands for his granddaughters, had thrown away his T-shirt and the shorts which were so restrictive, and was going home. He'd realised he could always get more money, when he needed it, by repeating the standing-at-the-roadside-wearing-just-a-loincloth routine, but there'd been less white tourists coming along since the earth had trembled. The men he had talked to in the *shambas* and villages had all been far more interested in the *shillingi* and dollars notes in his bag than in him or his granddaughters.

He had briefly ventured into Arusha town where he had bought some tobacco and a box-that-talked, which the man who'd sold it to him called a *radio*, but De/ne had felt so uncomfortable amongst the many bustling people that he'd not even stayed for one night. Towns were no place for him and he knew it would be useless looking for worthy husbands or even guidance from Mantis there.

Now he trotted along a dusty road, elated at the thought of returning to the Place of Peace and seeing his lovely granddaughters again but frustrated by the failure of his mission.

Lars and Ryan raced each other for ten lengths of the pool at the Riverside Hotel, then sat on a poolside bench, drying off in the sun and watching the brilliant orange-and-blue African starlings flitting from tree to tree against a background of bright blue sky, speckled with tiny, high, white clouds.

'You know, Lars, we're really lucky being here. Imagine having to live in a big, cold city like London or New York.'

'People don't have to,' Lars replied. 'The world's a big place. It's just that they all want more and more money and that's where it is – in the cities.'

Ryan stood up and rubbed the back of his legs with his towel. 'It's *oil* that's behind it all, you know. Oil and the stuff they make from it – petrol, diesel, and the like. That and what they like to call *natural* gas.'

'Lecture coming up!'

'I've got to talk to someone about it, and you're the best friend I have. *And* you're the only one here.'

'Go on then!' Lars sighed.

'Our whole, so-called global economy is based on oil and gas. Now, I want you to imagine that the world – planet Earth – is like a big living body crawling with harmless parasites – humans – not doing any real harm and perhaps even doing some good. Now, these clever little creepies learn how to drill holes down into the guts of this big body and suck out the crap and the farts through pipes. They burn it or trade it with others, until there are far too many creepies, most of them living off nothing but the waste products of the big body and not growing any food for themselves. Eventually, there are so many creepies and so much pollution from the burning crap, that the body itself gets ill and dies. *That's* what's happening to the world right now!'

'And what would be *your* solution?' Lars asked, stepping into his shorts.

'Well – If there was no oil or gas coming out of the ground, everything would grind to a halt within days. People wouldn't be able to get about, and would start robbing and even killing other people for what they had – or at best perhaps they'd realise they had to get busy growing or finding food and wouldn't have time to do things like that. No drugs – legal or otherwise – could be moved around the world. There'd be no more tourists flying all over the place, corrupting local economies and teaching other people to be greedy consumers like we, so-called *civilised* people, are.'

'That's *us* out of a job then,' said Lars. 'And the cities would starve. I read somewhere that western cities have only enough food for about three days. If you couldn't get it from the storage depots into the cities, the people in them would soon die of starvation.'

'Serve 'em right. I've never liked city people.'

'You're a hard man, Ryan Kavanagh. It's a good job you're not God.'

'Sure, I'm glad enough of that, too. I'm far too soft. And I don't think heaven could be better than *this*.' He waved his hand to include the pool, the trees and the distant mountaintop. The starlings, which had come down to scratch and poke about among the leaves on the grass, flew up in a cloud.

'Africa – it's magic,' he exclaimed.

'If one has a job!' Lars retorted. 'Cash reserves can run out surprisingly quickly living here. We should go into Arusha and ask about. There maybe something going.'

He stood up and started to walk to his room. Ryan picked up his towel and followed. 'See you at the bar before lunch,' he called after his friend. 'Thanks for listening while I shoot my mouth off.'

'That's what friends are for. One of the things!'

Peter the barman was talkative. He greeted them with, '*Sijambo*, *Bwana* Petersen and *Bwana* Kavanagh.' The *Bwana* he usually kept for overseas visitors who enjoyed being called by the title once reserved for white men, and which they had heard used in films such as *Out of Africa* and *The Snows of Kilimanjaro*. During a lifetime of serving drinks to guests he had fine-tuned ways of increasing his gratuities.

He didn't wait for their orders – their pre-lunch refreshment was always a small bottle of chilled beer each. As he poured the beer he asked, 'Have you heard about the American hunter and the elephant's tusks?'

Lars sipped from his dewy glass. 'I'm sure I'm about to. Is this a joke, Peter?'

'Oh no, *Bwana*. There is a rich American in Arusha – a *very* rich American – who is going back into the bush after some very big tusks.'

'The cigar guy!' Ryan said. 'It must be him.'

'From what Moses Jackson told us I would have expected him to have been on the next plane back home.'

'Yes, Sir,' said the barman. 'That would be the one. His name is Mr Walter Schwiner. He has hired Moses Jackson to take him to get some very big tusks. They're all talking about it in Arusha.'

Lars looked at Ryan who was obviously also thinking about the tusks from the ice-cave on the mountain behind them.

'Tusks?' he asked, trying to sound casual.

'Oh yes, Sir. Their cook was saying that the American shot an elephant in Maasailand and that elephant was with others who were carrying very big tusks. The elephants went to their camp and smashed it all up and wrecked their vehicles too. Very bad elephants those.'

'When did Moses and the American leave?' Ryan asked.

'Very early this morning, Sir. In one of the Land Cruisers Mr Burns has been buying for very little money.'

'Just the two men?'

'That is what people are saying, Sir.'

'Are they saying where these elephants are now – the ones carrying the big tusks?'

'The cook said they were hunting up towards Olsandura when the elephants with the big tusks made *fujo* of the camp.'

Lars and Ryan ordered the lightest of lunches.

'When can we leave?' Ryan asked.

'This afternoon. Get your kit packed and we'll stock up on food and fuel in Arusha.'

Once more, Walt had to admire Moses' driving. Although the surface of the red murram road was pitted with holes of various sizes and, in places was corrugated with transverse ridges, the African effortlessly steered a course that avoided the worst of it, sometimes even leaving the main track and taking a parallel route through the bush.

On one of the better stretches they could see a small man walking ahead of them. He was dressed in a yellowy coloured loincloth and a pointed cap sat at an angle on his head. He stepped back from the road and watched them pass.

'*Hadza*,' Moses said, contemptuously.

'Bushman?' Walt asked.

'Yes. They live by scratching up roots and trapping animals and birds.' The contempt was again evident in his voice. 'Those people never own cattle! They never have. They are thieves too. Pah!'

They drove on, the dust from the wheels billowing out behind them and off to the side of the track, enveloping the little man.

'Pah!' said Moses again, looking in the rear-view mirror.

Moses pulled off the road to set up camp before it got too dark. Walt told him not to bother to put up the one-man toilet tent. 'I'll use the bush-toilet like you do,' he said and, after Moses had lit a fire, cooked their meal and they'd eaten, Walt leaned back in his director's chair by the fire, took out a cigar and asked, 'Do you mind?'

Moses made the 'You are the visitor,' response with his hand and got up to fetch more firewood as Walt flicked his lighter, the flame lighting up his face. Moses threw some wood on the fire and sat on a log, upwind of the smoke.

'Tell me about *your* people,' Walt asked. 'I've read that cattle are important to you. My uncle had a ranch out west.'

'To a Maasai, his cattle are everything.' Moses made an expansive gesture with his hands. '*You* rate your wealth by how many dollars you have in the bank and how big your houses and your cars are. The Maasai count their cows – and their wives. But the cows first!' He laughed, and Walt joined him.

'I count my wives, and call them *cows*.'

'You have more than one wife? I thought—'

'Only one at a time. None at the moment, thank God. How many wives have you got?'

'Me? None.' Moses looked uncomfortable. Walt sensed his discomfort and pushed a bit. It was a technique that had stood him in good stead in business – get your salesman or customer wrong-footed and you can screw a better deal out of them.

'Why's that?' he asked. 'I'd have thought a handsome guy like you would have the women lining up.'

Walter glanced at his watch. It would be a couple of hours before he'd want to go to bed. He would find out more about what motivated this man. The knowledge could well be useful to him sometime.

'Do you remember where you packed the whisky?' he asked.

Moses brought a bottle from the Land Cruiser and poured a generous amount into the coffee mug Walt held out towards him before the American said, 'Have some yourself. Be *my* guest.'

Moses was about to refuse, remembering the strict warnings against the evils of drink that had been a regular part of his teenage years at the mission. But to refuse would have made him look as though he couldn't take it and, in truth, he *had* learned to enjoy getting drunk in the bars of Arusha when he was trying to forget how useless he was with women. He walked round the fire and picked up his empty mug.

It may have been the delayed reaction from seeing The Collector outside his house, the intimacy of the firelight, the effect of the whisky, or even Walt's skilful interrogation, but before long the Maasai was telling the American what he had never before admitted to anyone, other than Mr Washington Jackson on his seventeenth birthday.

'I blame my half-brother mostly. His name was Sambeke and he was older than me and already a warrior. He sat through his *emorata* without a murmur and he kept taunting me, telling how much it hurt and how he was sure that I would cry out and bring disgrace on the family. He would pull out his *eniwatok* and make chopping actions with his *simi* – that's the sword that Maasai warriors carry. Of course it's not done like that. The *alamoratani* uses a sharp knife. Even so, it takes about five minutes and you have to keep absolutely still and not make a sound.'

Walt grimaced in the firelight, and encouraged Moses to continue.

'Well, a few days before it's your turn, the *alamoratani* gives you the knife to sharpen yourself. I started to do this and kept thinking about *why* I was doing it. I wanted to be a man – a warrior like my brother – but I was scared.'

Walt poured another generous shot of whisky into Moses' mug.

'Well, I decided to hide the knife in case my brother found it and blunted the edge – Sambeke could be like that –

and I went to put it where he wouldn't find it, on a ledge in one of the holes in a termite mound. Perhaps my hand was trembling, but the knife slid down inside and those holes go deep into the earth. I panicked – Maasai are not supposed to do that – and ran away to Arusha.'

'To the mission?'

'Yes. They were always glad to be able to take in boys to convert to be Christians. They didn't ask questions when I said I was an orphan and that a lion had eaten my parents. I don't know if they believed me or not – they just wanted to save my soul. The Superintendent was Mr Washington Jackson – he christened me *Moses* and gave me his name.'

'So you still have your . . .?' Walt paused.

'Oh no.' Moses felt the resentment rising in him. He didn't want this man to think he really *was* a coward. 'When I was seventeen I decided that I would go back to my family and have my *emorata* done and be a proper Maasai man. I told Mr Jackson, and he said that he understood – but he didn't. He was a very kind man really and he put something in my cocoa that night and took me to the hospital. They did it with anaesthetic while I was too drowsy to realise what was happening.'

'Sounds good to me,' Walt said sympathetically.

'*You* don't understand either. The pain *has* to be part of it. Only by showing that you can stand the pain of the *emorata* without crying out, that you can ever really be a Maasai man – a warrior. Now I can *never* be that. The most I can be is a guide to people like you.'

'You're a Christian – the same as I am. That's better than being a warrior, surely?'

'I'm not even a good Christian.' Moses stood up and reverted to his role as guide.

'I think that it is time we went to our tents, Sir.'

'*Walt* to you. *Buddies*, remember?'

De/ne saw the light of the campfire from the track and slipped across to investigate. He circled the camp, keeping just out of the firelight and watched as the Maasai and the white man sat talking. He was just too far away to hear what was being said but watched the white man ply the Maasai with liquor from a bottle. He did not covet the alcohol – Mr Fotheringay had told him of the effect drink had on others of his race – but he did envy the white man his cigars . Although he had some cheap tobacco in his skin bag, he reckoned these men owed him something for not slowing down when they'd passed him earlier in the day. Somewhere, there would be more of those cigars. The white man was smoking them almost continuously, so he must have brought plenty with him. They'd probably be kept in the *gharri* rather than his tent.

De/ne crept round to the Land Cruiser and silently opened the door on the dark side. There was just enough light from the fire to enable him to scan the stacked boxes and crates for the most likely one. Finding them, he helped himself to three packets, then thinking that the insult had not been worth *three*, put one back before closing the door and returning to the track. Here he turned back for a short distance and, because he had heard a lion coughing not far away, he selected a tree in the moonlight, climbed it and slept lying along a branch with his feet hanging down either side like a leopard.

The elephants had spent a restful day in the shade of the trees lining the riverbank. Without prompting from M'zee, the older tembulls and the tembellas had taken up positions around the outside of the herd to watch for any approaching danger, while the younger elephants and the females with babies stayed in the centre. The jostlers roamed about restlessly, wanting to be on the way to new adventures, while Tembas Kindness and Comfort took over the preparation of food-wads for M'zee. This allowed Kidogo to forage for herself, accompanied by Rafiki who kept reaching out his trunk to touch her as if he was afraid she might wander off without him.

The free ivories the elephants had carried were laid reverently at the foot of the densest trees where they could not be seen from over-flying aircraft.

When M'zee felt it was time to move on, he gave the signal and each family or group drank at the pools in the riverbed before following him up the far bank. Turning at the top of the bank, he could see that nearly all of the elephants, except those with the youngest babies, were carrying tusks from dead tembos. The sun had set in the west and he chose a path towards the last red glow on the horizon. The rest and the plentiful supply of food-wads had given him new energy but he set a pace that would not be too hard on the babies and the carriers, as he pushed his way through the bush or led the way along any game trails he encountered.

Lars and Ryan discovered that there was a shortage of fuel in Arusha and visited several filling stations before finding one that had any for sale and even then they had to queue for an hour before they could fill the Land Rover's tank and their reserve cans.

As they swung the last can into the back of the vehicle, Lars said, 'It's only when you have to search it out and hang around for it that you realise how dependant we are on petrol, diesel and the like.'

'That's what I was trying to tell you back at the Riverside,' Ryan replied with a grimace.

They'd driven very hard and camped in a glade closer to Walt Schwiner and Moses than they knew, and even closer to De/ne, although they were totally unaware of the presence of any Bushmen in that part of the country.

After they'd eaten their evening meal, Ryan asked, 'Just *what* are we doing here?'

'I was asking myself that,' Lars replied. 'I suppose we're trying to stop the American guy getting those big tusks. They've *got* to be the ones we found in the cave.'

'Why do you think the elephants have carried them this far?'

'I've been wondering about that too. But it's their business. They must have a reason.'

'So, do you have a plan?'

'Not much of one. Just stay on the tracks of Moses Jackson and the Yank and try and bugger up any ideas they've got to steal those tusks. Sort of make it up as we go along.'

'No Plan B, then?'

'No – even Plan A is very sketchy.'

'Did Oi ever tell you about the Oirishman at the business meeting?'

Lars always knew what was coming whenever Ryan put on his stage-Irish accent. 'Go on then,' he said, grimacing in the light from their fire.

'Well, when the meeting was just finishing Paddy turns to the chairman and asks, 'Why don't we save time and be implementing Plan B *first*?'

'Definitely time for bed,' Lars replied.

After packing up their camp in the morning, they were delayed in starting when Ryan found that there was a flat tyre on the Land Rover, caused by an acacia thorn which had penetrated the thick rubber tread. After changing the wheel, Lars decided to repair the puncture while the air was still cool.

Walt Schwiner had lain awake much of the night, thinking over what he had learned about Moses. It had stirred long-suppressed painful memories of his own childhood.

When Walt had stayed on his uncle's ranch, the local boys all met each afternoon at the swimming hole downstream from the gorge. Here they swam naked and romped in and out of the water. If any local girls knew of the pool they kept well away – it was a boy's place.

Walt, whose uncle owned the land for miles around the pool, was made welcome during his vacations, until it was time for his 'initiation'. The gorge was not wide, the drop from the log which bridged it was only about fifty feet and the pool below the log was deep enough to make a fall scary – but not dangerous. Walt knew all this and was a strong swimmer but, when it was his turn to run across, he had pleaded a stomach-ache.

'I'll do it tomorrow,' he'd told the jeering boys but the stomach-ache had persisted over the few remaining days of his stay, only miraculously getting better when his uncle took him to the Greyhound Bus terminus for the homeward journey. The tone of his uncle's 'Goodbye, Walt,' clearly indicated that word had reached him about his nephew's cowardice.

'Who cares now?' Walt asked himself as he lay in the tent. 'I'm a hunter of wild animals, and a very rich man who can buy whatever I want.' Even so, he could remember many years later feeling more relief than remorse when his uncle died and took with him to the grave the knowledge of his nephew's lack of courage.

Walt woke early, got out of bed, shivered in the cold morning air and made enough noise to ensure Moses woke too. Walt was cross, having been thirsty in the night and unable to find a water bottle in the tent. He complained about this and Moses apologised. It was normally the camp-cook's responsibility to place a bottle of drinking water in each guest's tent and, in the absence of a cook, he should have done that.

Walt grudgingly accepted the apology and, while Moses packed up the camp, Walt stoked up the glowing embers of the previous night's campfire and brewed coffee for them both.

A dawn-dove called from the tree above their campsite as they drove away. Ten minutes later, Moses slowed to avoid a puff adder sluggishly wriggling across the road.

'Kill it! Drive over it!' Walt shouted.

Moses started to protest. He had been taught at the Guide School that snakes were to be avoided, not killed.

'Kill it! I hate them. Kill it!' Walt repeated, and Moses, thinking of the money this man would give him, steered so that the wheels passed over the snake's back, just behind its head.

Lars was mending the puncture when another dove called from the tree above where he was working. '*Dee-daadaa, dee-daadaa.*'

'Damned bird,' he remarked to Ryan. 'They always sound as though they're saying, "**Work** harder, w**ork** harder."'

'*I've* always thought it sounded more like, "**Drink** lager, **drink** lager."'

'That's the difference between you and me,' Lars said, laughing as he stood up and dusted his hands on his trouser leg. 'Give me a hand to lift this wheel onto the bonnet, please.'

When the wheel was securely bolted down, Lars drove the Land Rover out of the glade where they'd camped, and onto the track. After driving for a few minutes he could see a small figure walking ahead of them who stepped back off the track to let them pass. Lars slowed down and stopped alongside the man who was smoking a cigar.

'Hadza,' he said to Ryan quietly. 'A Bushman.' Then pushing the side window open, he greeted the man in Swahili.

'Good morning, gentlemen,' the Bushman replied in refined English. 'Can I be of assistance?'

Taken aback, Lars stared at the man who was wearing a soft-leather loincloth and carrying a leather bag hanging from a strap over his shoulder. Even the pointed cap on his head was made of leather. The man's wrinkled skin was an apricot yellow and what one could see of his scalp was covered in little knobbles of grey hair. He could have been any age from forty to a hundred. His eyes sparkled mischievously as he drew on the cigar and repeated, 'Can I be of assistance, gentlemen?'

Lars answered in English. 'Perhaps you can. Do you know if a vehicle with two men in it has come this way recently?'

'Yes, Sir, – yesterday – in the afternoon. They were going very fast. One of the men smokes very fine cigars.' He took another pull and blew the smoke into the air, making a perfect smoke-ring in the morning stillness. '*Very* fine cigars. But I am used to a coarser mix of tobacco myself. Might I avail myself of a ride with you?'

'Put that thing out and jump in the back,' Lars replied. 'Where are you going?'

'Home,' said the Bushman, carefully extinguishing the cigar and putting the half-smoked remainder in his bag. 'Home.'

The elephants were making slower progress than M'zee had hoped. The presence of the babies and the number of tusks being carried all delayed the herd and once the moon had set he feared he might lead them over the edge of a ravine in the darkness. When the first light touched the highest of the clouds, he called a halt in a clump of flat-topped Acacia trees and sent the three jostlers forward to see what kind of country lay ahead.

They reported back as the sun rose. 'The trees thin out as the ground slopes downwards,' Three Eyes told him. 'Then there is a wide, wide valley with no trees at all. The tall humans who love cattle have a camp there. We could see their huts but there was no smell of fire-smoke and we could see no people or cattle. There is no water nearby, so maybe they have left their camp and taken their cattle away to another place.'

M'zee decided they would stay under the trees even though there was no water. Tembos could go without drinking for several days and they had all had their fill the evening before. It would be good when the rains came and made plentiful pools to drink from, which wouldn't be long now. In the night, so far to the north that M'zee could hear no sounds of the storm, he had seen tiny flashes of light.

'We stay here today,' he announced and the tembos started to browse on the bushes and graze on the dry grass under the trees.

When Moses and Walt reached their previous campsite they drove slowly past the Land Cruiser where it lay forlornly on its side, and on along the winding track to the pass where the ambush had taken place. Here, Moses stopped and got out cautiously but there was no fresh dung about. Walt opened the door and stepped down, holding his new rifle at the ready.

'Which way have they gone?' he asked.

Moses didn't reply. He was standing still, listening.

'Which way have they gone?' Walt asked again.

Moses held up his hand. 'Shuss,' he said quietly. 'I've got to get the feel of the place again.'

Walt walked across to a patch of shade under a tree, examined the ground carefully to ensure there were no snakes about, sat on a rock and lit a cigar, his rifle resting across his knees. Moses walked about slowly, his whole body tense and alert, retuning himself to the sounds, smells and sights of the bush and trying to put himself into the mind of an elephant.

The big old bull had not been up here when the elephants had attacked the Land Rover – there had only been the younger ones and the tuskless female. Once they had taken the tusks, they would most likely have gone back to where the American had shot the smaller bull.

'First, we will go to where you killed the elephant, and start tracking from there,' he told Walt.

Lars drove on with the Bushman seated on the pile of gear in the back of the Land Rover. After a while Ryan half turned and asked, 'So – where is *home*?'

The Bushman pointed forwards through the windscreen. 'Up there, over the hills and far away.'

'Where did you learn to speak English?' Lars asked.

'A man from England lived with my people for many years. He taught us all to speak pukka English. But I have discovered they do not speak English that way in Arusha.'

'What's your name?' Ryan asked. 'I'm Ryan, and my friend here is Lars.'

'You may call me De/ne,' the little man replied pronouncing it *de–tch–ne*. 'My full name is more complex. Not even Mr Fotheringay could pronounce that. He said that Bushmantaal is difficult for people from Europe to speak.' De/ne spoke a word that consisted of a variety of clicks with the sound *De/ne* buried within it. 'That is my real name. It

253

means, 'He who was born when the ostrich was calling.'

As Lars swerved to avoid the body of a puff adder lying in the road, he was wondering who Mr Fotheringay had been, and why he had spent many years teaching some Bushmen to speak English. If the Bushman was going home and *home* was in the direction they were going, he might be very useful to them. His people were said to be the finest trackers in the world.

Moses drove the Land Cruiser towards the corpse of the elephant that Walt Schwiner had shot. Sated vultures sat around the sagging body, and hyenas quarrelled over pieces of flesh that they had torn from it. Two jackals scurried away at the sound of the vehicle, and the hyenas slunk out of sight into the bush. The stench of rotting flesh reached Walt and he retched.

'Get us away from here,' he said to Moses.

Moses drove round to the upwind side, stopping the vehicle where the body was hidden by scrub, and got out.

'I will look for the tracks made by the other elephants,' he said, 'then we will follow them. Will you drive ? It may take us some days to catch up with them and we know that these are *kali tembos*.'

'What in hell are *kali tembos*?'

'Fierce elephants. Dangerous ones. Remember how they attacked us before.'

'I'm not likely to forget that! Yeah. I'm sure I can drive this Jap jeep. Just keep behind you, right? What if the jumbos ambush us again?'

'I can tell by their droppings how far ahead of us they are. When we begin to get close we will leave the vehicle and stalk them on foot. We are quite safe at the moment. I'll just top up the fuel.'

He climbed up onto the roof rack, unstrapped one of the

cans and passed it down to Walt. As he poured the diesel fuel into the Land Cruiser's tank, a shift of wind brought the stench from Lonely's body to them and Walt retched again. 'Hurry up,' he said. 'That thing stinks.'

Moses pushed the empty can into the back as Walt swung himself up to the driving seat, started the engine and tried out the gear lever. 'Just checking where reverse is!' he told Moses as he let the clutch up for a moment and the vehicle moved backwards.

Moses stepped up onto the bumper to the side of the winch-housing and indicated to Walt that he should drive on, then stepped down again and led off in the direction the elephants had taken.

Lars stopped beside the Land Cruiser that One Eye and Kidogo had tipped on its side in the abandoned campsite. The three men got out and examined it before walking around the remnants of the camp.

'They made a good job of this,' Lars remarked to Ryan.

De/ne was walking about looking at the ground, then he walked over to where a fallen tree was lying. He studied it for a while and went back to the others.

'All this was done by *two* elephants, one a male, the other a female, neither of them fully grown,' he told them. 'A man was hiding in that tree before the male elephant pushed it down – but he did not hurt the man.' De/ne touched the overturned Land Cruiser. 'The one of *these* we are following is ahead of us today. It passed through here about three hours ago, going *that* way. May I ride on with you, gentlemen?'

Lars smiled to himself at the Bushman's pukka English, and could see that Ryan was equally amused.

'You may indeed ride on with us, De/ne,' he replied. 'You are very welcome.'

Farther on, where the track passed through a rocky defile, De/ne, who had been studying the track over Lars' shoulder as they drove, said, 'Here there has been much activity. Perhaps we should examine the ground and see what is to be learned.'

There was still a faint smell of spilled diesel oil where a small tree had been uprooted and now lay beside the track, its leaves dried by the sun. 'Much has happened here. There were more elephants,' De/ne pronounced. 'Two more, in addition to those who caused much havoc at the camping place we so recently visited. They all went in *that* direction. And that day the bwana smoked a cigar sitting on *that* rock while some Maasai man walked about *here*, and around *here*. Then the white men went after the elephants in their *gharri*.'

'What's a *gharri*?' Lars asked.

'I am sorry, Sir. It is a word Mr Fotheringay used for vehicles with wheels. Perhaps the word is not used now. I had never before seen such a vehicle until I left my home after the last short-rains.'

'You'd never seen a vehicle with wheels until this year?' Ryan was incredulous.

'That is a truth, Sir. Where my home is there are no such things. And for that I am truly glad.'

'You don't have to call me – or Lars – *Sir*. Please just use our names. Tell me about your home.'

De/ne hesitated, as though wondering if he could trust these men. 'It is far away over there,' he said with a sweep of his arm that covered a quarter of the horizon. 'There the land is still as Mantis loves it. It is a place we share with the elephants and the lesser creatures. I would never have left it except that I wished to find worthy husbands for my grand-daughters.'

'And did you?'

'Alas – no. Most of those I met were rogues who thought only of money. Other men only wanted more and more possessions, which is not the way of my people. Such men as those would lie and cheat to get more possessions for themselves and I would rather my granddaughters were to die and not have grandchildren for me, than for them to be married to such men.'

He looked sad and kicked at a tuft of dry grass with his foot.

Ryan said, 'There are some good ones left, surely?'

'I found none, and am returning to tell this to my granddaughters. They will be very disappointed, for when we three die it will be the end of my family and there will be no more guardians of the elephants' secrets.' He reached into his skin bag, drew out a two-litre plastic bottle of water and drank from it.

Ryan smiled at the incongruity of this and was about to ask more when Lars interrupted him. 'I think we should be pressing on to catch up with the American and Moses Jackson. Perhaps De/ne will tell us more when we camp tonight.' He turned to the Bushman. 'Will you be our guide, De/ne? If you were to sit on the bonnet of the Land Rover you could show me which way to drive. You are welcome to stay with us and share our food for as long as you wish.'

De/ne looked at the Land Rover and asked, 'Is that canvas part on top, the *bonnet* of the gharri?'

'No. *This* part is called the bonnet,' Lars replied, slapping the flat metal engine cover and thinking how illogical the English language can be.

De/ne smiled politely and clambered up to sit on the front like a giant mascot, grinning at an idea that was forming in his mind.

257

CHAPTER TWENTY-THREE

Tembo Boy and Temba Girl were some distance away from the other elephants, browsing on sparsely leaved shrubs.

'I could do with a hatful of pony nuts,' Boy said.

'I often think that,' Girl agreed. 'Being a real elephant is exciting though. I'd always thought the wild ones lived dull lives – mostly just eating and sleeping. I had no idea they carried tusks all over the country like this.'

'Ever thought of going back?' There was a touch of wistfulness in Boy's voice.

'Quite often. You?'

'Quite often. Doug and Jayne will be missing us terribly.'

'We could go back. There are plenty of other tembos to carry the tusks now.'

'Should we say *may you fare well*, to the others?'

'I think not. We can just slip away. They might not even notice we've gone.'

'Now?'

'Now!'

Kidogo was relieved when Temba Kindness and Temba Comfort took over the role of foraging and preparing food-wads for M'zee, and was happier now that Rafiki was mostly at her side. Her mind returned to what Tembo Lonely had told them. First, there was the whale's prophecy.

When the stone mount ~ breathes fire and smoke,
Mana will ask ~ a Gift of Love.
Tembos *give this ~ though it hurts them.*

Only the Love ~ of Tembo Jay
Can save the world ~ from human greed.

Only the first part made any sense to her. She remembered fleeing with M'zee down the snow-covered
mountainside, losing her hold on the sacred tusk and finding
it again at the edge of the snow-slope as the mountain
breathed fire and smoke behind them. But what was the *Gift
of Love*? Some great *Gift* must still be needed and the
prophecy said *Tembos give this*, not a temba on her own. She
felt relieved – the responsibility would not be hers alone.

She pulled down an acacia branch and chewed it thought-
fully. Tasty new shoots were beginning to grow between the
thorns, which meant the rains would come soon. How strange
it was that new shoots appeared on the trees *before* the rains
came. It would make more sense if they came after, as with
the grass, but before. . . . Could the trees know when the
rains were due? Life was full of such mysteries.

All around Kidogo other tembos were browsing, grey
shapes glimpsed between the yellow bark of the acacia trees.
She felt safe in their company and could feel the Love that
encompassed the group. A baby left its mother's side and
made a mock charge at her, its tiny trunk swinging loosely
from side to side. She held out her trunk to greet it and the
baby skidded to a halt, turned and ran back, to peer at her from
beneath his mother's belly.

How sad that Tembo Lonely couldn't have been here to
share all this. Kidogo thought about the whale's song which
Lonely had sung for them that night, such a short time ago.
That wonderful song was now lost for ever, like the *Song of
Tembo Jay* that Tembella Grace had told her about. Or was
it? She signed to Rafiki to come with her as she walked to
where the free tusks were laid out under a densely foliaged
tree, guarded by three jostlers who stood back to let her
pass. Lonely's tusks were easily identified by the scraps of

flesh that still adhered around their roots, attracting swarms of buzzing flies. The white, wriggling babies of the flies would soon clean up the tusks, she thought. Everything is part of a plan – nothing has been left out, nothing wasted.

She chose Lonely's right tusk and ran her trunk along it. Soon, images were flashing through her mind but she paused at the vision of blue water between tall, single-trunked trees. This must be the sea Lonely had reached in his wanderings. She moved her trunk very slowly until she could see the dark back of the whale in the water.

'What are you doing?' Rafiki asked, and the picture faded.

'Reading the tusk. I'm looking for—' Kidogo stopped. She herself had only been taught to read by M'zee in the cave on Holy Mountain *after* Rafiki had left to return to the Sacred Grove. Did he know about reading?

When she asked him he replied, 'The Sisters spent much time caressing the tusks of Tembella Grace when we were resting on our way here. Perhaps that is what they were doing. I didn't ask – it would have seemed an intrusion.'

Kidogo began to tell Rafiki how reading tusks tells you all about the life of the tembo whose tusks they are. Rafiki lifted his trunk and felt along his own remaining tusk.

'It only works with tusks after they have been freed from a tembo who has stepped-over,' she told him, aware that many other tembos had silently come closer to hear what she was saying. Perhaps none of *them* knew how to read. When the time was more suitable she would have to teach them – but not now. She needed to be on her own, or just with Rafiki, if she was to find what she hoped would be stored away in Lonely's tusks. She touched them both reverently and turned away. The other tembos parted to let her through, with Rafiki following her.

Rafiki was so happy to be with Kidogo again he wanted to be at her side all the time. He had thought of her often during his journey to the Sacred Pool and onwards from there. He knew he had grown physically since he had seen her last and his remaining tusk was notably longer, thicker and heavier. If tusks *were* the way tembos stored up Love, then his must have absorbed the Love of the Sisters and of his friend, Kidogo. He knew she had a great Love for him, for old M'zee, and indeed for all the other tembos and that they all loved her but, without tusks of her own, she could not store it. This puzzled him and seemed most unfair.

He had also noticed how much more confident she was. Most of her old fears had gone and she was certainly respected, as well as loved, by the other tembos. He was intrigued by what she'd told him about *reading* freed tusks and was sorry her lesson had been interrupted. He was greatly excited at the thought of it continuing.

De/ne, sitting on the bonnet as Lars drove the Land Rover slowly through the bush, smelled the stench drifting downwind from Tembo Lonely's body which was still being torn apart by the hyenas and vultures. He leaped off to the side of the moving vehicle and ran ahead towards the corpse, the hyenas scattering as he approached. One quick look and he turned and ran back, signalling to Lars to drive off to the side and stop upwind of the smell.

'This elephant has been dead for several days,' he said. 'Its tusks were taken from it soon after it was killed. The other gharri has been here today and has now gone *that* way – following the tracks of the other elephants who were with this one when it was shot. Are we to follow?'

Half an hour later, with De/ne once more sitting on the bonnet, a flock of speckled, grey guinea-fowl ran across the path of the Land Rover. With one move, De/ne swept off his hat and his leather bag, and leaped forward, running in amongst them as they tried to fly up to safety. He grabbed a bird by the neck with each hand, swung them in a circle to break their necks, dropped them and had snatched another out of the air even before Lars had time to stop the vehicle.

De/ne walked back, carrying the three limp birds and dropped them into the footwell in the rear of the Land Rover.

'My contribution to this evening's dinner, gentlemen,' he said with a grin before climbing back onto the bonnet. He put a spotted grey feather into the side of his hat and perched it jauntily on his head before signalling that he was ready for them to go again.

Walt was driving the Land Cruiser, keeping a couple of metres or so behind Moses, when the guide held up his hand to signal they should stop and rest. The dung piles he was finding were not fresh and the tembos were at least one or two days ahead of them.

Walt got down stiffly from the driver's seat and asked if there was any beer in the icebox. Moses fetched two cans, glad of the small refrigerator that ran on current drawn from the vehicle's batteries. Walt drank his beer, took his new rifle from the cab, loaded it and walked a hundred paces back the way they had come, before standing the empty can on the ground in front of a tall termite mound.

'I need to sight this in,' he told Moses when he returned. He raised the rifle to his shoulder and squeezed the trigger. The shot sounded sharp and harsh amongst the natural sounds of the bush and the birds stopped calling. Dust spurted up on the left-hand side of the can and Walt fired again. The can rolled over. He fired several times, reloading as fast as he could and each time the can jerked and jumped.

He knew he was showing off but was mighty pleased that he had not lost any of his skill with a gun – and Moses was clearly impressed.

De/ne, once more guiding from his seat on the bonnet of the Land Rover, heard the distant shots and, putting his finger up to his lips, he turned towards Ryan who was driving. Ryan cut the engine as De/ne jumped down and came round to stand by his window.

'I can hear the sound of shooting ahead of us. I will go and find out what is happening,' he said and loped off into the bush at right angles to the route they had been travelling.

Lars and Ryan got out of the Land Rover and moved into the shade of a baobab tree, glad of the chance to stretch their legs. A monkey scurried along a branch above their heads and leaped into a neighbouring tree.

'Do you think they're shooting at the elephants?' Ryan asked.

'I hope not. It'll be bad enough if they get hold of the tusks from the cave. I really hope not. But we'll know when De/ne gets back.'

'I like him,' Ryan said. 'He fits in here with the same ease as the animals.'

'I like the way he seems to be enjoying himself so much. I've heard that Bushmen have a great sense of humour.'

'We *still* don't have a real plan,' said Lars, expressing what they were both thinking. 'They're armed and we're not. They could shoot us both if they wanted to and most likely get away with it.'

'I don't think it would come to that,' said Ryan. 'This may be Africa, red in tooth and claw, but our Mr Schwiner is an American and Moses was brought up by missionaries. But I think we should try to prevent any more killing and help the elephants do whatever it is *they* want to do with those tusks. All we can do is tag along behind and play it by ear.'

'De/ne is a godsend.'

'Synchronicity!' said Ryan.

'Synchronicity? What's that?'

'I was reading about it just before I left Nairobi. It's a kind of special coincidence – like *serendipity*.'

'Good things happening by accident?'

'It's more than that. But I once heard a lovely example of serendipity. It's like looking for a needle in a haystack – and finding the farmer's daughter!'

The two men laughed and Ryan said, 'No, seriously, synchronicity is when you set yourself on a benign path, good things happen to help you along it. Much more than sheer coincidence! Serendipity plus.'

'Are *we* on a benign path?'

'Helping the elephants could be called that.'

'I'd like to think so.'

An hour later, De/ne returned carrying the remains of a beer can torn to pieces by several high-velocity bullets.

'The two men had been shooting at this,' he said. 'Then they each drank another beer before the Maasai-man came looking for it.' He held up the can with a grin. 'But it wasn't there,' he added, tossing the can from hand to hand. 'He was much puzzled by that. Now they have driven away after the elephants.'

'A beer sounds good to me,' Ryan said and went over to the polystyrene cool-box in the Land Rover. He took out three cans, tossed one each to Lars and De/ne and pulled up the opener on the third.

De/ne climbed back onto the bonnet, holding the can in his left hand, occasionally drinking from it while guiding Lars by simple hand-signals with his right.

When a puzzled Moses had finally given up looking for the missing can that Walt had used as a target, he suggested he could as easily follow the elephants' tracks while sitting on the bonnet of the Land Cruiser as he could by walking in front of it in the heat. That way they'd be able to travel much faster and catch up with their quarry sooner.

Shortly before nightfall, Walt and Moses reached the riverbed where Rafiki's group of elephants had joined those led by M'zee. Moses jumped down and scouted around.

'The elephants were here last night,' he told Walt, who had stayed in the vehicle at the top of the bank. 'The ones we've been following were joined here by many others. The new ones have some calves with them, which will slow them down. They dug holes to get water and I think, by their tracks, that they stayed here for two days. Then they all went *that* way.' He pointed towards the setting sun. 'We will go farther up the bank to be away from the elephant dung and make our camp.'

When they stopped, Moses drew Walt's attention to a distant mountain, its summit catching the last rays. 'That's Oldoinyo Lengai, a dormant volcano. It's a mountain sacred to the Maasai people. They believe it is where God lives.'

'Do *you* believe that?' Walt asked him.

'Of course not. I am a Christian. Not a Maasai.'

Lars and Ryan made camp well before it got dark. Lars didn't want to be driving with his headlights on, as they might be seen from the vehicle ahead of them. He stopped when they reached a patch of open ground backed by a fallen tree, and asked De/ne if he would like to stay the night with them.

'It would give me much pleasure to share a camp with you,' he said. 'But first I will find out how far away the other men are camping. I suggest you do not light a fire until I return.' He loped off into the bush without waiting for a reply.

Lars and Ryan cleared the ground of any logs that might harbour a snake, set up their tent, dug a hole for a latrine away from the camp, collected a large pile of wood and made a fire ready for lighting.

When De/ne returned he was carrying awkwardly a small but obviously heavy wooden box. 'They are camped on a riverbank far enough away for us to safely light the fire,' he told them as he put down the box and sat on it, grinning. 'I had hoped to acquire their two guns but the white man holds one of them all the time and carries spare bullets in loops on his belt. The other rifle in the gharri is for the Maasai man. I could easily have taken it – but it will be of little use without these.' He smacked the case on which he was sitting and grinned again. 'This is almost all their ammunition. Only one box of cartridges had been taken out of here and I have that too – it was in the front of the gharri.' He took a cardboard carton from the skin bag he always carried, tipped the contents into his hand and held it out towards Lars and Ryan.

'I have counted these,' he said. 'I also counted eight shots that were fired at the tin. So Mr Big-shot has only ten bullets left. He will be unhappy when he discovers that. What shall I do with these?' He slapped the box again.

Lars and Ryan discussed the possibilities and eventually decided to bury the ammunition in its case near a prominent kopje not far from their campsite. Lars took the *panga* to dig a hole, and De/ne carried the box.

At the foot of the kopje, De/ne put down the box and walked to where one of the huge rocks formed a natural shelter.

'Here was once the home of some of my people,' he said, 'before the *Others* came many hundreds of years ago. See. Here is where my people would have slept – and here is where the women would have broken open the nuts.' He pointed to small hollows in the rock floor, darker than the surrounding rock. Lars touched one and could feel where the nut-oil had impregnated the stone.

'Here is not a good place to bury such a box, the spirits of my people would not like it,' De/ne said as he picked up the box and walked away from the kopje, eventually dropping it near a large acacia tree.

Lars dug a hole between the roots and the box was buried. De/ne scattered the surplus soil, pressed down the earth covering the box with his feet and dragged a dead branch over the burying place to conceal it.

By the time they returned, Ryan had lit the fire, plucked the three guinea fowl and was boiling them in a cooking pot with some dried herbs from his pack. De/ne squatted by the fire, smoking one of Walt Schwiner's cigars as darkness fell and the night-birds started to call.

'Guinea fowl are supposed to be tough,' Lars remarked.

'I'm using an ancient African recipe,' Ryan said, trying to hide a smile. 'You put the birds in a pot of boiling water with three stones and boil them all together for one hour. Then you pour the water away, put more in and boil for another hour. You do this four times. Then you throw the water *and* the birds away and—'

'Eat the stones!' De/ne finished the story. 'That is a recipe Mr Fotheringay told me, many years ago. I think it is what he called an *old chestnut*.'

The birds were quite tender and tasted good. When they had eaten them and thrown the bones onto the fire, Ryan asked, 'Should we keep watch?'

'I don't think we need to,' replied Lars. 'They don't know

they're being followed.'

'They may, if they notice their ammo has been taken.'

'It could have been taken by *anyone* wandering in the bush. There's no way they'd think it would be us.'

De/ne pulled on the tiniest remnant of his second cigar of the evening and dropped the smallest butt-end Ryan had ever seen into the fire. 'You gentlemen do not need to worry,' he said. 'I will hear if anyone is approaching this camp and I will wake you in good time. You may sleep in peace.'

It was almost dark when M'zee led the herd out of the bush and onto the wide-open grazing lands. The air was heavy and far to the north the lightning flickered silently along the horizon. He had seen no humans and no cattle on the grasslands all day, although there had been many antelope nibbling at the sparse tufts of dry grass. The jostlers had probably been right – the herdsmen must have taken the cattle to where water was available, and antelope never seemed to have the same need to drink in the same way that cattle and tembos did.

When he had asked earlier if any tembos knew the area or had ancestral memories of water sources ahead, none of them had. So he had to risk crossing the plain *and* the hills beyond in the hope of finding water on the other side of them. If only the rains would break, there would be plenty, but the lightning was still a long way off.

Boy and Girl were hurrying back along the trail, following it easily by the scent and the droppings left by the herd when they had come that way. Half of the night had gone and the moon was rising when Girl slowed down and asked, 'Do you think Doug and Jayne will be happy when we get home?'

'I am sure they will.'

Girl stopped suddenly. 'Do you remember what Jayne and Doug were saying before we left?'

'About wanting to have babies?'

'No. About *holydays*. Wanting to go away – for a *change*.'

'I remember that. Jayne was saying she wanted to have a *holyday* with Doug but they couldn't leave us.'

'It may be that they are now having a *holyday* and they will not be there when we got home.'

'If it is a *holy day* they will be back now.'

'A *holyday* must mean *many* days. They often left us for just one day. Hush!'

Boy held up his trunk and moved it around slowly, testing the air. He could scent smoke from a fire and a faint trace of the smoke that comes from the back of a vehicle and lingers in the air long after its engine has stopped. His heart leaped. Doug and Jayne had followed them after all – and had come to find them. But then there was another lingering smoke scent – tobacco. Neither Doug nor Jayne ever used the fire-twigs that so many humans held between their lips, and which they called *cigarettes,* or sometimes just *cigars* when they were the very fat ones. The scent was from one of the fat ones – he was sure of that.

Girl was also scenting the night air. 'There are two humans there,' she said. 'I remember the scent of each one of them from where we found the tusks of Tembo Lonely. What shall we do?'

'We must get closer to their camp. The men will be asleep now. Follow me. Walk with care.'

They circled the camp, noting the two tents and the glow from the dying fire, before stepping some way back into the bush to talk, mostly using their sign language in the moonlight.

'They are following M'zee and the other tembos,' Boy said. 'Their vehicle tracks are covering the ones we made as we came this way. *These* are the men who killed Tembo Lonely the day after he sang that wonderful song we heard in the night. They are *rogues*.'

'We must warn the others!'

Boy and Girl turned as one and headed back westwards, quickly picking up the scent of their own tracks and hurrying on.

They caught up with M'zee and the other elephants before dawn as they were nearing the hills on the far side of the wide grazing lands. M'zee had been a little concerned about the footprints the group had left in the dusty ground but decided that it was not worth linquing for rain as there was no real evidence after all that time that any humans were following them.

Boy and Girl were breathing hard as they passed the column of tembos and came up alongside M'zee, Kidogo and Rafiki.

M'zee continued the steady pace he had set to let the tusk carriers and the babies keep up. 'So,' he said quietly, without turning his head. 'You have chosen to rejoin us. I am sure you had a good reason for turning back.'

'There are humans following you—' Boy said urgently – 'two of those who killed Tembo Lonely. They are less than half a day's travel away if they use their *four-by-four* – which they're sure to do. It will carry them swiftly across this open country.'

'Thank you,' M'zee answered, his voice low. Then he added, 'If you choose to leave us again, I would like to know about it *before* you go, so I can plan who carries each tusk and not waste my time nor endanger the tembos who wasted *their* time and energy looking for you last evening.'

Boy and Girl lowered their trunks in apology at the rebuke as M'zee walked on. He was thinking hard. With the elephant killers so close behind them, he must not stop when they reached the wooded ridge looming up not far ahead of them. His plan had been to hide among the trees so that the herd could rest before walking over the top. But, if the ground was as rocky and steep as he expected it to be the humans would not be able to drive their vehicle up there. They would either have to follow on foot or give up and turn back.

He called over his shoulder, urging the others on.

Walt had another uncomfortable night and, soon after midnight, he needed to relieve himself. He pushed aside the light bedcover, found his flashlight and shoes, and pulled the heavy zip-fastener on the tent-flap almost down to the ground. Moses had told him never to leave the flap open, as snakes were known to wriggle inside tents in search of warmth – but he'd only be outside for a minute at the most. He stepped out through the opening into a close darkness broken only by the faint glow from the embers of the fire, and shone the torch around the campsite. To his immense relief there were no reflections from eyes in the surrounding bushes, so he peed not far from the tent, ducked quickly back in through the opening, and zipped it up securely behind him before sitting on the mattress to take off his shoes in the darkness. He lay back, wondering whether it was too hot in the tent to pull the thin blanket over him or whether he would be warm enough in just his pyjamas. He reached his hand over to his right side for the blanket and froze, his heart racing.

His hand was around the smooth, cool body of what . . . a puff adder?

He willed himself to lie still, sweat breaking out all over him, not daring to move his hand and wondering if the snake's head was at the end of the bed where his feet were or, horror of horrors, right next to his face. Oh God, this was terrible! Was it really a puff adder? Like the one they'd run over, slow and reluctant to bite, or could it be a black mamba? The one the natives called the *fifteen-steps* snake because, once bitten, fifteen steps was as far as you'd get before you dropped dead? All this passed through his mind within seconds. His heart was pounding as he wondered what the snake would do if he called out for Moses. He decided not to. Could he find the flashlight with his other hand? But that wouldn't help him and, if it turned out to be a spitting cobra, the snake would be able to see his eyes and shoot its venom to blind him.

His pyjamas were drenched with the sweat of fear – but still the snake didn't move. Perhaps it was asleep and he'd be able to get out of the tent without waking it. Nerves tingling, he opened his hand and quickly rolled to the left, feeling urgently for the zip-fastener of the tent flap. He jerked it down and dived out through the opening, any possible dangers outside being infinitely preferable to the known horror in the tent. He turned, grabbed the zip and pulled it up to trap the snake inside the tent. Only then did he call out for Moses.

He stood in the dark, shivering in his damp pyjamas, his legs feeling very weak as he saw a light come on in Moses' tent. As the guide's head emerged, Walt blurted out, 'There's a snake in my tent!'

Moses walked barefoot towards him, scanning the ground between them with the torch.

'How do you know?' he asked calmly.

'I felt it. I put my hand on it. It was as fat as this.' Walt made a circle with his hands in the torchlight.

Moses pulled the tent-zip down a few inches and shone his torch inside, then he pulled the zip all the way to the ground and stepped into the tent.

A moment later he emerged holding a plastic bottle of water.

'Here's your snake,' he said, trying to keep his voice level.

Walt turned away and was sick into the dry grass behind him.

Ryan and Lars were woken by the insistent calling of a dawn-dove, and found two mugs of coffee waiting for them outside their tent. De/ne was sitting on a log by the fireside, imitating the dove's call and looking to Ryan exactly like the drawings of leprechauns in the picture books of his childhood, even down to the conical leather hat with its jaunty feather. De/ne raised a hand in greeting, stood up and walked over to them.

'The greedy men have not made an early start today,' he said. 'The white man has vomited on the grass outside his tent in the night. Two elephants came to look at their camp but have gone back to speak with the other elephants.'

'Do you mean *speak*?' Lars asked.

'Oh yes, elephants talk to one another as we do. But, of course they use a different language. I can speak the language of elephants, just as I can speak the language of English people.'

Lars glanced sideways at Ryan, then looked back to De/ne.

'You can speak the language of elephants? How does it sound?'

De/ne crouched slightly, put his left hand behind his ear, pushing it forward and swung his right arm like a trunk. Within a moment he was exuding the essence of elephant. He wiggled his ear by moving his fingers behind it, lifted and lowered his *trunk* and made a series of little grunts and squeals. Then he stood upright and was once more a human.

'I've just said, in the language of the elephants, *These humans do not believe I can speak to you,*' he told them, and added, 'Elephants speak as much with their trunks and their ears as they do with their voices.'

'Where did you learn to do *that*?' Lars asked.

'At my home there have always been elephants. I learned their language as a child – at the same time as I learned Bushmantaal from my mother – and a long time before Mr Fotheringay came and taught me to speak the Queen's English.

CHAPTER TWENTY-FOUR

M'zee and the herd were resting amongst the cactus-like euphorbia trees on the very top of the rocky ridge. The air was hot and sultry and the climb up through the rocks had been hard, especially for the babies and the tembos carrying the heaviest tusks. Fortunately, there were enough elephants to share the carrying but they were all glad to be able to rest and spread their ears to catch the occasional cooling breeze.

M'zee called Kidogo to stand by him and describe what she could see. 'My eyes were never as strong as yours,' he reminded his granddaughter in a fond voice. 'Tell me what you can see ahead of us.'

Kidogo described the scene. 'The far side of the ridge we have just climbed slopes down to another wide valley with many scattered trees. In the centre of the valley there are more trees, growing close together – winding about like a snake. I am sure there is a riverbed down there but it is too far away for me to see if there is water in it. Beyond that there is more grassland with a few trees and some small kopjes, then the valley slopes up and finishes far away at the foot of a high wall of rock.'

'Are there cattle in the valley?'

'I can see no cattle, but many antelope, some zebra and three ostriches – all males.'

'No humans?'

'None that I can see.'

'What is to our left?'

Kidogo turned sideways and looked southwards. 'I can

see, through the trees, that the ridge rises towards some higher hills which are hiding their heads in the clouds.'

'And to our right?'

'The ridge runs far to the north, getting lower all the time, until it ends in a plain of dry grass. Beyond that there may be a lake – but I cannot be sure of that.'

'And behind us?'

Kidogo turned again. 'Behind us is the wide, flat valley we have crossed, with the trees along the riverbed where we rested until last evening.'

'Can you see the *four-by-four* that Temba Boy and Temba Girl saw in the night?'

Kidogo strained her eyes to see anything that might be it, until Tembo Three Eyes, who was standing within ear-twitch, pointed with his trunk and said, 'There. Look there. *That* dust is made by a *four-by-four*.'

Kidogo could see it now, heading directly towards them and travelling fast.

Moses was driving the Land Cruiser, easily following the tracks of so many elephants across open ground. Beside him, Walt was silent, still embarrassed by the affair of the 'snake' in the night.

Nearing the foot of the ridge, Moses slowed and steered between some small rocks and scrubby trees. The elephants had obviously gone up the ridge and were probably already going down the other side. It would take many hours to follow them in the vehicle – even if it was possible, and he doubted that. But he knew this whole area – he had helped herd his father's cattle here when he was a young boy. The grass in this and the parallel valley to the west was always lush after the rains, which were late this year. As he selected the best route, he realised how little the timing of the rains had meant to him while he lived in the town, and how vital they were to everything that happened out here. Part of him longed to be back, living a simple life where such things mattered. He spun the wheel to the right.

'What the—?' Walt muttered.

'I know this country,' Moses said. 'Have you noticed that the elephants have been heading almost due west? This ridge runs from south to north and finishes well before the lakeside flats. We can go round the end and catch up with the elephants as they come down the other side.'

'The *four-by-four* is turning north,' Tembo Three Eyes reported. 'They are heading towards the end of these hills and will try and meet us as we come down into the next valley.'

M'zee looked concerned. The tembas with the babies could never get down the far side of the ridge before the *four-by-four* got there. Then the humans could come up with plenty of cover to where they were and stalk them. They could shoot the tembos one by one until they got what they wanted, which he was sure were the tusks of Tembo Jay. He thought of turning left and following the ridge southwards to the distant hills and looked in that direction. Lightning was now playing amongst the dark clouds around the hilltops – but that way would be very hard for the mothers and babies. The voice of Mana had clearly said, *'Follow the tired sun.'* To do that meant going on towards the west. He was sure Mana would try *his* best to keep them all safe – but it was on him, an ageing, toothless tembo, long past his best years, that the immediate decision rested.

Tembo Three Eyes touched M'zee's shoulder with his trunk. 'I have thought of a plan,' he said. 'Those humans want the tusks of Tembo Jay – I am sure of that. If we three jostlers were to take the tusks and show them to the humans they would follow us and leave the rest of you in safety.'

'What if they catch up with you? You won't be able to run fast with such heavy tusks? They will kill you and take the sacred ivories. Down in the valley, the four-by-four can run much faster than you can.'

Kidogo said, 'If the humans *think* the jostlers have the tusks they will follow them, and if the tusks *aren't* heavy, the jostlers will have some chance of escaping.'

'Explain more,' M'zee signalled.

'If we can find some branches similar in size to the sacred tusks and strip off the bark, the jostlers could show them to the humans at a distance, then lead them away while the rest of us cross the valley.'

M'zee looked at the eager faces of the jostlers. Having no better plan, he signalled, 'Do it now!'

The three young tembos immediately started to search for suitable branches, pulling the most likely ones down from young trees, tearing off projecting twigs and working their tusks in under the bark to strip it off. Soon two realistic dummy tusks had been made and Three Eyes and Two Eyes took up one each, leaving One Eye looking envious – but he wasn't going to left out of the action.

'Follow me,' Three Eyes called and ran off down the hillside, weaving between the trees, closely followed by his fellows.

M'zee watched them go. It was true – from a distance the raw, white branches did look just like the tusks of Tembo Jay, and he was glad he had given the youngsters a chance to distinguish themselves back on Holy Mountain.

'Fare well,' he called out after them.

The second part of the plan called for him to lead the remaining tembos down from the ridge and across the valley, but going downhill was far more difficult for him than climbing, and the plan was far from complete. But if he and Kidogo were to stay here, with his Shadow acting as his eyes, and reporting what she was observing, he could direct what was happening by using low~sound. Who would lead the others down? Tembo Lusty was the largest of the males but he had proved to be unreliable – it would need to be the one-tusked tembo, Rafiki. He called him over and told him his plan.

'I want you to chose strong, reliable Tembos to carry the tusks of Tembo Jay and Tembo Steadfast then lead the females with their babies and the tembos carrying the other tusks down to the valley floor and wait in the cover of the trees until you hear me call in low~sound. Then follow my directions. My Shadow will stay here with me. Do you understand?'

Rafiki looked at Kidogo, obviously not wanting to be parted from her again. When she flicked her trunk to indicate he must go, he turned and called the others to follow him.

The jostlers were enjoying themselves. They had been given a vital job to do and knew if they did it well they would earn the praise and respect of all the others. The branches were so light compared to the heavy tusks they had been carrying they hardly had to slow down at all, even in the roughest places.

'Head north and west,' Three Eyes commanded when they reached the open grasslands. 'Run towards the riverbed. We want the humans to see *us* long before they get near the other tembos.'

Moses and Walt drove past a number of unoccupied *manyattas*, the Maasai families evidently having taken their cattle much farther north. Moses was glad of this. He had no desire to be seen here, where he was sure he would again be reviled as a coward.

As soon as the last of the ridge petered out into isolated patches of rock and scrub, he turned left and followed a cattle track into the western valley. Once onto open grassland, he accelerated in his attempt to head off the elephants. The Land Cruiser bucked and rolled as he tried to avoid rocks, fallen trees and, especially here, the burrows made by warthogs. Moses was remembering watching warthogs when he was a boy herding his father's cattle, and was startled when Walt suddenly yelled, 'Over there – look over there!'

Close to the ribbon of trees marking the riverbed, were three elephants – and two of them were holding the largest of the tusks they were seeking. Moses turned towards them as the elephants slipped in amongst the trees and disappeared.

Up on the ridge, Kidogo reported to M'zee. 'The humans must have seen the jostlers. Their four-by-four has turned away to follow them towards the river trees a long way to the north of us.'

M'zee deliberated. Should he order Rafiki to lead the others across the valley while the humans were pursuing the jostlers who were carrying the wooden tusks, or should he hold back until they were certain the humans had been fooled? Action was usually better than inaction, but then another wise saying advised, *If you don't know what to do – do nothing.* Since the first of the choices did not involve *him* in any immediate physical action, where his infirmities might 'let the team down', he decided on *action* and sang down to Rafiki in long-distance low~sound.

'The humans are ~ far away now.
Hurry to the ~ riverbank trees
Cross over there ~ and hasten on.'

M'zee asked Kidogo what she could see. She told him Rafiki and the other tembos were heading across the valley but she could not now see the jostlers nor the humans.

By the time Moses had driven the Land Cruiser to the edge of the trees lining the riverbed, the three elephants carrying the tusks were nowhere to be seen. He stopped and got out, and went to fetch his new rifle from the back of the vehicle. He slid it out of its case and looked for the open box of bullets. Unable to find it, he went to fetch a new box from the case but that was not there either. Walt, meanwhile, had taken his rifle and loaded it with ammunition from the loops in his belt. 'Bring me some more bullets,' he called to Moses.

'Where have you put them?'

'I haven't moved them. *You* must have.'

Moses searched through the boxes and other gear in the back of the Land Cruiser while Walt watched the riverbank, his rifle at the ready. Eventually, Moses had to admit that the ammunition was not in the vehicle.

'We've been robbed,' he announced. 'Some *klefti-wallah* must have taken them.'

'What in hell is a *klefti-wallah?*'

'Sorry – it's a Swahili word for a *thief*. How many bullets have you got?'

'Ten – including the ones in here.' Walt tapped the rifle.

'This is not good. I think we should turn back.'

'Like Hell we do! We can share these.' He handed three bullets to Moses.

'If I'm going to follow and find the elephants, I should have more than three!'

Walt reluctantly handed him two more and sat in the driver's seat as Moses walked cautiously down the bank and onto the sandy riverbed, rifle at the ready.

Farther up the valley, Rafiki had also reached the dry riverbed, and urged the tembos to cross. Some wanted to dig in the sand for water but he forbade them, and said, 'We must hurry on.'

Temba Comfort and Temba Kindness were bringing up the rear, helping the smaller youngsters up the steep bank, when Rafiki had an idea. He called on the others to come back and join him.

'Rain is not far away,' he said. 'If we can call it down, the water might stop the four-by-four from crossing the river just long enough for us to get across the valley.'

'What about Tembo M'zee and his Shadow?' one of the mothers asked. 'They'll be on the wrong side.'

'They can wade across when the four-by-four is somewhere else. Let us all linque trunks.'

Some of the tembos had never called for rain before but all were ushered into circles by Rafiki and the Sisters, and shown how to linque.

'Now shut your eyes and think of rain. Nothing else – just rain – wet and cool – bringing life to the land.' Rafiki repeated the words he had learned at the Sacred Pool.

He had only ever done this before with Tembella Grace and the two Sisters. Now, there were many tembos all linqued. The riverside trees shook and the branches moved as though there was a strong wind blowing, yet the air was still. Over the distant hills, the lightning flashed more violently and when the trees grew quiet again they could all hear the rumble of thunder coming from that direction and feel the waves of low~sound it caused – but no rain fell around them.

'Try harder,' Rafiki demanded. 'Clear your minds. Think only of rain. Nothing else – just rain – wet and cool – bringing life to the land.'

The trees rustled again, even more violently, but still no rain came. Rafiki was now concerned. He had wasted too much time on the unsuccessful attempt to call down rain to stop the four-by-four crossing the riverbed. The vehicle had probably crossed over by now and would be on the same side as they were. The humans may even have discovered the trick played by the jostlers and be coming up *this* side of the river to head them off. Should he lead on across the open grassland where they would be in full view? Should they all turn back and join M'zee and Kidogo on the ridge? Or should he tell the others to hide in the trees along the riverbank where they were now? He knew he should have followed M'zee's instructions and hurried on across the valley – but to do this now might cause them all to be caught in the open.

He made his decision. 'Stay in the trees,' he told them.

Walt waited impatiently in the Land Cruiser for Moses to return. He considered getting a beer from the refrigerator in the back but decided not to get out while there were fierce elephants about. What was it Moses had called them? *Kali tembos*, that was it. He didn't want to face any *kali tembos* with only five bullets. Where was Moses? Noticing that Moses had left the ignition key in the lock he turned it, put the vehicle into gear and edged forward to where he hoped he could look down into the riverbed without getting out.

Close to the edge he turned parallel to the bank and switched off the engine. He was peering out of the window, trying to see Moses or the elephants, when the bank beneath the wheels suddenly crumbled and the Land Cruiser slid gently down into the bed of the river and came to rest lying on its side in the soft sand.

Walt swore and struggled to climb up and open the passenger-side door above him. Opening it upwards was far harder than he expected and his heart was pumping hard and erratically by the time he clambered out. He dropped down onto the sand, realising as he did so that he'd left his rifle in the cab.

He swore again, cursing *kali tembos*, Moses, *klefti-wallahs*, Africa and finally, his own stupidity before slumping down with his back against the remaining fuel cans strapped to the roof-rack. One of the cans was dripping fuel onto the sand but he was too exhausted to do anything about it.

Tembo Three Eyes had seen the Land Cruiser swerve in their direction. Clearly their ruse had worked and the humans believed they'd seen the tusks of Tembo Jay. He led the other two tembos into the trees and across the dry riverbed, making sure they left clear tracks in the sand. At the top of the far bank they stopped, put down the wooden tusks and listened. They heard the engine noise of the four-by-four getting louder, then stop.

'Be ready to take up the *tusks* and run towards the lake when I call,' said Three Eyes, moving to where he could peep through the trees. He watched the tall dark-skinned man come slowly down the far bank, holding a gun. He soon found their tracks and stood still, looking all about him.

Three Eyes stepped back out of the man's sight but trumped loudly to let him know they were nearby. He then ran to catch up with the other two jostlers as they trotted across the grassland towards the distant lake, avoiding the bends in the meandering riverbed. He was sure the humans would try and follow and he wanted to be far enough away from that gun for it not to be able to hurt them.

Once Moses had found the tracks and established that they led up the far bank, he knew he would have to find somewhere for the Land Cruiser to cross. Upstream looked most promising and he started to walk that way when he heard an elephant trump. With his nerves on edge, only five bullets for the rifle and an unpredictable hunter, he decided to go back to the vehicle and consider their options. He back-tracked, frequently glancing behind him, alert for any action by the elephants. He used a blasphemous word when he saw the vehicle lying on its side, and Walt Schwiner sitting with his back to the vehicle roof.

The fool of a man must have driven closer to the riverbank not realising that fast currents frequently undercut such banks in Africa during the rainy season.

'I'm sorry about this—' Walt started to say but Moses cut him short with a wave of his hand.

'We've got to get this upright – *fast*! Those elephants are not far away,' he said, going to the winch on the front bumper and releasing the snap-hook. 'Walk backwards, pulling this,' he growled at Walt who'd got to his feet, but Walt stood still, anxiously looking around and obviously reluctant to leave what cover the Land Cruiser provided.

'All right. Come and push these buttons while I do it. *That* one is for playing out – *this* one for hauling in.'

With the winches' electrical motor whining behind him, Moses walked away from the vehicle towards a tree lying halfway across the riverbed but with its roots still in the crumbled bank. He was carrying the snap-hook with its trailing steel cable in one hand and his rifle in the other. When he reached the tree, he called back to Walt to stop paying out the cable. Moses looked around carefully, could not see any elephants, so leaned the rifle against a branch of the tree and secured the wire with the snap-hook where he calculated that when the winch drew the cable back the vehicle would slide round and right itself.

M'zee, standing at his lookout point on the ridge, kept asking Kidogo to report what was happening. After she'd told him the four-by-four had turned to follow the jostlers into the trees by the riverbed, and he had sung to Rafiki to lead the others across the valley, there was not much for her to tell. She had seen the main herd reach the riverbed trees and was worried when they didn't emerge onto the open ground on the other side – but she didn't immediately tell M'zee that. Then she noticed the lightning flashes over the distant hills were making an almost continuous wall of light and could feel intense waves of tremulous low~sound rippling along the rocky ridge from the thunder in that direction. M'zee had felt it too and asked her where the herd was now.

Kidogo had to admit that they hadn't yet left the shelter of the trees, and M'zee immediately sang out a warning in low~sound.

'A flood may come ~ stay on high ground.'

But he was terribly afraid that his call would be lost in the waves of low~sound from the storm.

One of the females with a two-year-old baby had succumbed to her youngster's pleadings of thirst after the linquing and, disregarding Rafiki's instructions, she'd gone back down to the riverbed to dig for water.

She was scuffling at the sand with her front feet and moving the loose sand away with her trunk when she heard the rustling of dry leaves in the channel upstream from her. She stood and watched, fascinated, as a tongue of brown water crept towards her, filling each hollow in the sand and overflowing into the next.

All of a sudden, it was more than just an interesting trickle – the brown, searching snout of the floodwater swept past her and her youngster, the water rising rapidly, filling the various channels, and carrying not just leaves but also small dead branches and ragged bushes on its crest.

'Out! Get out,' she bawled at her young one, who was standing motionless as the water rose around him. She reached out her trunk and slapped his rump as a snake swam past, flushed out of its burrow by the flood. He turned and quickly followed his mother up the crumbling bank as another snake was swept past.

Moses had just secured the wire cable around the tree when, out of the corner of his eye, he caught sight of a tiny movement in the riverbed. A leaf lifted and fell back again. He turned his head and saw a sloping wall of brown water sweep around a bend and rush towards him, carrying all kinds of debris on its crest.

'Get up the bank!' he yelled to Walt, but the American was bending over the winch, having just pressed the 'haul in' button and did not hear him over the whine of the motor. The water was already up to Moses' knees as he reached up, grabbed a branch above his head and pulled himself up and out of the rushing water.

In a moment, the spate caught the Land Cruiser, lifted it upright, swung it round and swept it downstream, the cable tethering it to the tree jerked tight. Walt, caught off-guard by the suddenness of the flood, climbed up out of the water breaking around the bonnet, and scrambled onto the roof-rack where he grabbed at the frame and clung on as the vehicle bucked and rolled. Eventually, after the first rush had passed and the current settled into a more even flow, he was able to haul himself right out of the water and sit on the reserve fuel-cans, holding onto their recessed handles and desperately hoping the securing straps would hold.

Moses climbed up through the branches as the water rose, all the time aware that the tree was twisting under the rush of the water around its trunk and from the drag of the Land Cruiser tethered to it. Remembering Walt, he turned awkwardly to see what had happened to him.

The American was crouched on the roof-rack, the only part of the Land Cruiser still visible. Walt was staring in terror at the head of a spitting cobra which must have been washed downstream and was now sharing the roof-rack with him. The snake had reared up, ready to spit venom into the eyes of the man if he made the slightest move.

Watching the back of the cobra's head, Moses recalled that his first duty as a guide was to protect the client. He lowered himself from the branch into the rushing water and was swept downstream towards the vehicle. His legs struck the submerged bonnet and he fumbled for foot- and handholds as he climbed up onto it. Here, the rush of the water was less, and finding a handhold he reached forward to grab the snake just behind its head.

As Moses reached out, Walt raised his hand to protect his eyes, and the snake reared up and shot a jet of venom at his face. Moses' hand caught the snake too far down. It turned its head and spat another stream into *his* eyes. Blinded and in agony, Moses threw the snake as far as he could, lost his balance on the bonnet and was swept away downstream.

Walt, with one eye burning painfully, lost his grip on the secured fuel can and was swept along after Moses as the roots of the tree, to which the Land Cruiser was still secured by the cable, were torn out of the riverbank, and the floodwaters carried both tree and vehicle downstream behind the men.

The three jostlers reached the wide stretch of hard-packed mud surrounding the shrunken lake and stopped, breathless. Long-legged pink birds were wading in the shallow water but were sufficiently far away not to be disturbed by the sudden appearance of elephants. Three Eyes was beginning to feel a little foolish about running so far and now having no idea where the men and their four-by-four were.

An arm of the lake reached inland towards the riverbed and he walked across the caked mud towards the water, while Two Eyes and One Eye waited, still holding the wooden tusks. Three Eyes tasted the water but it was bitter and salty. He was about to turn away when he noticed it was being stained brown by water coming down the riverbed. He stepped backwards slowly as the water rushed ever faster into the lake and spread out across the mudflats. By the time he reached the other two jostlers on slightly higher ground, a torrent of floodwater was rushing out through the river mouth with uprooted trees and bushes swirling around in it as lightly as if they were mere twigs.

One Eye and Two Eyes had put down the wooden tusks and the three stood side by side watching the ever-increasing flow. At the height of the onrush the Land Cruiser floated into sight. It seemed to be connected in some way they could not see to an uprooted tree, and was washed out onto the now submerged mudflats, where it stood forlornly, draped with broken branches, as the brown floodwaters that had carried it there filled the lake.

'What do we do now?' Two Eyes asked.

'If the two humans are still alive they will be more interested in finding their four-by-four than chasing after these,' Three Eyes said, touching one of the wooden tusks. 'We'll leave them here and go back and find the other tembos. They may have crossed the river and be on this side.'

They'd not gone far when they saw three men on the riverbank upstream of them. A dark-skinned man was lying motionless on the ground above the tangle of debris left by the now receding floodwaters, and a pale-skinned man was sitting by his side. A third man, who was tall and dark-skinned, stood talking to the other two. The jostlers could not see any guns, although the tall man carried a long stick with a wide metal blade at one end. None of the men appeared to have seen the three jostlers so they turned slowly and walked in a wide semi-circle to avoid them before continuing up the riverbank in the hope of finding the other tembos had crossed safely.

Moses had a vague recollection of someone – and it must have been Walt – grabbing his shirt as he sank in the raging river, someone who'd held his head above the water until they were washed up against a bank, where he'd been hauled out, coughing and retching, onto the warm dry grass. He was completely blind and the pain in his eyes was intolerable but he kept silent, sure he could hear someone talking, even though the voice seemed to be coming from far away.

Someone – and he could have sworn it was his half-brother Sambeke – was saying in English, presumably to Walt, 'I thank you, Sir, for what you have done today. I saw it all.' Now he heard the voice speaking in Maasai, as though to him, 'Not such a coward after all, little brother. Not such . . .' but the voice faded as Moses coughed up more water before losing consciousness.

Rafiki was watching the water level recede when the jostlers appeared and excitedly told him what they'd seen. He agreed that the bad men were no longer an immediate threat to the tembos and, as soon as he was sure it would be safe for a large tembo to wade across, he called Boy and Girl to join him.

'M'zee will need to know we are all safe,' he said. 'He and his Shadow should come and join us and tell us what we should do now. Are you two willing to go back over the river and lead them to us here?'

CHAPTER TWENTY-FIVE

So far, De/ne's plan was working well. Lars and Ryan had slept soundly before he woke them with mugs of coffee. By not waking them early, he was sure he'd let the two *bad* men get far enough ahead in their gharri to make it unlikely that these *good* men could catch up with them today.

He had created another minor delay by demonstrating how he could talk with the elephants but after that, Lars had hurried breakfast, and driven off with Ryan next to him and De/ne seated on the bonnet, the Bushman once more directing him to follow the tracks of the elephants and the Land Cruiser.

Lars began to suspect that De/ne was not doing his best to find the tracks. On two occasions, although even *he* could see the tracks clearly ahead, the Bushman had signalled for him to stop the Land Rover while he made a pretence of searching. Lars was beginning to think of the little man as a *skelm*, a South African word for a rascal, a word he'd not used for many years. But why? What benefit could it be to the Bushman to delay them?

At noon, Lars called a break for cold drinks and a snack of biscuits and, as they prepared to move off, with Ryan driving, Lars said to De/ne, 'You can ride inside. I think I can follow the tracks over this easy ground from the front seat.'

De/ne didn't argue, but climbed into the back.

It was, as Lars had expected, easy enough to follow the tracks and direct Ryan. They were making better time when, an hour later, they approached a high rocky ridge that looked like difficult terrain to drive over. Lars told Ryan to turn to the right as the Land Cruiser's wheel-tracks veered that way.

After another half hour they came to the end of the ridge, followed the tracks round and into another valley. Ryan, turning sharply to avoid a klipspringer, drove through a patch of long grass. The nearside front wheel dropped into a warthog hole and the Land Rover's engine raced as the opposite rear wheel spun in the air.

He reached down to the lever that would lock the differential gears but it wouldn't move. He tried again and again but with no success.

They all got out and looked into the hole, then under the Land Rover.

'It'd be nice to be having a winch right now,' Ryan said. 'But it's the digging it'll have to be.'

'Has that lever stuck before?' Lars asked him.

'Only the once – but they were supposed to have fixed it when it was serviced in Nairobi.' He fetched the spade from the back of the vehicle.

When the vehicle was once again on level ground Ryan stowed the spade and they all enjoyed a cool beer while watching a storm raging around the hills to the south. When they moved off, across open grassland with a few scattered trees, De/ne was again perched on the bonnet, watching out for more warthog holes as well as following the tracks of the Land Cruiser.

It was mid-afternoon by the time they reached the bank of the river and found it to be in full flood. The brown torrent had filled the whole channel and was gnawing away at the bank where the Land Cruiser's tracks disappeared. The three men looked over the rushing water.

'They must have got across before this started,' Lars said. 'It could be a couple of days before this lot goes down enough for us to get across – although it might be easier upstream.'

As they drove between the riverbank trees, following the course of the river, they could see the water level was already falling but found nowhere that offered any chance of a safe crossing.

When they came upon elephant tracks leading to the bank where the herd had crossed, Ryan stopped and switched off the engine while De/ne went to examine them.

'All the elephants crossed here earlier today, except for the biggest one and a small female. I cannot find *their* tracks.' He took the plastic bottle out of his bag and drank deeply. 'I suggest we go farther upstream and camp until the water has gone down enough for us to cross.'

It seemed about the only choice they had and, with the three of them back in the Land Rover, Lars turned the ignition key. There was a small whirring noise, then silence. He tried once more but there was no response at all.

'Ominous!' he said and tried again with the same result. Ryan got out and opened the bonnet.

'The sodding battery must be flat and I had a new alternator fitted before I left Nairobi.'

'By the same guy who fixed your diff lock?' Lars asked him. 'Had you told him you were leaving Kenya to live in Tanzania?'

Ryan nodded glumly. 'We'll have to radio to Mr Burns and see if he can send out a four-by-four with a new battery.'

'And what do we need to make the radio work?' Lars asked with a touch of sarcasm in his voice.

Ryan grimaced. 'This is a fine mess I've got you into,' he said, mimicking Oliver Hardy. 'Anyway we'll have to camp here tonight.'

'And hope that the magic of synchronicity produces a fully-charged battery in the night!' There was more than a touch of sarcasm in Lars' comment.

Ryan wondered how this might materialize and decided what he would really like would be for a Land Rover to come up the track and tow them home. Home! Now would that be the Riverside Hotel or his dream cottage on the west coast of Ireland? It would be his cottage – with a dark-haired, smiling colleen waiting to welcome him, her face and bare arms tanned golden by the wind and the sun.

'Ryan? Ryan?' Lars voice seemed to come from far away.

After M'zee had sung his warning of the danger of a flood, there was little else he could do except wait on the top of the ridge and listen to Kidogo describe what she could see. Much of what was happening was hidden from her by the trees along the riverbank, but when she told him of glimpses of brown water between the trees it confirmed that a flood *was* sweeping downriver as he'd feared. The herd remained hidden by the trees but she had seen the three jostlers make their dash for the lakeside, and return less hurriedly up the other side of the flooded river to where the herd must still be. There was no sign of the bad men's four-by-four, nor of the men themselves, although she had seen another man emerge from the rocks beyond the river and walk into the trees towards where she had last seen the four-by-four. She reported this to M'zee and told him the man was wearing a red-coloured cloth around his body and was carrying a spear or perhaps a long stick.

Later, she reported seeing the same man walking down the far riverbank towards the lake *without* the stick, or spear, and not wearing any clothing.

'That is unusual,' M'zee remarked. 'Humans always want to cover their bodies in *some* way.'

Kidogo was feeling odd. A discomfort she'd not known before was suffusing her whole body and she put it down to the strain of the last few days. She moved away from M'zee and passed water, but only a small amount, having drunk so little recently. She was missing her friend Rafiki but also found herself thinking of that useless lump of a tembo, the one they called Lusty. He was so big, with good-sized tusks. Why was she thinking of him?

Preoccupied by her own strange feelings, she failed to notice the other four-by-four coming up the nearside of the river.

M'zee caught the scent of Kidogo's urine and groaned to himself. His Shadow was in joyneed and, although he knew she had no control over the timing of it, he realised that it complicated his whole plan. But what plan? His herd and the sacred tusks that had been entrusted to him were on the far side of a flooded river, as were the bad men who were trying to take them for themselves.

He had little knowledge of what was happening over there – and before very long it would be dark. Clouds were rolling down from the hills, so tonight there would not even be a moon. What a mess he had made of his Trust! *Mana help me*, he pleaded in his mind.

'I think it might be best if we went and joined the others,' Kidogo was saying. 'We can probably cross the river before it gets too dark.'

Walt had watched the Maasai man walk away, dignified even in his total nakedness. Between him and Moses lay the man's *shuka* cloak, his spear, his sheathed sword and a short stick with a round knob at the end. Walt tried to remember exactly what it was he had to tell Moses when he recovered consciousness.

'You are to give him these,' the man had said. 'I am on my way to be initiated as a junior elder. His courage in saving you from the snake has earned him the right to use them and be a warrior. One day – when our father is dead, he may come back to live amongst us – but not yet.' He had added that his brother and Walt must bathe their eyes every couple of hours with milk and said he would send a cow up to them as soon as he could.

Walt knew it was true what the man had said about his guide's courage. When Moses had distracted the snake's attention he had prevented all but a tiny portion of its venom reaching Walt's eyes and had taken the full force of the next jet in his own face. Walt felt his own actions, in saving Moses from drowning and giving him mouth-to-mouth resuscitation, had been merely an instinctive act due to his practising for the coveted Lifesaving Medal at the local swimming pool when he was a teenager. When the other Masaai man had appeared Walt felt somewhat embarrassed to be found giving Moses the kiss-of-life, and stopped doing it. But by that time he already knew his guide would be able to continue breathing on his own.

Feeling awful himself, he now needed to make a fire and dry their clothes. His left eye was hurting terribly and he wondered how long it would take for the promised cow to arrive.

The water level was up to their bellies as Tembo Boy and Temba Girl waded across the river on their way to report to M'zee. On the far side was a stationary four-by-four, near which two men were setting up a tent. A third, smaller, man was trying to attract the tembo's attention. He was bending forward, swinging his arm like a trunk and moving his ear with his other hand. Having lived with friendly humans for most of their lives, Boy and Girl had no fear of these three and stood watching the antics of the smallest one.

'He's speaking tembotalk,' Boy whispered to Girl. 'I've

never seen a human do that before!'

'He's telling us not to be afraid,' Girl whispered back. 'Shall I reply?'

'You can try,' Boy said. 'You may need to speak slowly.'

'We – are – not – afraid,' Girl said, making the words with her trunk and her voice. 'But we have never known a human who speaks the language of elephants.'

'I have lived amongst your kind all my life,' De/ne replied. 'It is not easy for me to do – with no trunk and only small ears – but I can converse a little. Did you see a *gharri* with two men in it on the other side of the river?' As he pronounced the word *gharri* De/ne whirled his 'trunk' hand to represent wheels.

'I think by *gharri* he must mean a four-by-four,' Temba Girl said to Boy.

Slowly, Temba Girl recounted to De/ne what the three jostlers had reported about the Land Cruiser and its two occupants, who no longer had any guns with them. She then told him that Temba Boy and herself were on their way to fetch their Leader and his Shadow.

De/ne signalled 'Fare well,' as the two elephants walked on. He was wondering how he might use them to further his plans as he turned to where Lars and Ryan were watching from beside the Land Rover. The Bushman straightened his back, took his hand away from behind his ear and spoke to them in English.

'Those two elephants told me the bad men's *gharri* is now far out in the lake and both men have had their eyes burned by a snake. One is otherwise well but his companion was nearly drowned. They do not have any guns with them now.'

'They must have met a spitting cobra,' said Lars. 'They'll need to have their eyes bathed in milk or they could lose their sight.' Then he added, 'How can we get across the river, De/ne?'

Despite the burning sensation in his left eye, Walt had collected enough dry wood to start a fire using his waterproof cigarette lighter. He was desperate for one of his cigars but they were now somewhere downriver, all soggy and ruined.

Moses had coughed up some water and was trying to sit up. 'You stay there, buddy,' Walt called to him. 'I've just made a fire to dry our clothes. *I'll* look after *you.*'

It was dark beyond the ring of firelight by the time Walt reckoned his woodpile was large enough to see them through the night. He hung his own wet clothes over the stacked wood and went to help Moses out of his. Once his guide's clothes were steaming in the heat from the flames Walt remembered the things the other Maasai man had left behind. He carried them over to where Moses sat and put them on the ground in front of him, then he took up the *shuka* and draped it around his shoulders.

Moses fingered the fabric and asked, 'Where did you get this?'

'A Maasai man left it for you. He asked me to tell you he was on his way to be made a junior elder. Then he said you had earned the right to be a warrior and to use the other things he's left for you . . . and that you can go back after your father is dead—'

Moses interrupted him, 'What *other things* did he leave?'

Walt guided Moses' hands to the spear, the sword and the knob-ended stick.

Moses felt along each of the weapons, concentrating on a deep notch on the blade of the spear. 'That man was my brother,' he said. 'Did he *really* say that, and leave these for me?'

'Sure did,' Walt replied.

'Where is he now?'

'He's gone to get a cow so we can bathe our eyes with milk.'

'Are you blind too?'

'I only got a tiny bit in one eye – thanks to *you*, Moses! How long will it be before the cow comes.'

Moses was silent, working out how far the nearest cattle would be at this time of year with the rains being late.

'Two days at best,' he replied, slowly getting to his feet. He tied the *shuka* in the proper way, over one shoulder and under the other, bent over and fumbled around to find the spear, then he stood upright, finding the point of balance in his hand.

Walt had never seen a prouder sight than this tall man standing before him in the flickering firelight.

Tembo Boy and Temba Girl had not gone far from the Land Rover when they met M'zee and Kidogo coming towards them in the fading light. Their greetings were swift.

'There are three humans down at the river, but they are friendly,' Girl said. 'We have spoken with them and they—'

'You have spoken with humans? Do *you* speak *their* language?' M'zee asked.

'No, one of them speaks tembotalk – slowly and not well, but enough for us to understand what he says. He seemed to understand what I said to him.'

M'zee shook his head. If humans and tembos really could talk to one another, how wonderful that would be for the future of both. But right now he had to ensure the herd was safe and that the bad men had not got the sacred tusks.

'Tell me all you know,' he said as they walked together towards the distant firelight that lit up the side of the Land Rover.

De/ne was waiting by the crossing place, clearly visible in the light from the fire.

He adopted his elephant stance and greeted M'zee. 'Love, live long and find sweet-water.'

'May Mana bless and keep you safe. Tembo Jay and goodness guide you.' M'zee replied, speaking in tembotalk rather than low~sound, which he knew humans couldn't hear. He was still unconvinced that this man could really understand what he was saying and said nothing more.

De/ne swung his arm-trunk into the *request* position and said, 'We need to help the other men. Will you carry us across the river?'

'Why would *you* wish to help them? They are bad men who kill tembos and want to steal our ivory.'

'Their eyes have been harmed by poison from the mouth of a snake. They need our help. If you help *us*, we promise they will go back to where they live and not harm you – nor take your ivory.'

'I have heard only bad things about the promises made by humans.' As M'zee spoke, he saw Lars and Ryan standing back in the shadows. 'Tell *those* men to step forward to where I can see them,' he commanded.

De/ne interpreted for Lars and Ryan. 'The chief of these elephants wants to see you. Please step forward slowly, keeping your hands clearly in front of you and carry nothing.'

Ryan whispered to Lars, 'I'm sure that these are the jumbos who pulled the tusks up from the cave on Kili.'

At the same time Kidogo was whispering to M'zee. 'They are the men who had made the sacred ivories ready for us on Holy Mountain.'

M'zee scented the air. He had already begun to suspect the same thing, and their scents confirmed it.

'My Shadow and I have met these men before and we trust them,' he told De/ne. Collect together whatever you need to take across the river and we will carry you all.'

De/ne translated this to Lars and Ryan, and suggested they take one pack each containing a little food, some cooking utensils, their sleeping bags and the First Aid kit. He turned and said something to M'zee in tembotalk while Lars and Ryan took the tent down and bundled it onto the front seat of the Land Rover before filling their backpacks.

When they were ready, Boy and Girl knelt, and were copied by Kidogo.

'What about the fire?' Lars asked De/ne.

'The chief of the elephants will see to that,' he replied and climbed nimbly from Kidogo's leg up onto her back, carrying just his small leather bag. Lars and Ryan, with their Bergen backpacks, followed his example rather less expertly. Lars climbed up onto Boy, and Ryan onto Girl.

As soon as the humans were in position, the three elephants rose to their feet.

Ryan called to De/ne, 'What do we hold onto?'

'If you have to, hold the top of their ears – but gently. They are very sensitive.'

M'zee walked to the river, drew up a trunkful of water, returned and dowsed the fire, then with him leading through the darkness and testing the depth at every step, they crossed the river and rested at the top of the bank.

Lars spoke towards where he thought De/ne would be. 'How can we ask these elephants to take us to where the *baddies* are?'

Kidogo, Boy and Girl all understood the question and Kidogo told M'zee what had been said.

'I will find the herd. You three carry the men where they want to go. Then come and find the herd. Fare well.'

The three elephants walked northwards, guided by the sound of running water to their right. They travelled in single file with Boy in the lead, his trunk outstretched ahead of him to feel for any obstacles in the darkness. Girl held onto his tail with her trunk and suggested to Kidogo that she hold onto hers.

When Tembo Boy eventually spotted firelight ahead he paused and the others came alongside him.

'Should we leave the humans here?' he asked Kidogo.

'I think it would be wise,' she replied. 'They may still have guns with them. The three humans we have carried can walk from here. They only have to go towards the firelight.'

She knelt down and De/ne leaped from her back. Lars and Ryan followed him as the other two elephants also knelt. Ryan was rubbing the inside of his thighs. 'I never was good at doing the splits,' he said, and turned to say some kind of 'thank you' to the elephants – but they had already melted away silently into the night.

Walt got up and threw more wood onto the fire. The state of excitement from the day's events had worn off and his eye was now throbbing with pain and his left eyelid was so swollen he couldn't see out of it. He felt cold despite his dry clothes, and was starting to imagine animals creeping up on him in the darkness. He was sure he could hear *kali tembos* and hungry lions all around him. He tried to pick up the spear the Maasai had left but Moses' hand was gripped tightly around the shaft, even though he appeared to be fast asleep. Perhaps he was unconscious again. What if the man died in the night?

Walt went to throw another log on the fire but hesitated, unsure now if he had collected enough to last right through the night – the pile seemed to be shrinking very fast. Suppose he ran out of wood before it was light – the lions were bound to attack him then.

There was a movement in the darkness – he was sure of it. He retreated round the fire to put it between him and whatever it was out there.

'Hello. Hello?' a voice called in English.

'Hello,' he replied, shaking with relief as two white men and a Bushman walked into the firelight.

Lars went past him and knelt beside Moses, feeling for his pulse. Ryan tidied the fire, pushing half-burnt logs towards the centre, while De/ne walked around the perimeter of the fire-lit area, listening.

Walt collapsed by the fire, and Ryan opened his backpack and took out his unzipped sleeping bag to spread over the man where he lay.

'How's *he* doing?' he asked Lars, pointing at Moses.

'His eyes look terrible but his pulse is strong. Can you get my sleeping bag for him? All the training manuals say one should bathe patient's eyes with milk when they have been hit by cobra venom.'

'I don't suppose powdered milk is any good?' suggested Ryan. 'I've got some of that.'

'I shouldn't think so.'

Walt's voice came weakly from under the sleeping bag. 'There was a Maasai man here. I think he was my guide's brother. He has gone for a cow. But Moses said it would take two days at least. I'm hungry – do you have any food with you?'

Ryan had prepared a meal of soup and biscuits and had boiled water for hot drinks before they noticed that De/ne was not with them.

'Where's that *skelm* gone now?' Lars asked.

'You don't trust him, do you?'

'Not entirely. He seems to have his own agenda.'

'Don't *we*? Although I've never been sure just what it is. He'll be back. Coffee or tea?'

It was getting light when De/ne returned, carrying his plastic water-bottle full of milk, which he held out to Lars.

Lars looked at him hard, took the bottle and immediately started to bathe Moses' swollen eyes, using a pad of cotton wool from the First Aid box. Ryan did the same with Walt's left eye.

De/ne sat by the embers of the fire, smoking a cigar. Walt smelled the smoke, pushed Ryan's hand away and sat up.

'Where did you get that?' he demanded.

De/ne took the cigar from his mouth and examined it. 'It came from a man who drove past me so fast that I was covered in the dust of the road. Would you like one? They are very good cigars indeed!'

'You thieving little bastard!'

'Steady now,' Ryan said, putting his hand on Walt's arm. 'He walked all through the night to get this milk for your eye.' And turning to De/ne, he asked, 'Where *did* you find a cow in the night?'

'It is not the milk of a cow. I was given it by an elephant.'

CHAPTER TWENTY-SIX

M'zee, who had followed the scents of the other tembos through the night and rejoined the herd, was pleased to find the Sisters had prepared many food-wads for him, and he swallowed them hungrily. Rafiki asked him where Kidogo was, and when he was told she'd gone north towards the lake with Boy and Girl, carrying humans on their backs, he asked M'zee if he could go to find her.

'You may,' M'zee replied. 'But she should be here with us by dawn.' Then he led Rafiki to one side and whispered, 'She is in joyneed. You and I will need to guard her. Tembo Lusty and several of the other tembulls, possibly even the jostlers, will try to joyn with her and that would not be good. It will cause rivalry and maybe even fighting. We must not allow that to happen.'

Rafiki hurried away into the darkness, horrified at the thought of Tembo Lusty, or any other tembull, joyning with his Kidogo. With little wind and no moonlight he wandered about for most of the night before he caught the scent of the humans' fire and approached it cautiously. Kidogo was not there but, as he circled the camp, he found the scent of the three tembos and followed it back towards the herd. Kidogo's normal scent was overlaid with a lighter tantalising odour that made him shiver with excitement. But there was something in Tembo Boy's scent that told Rafiki that Boy, too, was excited by Kidogo's condition. He hurried on to catch up with her.

It was beginning to get light when he finally glimpsed

Boy's tail between the trees ahead of him. As he got nearer he could see that Boy was close behind Kidogo, his trunk stretched out towards her as she hurried along behind Temba Girl. Rafiki trumped to catch her attention and she wheeled round past Boy and galloped to his side.

'Stay by me,' she whispered. 'Tembo Boy won't leave me alone.'

When a dull dawn broke over the camp, De/ne put the last of the wood on the fire and woke Lars and Ryan. They had slept wrapped in their emergency survival sheets since their sleeping bags still covered 'the baddies' as Ryan now referred to Walt and Moses.

'Gentlemen,' De/ne addressed Lars and Ryan. 'Today the rains will fall here and not just in the hills. Farther up this valley is a shelter that is used by the Maasai herdsmen when the grass is good and they graze their cattle here. It was once a home for *my* people before the Maasai came. We should go to this place now. I will make coffee while you prepare *the baddies* for the walk.'

Lars woke a grumbling Walt and a silent Moses, and he and Ryan again bathed their eyes with elephant's milk warmed by the fire.

'We are going to move up the valley to a rock shelter before the rain starts,' Lars told them. 'De/ne will lead, Ryan and I will carry the gear, and you, Mr Schwiner, are to lead Moses and take care of him.'

'*Walt.* Call me *Walt.* Look, I'm sorry to have gotten you into this mess. We were very lucky you two chanced along. I'll see you OK when we get back to Arusha.'

'It was no chance—' Ryan started to say but Lars glared at him to shut up, and they began walking in the direction De/ne had pointed out as he made sure the fire was safely doused.

They walked between scattered groups of trees and rocky outcrops, frequently disturbing small herds of zebra who ran a short distance braying wildly before curiosity overcame them and they turned to watch the five men pass by in single file, the last one walking with his hands on the shoulders of the man in front of him. Antelope virtually ignored the men, just trotting a short distance away, then resuming their grazing on the dry grass.

After walking for about three hours, with occasional rests, De/ne told them, 'The elephants are waiting for us at the shelter.'

'Is that good or bad?' Ryan asked.

'I will find out,' De/ne replied, and signalling them to stop he walked forward.

'What in hell is he doing?' Walt asked. 'Is he mad. Those are *kali tembos* – fierce elephants.'

M'zee had just arranged for all the tusks to be brought together into the rock shelter the jostlers had found. With the rains imminent and good browsing available on the riverside trees, he thought it would be wise for them to rest here for a while. The *bad* men down by the lake could not harm them now that they no longer had guns. And he was also sure that the *good* men, who had helped with the tusks of Tembo Jay on the mountain, would keep the bad ones away from his herd.

But now he could see all of them, including the little man who could speak tembotalk, coming straight towards where all the tusks were stored. He moved forward, head up and trunk raised defensively. The little man stopped, bent forward, put a hand behind one of his ears, swung his other arm like a trunk and spoke to him.

'Love, live long and find sweet-water.'

'May Mana bless and keep you safe. Tembo Jay and

goodness guide you.' M'zee replied, once more intrigued to meet a human with whom he could talk, and who also knew the correct form of greeting.

De/ne spoke again. 'Two of the men behind me are those who tried to harm you and your fellow tembos. They are sorry for this now and would like to thank you for the milk given by one of your tembas to heal the hurt to their eyes. The other two men are known to you as good and kind. They have told me how they found the special tusks on Holy Mountain and prepared them for you to carry away. I know – but they do not – where you are taking them, for my family have been friends to the tembos at the Place of Peace since the days when the Yellow Tusks were frustrated by the Love of Tembo Jay.'

M'zee did not respond immediately. This man seemed to know more than *he* did about their journey. He had not heard any tembo speak of the Place of Peace since he had been ousted from his family by his mother, Tembella Grace, so long ago. Was the Place of Peace real or just somewhere in a tembo legend? He reached into deep memory and recalled his mother telling him it was where tembos used to go to step-over, a place where their tusks would be safe. He had not really believed it to be true, because most of the tembos he'd known were killed before they were old enough to step-over with dignity, and their tusks had been taken only-Mana-knows-where.

Perhaps the little man was right. M'zee, and the other tembos with him, were carrying many tusks to *somewhere*. What better place than the Place of Peace, where these tusks would be safe? It all made sense now.

He made the sideways flick of his trunk that meant, 'Say more,' and waited.

The little man continued in tembotalk. 'Soon, the rains will come. Humans do not have thick skins like tembos and will chill and die if they sleep in the rain. I have brought these people here to where my people, the First People of Africa, have sheltered from the rains from the beginning of time until the tall men came with their cattle. I have seen that you have placed your ivories in our shelter, and these humans have no wish to disturb them. It is a large shelter and there is plenty of space for all.'

M'zee answered, 'How can I trust you? It is the experience – the painful experience – of tembos for many generations that most humans are greedy for our ivory and arrogant in believing that they have more right to it than we do.'

De/ne replied. 'What you say is true. But two of these men with me are *good* men, and known to you as such. One of the others has no sight and the other is from far away over the sea and is afraid of Africa's ways. *They* can do no harm. As for myself – I can give you directions to the Place of Peace and the guardian tembo there can tell you that I speak the truth about myself and the First People.'

As De/ne said this, rain started to fall and he made the signal with his trunk-arm that asked for a decision.

What he had said seemed fair to M'zee – and he *was* obligated to the two men who had done so much to recover the tusks of Tembo Jay on Holy Mountain, so he signalled his assent and stepped back to allow the humans to pass.

De/ne led them into the shelter of the overhanging rock. It was high enough even for elephants to walk under and there was plenty of room for him to choose a place, away from the stacked tusks, for Lars and Ryan to unpack and spread their gear. Walt found a rock for Moses to sit on and wrapped Lars' unzipped sleeping bag around the Maasai's shoulders.

'Thank you,' Moses murmured.

De/ne left the shelter and walked fearlessly among the elephants to find M'zee, who was talking with Kidogo and

Rafiki. He saluted the old elephant, adopted his talk stance and said, 'My companions are cold and need a fire. There are some little pieces of wood in the shelter – but that will not last long and soon the dead trees which are out in the open will be wet from the rains. May I ask if some of your fellows will be so good as to collect more for us?'

M'zee spoke. 'It will be but little effort for us to do that. But, I must ask that you keep the fire small and away from the ivories. Some tembos fear fire but *I* know it is essential to the wellbeing of humans. While others collect the trees for you, I wish to hear the directions to find the Place of Peace.'

He turned to Kidogo and said, 'All tembos who are not mothers with babies are to find a dead tree and bring it to where the humans are taking shelter. The wood is to feed their fire. Please tell them this.'

Kidogo left his side, closely followed by Rafiki. Not far away, Tembo Lusty was waiting for her. As she walked towards a group of tembos to pass on M'zee's instructions, she was surprised by Lusty coming up behind her and trying to mount her. She was equally surprised that part of her wanted to accept him, while another part was screaming, 'No, No!'

Rafiki was in no doubt what to do. Using his single tusk he prodded viciously at Lusty's rump, causing him to bellow, 'You keep out of this, you one-tusked runt!'

M'zee heard the commotion and trundled over towards them.

Tembo Lusty faced him. 'This is nothing to do with *you*, Old Fellow,' he bawled.

M'zee's heavy trunk snaked out and struck him a stinging blow across the tender upper part of his right ear. '*Everything* that happens here is to do with me,' he replied coldly.

'Fancy the little one for yourself, do you?' Lusty sneered.

M'zee's trunk snaked out again, this time to Lusty's left ear.

'Now is *not* the time and this is *not* the place. Recognise that or leave us,' M'zee hissed. 'And, as to your last rudeness, Temba Kidogo is kin to me.'

Tembo Lusty turned and stalked off between the silent elephants.

Lars was doing a stock-check of what they had brought with them from the Land Rover. 'Did you say it would take two days for your brother to bring the cow?' he asked Moses, who was sitting silently on the rock ledge.

Moses, who was wearing his brother's shuka and gripping the spear and the knob-ended *rungu*, did not answer immediately and when he did, it was as though his voice came from far away.

'I do not expect my brother to return. He will send a boy with the cow,' he replied. 'It will be at least two days more.'

'We have food for three days,' Lars told Ryan. 'But we could do with more things from the Land Rover. Are there any blankets in it?'

'I packed some spare ones in case we ended up on the High Lands.'

'We could use those and more clothes. Water's OK – see how the rain trickles off that rock – we can catch that. Would you go with De/ne down to the river and see if it's safe to cross on foot. If not, he may be able to work his magic with the elephants again. I'll look after things here while you two go back to the Land Rover.'

Lars stood up as the first of the elephants arrived, dragging a whole dead tree, which he left under the extreme outer lip of the overhanging rock. Many more followed during the time Ryan and De/ne were away. Lars chopped off branches with the *panga* and built a generous fire to dry their clothes when they got back.

Ryan returned alone, riding on the back of an elephant whose name De/ne had told him was *Girl*. He had brought a bundle containing the spare blankets and other things to make their stay in the rock shelter more comfortable.

Lars walked down from the camp to meet Ryan out of earshot of Moses and Walt. 'Where's De/ne?' he asked.

'He's gone on down the riverside, riding an elephant he says is called *Boy* to find out where the Land Cruiser ended up. I thought we might be able to get its battery out and fit it into the Land Rover. Then we can leave the elephants to do what they have to – and we can get Walt back to Arusha. I expect Moses will want to go to his own people.'

'Good thinking,' said Lars. 'Have you worked out a Plan B if the battery's no good?'

'Not yet I haven't. That can be *your* job!'

'So, what's Plan B then?' Ryan asked Lars when De/ne returned two hours later, riding Boy, and told them the Land Cruiser was slowly sinking into the lake bed. Only the top of the roof-rack and the spare fuel cans were visible when they found it.

'I suppose we'll have to walk out, once Moses' people have collected him. Unless De/ne can persuade the elephants to carry us.'

Moses, who had been listening, said, 'I cannot go to my people yet. I will stay *here* with the cow until my eyes are better.'

'We can't leave you on your own, Moses,' Ryan said at once. 'Anyway, how will your people know you are up here?'

'They'll just follow our tracks – but they will guess we would be here in the shelter.'

'We don't have to decide anything more today,' Lars

pointed out. 'Let's just make a good meal and have a warm night. Heaven knows, thanks to the jumbos we've enough wood now to last us a month.'

After Lusty had been humiliated by M'zee, he walked down to the river, furiously pushing over any tree he thought would yield to his massive bulk. He splashed through the water and stumbled up the far bank, now slippery where the water had receded. Beyond it, he saw the humans' four-by-four and lunged at it, piercing one of the doors with his tusk. Still angry, he deliberately punctured each of the tyres in turn, and in a final savage act he succeeded in turning it completely over onto its roof.

Three nights later, crossing the road from Arusha to Nairobi, he was hit a glancing blow by a truck even larger than he was, and died by the roadside. By the time it was light and the vultures had begun to gather for their feast, his tusks had been hacked out and commenced their long and illicit journey to Japan.

313

CHAPTER TWENTY-SEVEN

The long-awaited rains were falling in the volcanic caldera known to the First People and to countless generations of elephants, as the Place of Peace.

Two young women bent over the ground they had cleared of last year's weeds and had then laboriously cultivated by digging with pointed sticks. The warm rain ran from their naked bodies as they pushed the individual mealie seeds into the carefully spaced holes and pressed the soil down with deft movements of their feet.

Like their mother before them they had skin of a delicate apricot colour and their faces had the same high cheekbones and almost oriental eyes but, unlike her, they were tall and willowy, genes which had evidently been inherited from their late father, Mr James Fotheringay.

Occasionally, the women spoke to each other, sometimes in the click language they'd learned from their mother and their grandfather, De/ne, but more often in the English they had learned from their father.

The clouds had retreated to the rim of the crater and the sun had broken through by the time they'd finished the planting and were walking back towards the rock shelter that had been the home of their ancestors.

'Grandfather said he'd be back *before* the rains came,' said the woman whose Bushman name was D/aw/a but who her father had always called *Sarah*.

'What do we do if he *doesn't* come back?' asked her twin sister Lo//te, who their father had always called *Ruth*.

'He'll be back. He promised that. And he will bring men to give us babies – *good* men, like our father.'

They stopped where a little stream ran over flat rocks, which were pitted with deep, round hollows. They washed their hands and feet, and let the sun dry off the water as they sat on the warm rocks and shook out their waist-length brown hair. Sarah combed out Ruth's hair with a wooden comb that lived in a dry hollow under a stone, before plaiting it into a single, long tail. Then she changed places with her sister and let Sarah comb hers and plait it into two tails.

They left the stream and walked up to the rock shelter that was their home. Ruth stirred the ashes of the fire into life and set two cobs from the previous year's crop of mealies to roast on the hot stones.

A flying ant, heavy with the eggs that would start a new colony, dropped near Sarah's feet as she stared out over the brown floor of the caldera to the steep crater wall beyond. She looked down and watched as the fat creature bit off its wings and searched for some suitable crevice in which to start a new nest.

'The ants are flying,' she told Ruth. 'When we've eaten the mealies we'll collect a basketful for supper.'

Several days' walk away, their grandfather De/ne was sitting in a similar shelter, reassessing his plans. His expedition to 'civilisation' to find mates for his granddaughters had been a bitter disappointment until, having given up and started his return journey, Mantis had delivered Lars and Ryan into his hands.

The elephants, and the men who pursued them, had been an unexpected complication. He was glad the tembos were once again finding their way to their Place of Peace – but the Maasai and the white hunter were just a nuisance. He must get rid of *them* without losing Lars and Ryan. If they all went together to the Place none could ever leave – and four men and just two women wouldn't work.

The Maasai could probably be persuaded to go back to his own people – so that would be him out of the way.

The white hunter from America was quite old compared with the two *good* men so he might not be such a problem. If he did go with them to the Place then he would have to be prevented from ever leaving, just as Mr Fotheringay had been.

Lars and Ryan were again bathing the eyes of the *baddies* with fresh, warm, elephant's milk De/ne had acquired earlier. Nothing could be done until the Maasai cow arrived and hopefully Moses would go away with whoever brought the cow. His plans would just have to wait until then.

His granddaughters would be wondering at his not having returned by the start of the rains – but they were quite safe in the Place of Peace. He reached into his skin bag and took out the tiny radio he had bought from the man in Arusha.

Lars and Ryan both turned their heads sharply when the sound of African beat music filled the space under the overhanging rock.

'What have you got—?' Lars started to ask, saw De/ne hold up the radio, and shook his head.

'I thought we'd left all that behind,' he said.

De/ne looked disappointed, turned off the radio and put it back in his bag.

M'zee stayed within sight of the tusks in the shelter, keeping Kidogo close by him. In her condition she might attract unwelcome attention from any one of the tembulls, especially those in a state of mustdo. Rafiki stayed nearby, too, but kept discretely just behind M'zee's tail.

With Tembo Lusty out of the way and probably heading back to Amboseli, the tembos most likely to prove a nuisance were the three jostlers. The little man had offered to give him directions to the Place of Peace where he had told him that the guardian tembo would speak for the little man's honesty. If the jostlers were to go *there*, it would ensure they were out of the way of temptation until Kidogo's joyneed had passed. That was a good idea!

M'zee swallowed several of the food-wads that the Sisters regularly prepared for him from the new leaves sprouting on the riverside trees, then spoke to Kidogo.

'Can you get the little man to come and speak to me?' he asked her. 'But keep within my sight.'

Kidogo circled around and approached the end of the shelter where the humans had their fire. De/ne noticed her immediately, and she beckoned him over with her trunk. De/ne jumped down from the ledge where he'd been squatting and went to her. She held out her trunk, took his hand with it and they walked hand in trunk to M'zee.

'He's here,' she said.

M'zee spoke slowly to ensure he was not misunderstood. 'You said you would give me directions to the Place of Peace so that the guardian tembo there could speak for you.'

De/ne adopted his tembotalk attitude and replied, 'That is true. The way is known to me. It is to the west of here.'

M'zee's ears came forward. West was the direction they had been taking to *follow the tired sun*. It boded well. He called over his shoulder to Rafiki to fetch the three jostlers.

When they had come and were standing facing him, M'zee said, 'You have all proved your worth, and I now have a new task for you. Listen and learn from this man who will tell you the way to the Place of Peace. I want you to go to this place and speak to the guardian tembo there. Ask the guardian if this man is a *good man* and can be trusted.'

De/ne turned towards the jostlers and spoke in tembotalk. 'The Place of Peace is three tembodays' walk to the west of here. Youngsters like yourselves may do the journey in two

317

days if you do not spend too much time feeding. Follow the tired sun through much flat land with many biting flies. When you reach a high, steep bank, at the foot of which are springs of fresh water, you must follow ancient tembo-paths to the top. The air is clearer there and cooler. Once more, follow the tired sun until you come to a *fire-hill* covered in trees from which a stream flows through a gorge that was cut by the waters. There, you will meet the guardian tembo. Speak of me to him,' said De/ne, 'then return to your chief here and tell him what the guardian has told you.'

'Repeat those directions to me, Three Eyes,' said M'zee, and the young jostler did so, faultlessly.

'May we leave *now*?' he asked eagerly.

'You may.'

As one, the three jostlers wheeled round and trotted off towards the west.

M'zee signalled to De/ne, who was watching the departing jostlers. 'I have an apology to make on behalf of we tembos. I sent a tembull away in disgrace, and it has been reported to me that he has vented his anger on the four-by-four across the river. It now lies on its back – dead. For this, his action, I offer my regrets.'

De/ne walked back towards the fire, thinking.

The jostlers hurried along, glad to have another important job to do and relieved to be away from the melee of mothers and babies. Three Eyes was also glad to be away from the scent of Kidogo's joyneed, which he found to be disturbingly attractive. He had no wish to be treated in the same way as M'zee had treated Tembo Lusty.

Biting flies troubled them, as the little man had said they would – flies that seemed to know their ears were the best place to drink their blood. But the tembos hardly slowed their pace, heading towards the setting sun until clouds came over and rain started to fall. Three Eyes called a halt for them to forage near a stream which he guessed would be fed by springs flowing from the foot of the high, steep bank they had occasionally glimpsed ahead of them.

Walt's eye had responded well to the regular bathing with elephant milk but there was no such improvement for Moses. His eyes, which had taken the snake's venom at close range, stayed closed behind swollen eyelids. He sat, immobile and silent, wearing the *shuka* and wrapped in Lars' sleeping bag with the sword, spear and *rungu* close at hand. He ate what was put into his hands but seemed withdrawn and apprehensive.

In the morning, on the day Moses had predicted someone would come with a cow, a voice was heard calling in the language of the Maasai, using Moses' birth name. Moses stood up and called back to him, also in Maa.

Shortly after this a boy of about twelve came into the shelter, ignoring the watching elephants. He carried just a stick, and a brown gourd decorated with zigzag patterns. He and Moses spoke for some time before Moses slipped off the *shuka*, folded it and handed it, together with the spear, sword and *rungu* to the boy, who then left, leaving only the gourd propped against the rock near Moses' feet.

In the silence that followed, Walt took Moses' safari clothes to him, laid them on the rock at his side and guided his hands down to them. Moses dressed slowly.

'I am *still* an outcast,' he said. 'My brother told the elders of what I had done in the river – but they were unmoved. I will never be a true Maasai. *Never.* And they would not send a cow,' he added.

Walt picked up the gourd and put it into Moses' hand. 'The boy left this,' he said.

Moses pulled out the wooden stopper and smelled it, then

stood up and felt his way to the end of the rock shelter. Here he poured the contents of the gourd onto the bare earth.

'What was that?' Walt asked him when Moses had felt his way back to the ledge and sat down.

'Saroi – it is milk mixed with the blood of a cow. A staple food for Maasai people. It was a gift from the boy – but I am now *not* a Maasai.' He tossed the empty gourd towards the crackling flames of the fire.

Walt stopped it rolling into the fire with his foot, picked it up, smelled it, then quietly rinsed it out with some of the rainwater they had collected, thinking that Moses might like to keep the gourd when he was feeling better.

As the sun rose on the following day, Kidogo felt less excited. What she now realised was her joyneed had abated in the night and she no longer felt that to joyn with a tembull was the most important thing to be done.

M'zee was still asleep, rocking gently on his feet. As usual, Rafiki was close by. The Sisters were down by the river collecting foliage and chewing it into food-wads for M'zee, while the other tembos and tembas were spread widely across the valley, either feeding or suckling their babies. Later, most of them would gather at the river to bathe. Perhaps M'zee would let Kidogo join in today as, thankfully, she would no longer be so attractive to the tembulls.

Rays from the sun were lighting up the new shoots of grass that were giving a green glow to the whole valley floor. The trees were all much greener, too, and the birds were fluttering from ground to tree and tree to tree, carrying wisps of grass to build their nests, constantly chattering and calling as they did so.

Kidogo had watched the young man come to the shelter, and then depart carrying the things that had been given to the man they called Moses. And now Moses was once more wearing the same kind of clothes as the other humans. She did not understand it, but it was *hapana shauri ango,* as her keepers would have said back at the orphanage in Nairobi – *not my affair.* All that seemed a very long time ago.

The jostlers had restarted their journey before the sun was up. They drank from the sweet water of the stream and followed it as far as the springs that gushed out where the ground rose sharply. What had seemed to be just a steep bank from a distance, now seemed to be a formidable obstacle. Above a slope of fallen rocks, the scarp rose almost sheer, some of it covered with clinging trees while in other places it was just bare rock with a few stunted trees growing from cracks and crevices.

'There *must* be a way up,' Three Eyes said. 'The little man wouldn't have sent us this way if there wasn't.'

After some searching, they found a track that zigzagged up the scarp, turning between rocks which had been stained a dark grey by the rubbing of generations of passing elephants. Wherever a tree grew that could be grasped to haul a tembo higher, the bark was smooth and polished by the grip of many trunks.

There was little cover from the sun as the jostlers climbed the steep, narrow path and, when they eventually reached the top, they rested, ears wide, in the shade of a tree, and enjoyed a cooling breeze that blew along the ridge.

'M'zee's going to have a problem if he tries to get up here,' One Eye remarked. 'Some of those rocks were very close together!'

After a short while Three Eyes urged them on. The air was fresher here and they passed through lush grasslands, green from the recent rains, past a place where a stream disappeared into a hole in the ground. Far ahead was the unmistakeable outline of what the little man had called a 'firehill' and they made their way towards it, following the stream until another, lesser, rock wall loomed ahead of them. Three Eyes led the way along a little used path beside the stream, walking out of the sunshine and into the shadow of a deep gorge through the rock. Here, every sound was magnified. The clatter from any loose stone kicked by a careless foot echoed from the steep walls and the splashing of water falling over rock ridges in the stream seemed to fill their ears.

'I don't like this place,' One Eye whispered.

'**Stand where you are!**' an unseen voice suddenly trumped.

The three jostlers stopped and huddled together, looking around them fearfully.

A trunk emerged from a cave in a sidewall, followed by the head and body of an ancient tembo whose huge bulk blocked the path ahead, his ivories almost sweeping the ground.

'I am Tembo Guardian – the keeper of the Place of Peace. Name yourselves.'

'Love, live long, and find sweet-water,' Three Eyes replied, his voice shaky. 'We are known as The Three Jostlers, Tembo One Eye, Tembo Two Eyes and myself, Tembo Three Eyes.'

'*Three* Eyes?' Tembo Guardian asked.

'An old joke – no longer funny.'

'What is your business here? You are too young to have come to step-over in the Place of Peace, yet you do not bring free ivory.'

'We have been sent by our leader, M'zee, to ask if you know of a little human, who calls himself, De/ne.'

'He is a good friend to me. His family and mine have shared duties here for many generations. The daughters of his daughter are waiting for him to return. What of him?'

Three Eyes told the guardian all he knew about De/ne and the other men and about M'zee and the other tembos bringing many free tusks, including those of Tembo Jay.

Tembo Guardian was clearly moved by this news. 'The tusks of *Tembo Jay*! Just let me read *those* ivories for a day and I could step-over with no regrets.'

'So,' Three Eyes said. 'We can report that the little man, known as De/ne, *is* a good man?'

'You may indeed. I look forward to his return and the coming of your leader, M'zee and his companions with the tusks of the blesséd Tembo Jay. Fare well.'

The jostlers did a shuffling turn on the narrow path and made their way out of the gorge and back into the sunshine.

Rafiki, knowing that nothing was likely to happen before the jostlers returned, asked Kidogo if she would show him *reading*. Not feeling that the time was right for this with the tusks all stacked in the shelter with the humans and feeling tired in her brain, Kidogo suggested instead that they might walk down to the river and view the 'dead' four-by-four. She went to M'zee and asked his permission to go with Rafiki.

M'zee, aware that he had been taking up all his Shadow's time and attention for a long time, agreed, relieved that he could relax his guard on her now that her period of joyneed was past.

As the two friends walked down to the river, Kidogo told Rafiki about the whale's song Lonely had sung to them on that memorable night before he'd been shot. She decided not to tell him Lonely had been killed by the white hunter who was in the shelter, although she suspected he would already have guessed.

'The song was wonderful,' she told him. 'I thought we tembos knew something about Mana – but the song went much further than even our knowledge. I wish I could remember it all.'

She sang snatches of it that had caught in her memory during Lonely's singing, and apologised for not remembering more of it.

'Could it be *read* from Tembo Lonely's tusks?' Rafiki asked, eagerly.

'I've been wondering about that,' Kidogo replied. 'But I have only ever found scenes in the tusks, never sounds.'

'Then is the whale's song lost for ever like the *Song of Tembo Jay* which the Sisters told us had been lost?' Rafiki asked.

'I can't believe Mana would wish that. Perhaps other whales know the song too. The whale also told Tembo Lonely a prophecy, and I remember that.

When the stone mount ~ breathes fire and smoke,
Mana will ask ~ a Gift of Love.
***Tembos** give this ~ though it hurts them.*
Only the Love ~ of Tembo Jay
Can save the world ~ from human greed.'

Rafiki repeated this to himself, before asking, 'Do you know what it means?'

'I believe *we* are involved in some plan of Mana's – *whatever* it means. M'zee and I were on Holy Mountain, carrying down the tusks of Tembo Jay, when the mountain breathed fire and smoke. But I don't yet understand what the rest of it will mean for us. I supposeMana knows.'

They waded across the river and scrambled up the bank to look at the 'dead' Land Rover. Kidogo felt a twinge of guilt that she had, however innocently, been responsible for Lusty's behaviour.

The jostlers had returned from the Place of Peace without resting on the return journey. They were just reporting back to M'zee when Kidogo and Rafiki also returned.

'We met the guardian,' Three Eyes was telling him. 'He said the little man who is called De/ne *is* a good friend to him and all tembos, and for many generations their two families have shared the duties at the Place of Peace.'

'That is good,' M'zee replied. 'Now tell me about the journey. What hazards are there for the tembas and babies?'

De/ne was hungry for meat and had found a porcupine's burrow. Having no spear now, he built a tapered trap with branches into which a porcupine would enter to eat the tuber he had left in it, but would be unable to back out because of its spines. He hid downwind of the burrow and watched.

He didn't have long to wait. Even as it started to get dark a porcupine emerged from the burrow and snuffled its way into the trap. He killed it with a sharp blow to the back of its head and apologised to the dead creature's spirit before plucking out its quills. These he buried, regretting that he had no immediate use for them, then returned to the shelter carrying the body, now bald except for a scattering of underhairs, which he singed off in the flames before preparing the meat for roasting. As he waited for it to cook De/ne once more reviewed his plans.

The Maasai man was *not* now going back to his own people, and the hunter man couldn't be left on his own. *He* would want to go back to Arusha and fly in an aeroplane back to his home in America. The two good men, who he wanted to come to the Place of Peace to become husbands to his granddaughters, would probably feel obliged to return with the hunter and the Maasai, walking out together through Maasailand and hoping to meet other men who could help them. That, he couldn't allow – they would *all* have to come to the Place with him and the elephants – but how would he persuade them?

After the ritual of bathing Walt and Moses' eyes with warm milk, the five men were sitting around the fire when De/ne asked Lars what his plans were.

'I'd like to tell you I have a clear plan,' he replied. 'But I don't. The obvious choice is for us to walk back the way we've come – but without you and the elephants it could take us forever. Moses can't see, and we would need the tent to sleep in when it rains. We don't know where the rock shelters are, like you do, and the tent's not a lightweight one. I don't suppose you could get your elephant friends to carry us out?'

De/ne made a pretence of considering this suggestion before he told them, 'The elephants are all on an important journey of their own, and I am awaited by my family. If you were to travel on with us, the elephants could carry your tent *and* yourselves. Our destination is near to the Endless Plains – the Serengeti. As you know, there will be a better chance of you meeting a passing four-by-four there than in Maasailand.'

Lars looked at Ryan, 'What do *you* think?'

'Sounds good to me.'

'Walt?'

'*Anything* to get me out of here and back to the States. I've had enough of Africa for a lifetime.'

'Moses?'

'I am in your hands. You must decide.'

Lars turned back to De/ne, who was gnawing the last of the meat off the porcupine's leg-bone. 'Would the elephants do this for us?'

'They would do it for *me*,' he replied.

In the morning, M'zee listened to De/ne's request and said he would consider it. De/ne strolled away, keeping his back to the elephants to show he was not overhearing their discussions. Soon, Kidogo appeared at his side.

326

'It has been agreed,' she said. 'Tembo Boy and Temba Girl will take you and one of the good men to the dead Land Rover, where you are to make two bundles of whatever you require to bring with you. We will leave in the morning after all the elephants have fed. Temba Girl will carry the man who cannot see, Tembo Boy will carry the hunter man and Rafiki and I will carry the two good men. Tembo M'zee said he would carry *you* if you wish it, as you are small and he is too old and weak to carry a tusk.'

'Please tell Tembo M'zee that I am honoured by his offer but I will be happier to be on the ground – where I have lived all my life.'

Ryan and Lars made up two bundles of gear from the Land Rover, one wrapped in the tent and the other in the canvas sheet they used as a camp shelter if it rained while they were on safari. Neither the tent nor the sheet appeared to have been damaged by Lusty's attack.

As Ryan was tying up the first bundle, Lars reopened the other one and put in the spade.

'What's that for,' Ryan asked. 'Planning to bury Walt?'

'He's mellowing,' Lars replied. 'I hated him at first but he helps Moses quite a bit now. Gratitude for what he did with the snake, I suppose.'

'And the spade?'

Lars laughed. 'I just had an odd feeling that I ought to bring it. The elephants won't notice the extra weight.'

He was pleased De/ne had presented him with a plan of action, even though he knew tourists' vehicles seldom visited the farthest northeast corner of the Serengeti Park. However, at least going there with the elephants would give his party some chance of meeting a park warden. De/ne had also promised to show him how to find bush-food, such as edible tubers, how to make snares to capture guinea fowl and small animals, and build traps for porcupines.

After returning to the shelter, they ate a late breakfast of tinned food from the Land Rover, repacked the two bundles and waited for the elephants to return from their feeding.

De/ne had briefed them all as to which elephant they were to ride and when the four came M'zee was standing quietly nearby. The rest of the herd milled about, watching as Lars and Ryan guided Moses up and onto the back of Girl, then helped Walt to get up onto Boy's back.

'How do I make him do what I want?' Walt called down as Boy rose to his feet.

'You don't,' Lars called back. '*You* do what *he* wants. We're the guests – remember that!'

When Lars was on Kidogo's back, she picked up one of the bundles of gear with her trunk and passed it up over her head to him. He positioned it on her neck in front of him where he judged it would be most comfortable for her.

When Rafiki, with Ryan on his back, had done the same, De/ne who was carrying just his leather bag and spear, told M'zee they were ready to move off.

Behind them, the jostlers were silently taking the tusks from the stack in the shelter and passing them to other elephants, retaining Tembo Jays and Tembo Steadfast's to carry themselves. Finding that he had kept four tusks back for the three of them, he had to call after a temba with a half grown youngster to come back and take up the second of Steadfast's ivories.

De/ne led the way, with M'zee close behind him, followed by the other elephants. He set an easy pace with frequent breaks for them to feed and rest. Once out of the valley they entered monotonous scrubland where there were few other animals about. Biting flies attacked both the elephants and the humans. Lars watched one circling around him and tried to swat it with his hand as soon as it landed on his arm, but missed it.

'They're tsetse flies,' Ryan told him. They're like the horse flies at home. You have to wait until they've landed and are about to bite you, then swat them like this.' He struck his arm with a sliding stroke. 'That kills them.'

When the flies started biting, De/ne dropped back to speak to Lars. 'These flies are a nuisance but they do not carry the sleeping sickness here. They do harm cattle though – which is why the Maasai don't come as far as this.'

Ryan slapped at his chest. 'That one was a titse fly,' he said, trying to keep a straight face. 'They're smaller – and bite your nipples.'

It was not yet dark when the elephants reached the stream where the jostlers had spent a night on their way to meet Tembo Guardian. M'zee arranged for the tusks to be laid out together in a line before they drank so that any tembo, who was not too tired, could read them. Rafiki found one of Lonely's tusks and asked Kidogo to show him how to read it. She ran her trunk along the tusk and stopped when she found the scene where Lonely first saw the whale. Then she guided Rafiki's trunk to the same spot.

'Relax your body, clear your mind, open your thoughts,' she said, using the exact words that M'zee had used when he had taught her to read in the cave on Holy Mountain. 'What can you see?' she asked him.

'Blue water,' he replied. 'Lots of blue water with a floating tree trunk in it.'

'That's not a tree trunk – that's the whale,' she told him.

Soon Rafiki was exploring other scenes in the tusk and saw the whale leap out of the blue water three times. When he looked up, many of the other tembos were reading the other tusks. He lowered his trunk and found the place where the dolphins came, and loved the speed and grace of these creatures as they swam around the whale. Then he came to the scene where the whale seemed to be singing in low~sound – but the tusk was silent. He guided Kidogo's trunk-tip to the place but the tusk was silent for her too. Perhaps free tusks couldn't hold low~sound. They did find the harrowing scene where Lonely was shot down as he stepped forward and took the bullet intended for M'zee. It seemed that the whale's wonderful song *had* been lost, other than the little of it Kidogo had remembered. They each stroked the tusk in a gesture of thanks and remembrance, then went down to the river to drink.

While Lars and Ryan were putting up the tent for Walt Schwiner to sleep in and hanging the canvas shelter on a rope between two trees, away from where the elephants were resting, De/ne slipped away. When he returned after dark he presented them with three guinea fowl.

'I'm sorry there is not one bird for each of us – the others could run faster than me – and I have not yet learned to fly,' he said, with his usual grin. 'Now I must visit my elephant friends for some milk for the eye-bathing.'

Later, Lars woke to hear human voices some distance away in the bush. Only when he heard a snatch of music did he realise that De/ne was listening to his radio.

It was midday when they reached the high rock wall, where springs of cool, clear groundwater welled up and merged to form the stream they had been following. In the shade of the tall trees which grew luxuriantly at the foot of the cliff, the men slid down from the backs of the elephants.

'There's no way we're going up there,' said Walt, looking up at the cliff. 'That's got to be a thousand feet high!'

'That's the side of the Great Rift Valley,' Lars told him. 'It runs from the Red Sea right down to Lake Nyasa. People and animals have climbed it for thousands of years. De/ne will know the way – but don't expect to ride up!'

The tembos and the humans drank their fill from the bubbling springs then rested in the shade, gathering their strength for the climb. When M'zee judged they were ready, he signalled to De/ne to go ahead and show the way.

Three Eyes pushed forward. 'We know this path,' he said.

M'zee nodded at the eager youngster and the other two jostlers close behind him.

'I may need you to help the mothers and the babies and there are heavy ivories for you to carry. It is best for the little man to go first. We will follow him.'

The youngsters moved away, obviously disappointed.

M'zee moved out into the direct sunlight. It was so hot on his back he wondered briefly if he should put off the climb until the cool of the evening. But then, if it took longer than he hoped they all might have to try and complete the climb in the dark. This would be even more dangerous. He looked at the lower part of the path which didn't seem too difficult. He could see the jostlers were already organising the tusk carriers and the mothers and babies into some sort of order and, despite his qualms, he signalled to De/ne to lead the way. De/ne signalled back that they should wait until it was cooler but M'zee misread his tembotalk and replied, 'Lead us now.'

De/ne moved off up the track and M'zee told Kidogo and Rafiki to stay close to the little man.

'My place is near to you, M'zee,' Kidogo reminded him quietly.

'I will be close behind you,' he replied. 'None of us will be able to climb quickly. Your job will be to call back and warn us of any especially bad places.'

M'zee looked back and saw the jostlers positioning themselves amongst the mothers and their babies so they'd be ready to help them on the steepest places. Behind the mothers and babies came the Sisters, Comfort and Kindness, readying themselves to look after any tembos who became exhausted by the climb and, at the very rear of the file were Boy and Girl, carrying the two bundles of possessions for the humans. The four other men were still in the shade of the trees.

Lars and Ryan watched the elephants starting their climb. 'I bet when I e-mailed you to climb Kili with me, you never thought it would lead to this,' Lars said with a half-smile.

'It was a bit of ice-climbing you promised me,' Ryan replied. 'And now, just a couple of months later, I've given up my job, been run off a mountain by an eruption, explored much of Tanzania, chased two elephant hunters across half of Maasailand, and now we're about to follow a herd of jumbos up the side of the Rift Valley, led by a Bushman who talks their language. I'm not sure if I believe it!' He looked up to where a column of elephants of all sizes zigzagged up the steep bank half hidden by clouds of dust.

Walt, who had been sitting on the trunk of a fallen tree with Moses, got up and joined them. His left eye was still partly closed. 'Are we really going up there?' he asked.

'Our best bet for getting out of here is to stay with the Bushman and the elephants. De/ne knows the country and they provide the transport,' Lars replied. 'And the milk to bathe your eyes!'

'How is your eye, Walt?' Ryan asked.

'Quite a lot better. It still hurts but at least I can see out of it. Moses' eyes are much worse. He's completely blind.'

'When the elephants are well ahead, we'll follow them up but keep our distance. We don't want any of them rolling back onto us if they slip.' Lars said. 'Ryan can help you if you need it. I'll guide Moses.'

M'zee was finding it increasingly hot and tiring, and was fervently wishing he had waited for evening before starting the climb – but it was too late now, there could be no turning back.

'Narrow place here, M'zee,' Kidogo called back to him as he approached a turn in the path where two huge boulders were close together, each smoothed and polished by the passage of elephants over many millennia.

M'zee felt the width of the space between the rocks with his trunk, judged that he could pass through, reflected that bigger tembulls than him had almost certainly got through before and pushed his huge body into the gap. He was nearly through when, without any warning his legs folded under him and his body slumped down, jamming him between the boulders. He tried to get up but knew he was totally trapped.

It must be time for me to step-over, he thought, and found he was not bothered by the possibility of doing so. Soon, I'll know the last hidden truth of Mana. If there *is* another life beyond this one, I'll know all about it soon, and I won't be sorry to leave this tired old body behind. If there *isn't,* then I won't know anything about it, and I won't even be able to feel disappointed!

Then, with horror, he realised where he was. He was blocking a path needed by the tembos behind him who were carrying the tusks, including those of Tembo Jay, on their journey to *follow the tired sun.* He would *have* to get up and out of their way. He tried and tried but his legs would not lift him.

The column behind had halted. The message, 'The old one is down and stuck between two rocks,' was passed back down the line. When it reached Three Eyes, he thought of what that old one had once said to him – *'Tembo Three Eyes, I sense you are intelligent and have the qualities that would make a fine leader.'* Now it was up to *him* to find a solution.

He worked his way up the track with the other two jostlers close behind him, passing the mothers and babies wherever they could find sufficient width and stepping precariously out onto bare rock where there was no other way past. When they reached M'zee, Three Eyes looked to see if there was any way to pass round their fallen leader. There was none.

In front of him, the huge wrinkled rear end of the old tembo filled the entire space between the two huge boulders, and he could see no way round either of them. The sun was blazing down from a clear blue sky, its rays radiating off the bare earth and stones which shimmered in the heat. Behind him, the mothers and babies were in the full glare and Three-Eyes knew if they stayed where they were many more would collapse.

'Tell the rest of the tembos to go back down to the trees and wait by the springs,' he told One Eye. 'Pass the message back. Tell them to take the free tusks with them – and not to leave them unguarded at any time.'

With some grumbling and much difficulty for many, they obeyed his instructions.

The men, who had stopped when they saw the elephants turning round and trundling back down the track, sat together in the shade of one of the sparse-leaved trees near the track, watching the elephants coming back towards them. Each of the elephants acknowledged the humans with a slight wave of their trunk as they passed by.

Hearing their movements, Moses turned his head and asked, 'What's happening?'

'For some reason, the elephants are all coming back down and bringing the tusks with them,' Lars told him. 'I'll catch up with De/ne and find out what's going on. It's probably best if you all stay here.'

When the last group of elephants had passed them Lars made his way up the track. De/ne had scrambled over the rocks where M'zee was trapped and was conversing with the three jostlers in tembotalk.

'The old one is stuck in a narrow place,' De/ne explained to Lars. 'The elephant they call *Three Eyes* is trying to think of a way to move him. It will be best for you to take the other men down to the trees and set up camp. Freeing the old one is going to take some time. I am staying here to see if I can help.'

Through the heat haze M'zee saw Kidogo and Rafiki coming back down the track towards him. They must have realised he was no longer close behind them. He spoke to Kidogo, his voice tired and weak. 'There is nothing you two can do here,' he told them. 'I want you to climb to the top and look for water. Take care of yourselves – *you* may soon have to lead the team.'

'My place is here with you,' Kidogo said. 'I am your Shadow.'

'Shadows have to do what they are told,' M'zee said kindly, reaching his trunk up to touch her forehead. 'Come back when the night is cool.'

She in turn touched the old one's forehead, hot from the sun, and turned back up the track with Rafiki, both of them looking back frequently.

The steep path turned and twisted between more great rocks and scattered trees but, as they neared the top and the slope lessened and a cooling breeze started to blow. For a moment Kidogo forgot what was happening out of her sight down the track and gasped at the beauty of the vast view over the plains to the blue faraway hills. Brightly coloured butterflies flitted around her head and spiky pink flowers grew up out of the fresh green grass around her feet. Far to the east she could just make out the white top of Holy Mountain with a plume of smoke streaming away from it.

Remembering that his sight was not as good as hers Kidogo described the scene to Rafiki but she knew they mustn't linger here. They had to do what they had been told to do – find water. She strode on across the level ground, hardly aware of how much cooler it was up here on the high plateau. The one-tusked Rafiki followed close behind, ready to step forward and protect his friend if any danger threatened.

M'zee gave up struggling, as his movements only seemed to jam him more tightly between the boulders and in such heat he would soon step-over. This was why he'd sent Kidogo away – if she watched it happen, she would suffer more than he did and there was nothing she could do. Then it came into his tired mind that by being stuck between the boulders he was preventing any of the other tembos from passing. He knew now he should not have been up in the lead – but that was where a leader should be – in the front. But if he stepped-over here, the others wouldn't be able to get past until his body had rotted enough for them to pull his bones out of the way – and that could take many days, even with the help of the inevitable hyenas and the eaters-of-dead-flesh birds. *They* would find his body soon enough. He shuddered, knowing that would happen if he was too weak to get back on his feet.

He *shouldn't* have tried to do the climb in the daytime. He *should* have waited until it was dark. He was a bad leader – making poor decisions – and now he was having to suffer the result, and not just him. . . . And he was so hot! The sun was scorching the skin on his back, weakening him even more. Oh, for some shade! He reached his trunk back into his throat to draw on his small reserve of water, sprayed it back over his head, and felt a little better. Then he felt another spray from behind him and another and another. The jostlers must be using *their* reserves to cool *his* back. How generous of them. Now he felt branches being laid over his damp skin.

'Hey, I'm not dead yet,' he called.

'The little man says it will help to keep your skin cool for longer,' Three Eyes called back from behind him.

The little man himself appeared before M'zee, his body appearing to quiver in the heat, and spoke to him in tembotalk, swinging his trunk-arm and moving one ear with his other hand.

'The three jostlers are going down to bring up more water,' he said. 'When it is cooler you may be able to stand up.' He looked around and asked, 'Where have the little tembo and the one-tusked young tembull gone?'

M'zee replied with difficulty, 'I sent them away. There was nothing they could do here and they would only have suffered in the heat. They'll be back when it is dark. If I don't survive, will you do your best to help them as you have helped me and others of my kind?'

De/ne made the tembo-sign for, 'You don't even have to ask!'

Three Eyes was glad the little man had suggested putting branches over M'zee but he knew it would not be enough to save the old one's life.

'Come on down with me,' he said to his fellow jostlers who had been waiting for him to tell them what to do next. 'We'll get *more* water.'

At the groundwater springs they again drank their fill, replenishing their throat reserves, and started back up the steep track, pleasantly surprised that many of the other tembos were doing the same..

On reaching M'zee, each tembo in turn sprayed water over the branches covering his back, where it dripped down in cooling trickles onto his skin.

When Tembas Comfort and Kindness saw what the others were doing, they wondered if they could call for rain to cool their leader. They tried but no matter how many of the tembos linqued together and asked, the small clouds that did form quickly dissipated in the heat from the cliff-face before any rain could fall. So they gave up trying and joined the others in carrying water in their throats and spraying it over their fallen leader.

Kidogo walked on across the plateau, fretting at having to leave the fallen M'zee and frequently sniffing at the cool air. When the wonderful scent of water reached her, she tracked it upwind to where a stream flowing from the west rippled over a rock lip and fell into a hole in the ground. She and Rafiki approached cautiously, listening to the sound of the falling water. They drank upstream away from the dark hole where the water disappeared, then turned back to report this to M'zee, stopping near the top of the cliff just long enough to gather some food for him. The sun was setting behind them and darkness was creeping across the plains below. In the farthest distance, the top of Holy Mountain held the last rays of sunshine as they started back down the track, each carrying a bundle of food-wads they'd made from the freshest of the grass and flowers. All too quickly the light faded and darkness welled up from the plains. Hampered by the bundles but not wanting to leave them behind, they carefully felt their way down.

When they approached M'zee he called out a greeting, his voice sounding stronger than when they'd left him. He told them what the other tembos had done to keep him cool and Kidogo put down the food-wads she was carrying, reached her trunk into her throat reserve and sprayed water from it into the old one's mouth. 'We have brought you food,' she said.

'Truly I chose my Shadow well,' M'zee said once more. 'I thank you both.'

Kidogo heard the jostlers talking behind the bulk of M'zee and called out to them in the darkness. 'We thank you, my friends, for what you have done.' Then she passed the food-wads, one at a time, to M'zee.

The old tembo held each one in his mouth to savour the sweet grasses before swallowing.

M'zee was soon feeling stronger but knew he would need help if he was to get to his feet. He could hear Kidogo talking quietly to Rafiki as they tried to think of a way to get him up, and he called to her. 'If your friend can get his tusk under my chest and one of the jostlers could get both of his under my belly from behind – and they lifted together, I just might be able to stand at least long enough to get clear of here and allow you all to pass.'

M'zee heard Rafiki grunt his assent and sensed the young tembo feeling his way forward in the darkness and kneeling in front of him. Then he heard Kidogo calling out instructions to Three Eyes and soon felt the jostler trying to push his tusks under his body from behind. M'zee could hear muffled grunting but Three Eyes' tusks were widely set and were either poking painfully into his legs or were grinding against the rocks that held him fast. He felt them being pulled back and then a different set, which M'zee realised must be One Eye's slender, close-set tusks, were sliding easily under him until the jostler's head was tight against his tail. He told Rafiki to wriggle his single tusk between his crumpled front legs.

When he could feel that all three tusks were in the best positions he braced himself, took a deep breath, focused his mind on standing up and called, 'Now, lift *now*!' He could feel the tusks pressing hard against his chest and his belly but he was still firmly stuck. He relaxed, let his breath go ready for another try and felt himself being lifted slightly. He took another breath and jammed tight once more.

'Breath *out* while we lift,' Rafiki grunted and, with him calling the timing to One Eye, together they eased M'zee up and onto his feet. Rafiki stepped backwards out of the way as the old one lurched forward for a few paces, then slumped down on his side as a round moon rose above the eastern horizon, lighting up the scene. M'zee breathed a silent 'Thank you' to Mana and said to Rafiki, 'You can tell the others they will be able to get past me now. If they start to climb as soon as it is light enough, they will pass before it gets too hot,' he wheezed, his aching legs twitching and shaking where he lay.

Three Eyes sent the other two jostlers to take the message down to the waiting tembos, reminding them to take care as moonlight can be deceptive.

By the time they and the humans approached where M'zee lay, the sun was just a trunk's width above the horizon and the air was still cool. Refreshed by the rest and the food-wads that Kidogo and Rafiki had brought him, M'zee thought he might now be able to make the rest of the climb.

'Go on by,' M'zee told the first of the carriers and the mothers and babies when they came to the narrow gap between the boulders. 'I will follow when I can.' He asked Rafiki to guide the herd and the humans to where he and Kidogo had found the water. 'Stay there with them until we come,' he said.

The Sisters came near and showed their concern, touching his head and feeling along his legs with their trunks. 'Go on up with the mothers and babies,' he told them. 'I am being well looked after by my Shadow and these three fine young tembulls.'

The morning was almost over by the time the five joined the herd at the place where the stream fell into the hole. Kidogo had led the way, pausing frequently for rests and choosing the easiest route for M'zee, who had been supported on either side by two of the jostlers as he'd staggered and lurched along behind her.

Tembas Comfort and Kindness came to meet the group and guide them to a patch of shade where they'd stacked foods-wads ready for the old one to eat. He took up and swallowed several before slumping down to sleep.

Three Eyes led Kidogo and Rafiki up to higher ground and pointed out the *firehill*. 'That is where we are going,' he told them.

'We will rest here by the stream and not move on until tomorrow,' Kidogo told him. 'There is plenty of water and good grazing. I am sure the mothers will have warned the youngsters to stay away from the place where the water falls into the ground, but if you three would stay near the hole and warn them to keep away, it would be a kindly act.'

She drew One Eye to one side and said, 'It must be the will of Mana that I have *no* tusks and that yours have grown closer together than those of most other tembos. Yesterday, we could never have lifted M'zee and freed him from the rocks if your tusks had not grown that way and if my friend Rafiki still had both his tusks. I know both you and I would rather have tusks like the other tembos but it seems we must accept that such things may be so for reasons we do not know.'

She touched his forehead, and he touched hers before ambling off to join his fellow jostlers

De/ne and the other men had followed the tembos past the fallen bull elephant and up to the top of the rock wall. At the summit, Walt had asked if he could remount Boy. Hardly had he finished speaking, when Boy stepped forward and knelt to allow the man to climb up onto his back. Soon Lars, Ryan and Moses were also mounted and were carried across the plateau. The elephants they were riding took care to avoid any overhanging branches and when they reached the stream where the other elephants were already grazing, they knelt for the men to dismount. In a routine that was by now familiar to them all, the men set up camp, and when M'zee and his helpers finally arrived De/ne went over to greet him.

The Bushman left the camp early next morning, and returned with a bagful of hard, round tubers, which he roasted in the ashes of the fire.

De/ne knew he would soon have to make his choice. His home was now very near. He could either guide the men with him southwest towards the northern edge of the Serengeti – or into the secret place his people and the elephants had always called the Place of Peace.

It would be no good sending the two baddies southwest *on their own*. The American and the blind Maasai could not survive in the bush for long, and he was sure the two good men would never allow it and would insist on going with them.

But, if he let *them* go southwest with the baddies, then his whole mission would have failed – his granddaughters would never have children and, when he and his granddaughters were dead, the Place of Peace would be without First People and elephants living together in harmony for the first time in many thousands of years. There was only *one* course of action De/ne could take.

CHAPTER TWENTY-EIGHT

Sarah and Ruth were sitting in the shade of their rock-shelter home, taking it in turns to read to one another from a well-worn, leather-covered bible. Each woman would read a passage out loud as their father, the late Mr Fotheringay, had taught them to do, then pass the book to her twin. This was the only book he had brought with him to the crater and the only book the two women had ever read – or even seen. They thought of it as their window onto the outside world.

Ruth had just finished reading *Psalm 121* when they heard the distant trump of Tembo Guardian's challenge echoing through the gorge.

'Grandfather must be back,' she said, standing up, closing the bible and placing it on a high rock ledge. 'We must put on some clothes.'

Each of the girls took their skirts from another ledge. They wrapped the soft tree-bark fabric around their waists and secured them with beaded belts. Their father had always made them wear sleeveless, soft-leather top-shirts as well as the skirts but, after he'd died, they had discarded them and reverted to going bare-breasted, as was the custom of their mother's people. It was so much more comfortable, and it felt right to them, no matter what their father had said.

They went together down the winding path, passing the wooden cross that marked his grave and waited by the tree-trunk that crossed a stream at the top of a small pool.

Tembo Guardian had trumped his joyful challenge when he heard movements and tembo voices in the gorge below his cave. After talking with the jostlers only a few days before, he had been eagerly awaiting De/ne and many tembos, especially since they would be bringing with them the tusks of Tembo Jay!

He greeted De/ne with a touch to his forehead for they had been friends since they were youngsters together. In those long-past days there had been many more tembos and First People in the Place of Peace but one by one they had stepped-over until he, De/ne and De/ne's two granddaughters were the only ones still living there.

De/ne introduced M'zee to Tembo Guardian, then introduced M'zee's Shadow, Kidogo.'

'It is good to know that older tembos still have Shadows – but a female Shadow is something new to me,' the guardian said.

'I could not have chosen better,' M'zee replied. 'She has kept me alive and safe for our whole journey. She deserves the love and respect of tembos everywhere.'

Kidogo looked around, embarrassed, and was glad to see that most of the others, who were waiting in line behind her on the narrow path, were out of ear-catch.

'I will escort you all up and into the Place of Peace. I am eager to see for myself the sacred Tusks of Tembo Jay.' Tembo Guardian then asked, 'They *are* with you?'

M'zee assured him that they were being carried safely by those close behind him and he slowly followed Tembo Guardian and De/ne up the path, forcing his weary legs to hold him up and carry him forward. Not far now!

Shafts of midday sunlight reached down between the high walls, lighting up the deep green pools and making the water sparkle where it poured over rock ledges. The spray from these falls formed rainbows, bright against the dark, wet walls of the gorge.

'Stand fast behind me.' The cry of one of the carriers came echoing up the gorge.

'What's happening back there?' M'zee called over his shoulder.

'The tusk I was carrying is in the water. It slipped from my hold.'

'Can you reach it easily?'

'No. It's in deep water.'

'Whose tusk is it?'

'Tembo Lonely's.'

M'zee knew if he stopped now he would never be able to start walking again.

'Let it lie,' he called back. 'It will come to no harm. We can collect it later. All tembos walk on.'

Moses, who had barely spoken for the past couple of days, suddenly called out, '*Yea, though I walk through the valley of the shadow of death, I will fear no evil,*' then was silent. Apart from that, the humans had not spoken as the elephants passed through the gorge. Talking while riding on elephant-back in single file was difficult, besides which the men were feeling such an overpowering sense of awe they had no desire to make conversation. Also, Moses' sudden outburst had been embarrassing.

What was ahead for them, Ryan wondered? They could have been in a scene from one of his favourite boyhood books by H. Rider Haggard, which were set in nineteenth-century Africa. The hero, Allan Quartermain – with the help of his cunning Hottentot servant, Hans, and the huge and fearless warrior, Umslopogaas always won through – whatever challenges and hazards had confronted them. It was probably through reading these stories that he had been drawn to Africa in the first place.

Ahead of them, the gorge was opening out and the sunlight was much stronger, shining through a mass of creepers that hung down on either side and trailed into the stream. Brightly coloured birds flew from one stem to another whistling and calling as the elephants emerged into the crater.

De/ne, aware of the effect it had on tembos to see their Place of Peace for the first time, stood to one side and watched the expressions on the faces of both elephants and humans as they stepped out into the full sunlight.

Ryan was riding Tembo Three Eyes and, as they came out of the shadow, Three Eyes turned to the left and stopped. In front of them, the broad caldera of the volcano was carpeted with grassland, bright with new growth, while to his right, a large pool of water was dotted with mauve-coloured water lilies and fringed with tall papyrus reeds. From this pool the stream ran down into the gorge and under the curtain of creepers behind him.

Beyond the large pool and a string of smaller ones, the ground rose gently towards a bare rock wall in which shadows suggested cool recesses. The rising ground might well have been cultivated once and parts of it looked as if it still was. Tembo Three Eyes was almost sure the patch of dark green vegetation at the foot of the slope was a clump of banana plants.

The whole crater, which Ryan estimated to be about two miles across, was encircled by a wall of rock several hundred feet high, rising to a peak on the far side, much of it covered in a tangle of trees and creepers. In several places the trees were spreading out to colonise the crater floor. But, set dramatically in the centre of the crater and looking like nothing he had ever seen before in Africa, was a round structure built out of large stone blocks. He guessed it must be about two hundred feet across and twenty feet high. It reminded him of the prehistoric Staige Fort he'd once visited in County Kerry but it appeared to have been built with much larger stones.

Ryan sat on Three Eyes' back trying to take it all in. But, beautiful as the whole scene was, its most captivating feature was not the trees, the grass, the pool, the stream, nor the stone structure, but an all-encompassing, intangible, sense of peace. Ryan felt as if, in some strange way, he had *come home*.

He turned to Lars, who was on Rafiki's back and said, 'Are you seeing what I'm seeing, then?'

Walt Schwiner, who was riding on Two Eyes, studied the scene with the eye of a big-game hunter and noted the absence of any animals, other than the elephants who had come up the track with them and were now spreading out and grazing on the fresh grass that reached almost to their knees. He would have expected antelope and zebra at least, with several giraffes, but there were none. The circular stone structure in the centre of the crater did not interest him as such, although it did bear some resemblance to the ruined walls at Machu Pichu which he'd once visited in Peru. He began to think what good cover it would provide for stalking game, but then realised that his attitude to shooting had changed dramatically. To shoot an elephant now was as unthinkable as shooting one of his uncle's horses just for fun. In fact, it was worse than that – it would be like shooting one of the board members of Schwiner Enterprises Inc. Not that he hadn't felt like doing that at times but, as majority shareholder he'd never needed to.

M'zee blinked his eyes in the bright light, seeing little but sensing the peace of the place. 'I could happily step-over here,' he whispered to Kidogo. 'I am so tired.'

347

She looked up at the gaunt features of the old tembo she had come to love so much and thought sadly that his wish was likely to be granted. Her trunk reached out and touched the centre of his forehead as she said, 'Mana owes that to you, M'zee.'

The humans were all dismounting from the backs of the elephants who had carried them through the gorge. Walt slid to the ground, helped Moses get down from Girl's back, then held his elbow and guided him to where the other men were standing, gazing in silent wonder around them.

As Ryan had done, Lars was trying to work out how far across the caldera was – but it was hard to do it with no buildings, other than the unusual round stone structure in the centre, to give it a true sense of scale. And the round building itself could be any size – it was difficult to judge. The crater was nothing like as big as the Ngorongoro crater had been. Lars estimated it must be about three kilometres from where he stood to the peak on the far side. But above all he felt almost overwhelmingly moved by the peacefulness of the place and, looking at the faces of the other men, he knew they felt it too.

When the last of the elephants had come out into the open, Tembo Guardian held up his trunk for attention and waited while those who had been grazing ambled over to him.

'Welcome to the Place of Peace,' he said. 'It is sacred to tembos and to the humans of the First People. We have shared the Joy of this place for longer than any tembo can remember, each respecting the needs of the other. Humans kill no animals within these walls and we tembos never eat the crops grown here by the humans. To avoid any such temptation, we tembos must never cross the stream to the part where they live.'

M'zee glanced at Tembo Three Eyes, who acknowledged the look with a tiny nod of his head and the slightest movement of his trunk.

'Although I, the Guardian, have been the only tembo here for many years, and the First People are now only three in number, we respect these customs and I expect you all to do the same. Tembos and First People may come and go from this place but humans, other than those of the First People, may never leave the Place of Peace in case they reveal our secrets. I am sure De/ne will have told this to his guests.'

Here De/ne fidgeted and looked uncomfortable, glad that none of the men, other than himself, could understand tembotalk.

'You may explore where you wish, on this side of the stream, and bathe in the pool nearest to us. May you all enjoy your time here.'

Most of the tembos made straight for the pool, led by the youngest, squealing with delight as they waded in and sprayed water about with joyful abandon. Kidogo, at M'zee's side, reminded him that Lonely's tusk was still in the stream halfway down the gorge.

'It will come to no harm there,' he replied. 'Let us go and bathe. It will be good after such a journey.'

CHAPTER TWENTY-NINE

Sarah and Ruth had watched their grandfather come out of the gorge, followed by many elephants, both large and small. Intrigued to see four other men riding on the backs of elephants the two women had crept down to stand behind some bushes where they could watch without being seen. When the men had dismounted and were standing beside De/ne, Sarah and Ruth could see that all the men were much taller than their grandfather, and were dressed in the sort of clothes their own father had worn in their earliest memories of him. When those clothes had worn out, Mr Fotheringay had taken to wearing a skirt much like theirs, except that his was made of soft leather and he'd called it a *kilt*.

Three of the men who had just come out of the gorge were pale-skinned like their father, but the other stranger, the tallest of the men, had a very dark skin. None of them looked at all like their grandfather, nor like they remembered their mother had looked. They were clearly not of the First People.

'I think we ought to put on our top-shirts,' said Ruth. 'These men may think like Father and not wish to see us this way.'

'It is best to be sure,' Sarah replied. So they returned silently to their shelter, frequently glancing back over their shoulders to where the elephants were listening to the Guardian, with the men standing in a group nearby.

De/ne, although keen to see his granddaughters, waited until Tembo Guardian had finished speaking. Not only did he want to hear what was being said, but he was beginning to have serious doubts about bringing the American and the Maasai into the Place of Peace. As Tembo Guardian had reminded him, no humans, other than First People like himself, could be allowed to leave. Once Lars and Ryan had met his granddaughters, De/ne was sure *they* would want to stay here forever – but not the other two – especially when they learned of the elephants' Secret. But there *were* ways to ensure they couldn't leave.

He waved towards the bundles the elephants had laid on the ground. 'We will leave the gear here and collect it later,' he said. 'Follow me, Gentlemen.' He led the way along the side of the large pool and several smaller ones to where a single tree-trunk made a simple bridge.

M'zee waded into the large pool, enjoying the coolness and the lift to his aching body as he got into deeper water. He turned to Kidogo, who had waded in beside him.

'I will be safe here,' he told her. 'I am sure this is the end of our journey and I relieve you of your duties as my Shadow. Join your friend – and *thank you,* Kidogo, for all the love and kindness you've given this old tembo.'

Kidogo paused for a moment, wondering if she should say anything, but M'zee had shifted his gaze to the far rock wall so she just brushed his shoulder with her trunk as she turned, and waded out to where Rafiki was waiting for her on the shore.

'Let's explore,' she said.

Tembo Guardian waited near to where the stream entered the gorge until the jostlers had come out of the water then, still keeping watch on the entrance, he walked over and spoke to Three Eyes, with the other two listening.

'It is clear to me that your leader, Tembo M'zee, trusts you with important jobs,' Tembo Guardian said. 'I have guarded this Place of Peace on my own for more than twenty years and now I feel it is time to pass this duty to others. Would you and your companions like to share this role between you? It is important, but not onerous, especially if there are more than one tembo to share the duties. You may arrange times to suit yourselves – but there must always be at least one *alert* tembo in the Guardian's cave where we first met, or close to the entrance here, where one can watch the top of the path.

Tembo Three Eyes recognised that his time of total *jostling* freedom was coming to an end, yet he felt no resentment. To take over this duty would mean taking the responsibility for at least a third of his lifetime – but if this old tembo had done it willingly on his own for so long, he could hardly refuse. He could tell by the expressions of his two fellow tembos that they too had made the same decision.

Before Tembo Three Eyes could give his answer, Tembo Guardian thought to add, 'Of course, *I* would no longer have my honourable title. I will decide on a new name for myself.'

'What exactly do we have to do?' Two Eyes asked.

'One of you must guard the path at all times. You may assume that any *tembo* is pure in their heart, but of all *humans* only those of the First People may pass either in or out of the Place of Peace.'

'Do many other humans come here?' One Eye asked.

'In that part of my lifetime here only one such came and he stayed to become father to the granddaughters of the little man of the First People, who is known to me as De/ne, and whose judgement I trust. And of course, those who came with you today'.

'So,' said Three Eyes. '*All* tembos can pass in and out, and *all* First People, but no other humans. If no others have come, except for the one who stayed and those with us today, is it worth the effort?'

'It is what the Tembo Guardian must do. Sometimes, wandering water-biters come up the path beside the stream. You must turn them back – or kill them with your tusks if they won't. They are creatures without Love or compassion. Such ones must never enter the Place of Peace.'

Kidogo led Rafiki back to the place where the stream left the valley through the gorge. She was walking with a lighter step than she had since M'zee had selected her to be his Shadow.

As they passed Tembo Guardian he greeted her as 'Temba Shadow.'

'No longer that,' she replied. 'I am now just Temba Kidogo – the *little* elephant – which in many ways is a relief to me, Tembo Guardian.'

'No longer *that*,' he replied. 'There are three new guardians. From now on you may call me Tembo *Carefree*!' He chuckled as he passed them, heading for the large pool which had already been churned into a muddy bath by the cavorting elephants.

They then passed two of the jostlers who were also heading for the pool. At the top of the gorge, Tembo Three Eyes was looking longingly after his fellows. Rafiki and Kidogo greeted him as Tembo Three Eyes.

'No longer that,' he replied. 'My name was a bad joke then – and has got no better.' He raised his trunk with a modest degree of pride. 'Please address me now as *Tembo Chief Guardian*.'

'That pleases me, Tembo Chief Guardian,' Kidogo told him, touching his trunk to confirm it. And Rafiki did the same.

Although eager to discover the purpose of the stone structure in the centre of the crater, the friends decided to walk round the wall of the crater first. In many places the trees at the foot of the wall were encroaching onto the flat grasslands.

'There have been not enough tembos here to keep the trees and grasses in balance,' Rafiki remarked. 'If we tembos don't push over some of these trees and eat many of their seedlings, the trees will take over and smother the grasses and flowers.'

De/ne had expected his granddaughters to meet him at the bridge, but when they didn't he'd realised that the four men with him were the only men – other than himself and their father, the late Mr Fotheringay – they had ever seen. It was hardly surprising they were keeping out of sight. 'This way, Gentlemen,' he said. 'My home is up here. My grand-daughters will be waiting for us there.' He leaped nimbly up onto the tree-trunk that bridged the pool.

Lars and Ryan followed, while Walt guided Moses as he stepped up and onto the bridge.

Halfway across, Moses stopped and sniffed the air. '*The Lord is my shepherd*,' he proclaimed. '*He leadeth me beside the still waters. He . . .*'

Walt gripped his arm and led him forward, helping the blind man as he stepped down at the far end of the bridge.

Watching from the rock shelter where they had always lived, Ruth reached out for Sarah's hand. 'I am afeared,' she said.

Sarah squeezed her sister's hand. 'And me also,' she said. 'But Grandfather would only bring good men to be married to us. I am sure of that.'

'He has brought four. Are we to marry two each?'

'In father's bible-book the men sometimes marry more than one woman – but never was one woman married to two men. He has brought more for us to choose from. We should be glad of that.'

They watched the group approaching.

'I am going to choose the tall man with the yellow hair,'

354

Sarah whispered. 'You can have the youngest of the dark-haired men for your husband. One of the others can't see and the other is much too old for you.'

'I like the dark-haired one better – so we need not quarrel,' Ruth whispered back, pulling at her top-shirt. It was uncomfortably tight. She realised she had been much smaller when she'd last worn it. It was all very well for her to choose one of the men but perhaps none of them would like *her* now she was bigger there – and then she would never have babies. And perhaps *she* wouldn't like any of the men when she got to know them. Her mother had once told her that she hadn't liked Mr Fotheringay when he had found the Place of Peace but, when he couldn't leave and there were no men of the First People, she had accepted him to be a husband to her. Would she, Ruth, just have to *accept* one of these men? She gripped Sarah's hand even more tightly.

De/ne left the other men as they walked up the path, and ran towards the shelter that was his home. Finding his grand-daughters hiding in the shadows, he embraced them in turn, noticing that they were wearing top-shirts which were far too tight for them.

'There are four men, Grandfather – *four* men!' Sarah exclaimed.

'I will explain later,' he replied. 'Only two of them are good enough for you. But first you must come and meet them all.'

Still gripping one another's hand they followed De/ne and met the men a little way down the track. 'These are my granddaughters,' De/ne said, and the women curtsied in the way their father had taught them so many years before.

Ryan shot a glance at Lars as De/ne continued. 'Their mother named them D/aw/a and Lo//te – but they were also named Sarah and Ruth by their father, the late

355

Mr Fotheringay. I am sure they will be pleased to be known by either name.'

Lars stepped forward and held out his hand, 'Lars Petersen,' he said, smiling. 'I am pleased to meet you both. I think I'll find Sarah and Ruth easier to say than your other names.'

The women both shook his hand solemnly, and he introduced Ryan. 'This is my friend, Ryan Kavanagh.'

He was not too sure how to introduce Walt and Moses but De/ne stepped forward quickly and spoke to his grand-daughters in Bushmantaal. They curtsied again towards Walt and Moses but did not shake their hands.

Sarah and Ruth led the party up to a large shelter under a projecting rock shelf which was divided into separate areas by low stone walls. Here De/ne allocated living spaces. Sarah and Ruth were to sleep in the area next to the hearth, then De/ne in a hollow place in the rock which was clearly already his own, and then Lars and Ryan. At the far end, Moses and Walt were to share a final recess. Walt complained. 'If any lions or hyenas come they'll get me first,' he said. 'Or any *snakes*.'

'There are *no* lions, snakes or hyenas in this place,' De/ne told him sharply. 'If there were, I would definitely put you here!'

Walt was only satisfied when Lars carried up the tent and erected it under the shelter for him to sleep in.

Kidogo and Rafiki walked around the side of the crater to where the stream trickled out of a boggy area. Beyond the stream was the part which Tembo Guardian – now Tembo Carefree – had told them was forbidden to tembos. It had obviously all been cultivated at one time but now crops were only growing in small patches, although there was a clump of banana plants on the other side of the stream. Bunches of the fruit hung down temptingly.

'Come on,' said Kidogo, turning away. 'Let's see what that is in the centre of this crater.'

The structure must have been built by humans a very long time ago, and was made of stones fitted together in a way neither Kidogo or Rafiki had ever seen before, not even in the days when they'd lived with humans. The walls were the height of a fully grown tembo and formed a circle, which was probably as far around the outside as one hundred tembos standing tusk to tail.

Unlike the crater wall, its walls were not covered in creepers, but only small plants and baby trees were growing from many of the cracks between the stones. Kidogo thought this was unusual, as all the kopjes she had ever seen had *large* plants, and even trees, growing out from the tiniest of crevices between the rocks. She pointed this out to Rafiki who agreed but had no suggestions as to why it should be so.

They circled round the wall until they found a stone-paved passageway leading through a narrow gap. Here the smooth stone sides turned inwards and narrowed until there was just enough space for a tembo to squeeze through and, as on the track up the cliff, the stones on either side were polished smooth by the passage of many elephants over a long period of time.

Peering through the gap they could see an ancient tembo-tree that grew in the centre of the stone-walled circle. 'Can we go through there?' Rafiki asked in a quiet voice.

'I don't see why not,' Kidogo replied. 'The guardian didn't say we shouldn't. Shall I go first?'

She passed through the narrow gap quite easily although Rafiki found it more difficult. Only when she turned to watch him did Kidogo realise how much he had grown since they had refound each other at the waterhole in Tsavo – and that seemed a lifetime ago. The area inside the walls was paved with stone slabs except where the tree was growing. This was so old that the trunk was clearly hollow and only a few of its branches still bore leaves. Beyond the tree, Tembo Carefree was standing on a ramp leading up to the top of the walls and was carefully tweaking out some of the seedlings that had rooted themselves between the rocks. Kidogo gave a gentle snort to let him know he was no longer alone – but not so loud as to startle him.

He turned and said, 'Welcome to the *Mount,* which is what we call this place. May I show you around? It is a very special place.'

Kidogo had noticed that the walls inside the circle were pierced in several places by cave-like openings just big enough for a tembo to enter and she was intrigued to know what they were for, but Carefree first took them to the ancient tembo-tree and poked his trunk into the hollow inside it. 'We lay free tusks in here when they are first brought to the Place of Peace,' he told them. 'Then we sacrifice the *right* tusk to Mana by dropping it down there.' He pointed with his trunk to a large hole in the paved area that sloped gently down towards it.

Kidogo signalled her wish to look down the hole, and Carefree nodded his approval.

She walked forward cautiously, afraid of slipping – the hole was big enough to swallow even a full grown elephant – and peered down. Far, far below she thought she could glimpse a tiny speck of light, which might have been fire, and she could definitely smell a whiff of the throat-closing scent she remembered from Holy Mountain. She stepped backwards, bumping into Rafiki.

'Do you really put the tusks down there, Tembo Carefree?' she asked.

'Only one of them,' he replied. 'The others are stored in those.' He pointed again at the cave-like openings in the rock wall.

Kidogo walked across to one and peered in. The cave sloped down into the ground beyond the entrance and its sides were lined with tusks stacked one on top of the other as far as she could see. A faint glow from the tusks lit up the cave and she stood back to let Rafiki see in.

He whistled through his trunk.

The next opening led into a similar cave, also lined with free tusks, as did the next, and the next.

Tembo Carefree followed them from one entrance to another, then said, 'This is the Secret of the Place of Peace. Tembos from all over Africa used to come here when they knew their time to step-over was approaching. They would pass their last days on the grassland, then when they had stepped-over, and the eaters-of-dead-flesh had flown in and cleaned their bones, other tembos would carry their free tusks up here.'

Kidogo tried to imagine how many elephants must have come here to die and asked Carefree where their bones were.

'No tembos have come for many years now,' he replied. 'At one time most came here to step-over and the grasslands were covered with bones but, as time passes, they crumble and are washed by the rains into the soil. There the crumbled bones feed the grasses and the trees – just as the grasses and the trees had once fed the tembos. It is a wonderful and a beautiful thing to happen.'

Kidogo recalled her mother's body rotting on the plain after she had been shot, and the eaters-of-dead-flesh tearing at her body. It was hard to see any wonder or beauty in that.

Rafiki was peering down the hole in the paved area. 'Why are only some of the tusks dropped down here?' he asked.

Carefree went and stood beside him. 'It is something we

have always done,' he said. 'It is a sacrifice to Mana. As I am sure you know, stored in the free tusks is all the Love a tembo has earned throughout his or her life. Mana needs this Love.'

Kidogo looked up sharply. She'd heard something like that before. It was the end of the whale's song that Lonely had sung to them. It came back to her clearly.

> Mana *needs the ~ Love we give him,*
> *Formed from Joy and ~ care for others*
> *For Love is the ~ magic power*
> *The force that linques ~ us all together*
>
> *Love that Mana ~ needs to function*
> *For the future of our planet.*

If only she could recall the rest of that wonderful song!

Thinking of Tembo Lonely reminded Kidogo that one of his tusks was still in a pool down in the gorge. She and Rafiki ought to go and find it, so she asked Carefree to excuse them without telling him why, and they left the Mount.

Rafiki, following close behind her as usual, was thinking about the Mount and wondering how it had been built. It would have needed a huge amount of joint effort from tembos and humans. And there were so many tusks . . .

CHAPTER THIRTY

Sarah and Ruth had already prepared a bed of dried grass for their grandfather after hearing from the Guardian that he would soon be coming home, and two more in anticipation of his bringing husbands for them. Now they asked De/ne if they should also make up soft beds for the men he had told them were 'baddies'.

'Men who kill elephants should not sleep well,' their grandfather replied in Bushmantaal. 'They can lie on the rock.'

Sarah blew the embers of a fire into a blaze as Ruth started to cook an evening meal of roasted mealies and small savoury cakes. De/ne knew these were made from crushed flying ants and, speaking once again in Bushmantaal, he warned the women not to tell the men this. 'Men who are not of the First People have strange ideas about what is good to eat,' he told them. 'Tomorrow, I will go out and get a buck.'

After they had all eaten and were sitting around the fire, De/ne reached into his bag and took out a cigar box. He opened it to show there were two cigars left, and offered one to Walt.

'You—' Walt started to say, then changed his mind, took the cigar and lit it with a burning brand from the fire. 'These are very good cigars. Thank you.'

'These are the last of them,' De/ne replied as he lit the other one.

Sarah reached out her hand and took the empty box,

opened it, sniffed inside, closed it, and opened and closed it again, before fondling the smooth wood.

'You may keep it,' her grandfather told her and, seeing the look in her sister's eyes, De/ne reached into his bag, glanced at Walt, took out a similar empty box and handed it to Ruth.

He stood up, saying, 'I will now get some milk from my friends the elephants.'

Moses spoke for the first time since they had reached the shelter. 'Do not go for my sake,' he said. 'It cannot help me now. I am like Samson. I will not see again.'

In the silence that followed this statement, Walt said, '*I'm* OK now. The pain is gone, and I can see as well as ever I could.' He touched Moses' arm. 'I'm sure *your* eyes will get better too.'

Tembo Chief Guardian was keeping watch at the gorge entrance when Kidogo and Rafiki came and asked him if he could describe the pool where Lonely's tusk had been dropped. He did so and allowed them to pass, but with sunset so close it was much darker inside the gorge than it had been before. Kidogo and Rafiki hurried down the track until they found the pool. Kidogo peered into the dark water but could see nothing.

'I'll wade in and feel for it,' Rafiki offered, and stepped into the shallowest part of the pool, sweeping his trunk from side to side in the water. He waded deeper but did not find the tusk until, beneath where the stream ran in from the pool above, he felt the smooth ivory tip of it jammed between two rocks. He tried to free it with his trunk but could not. Then, kneeling in the water and breathing through his upraised trunk, he poked at it with his own tusk but still it wouldn't move.

He tried again, and as his tusk touched Lonely's tusk under the water his head was filled with a song in low~sound.

362

We can all be ~ part of Mana
We will all be ~ part of Mana
If we share the Love within us
Love that Mana ~ needs to function
For the future of our planet.
For the future of our planet.
For the future of our planet.

He raised his head above the water and asked Kidogo if she had spoken or sung in low~sound.

'No I didn't,' she replied. 'Why do you ask me that?'

Rafiki didn't answer her but just looked up at the dark sides of the gorge and up and down the path which was now in deep shadow.

'Come up out of the water,' Kidogo said. 'We should leave now before it is so dark we can't see. We'll come back tomorrow when it is light.'

Rafiki climbed up from the pool and followed Kidogo along the path, frequently looking back over his shoulder.

There was a gathering of tembos by the gorge entrance, with M'zee at its centre. Many of them had also explored the Mount and were telling the old one about the caves filled with tusks.

Tembo Carefree told them, 'That is the store for the Love of Tembokind. Here tembos have come, whenever they could, to step-over and leave their Love-filled tusks in safety, away from the greed of humans. That is why no humans, other than those of the First People, are allowed to leave here. We fear they may betray our secret.'

Tembo Boy said, 'Not *all* humans would betray the secret. Girl and I knew two humans who *could* be trusted.'

'I am sure there are many others too – but how could a guardian know which they are.'

Boy didn't answer, but Girl asked, 'If this is so, how is it we can we trust the little people?'

'The First People, as they like us to call them, have lived in here since *before* tembos even discovered this place. They have no desire to take our ivories. It was told to me that they welcomed us here and together we built the Mount in the days of the Yellow Tusks. Later, when the men they called *slavers* were using other men to carry away our free tusks to the sea, we were glad that they never found this place. None of those men – the ones who carried the tusks – ever came back to their homes. Those men, and the ivories they had carried, were taken away in *dhows* which floated on the sea. It was a bad time, both for humans and for tembos.'

'What will happen to all the tusks which are kept here in the Mount?' one temba asked.

'Only Mana knows that, but for the time being I think the ivories you have brought with you should be laid inside the empty tembo-tree.'

'Will we still be able to read them there?' a tembo asked.

'Of course. Any tembo who can read can learn from the ivories of those who have stepped-over. It is a heritage of knowledge for us all. When there were other tembos here to share the duties of guardian I, myself, have borrowed tusks from the Mount and passed many a day and night reading them in the Guardian's cave.'

No tembo mentioned the tusk of Tembo Lonely which had fallen in the stream, and Kidogo whispered to Rafiki that he should not speak of it. There was something about it she still had to find out – something that intrigued and excited her.

When the other tembos moved away Kidogo asked M'zee how he was feeling.

'Very tired,' he replied, 'but very happy. We have all come

safely to this Place of Peace, and the Sisters are feeding me well. The grass here is very sweet – and I discovered a joyful thing that I had wanted to know almost all of my life.'

'Is it something you can tell me and Rafiki – or is it for you only to know?' Kidogo's voice was low and gentle.

'You may think I am a stupid old tembull, but ever since my mother, Tembella Grace, pushed me out of the family I have wondered if she had loved me as much as I had always believed.'

Kidogo was about to speak but M'zee raise his trunk to silence her.

'I know. You are going to tell me that *all* tembellas must do that when their sons have come to the age of jostling – but I couldn't believe it would apply to *me*. Well – today, when you were elsewhere, I read my mother's ivories, the ones the Sisters carried here. I sought the scenes where I was made to leave the family and learned that I had been a troublesome and selfish youngster. But I also learned that my mother loved me despite all my faults – and that she suffered within herself at having to do what *all* Tembellas have *always* had to do. To know this has given me great regret for my behaviour – but joy at knowing of her enduring Love.'

Kidogo touched his forehead and said, 'Sleep well. You have brought us all safely to this wonderful place.'

Lars and Ryan lay in their sleeping bags on beds of sweet-smelling dried grass. Light from the dying fire flickered on the underside of the projecting rock that roofed the shelter and beyond this, stars glowed in a purple-black sky.

Ryan spoke quietly to Lars. 'Some place this, eh?'

'I think I must be in another of those dreams,' Lars replied.

'How about those girls, then? Aren't they a couple of crackers?'

'One shouldn't call grown women *girls*,' Lars reminded him.

'To hell with you and all that PC nonsense. They're two lovely girls and they fancy us. I know that.'

Lars was silent for a minute, then said, 'Tomorrow, I want to look at that circular stone place in the centre of the crater. How long do you think we'll be staying here?'

'Forever – if I have my way. Have you ever been in a better place in all your life?'

Lars ran through in his mind the places he had loved. The view of Table Mountain from across the bay at Cape Town must surely be one of the most dramatic and beautiful in the entire world, and he had loved the time he'd spent climbing on that mountain and on Kilimanjaro. He had been thrilled by the spectacular views of the fjords in Norway when his father had taken him there as a boy – but each had been just views. There was something else here, something he couldn't quite place.

'No, I haven't,' he finally replied. 'But I won't mind when we set off back to Arusha.'

'You don't know when the Good Lord has given you a treat.'

'You told me you didn't believe in God!'

'Perhaps I'm beginning to, and wondering what I've done to deserve this. I'm looking forward to seeing that stone fort thing. I visited a place that looks like that in County Kerry once. But 'twas a long time ago . . .

De/ne listened to the conversation from the next recess. With his acute hearing and an acoustic aberration in the curve of the rock overhead, he could hear every word. He liked what Ryan had been saying about staying but was less happy with Lars' talk of going back to Arusha. But then, this was only their first day here.

Sarah and Ruth had also been talking quietly to each other in the recess on the far side of the fire.

'I think I've chosen the nicest one,' Ruth said, with just a touch of smugness. 'Yours is a bit cold – like father could be.'

'I'll warm him up,' Sarah replied, not quite sure what she meant. 'When do you think Grandfather will let us marry them?'

'Remember what he told us. We are to take our time – not to appear to be in a hurry. Like he told us *he* has to be when he is stalking a buck. Move too quickly and you will frighten it away.'

'Don't you think they will *want* to be married to us and give us babies?'

'I don't know. Men may not think the way we women do.'

Walt lay in his tent, uncomfortable on the hard ground. He had noticed that Lars and Ryan had been given beds of grass to sleep on but there had been no such luxury for him. He would complain to the god-damned management! Then he smiled at his automatic reaction. Here, he was not the wealthy guest at some five-star hotel. Here, he was the guy who had shot one of the jumbos that these men treated as equals, elephants who had carried him and his guide to this place where, for the first time since he had left the States and come to Africa, he felt safe. Perhaps he shouldn't complain after all. Outside his tent, he could hear Moses humming hymn tunes quietly to himself in the darkness. The Maasai had not been given a grass bed either. Was the poor guy losing his mind? He felt responsible for him but there was nothing he could do for him here. Perhaps, when they got back to Arusha . . .

Moses was thinking of the American sleeping in the tent next to where he lay on the hard rock floor, covered only by a blanket. This didn't trouble *him* – he had spent many such nights in his life, especially when he was a boy herding his father's cattle. He hated his blindness but was beginning to accept it. The American was showing him some little kindnesses, guiding him by the elbow across hazards he could not see and passing him his food.

Perhaps his blindness was a punishment from the God of the Maasai, Lengai, who lived on the volcano to the north of where they were now, for abandoning Him and worshipping the Christian's God. Or it might be a punishment from *their* God because he had left Him behind at the Mission. He started to sing one of the hymns he had learned there.

Temba Kidogo slept between Old M'zee and her friend, Rafiki. It was good to know they were all safe here in the Place of Peace, with the only entrance guarded by at least one of the jostlers. 'Not jostlers now,' she corrected herself. 'Tembulls.' All three had matured into fine bulls with worthy tusks and she was sure they could be relied upon to protect them all.

In the morning Kidogo woke Rafiki at first light and guided him sleepily towards the entrance to the gorge. Clouds were gathering around the rim of the crater but the sky over the grasslands in the centre was clear. There will be rain later, she thought, and was pleased. Regular rain would keep the grass growing to feed the many tembos now living within the sheltering walls.

At the entrance to the gorge, Tembo Two Eyes was alert and challenged them. Kidogo greeted him and asked why he and Tembo Chief Guardian didn't use the guardian's cave further down the gorge.

'It's spooky down there,' he replied. 'And up here I can watch what the other tembos – and the humans – are doing. Today, before it was fully light, the little man who calls himself De/ne, went down into the gorge carrying a bow for hunting and a long, round box, which I believe held arrows. I prefer it up here, and I can watch the entrance just as well.'

When Kidogo and Rafiki reached the pool where Lonely's tusk was wedged between the rocks, Rafiki waded in, the cool water rapidly washing away any remnants of sleep.

'I want you to do exactly what you did last evening,' Kidogo called to him and, if you hear any singing, tell me.'

Rafiki waded deeper, found the trapped ivory with his trunk and touched it with his single tusk. As before, his head was filled with singing.

> Mana *needs the ~ Love we give him,*
> *Formed from Joy and ~ care for others*
> *For Love is the ~ magic power*
> *The force that linques ~ us all together.*

He moved his tusk, touched a different place with it and again his head filled with song.

> *In the dim and ~ distant ages*
> *This our planet ~ was quite lifeless.*
> *Came a time when ~ it was ready*
> *Ready like a ~ flower open,*
> *Craving for a ~ speck of pollen.*

Still holding his breath and moving his tusk again to another place, he heard more.

Gaia chose from ~ all her creatures
Four to serve our ~ planet's interests
Four to give it ~ thought and focus
Four to save it ~ from destruction
Four were given ~ souls and duties.

Rafiki tried another place and, as he did so, Lonely's tusk came free. He grabbed at it with his trunk and grasped it firmly to stop it dropping to the bottom of the pool, then holding it above the water he waded backwards out of the pool, and lay the tusk at Kidogo's feet.

'Did you hear any singing this time?' she asked him.

'Only when I touched it with my tusk,' he replied. 'Then it seemed as if there was a singing inside my head. But it stopped whenever I moved my tusk away.'

'What was the song?' she asked, almost trembling with excitement.

'I can't remember much,' he replied. 'Last evening, the song was about *Mana* and *Love*. Today, it was about someone called *Gaia* choosing four creatures – and there was a bit about flowers and pollen.'

'That was the whale's song!' said Kidogo. 'And you were away with the Sisters at the Sacred Pool when Lonely sang it. You've found the whale's song!' She picked up the tusk and hurried up the path, followed by a bemused Rafiki. She acknowledged Tembo Two Eyes as she passed and placed Lonely's tusk on the grass in the open.

'Now,' she said. 'Now touch the ivory with your tusk and tell me just what you hear – as you hear it.'

Rafiki lowered his head and moved his tusk slowly along the one lying on the ground.

'Nothing,' he said. 'No singing at all. I must have imagined it.'

'You can't have,' Kidogo insisted. 'What you told me you heard was all in the whale's song, and *you* weren't there to hear it when Lonely sang it for us. You couldn't have imagined it – nor remembered it. Please, Rafiki, try again.'

Rafiki knelt on the warm grass and moved his tusk backwards and forwards against Lonely's tusk, but with no results. Kidogo found she could as usual *read* the tusk with her trunk, even the scene where Lonely was in the water with the whale, apparently listening to his song. But, try what they might, the tusk remained silent for them both.

They left the ivory on the grass while they grazed nearby. Seeing De/ne return from his hunt, carrying a small, dead, antelope over his shoulders, Kidogo and Rafiki lifted their trunks to acknowledge him, and he raised his hand in return as rain started to fall. Kidogo was sad for the animal, which had given its life to feed the humans and, as she watched De/ne cross the grassland past the families of elephants grazing in the warm gentle rain, she felt glad that Mana had made tembos able to live on the leaves of trees and grass, but she knew that many creatures had to kill others to eat – or die themselves. Whatever *she* felt about such killings would never change *that* fact.

She swallowed her mouthful of grass and turned her attention back to Lonely's tusk. The rain was pleasant on her back and tickled as it ran down her sides but she ignored it.

'Try once more,' she urged Rafiki. 'The song must be in there if you have heard it twice.'

With a look that said, 'It's a waste of time but I'll do it for *you*,' Rafiki knelt again and moved his tusk slowly along Lonely's where it lay on the ground, beaded with raindrops.

'I can hear it *now*!' he said. 'But only faintly. The song is saying:

> *'In the dim and ~ distant ages*
> *This our planet ~ was quite lifeless.*
> *Came a time when ~ it was ready*
> *Ready like a ~ flower open,*
> *Craving for a ~ speck of pollen.*
>
> *Floating in from ~ where-we-know-not*
> *Came a drift of ~ cosmic pollen*
> *Carrying the ~ sacred Life-force*
> *To this silent ~ waiting planet.*
> *Like the flower ~ gaining pollen*
> *Earth responded ~ to this Life-force.'*

Rafiki lifted his head and got to his feet. 'You were right, Kidogo. The song *is* there. Perhaps I can only hear it when the ivory is wet.'

De/ne walked over the log bridge with the buck he had killed slung across his shoulders, and his bow and the quiver of arrows in his hand. In the leather bag he always carried, was his radio.

After killing the buck, he had turned the knob on the front until he heard the voices he recognised as those of the BBC World Service. He had listened to the whole news bulletin, while wondering all the time why Lars wanted to return to Arusha.

De/ne had tried to make sense of the various news items but the idea of suicide bombings, war, and threats of war between neighbouring countries was as alien to him as the reports that had followed, detailing the movements of stock markets and the soaring price of oil and gas. He shook his head, turned the radio off and asked the Mantis on the bush near him if he should smash the set and bury it. Mantis stared back at him and De/ne knew the time was wrong for him to do that. He put the radio back into his leather bag, picked up the buck and turned towards his home.

The rain, which had started to fall as he had re-entered the crater, hadn't bothered him. His granddaughters had finished planting the maize and the rain was needed to start it growing. He pictured the bright green shoots that in a just a few days time would push up through the warm, damp soil. Twice a year this miracle of growth was a joy to him and he never failed to be moved by how one small seed could produce such a large plant with so many more seeds for his family to eat.

At the shelter he hung the dead antelope by its hind legs on a wooden peg hammered into a crack in the rock and joined the others for breakfast. His granddaughters had put aside a portion of mealie porridge for him and there was a bunch of newly picked bananas hanging from another peg near his head.

He was glad to see that the girls had discarded their shirt-tops this morning – women of the First People had no need to hide their breasts. It had only been the strange idea of their father that had led them to make shirt-tops for themselves at all.

De/ne studied the faces of Lars and Ryan as he ate his porridge from a bowl made of a half gourd. Ryan was looking at Ruth with evident admiration but Lars seemed to be avoiding Sarah's attempts to attract his attention.

Walt was eating a banana and looking bleary-eyed and tired, but Moses had finished his porridge and was staring blindly out across the crater.

Ryan was first to speak. 'Will you two young ladies be so kind as to take my friend and me to see the sights?' he asked.

'What are "the sights"?' Ruth asked.

'Sure, it is your plantations and the stone circle thing down there,' he replied.

'We would be pleased to do that,' Ruth replied making a little curtsy.

'Sure, an' I love the way you do that,' he said.

Lars said, 'Will you stop being so bloody Irish.'

Ryan looked at him in amazement and said, 'What's eating you, then?'

'Oh, sorry, Ryan,' said Lars, and turned to the girls. 'We *would* like it if you would show us "the sights".' Then, lightly touching the Maasai man's elbow, he asked Walt and Moses, 'Are you two coming?'

Walt shook his head. 'I'm going back to my tent. I didn't sleep much last night.'

Moses said nothing and did not even acknowledge the invitation.

De/ne, who had finished his porridge and was sharpening a small knife with a piece of stone, waved to indicate that the four should go without him as he was staying where he was.

CHAPTER THIRTY-ONE

The rain had stopped by the time the girls were ready to lead Ryan and Lars on their walk.

They followed a path from the rock-shelter, passed several other such shelters, now abandoned, where pictures of animals, mostly elephants, were painted on the walls. The girls then led them alongside patches of cleared ground and past trees with horizontal hollow logs hanging from their branches, each log humming with the buzz of many bees. Ryan showed great interest in the clearings, asking Ruth what was planted in each patch. They passed the melon and the pumpkin plantations and walked through many patches which had once been cultivated but were now neglected and overgrown, until they came to the banana grove near the stream.

'There must have been many more people here at one time,' Ryan remarked.

'There were,' Sarah replied. 'But that was long before we were born. We were the last babies here. I would like it if more were to be born here.' She was looking at Lars as she said this but he avoided her eyes and walked off down the path.

The others followed and stopped by the patch of ground where the girls had planted the mealies the day before.

'Now, that's a big patch to be feeding just the three of you,' Ryan said.

Ruth looked at her sister and said, 'Some are always taken by the birds of the air and others by small animals –

but Grandfather told us to plant more this year in case we were to have guests. And now we have. Come. We will show you the Mount.'

'What's the Mount?' Lars asked, knowing he had been rude in walking away and wanting to make amends by joining in again.

'You are teasing me,' Sarah said with a smile and a wave of her hand towards the stone circle. 'Over there. You asked to be shown *the sights*.'

Groups of elephants, mothers and babies of various ages, were grazing or wallowing in the lake as the four humans strolled through the waist-high grass towards the stone circle. White storks walked close to them, snatching at grasshoppers and other insects, while a secretary bird, with long plumes hanging down behind its head, strutted about with great dignity.

'The birds don't seem to be afraid of us,' Ryan remarked.

'Why should they be? We're not going to hurt them,' Ruth replied. '*You* won't, will you?'

'Of course we won't,' Ryan told her.

As they neared the Mount, Lars hurried forward excitedly to study the way the stones fitted together. He ran his fingers along the tightly fitting joints then turned to Ryan. 'These are just like the walls at Machu Pichu, in South America. I saw pictures of it in a *National Geographic* magazine once. It said no one knew how they were made to fit together so perfectly. Look – you couldn't get a sheet of paper between them.'

'Aren't all high stone walls made like that?' Sarah asked innocently.

'Oh no,' Lars replied. 'Most are made of blocks like this.' He made the shape of oblong-shaped block in the air with his hands.

376

'Don't they all come apart when the ground shakes?' Sarah asked.

'They're stuck together with stuff we call cement,' Lars replied defensively.

Ryan laughed. 'Even so,' he said. 'They *do* come apart if the ground shakes enough.'

Lars walked around the wall ahead of them looking for an entrance. When he came to it, he remembered his manners and waited for the others to catch up.

'Can we go through here?' he asked Ruth.

It was Sarah who replied. 'The Mount is special to the elephants but they have never minded if *we* come here. I am sure they won't mind if you come too. Follow me.'

As they entered the enclosure, Sarah waved to Tembo Carefree who was searching the paving for errant seedlings, and he raised his trunk in greeting. She stooped into the tembotalk stance and moved her arm-trunk rapidly while wiggling her left ear with her finger and making noises in her throat.

Tembo Carefree spoke back to her when she'd finished.

'What was the old fella saying to you?' Ryan asked.

'He said we are welcome to go where we wish, but to warn you not to fall down the fire-pit. Over there,' Sarah added, pointing. 'The elephants sometimes call it the Mouth of Mana.'

Ryan walked cautiously over to the hole, which was set around with smooth stones that sloped gently down towards the opening. It was certainly large enough for a man or even an elephant to fall into. He looked down into the darkness and saw what might have been a tiny fire far below, then gagged as a wisp of burning sulphur caught in his throat.

He coughed as he rejoined the others. 'That's scary! It must be a vent down to the guts of the volcano. This one must be just dormant like Kili was.' After a moment, he asked Sarah, 'Why do the elephants call it the Mouth of Mana?'

This time it was Ruth who replied. 'Mana is like the God in the bible that Father left for us. In the old days when lots of elephants came here to die, one of their tusks would be dropped down into the fire-pit as a gift to Mana. It was like when Abraham thought he had to sacrifice his son, Isaac, to Jehovah.'

'What did the elephants do with the second tusk?' Lars asked.

Sarah led them to the nearest cave in the inner wall and stood aside to let Lars and Ryan see inside.

Ryan whistled, much like Rafiki had done the day before. 'Holy Mother of God, can you see all that ivory? There must be thousands of tusks in there.'

Lars had gone to the next entrance. 'There's more in here,' he called to Ryan.

'You know what this place is?' Ryan called back. 'Tis the fabled elephants' graveyard. I should have guessed that's where we are.'

The men walked round the inner wall peering into each of the caves, followed by the two girls, then went across to the ancient baobab at the centre. In the hollow, lying on beds of freshly picked grass, were some of the tusks which the elephants had carried with them into the crater the day before and must have brought here. They were laid in a row within the huge hollow of the tree, the two largest – which Lars and Ryan had found in the cave on Kilimanjaro – enclosing the others like a set of brackets.

The girls marvelled at the size of them.

'There is much Love here,' Ruth said.

Sarah stepped inside the hollow tree and ran her hands slowly along one of the huge tusks. 'These are the tusks of Tembo Jay,' she said.

'Who was Tembo Jay?' Ryan asked, and Sarah told the men what Tembo Carefree had once told her and Ruth about the gentle giant who had challenged the rule of the Yellow Tusks so long ago, and had apparently lost. 'It was then the First People and the Tembos built this secret place.'

'Will you ask the elephant if he knows how they got all the stones to fit together so precisely?' Lars asked.

Sarah walked across to where Tembo Carefree stood quietly watching them, stooped, swung her arm and spoke to him. When they'd finished talking she came back and told Lars, '*He* doesn't know but thinks that our grandfather may. Is that important to you?'

'Not important – just interesting.'

Ryan said, 'And I was wondering what he is doing. It reminds me of weeding the garden.'

'Before Grandfather went away he used to stand guard at the gorge whilst this elephant did what you are calling *weeding the garden*. If this is not done the greedy trees will grow in all the cracks and their roots would push the stones apart. It has not been done since Grandfather left.'

They left the Mount with a fare-well wave to Tembo Carefree and walked together across the grassland, over the tree-trunk bridge and back up towards the shelter. The girls turned off the track, saying it was time for them to wash themselves and comb their hair, while Lars and Ryan went on and arrived as De/ne and Walt had just finished skinning the antelope. Walt was quite expertly cutting the carcase into joints while Moses was sitting morosely on his own at the far end of the shelter.

De/ne looked up at Lars and asked what he thought of the Mount.

'Did your people really build that place?' he asked.

De/ne's grin faded. 'Don't you think we could?' he asked.

Lars realised he had been clumsy with his question. 'No, it isn't that,' he replied. 'It's just that the way the stones are fitted together reminds me of a place in South America. Do you know how it was done?'

'That's simple,' he said. 'But you must remember that when my people built it we had no metal tools – only stones harder than those that make the walls.'

Lars and Ryan sat down on a rock in the shade of the shelter to listen and Walt stood, with his knife still in his hand. De/ne was warming to his story and moved about, illustrating every point with fluid movements of his hands.

'The tembos who lived here were afraid of the big bulls, who they called the Yellow Tusks,' he said. 'They were horrible, idle, greedy elephants, interested only in their own comfort and pleasures. The tembos from all around here asked my people to build a place where they could be safe if the Yellow Tusks came, and to build it around the fire-pit where they had always made gifts of ivory to Mana.

'Often the ground here shakes and moves. I believe you call this an *earthquake*.' He looked at Lars, who nodded in confirmation but didn't speak, not wanting to spoil the flow of the little man's story.

'My people had to find a way to stop the stones falling down from on top of one another when these *earthquakes* happened and also to stop the Yellow Tusks pushing them over if they did find their way in here. So the stones would have to be of different shapes and fit closely together.

'In those days there were many more families of the First People living here, and if we wanted more people to come, we only had to light a fire up there.' He pointed to the peak on the rim of the crater.

'The stone here inside the crater is quite soft – you can see how this shelter has been carved out by the winds of ages, but outside, down in the riverbeds, it easy to find round stones that are much harder and my people used these stones to hammer at the softer ones which lay about in here, until they were the shape we wanted them to be.

'While the men were doing this, the women made ropes from twisted grasses and reeds from the lake, and the tembos pulled the stones to the Mount and together they levered them up into their places.'

He stopped as though that was the end of his story and Lars asked, 'But how did they get the shapes to fit together so well?'

De/ne picked up the antelope skin from where it was draped across a rock, smothered in flies. 'If we want to make things with these skins, we have to treat them in different ways.' He fingered his loin-cloth. 'I can make an animal skin as soft as this or as hard as a Maasai shield. I can make it so that the hairs stay on, or the hairs come off. In the days when my people shaped the stones, they took many skins with the hair off and sewed them together with the tough strings you find in a giraffe's neck.

'They then put the skins into the lake until they were soft and laid them over the tops of the stones that were already in place and pushed the soft skin down tight into any cracks and hollows. Then I am sure they would have walked away and played with their children in the sunshine or lain in the shade and slept.' He mimicked sleep by putting his hands together against his head, tilting it to one side and closing his eyes.

'When they came back the skins would have dried hard and be the shape of the stones underneath. It is a simple thing to do.' He stopped, sat on a rock and looked at Lars as though the story was over.

'And then?' Lars asked.

De/ne shook his head slightly and said, 'They shaped more stones until they fitted into the *other* side of the skins.'

'Good God,' said Lars. 'It's as simple as that. To think that learnéd scientists have puzzled over how that was done at Machu Pichu for decades.' He paused. 'You've still got to get the stones into position.'

De/ne stood up again and performed another little pantomime. 'The tembos pulled them with the ropes the women had made. They pulled the shaped stones up slopes made of earth and rolled them over on top of the others that were already there. They always fitted into their position – and they are still there, as you have seen today.'

'When I get back to civilisation I will astound the waiting world by explaining how the rocks of Machu Pichu were made to fit together.'

'There aren't any elephants in South America,' Ryan pointed out.

'There don't need to be. Not if you have enough men with levers – and they probably used llama skins to make the moulds – the templates – or whatever *they* would have called them.'

De/ne was looking down the path at Sarah and Ruth who were walking up towards them, holding hands and laughing together. He didn't like this talk of 'getting back to civilisation'. His plan wasn't working yet, at least not as far as Lars was concerned. But now he had to make biltong and he busied himself cutting some of the antelope meat into thin strips and hanging them up to dry in the warm breeze.

CHAPTER THIRTY-TWO

'We must tell M'zee,' Kidogo said when she realised Rafiki had rediscovered the whale's song hidden in Tembo Lonely's tusk. She wanted to share this exciting news with the old one and was sure he would be as pleased as she was. How strange that the tusk had to be wet!

'Will you bring the ivory, Rafiki?' she asked, and hurried off to where M'zee stood as she had first seen him, up to his belly in a swamp. But now, he appeared even more gaunt and had difficulty lifting his head when she called out to him.

'Wait here for me,' she told the ever-patient Rafiki. 'We mustn't risk losing that tusk in the water again.'

Kidogo waded out into the lake, passing the mothers and their babies romping and playing in the shallows, until she was within trunk-reach of M'zee. His head had drooped again and he appeared to be asleep. She spoke to him quietly and touched his forehead respectfully as he opened his eyes.

'Greetings, daughter of my daughter,' he said.

Kidogo was sad he no longer called her 'my Shadow', but knew that role was over for her.

'May Mana bless you,' she replied, and rushed into telling him that they had found the whale's song hidden in Lonely's tusk and that the ivory had to be wet for—

'Not so fast, not so fast,' he said. 'My brain is still half asleep.'

She waited while he sprayed water onto his face and over his back. 'Now, tell me again. Just so.'

It had been a long time since she had heard him say 'Just so.' How she loved this old tembo!

She repeated what she had already said about the song, and M'zee agreed that it should be taught to all who would listen.

Then he said, 'You have been to the place they call the Mount, I believe. Will you tell me about it? I heard some words from the other tembos yesterday but you describe places and things so much better than they do. You can tell me as we wade ashore.'

By the time they reached the bank where Rafiki stood with Lonely's tusk between his feet, Kidogo had described the Mount with its caves full of tusks and the fire-pit.

'Let me rest here for a while, then, if it pleases you, will you take me there?'

'It will please me very much,' she replied.

While the three rested, the two Sisters, Comfort and Kindness, came and joined them, each carrying a bundle of food-wads, for which M'zee thanked them and swallowed the wads before they all moved off together towards the Mount.

Kidogo noticed Tembo Three Eyes – No! She mustn't call him that – Tembo Chief Guardian walking amongst one of the families of females, to the obvious annoyance of their Tembella. There was a dark trickle of fluid running down the side of his head and he was scenting under each of the tembas with his trunk. Kidogo was glad she was not in joyneed and watched the Tembella driving him away from her sisters and grown-up daughters with savage jabs of her tusks. Trouble there, she thought, and looked back at the entrance to the gorge where Tembo One Eye was on duty.

Was it still M'zee's responsibility to keep order – or was it perhaps hers? No. The Tembellas were older and probably much wiser than she was. She was no longer a Shadow to the old one – it couldn't possibly be *her* responsibility.

At the Mount, M'zee had to stop for a while to gather enough strength to squeeze through the narrow part, then he stood and looked about him. Tembo Carefree was there and came forward to touch the old one's forehead. 'Welcome to the Mount in the Place of Peace', he said. 'You will have come to read the tusks of Tembo Jay, I expect. They are in the belly of the tembo-tree.'

M'zee peered into the hollow. He could see the tusks of his friend Steadfast, one of Tembo Lonely's tusks and the ivories of his mother, Tembella Grace, lying between those of Tembo Jay. 'Where are the others?' he asked.

Tembo Carefree replied, 'They are stored safely here with the tusks of many more tembos who have stepped-over. Later, when you have rested, I will show you where they are.'

'I *would* like to see them,' M'zee replied, every word seeming an effort. 'But now I must rest in the shade of that tree.'

When he was settled, watched over by the two Sisters with the same Love and respect they had shown to his mother, Rafiki approached Tembo Carefree with Lonely's tusk. I would like to leave this here in your care,' he said. 'It holds the song of the whale which tells us much about who we are – and what we are. And not just tembos – but all the creatures in this world.'

'That must be some song,' Carefree replied. 'Is it like the *Song of Tembo Jay*, which my own dear Tembella told me had been lost for ever?' Without waiting for an answer he went on, 'But I am no longer a guardian – I am Tembo *Carefree*.' He waved his trunk in a light-hearted way, then seeing the expression on the faces of the other tembos he lowered it, and said, 'I would be pleased to guard such a treasure.'

'We thank you,' Kidogo said. 'We know you will guard it well. When it next rains, Rafiki will hear the whale's song, tell it to me and I will sing it for all tembos to learn.' She looked up at the sky. Clouds were forming above the crater rim. 'I think it will be tonight,' she said.

With Rafiki once more close behind her, she walked out of the Mount and they grazed together as she explained how she wanted him to repeat each part of the whale's song to her and wait while she sang it in low~sound from the walls of the Mount so that all the tembos in the crater could hear and remember it.

'Do you think I can do that well enough,' she asked her friend.

'Whatever you do, you do well,' replied Rafiki. 'Shall we go back now? The rain may start to fall soon.' They walked back through the passageway as the sun slid down behind the crater rim and darkness started to fill the caldera. M'zee was still leaning against the tembo-tree with his eyes closed. Tembo Carefree stood nearby.

'You have come for the singing tusk,' he called to them. 'I will get it for you,' and he reached into the hollow of the tree and drew it out, holding it carefully. Overhead the few leaves of the old tree rustled gently. 'Where do you want me to put it?' he asked.

'On the wall, where it will get the most rain when it comes,' Kidogo replied.

Carefree lifted the tusk with his trunk, reached up and laid it on top of the wall and held it there while Rafiki and Kidogo walked up a stone-paved ramp leading up to the top of the wall, glad of the light from the moon which was rising over the eastern rim of the crater and shining through gaps in the clouds. 'Go carefully,' Rafiki told her.

When they reached the place where Carefree was still holding Lonely's tusk, Rafiki took it and laid it across the top of the wall, holding it lightly with his foot so that it could not fall and waited for rain that did not come, the few clouds drifting away in the moonlight. 'What now?' Rafiki asked her.

Kidogo called down into the hollow of the Mount. 'Temba Care and Temba Kindness, will you linque with M'zee, Carefree and the tembo-tree and ask Mana for rain?'

After he had sent the e-mail to America, Mr Burns sat in his empty office in Arusha, looking out of the window into the yard beyond, which was full of the safari vehicles he had acquired at giveaway prices from operators who had already left Tanzania. His latest plan had been to drain the tanks of all of the vehicles and transfer what fuel was left in them to just one of the vehicles but *klefti-wallahs* had cut through the compound's wire fencing in the night and beaten him to it. Now there was unlikely to be enough to get him to the coast, let alone South Africa or Botswana. News from there was not good either.

The Directors of Schwiner Enterprises Inc. were seated around the polished oval table in the luxurious boardroom on the twenty-seventh floor. In a sombre tone, the Vice President announced that nothing had been heard from their CEO since he had left the International Hotel in Arusha with a Maasai guide to shoot a trophy elephant. An unconfirmed report had been received that a Land Cruiser, similar to the one hired by Walt, had been seen by local tribesmen in a lake following a flash flood, and there may have been two survivors. The Vice President said he was arranging for all action to be taken to locate and facilitate the return of their CEO.

Meanwhile, he was pleased to report that, with the demand for oil and gas running at unprecedented levels and sales at record prices, the profit expectations of the company were anticipated to be at an all-time high. 'Our share price, gentlemen, is going through the roof.'

Walt's PA tapped at the door, came into the boardroom, and handed the Vice President a sheet of paper. He read through it and grimaced.

'Gentlemen. This e-mail has just come in from a Mr Burns in Arusha, Tanzania. Mr Burns is the agent who organised Walt's safari.

'It reads, *"I regret that little can be done to locate Mr Schwiner and his guide, as Tanzania is suffering from an acute shortage of all forms of fuel. The government here is telling us that businesses in Africa can no longer afford to import oil supplies as the demand from the USA and China is so great that it has put the prices beyond our reach. Our police service, army and the independent safari operators have virtually exhausted their fuel stocks, and tankers bound for Dar es Salaam have been diverted to Shanghai and America. Search aircraft, and even commercial airliners, have been grounded and all normal commerce is coming to a halt. I will keep you informed of any developments but have to warn you that it is unlikely that resources can be made available to find Mr Schwiner."*

'I suggest we reply, *"Spare no costs. Make whatever arrangements are needed to locate Mr Schwiner and find ways to return him to this country. I repeat, spare no costs."* Are we agreed, gentlemen?'

And after their murmured approval, he added, 'Would you minute that please.'

CHAPTER THIRTY-THREE

From her position on the wall, Kidogo could see the shapes of tembas and youngsters making their way towards the Mount in the fitful moonlight, and wondered how they had known that a linquing was to take place. As many as could came up the narrow entrance path and crowded into the space around the tree, keeping well clear of the fire-pit, while later arrivals formed linquing groups outside the walls. Tembo Carefree, M'zee, and the Sisters had their foreheads pressed against the twisted bole of the tembo-tree. When they were all in place Rafiki called out, as he had done at the riverbed before the flood, 'Now, shut your eyes and think of rain. Nothing else – just rain – wet and cool – bringing life to the land.'

The clouds moved across the moon and shortly afterwards a gentle rain fell, wetting their backs, the warm stones of the wall, and Tembo Lonely's tusk.

'Now,' Kidogo whispered to Rafiki. 'Now. Touch your tusk to the ivory and make it sing for us all.'

As the clouds cleared again she saw Rafiki kneel and touch the wet tusk with his own. As if from far away, Tembo Lonely's voice was singing. Kidogo didn't need to repeat the words as she had planned; all the tembos could hear it for themselves.

In the dim and ~ distant ages
This our planet ~ was quite lifeless.
Came a time when ~ it was ready
Ready like a ~ flower open,
Craving for a ~ speck of pollen . . .

In the shelter across the grassland, above the plantation, the humans were eating roasted antelope meat and listening to the drip, drip, drip of the rain from the rock overhang. Suddenly, Moses stood up, threw the bone he was gnawing onto the fire and spoke towards where he knew Walt was sitting.

'That gourd,' he said. 'The one the boy used to bring me *saroi*. I know you have kept it, because I found it near the tent. I need it now.'

Walt got quietly to his feet, disappeared out of the firelight towards Moses' sleeping area and returned carrying the gourd, which he put into Moses' hands. The Maasai, guiding himself by keeping the warmth and crackle of the fire on his right, stepped outside into the damp air. He knelt on the soil, upturned the gourd so that the opening was on the ground and put his ear against the closed end.

'An elephant is singing tonight – and I can hear it.'

Lars, his senses reeling from the events of the past few weeks and surprised by Moses' unexpected activity, asked, 'What is it singing?'

But Moses hushed him with a wave of his hand, and said, 'It is telling of the days when there was no life on Earth and how Life came.

> *'Floating in from ~ where-we-know-not*
> *Came a drift of ~ cosmic pollen*
> *Carrying the ~ sacred Life-force*
> *To this silent ~ waiting planet.*
>
> *Like the flower ~ gaining pollen*
> *Earth responded ~ to this Life-force.*
> *Simple plants and ~ simple creatures*
> *Flourished here in ~ great abundance*
> *Making from this ~ sterile body*
> *Something more than ~ rocks and water.'*

'That's a beautiful song,' Ryan said, but once more Moses waved him to be quiet and continued to interpret the song for them.

> *'As time passed these ~ plants and creatures*
> *Grew more complex ~ found their places*
> *Leading to a ~ wondrous richness*
> *Making up the ~ world around us.'*

On the wall of the Mount, Kidogo had laid her trunk along Rafiki's back, pleased that she didn't need to sing the song herself as she was sure it was more poignant when heard in the voice of Lonely himself.

> *We can all be ~ part of Mana*
> *We will all be ~ part of Mana*
> *If we share the Love within us*
> *Love that Mana ~ needs to function*
> *For the future of our planet.*
> *For the future of our planet.*
> *For the future of our planet.*

As the song ended, to a murmur of appreciation from the assembled tembos, Kidogo lifted her trunk, wiped her eyes, and thanked her friend. Rafiki was standing, shoulders hunched, in an attitude of great exhaustion, while she felt hugely elated and excited by the experience. She reached out to share her feelings with him, but as he half turned and raised his trunk to meet hers the tusk he'd been holding slid from his grasp and fell over the inner edge of the wall. It bounced with a hollow thud on the paved area below, bounced twice more, then slithered like a snake down the sloping stones, paused momentarily at the edge, then fell into the fire-pit.

A young tembo stepped forward to peer down the hole but was pulled back sharply by his mother who'd quickly wrapped her trunk around one of his legs.

The word 'sacrifice' came into Kidogo's mind but that was not right. A sacrifice is deliberately made – the loss of Lonely's tusk had surely been an accident. She reached out her trunk again to touch Rafiki's forehead.

'It was probably meant to be,' she said.

When Moses had repeated the last line of the song three times, lowering his voice on each line, he stood up, leaving the gourd on the ground, and walked into the darkness towards where he slept.

No one else moved.

Eventually, Sarah spoke. 'I liked that song better than the stories about the beginning of the world in the first part of the black book. Can *both* be true?'

No one answered.

Shortly afterwards, Walt stood up and said, 'I think I'll go to bed now.'

Lars looked at Ryan, who nodded, and they both left the fireside.

Sarah repeated her question to her sister and grandfather. Ruth's sympathetic smile told Sarah that she'd been wondering the same thing, while De/ne sat smoking some rough tobacco in a short length of tube he kept in his leather bag. The faraway look in his eyes told his granddaughters they could not expect an answer from him tonight.

At breakfast the following morning, eating fresh mealie porridge the girls had prepared, Lars finished his bowlful and asked the question De/ne had been waiting for.

'When are we leaving here?'

De/ne didn't answer for a while, pretending he hadn't

heard the question. He saw the faces of his granddaughters both showing undisguised disappointment. The American had leaned forward, obviously eager to hear his reply, while Moses spooned porridge into his mouth as though he didn't care.

But it was the faces of Ryan and Lars that De/ne studied most closely. Ryan was looking at Lars as though he had uttered some obscene oath – that was good – while Lars was now looking uncomfortable.

De/ne knew he would soon have to tell them they couldn't leave. Now was probably as good a time as any. A quick kill was best. 'You *can't* leave here,' he said, watching Lars' face.

Lars looked at Ryan, then asked, 'And why not?'

'You have seen the ivory in the Mount. If you leave and tell other people, they will come here to steal it. My people have sworn to help the elephants protect their treasure. You cannot be allowed to leave.'

'If I want to go – I shall,' Lars said belligerently. Ryan put his hand on Lars' arm but he shook it off.

'Then I will have to stop you,' De/ne said calmly.

'How will you do that?' Lars demanded.

Ryan put his hand on Lars' arm again. 'Will you leave it for now?' he said. 'We can talk about this another time. I'm going down to the pool. Are you coming? We both need a bath.'

When they had finished washing themselves and their clothes, and spread the latter out over bushes to dry in the sun, Ryan said, 'Sure, and you were upsetting the little man up there. Do you really want to leave here? I could stay for ever. I'm going to ask young Ruth if she'll be my wife. I'm sure that you will have seen how we're feeling about each other. And that Sarah would make a lovely wife for *you*.'

'Hell, Ryan! We've only been here a couple of days and you're talking about getting married! I'm not saying that Sarah isn't a lovely girl, but she's *not* for me. I can't stay here – it's too small – too restricted. You know me – I'm one for high mountains – open spaces – freedom. It hasn't worked for me before – being tied, I mean.'

'Time's passing,' Ryan said. 'You're not getting any younger. Are you looking forward to a lonely old age with lots of freedom but no family – no children? And you know what it's like outside – compared with this place.'

Lars was peeling a small stick with his fingernails and flicking the slivers of bark into the pool.

'I might just consider marrying her if we could leave here,' he said.

Ryan turned on him angrily. 'You're a prat,' he said. 'You may be my best friend – but you're still a prat – a prat of the first order. Can you imagine how a lovely, innocent girl like Sarah would take to the outside world? She'd hate it. I'm hating it myself, with all its greed and selfishness and violence. 'Twas the best thing that ever happened to me to come here. If you go – you go without me – and without Sarah.'

Kidogo had spent the night consoling Rafiki, who believed it had been his fault that Lonely's tusk had fallen into the fire-pit.

'I'm sure it was meant to be,' she told him yet again. 'Remember what Tembo Carefree told us about how they used to sacrifice tusks to Mana by dropping them down that hole. You may have been guided to make a sacrifice of Lonely's tusk. After all, it didn't happen until *after* the whale's song was safe in the memories of many tembos.'

They were walking around the bottom of the cliffs that surrounded the crater, snatching at tasty twigs from encroaching trees. As they passed the entrance to the gorge where the path by the stream led to the outside world, she noticed that none of the three guardians was in place at the opening. Whoever was on guard must be down in the cave where they had first encountered Tembo Carefree, she thought – but later, having seen the three jostlers together reading from a tusk which they must have borrowed from the Mount, she wondered who *was* on guard and walked over to them and asked.

Tembo Chief Guardian told her, 'It's no business of yours. You're not Shadow to the old one now. And *we* are the guardians – but the whole thing was a waste of time. Nothing ever happened.' He turned back to running his trunk along the tusk they had been reading.

Kidogo hesitated. He was right. She was no longer M'zee's Shadow. Did she have the right to challenge them? If *she* didn't, who did? But surely it could not be right to leave the Place of Peace unguarded?

Rafiki touched her hindquarters in a way she understood to mean, 'Come away now,' and she turned and walked with him towards the Mount.

M'zee was dozing within the Mount, leaning against the trunk of the hollow tembo-tree where the shape of the tree fitted as comfortably against his body as the stones in the walls fitted against one another. He had been having more dreams and found it increasingly hard to distinguish between what he'd dreamed and what had really happened. The Sisters were looking after him well, bringing him food-wads which he didn't have to chew and even carrying water for him in their throat reserves and squirting it gently into his mouth. He wondered what he had done to deserve such attention. Soon he would step-over and, in truth, with his body aching so much, he wouldn't mind at all. How well

Mana had ordered such things. He wondered again what would be on the *other side* when he did step-over. Perhaps even the whale, whose wonderful song he had heard once more, didn't know that. It would have to be either another great adventure like his present life had been or – nothing, as some of his long-dead tembo friends had believed. He hoped for the *great adventure*, but if it *was* nothing that would be fine too, for he would know nothing about it. Truly Mana had ordered things well.

He could hear tembos coming up the slope and into the Mount. One of the jostlers – no – one of the *guardians* had been there only the day before to borrow one of Steadfast's tusks to read but this wasn't one of *them*. He lifted his tired trunk, sniffed the air and opened his eyes. Yes, he'd been right, it was his beloved Kidogo and her faithful friend, the young tembull, Rafiki. He was always glad to see them. But they weren't coming towards him. They were going to where Tembo Carefree was again pulling seedling trees from between the rocks. M'zee shut his eyes again and listened.

Kidogo was speaking. 'We have come to you,' she was saying, 'to ask what should be done. There are no guardians in the gorge nor at its entrance. You served there for many years as guardian. Surely this is a bad thing?'

Tembo Carefree snorted angrily. 'You two go to the entrance immediately and act as guardians while I find those who have neglected their duties.'

M'zee listened to Carefree's angry footsteps going down the stone path. He would need another name soon, he was sure.

Carefree found the three tembos he was seeking. They were reading together from Steadfast's free tusk, nudging each other and chortling, so did not hear him coming up behind them. Two Eyes was saying, 'Look here, that huge tembull is about to mount that skinny temba. She'll fall flat on the ground!'

One Eye was eagerly reading another part of the tusk. 'There's a big fight going on here,' he was saying, and Tembo Chief Guardian moved his trunk to where One Eye was reading.'

Carefree trumped in anger, louder than he had ever done before and the three turned to face him.

'What are you doing?' he roared.

'Just reading a tusk,' Two Eyes said meekly, and One Eye added, 'Actually, we call it *viewing*. It's easier than reading and more fun. You leave out the dull bits and just find the fights and the joynings.'

Tembo Chief Guardian was aware that his fellows were digging a pit big enough to trap them all. He had guessed why the Tembull had come to find them and he tried to excuse their absence from their duties.

'There was nothing to do in the gorge,' he said. 'It's all very well being guardians but there was nothing for us to guard against.'

Carefree resisted an impulse to sink his tusks deep into the belly of this insolent young tembull – but that was not the way of Tembo Jay, which he had always tried to follow, and he turned away. 'You three are no more worthy than as many heaps of dung,' he hissed, and walked away towards the gorge entrance where Kidogo and Rafiki stood side by side.

'Will you two share the guard duties with me in future?' he asked. 'I need tembos who can be trusted!'

CHAPTER THIRTY-FOUR

One of the tembo babies splashing in the shallows of the pool cried out in fear when he saw a water-biter gliding towards him. His mother dashed in and pushed him towards the shore, stepping between her baby and the scaly shape she knew was so dangerous. The mother trumped an alarm to the other tembos in the pool as the crocodile turned and swam underwater to the far side of the pool, where it lay submerged among the water lilies with just its watchful eyes visible.

The crocodile was in no hurry. He had eaten the best part of a zebra carcase before leaving to find a new territory and could go for many more days without *having* to feed.

Later, it moved off to explore farther upstream, where there might be other prey, and it was always as well to know what potential meals a new territory held.

Sarah and Ruth walked down the path through the cultivated patches of ground towards Lars and Ryan who were sitting naked in the sun waiting for their clothes to dry. Ruth called out to them, and she and Sarah were highly amused when the two men scrambled up to dress themselves. .

'Father was like that,' Sarah remarked. 'He hated us to see him without his clothes, even when we were small.'

'Wearing clothes must be a custom for all but the First People. Even in the black book the ones who were named Adam and Eve sewed fig leaves together to make themselves aprons.'

'But King David watched Bathsheba as she bathed, so men must like looking at women who are not wearing clothes.'

Lars and Ryan were what they would have called 'decent' when the two girls reached them and sat on the warm rocks nearby, Ruth splashing her bare feet in the water.

After a few minutes, Sarah looked straight at Lars and asked him why he wanted to leave.

Reluctant to offend her by answering, he asked instead, 'Your grandfather, De/ne, said he would have to stop us if we tried to go. How would he do that?'

Sarah glanced at Ruth with a look that clearly asked if she should tell, then she said to Lars, 'The same way he stopped our father, Mr Fotheringay, from leaving.'

Ryan asked, 'Did *he* want to leave then?' and was rewarded with a look from Lars that said, 'Let her answer *me*.'

Sarah paused, and choosing her words carefully she replied, 'Father came here, without planning to do so, while looking for pagans so that he could save their souls. He had been bitten by a lion and all the other men who had been with him had run away. And it came to pass that an elephant found him when he was very ill, picked him up and carried him here, where my People made him well. At one time, many of the First People were healers – our mother was one of them – but they are all dead now. Father tried to save the souls of our People who were here, but they said they were happy with Mantis and they wouldn't listen to him.'

Ruth took up the story. 'At first, Grandfather tried to get Mr Fotheringay to promise that he wouldn't try to leave, but Father said he *couldn't* promise that, in case he *had* to go. He told Grandfather – who, of course, was a much younger man then – that an Englishman's word was his bond, and he *couldn't* promise, so grandfather did something to make sure he couldn't leave.'

Lars leaned forward. 'What was that?' he asked.

Ruth lifted her foot out of the water and touched the tendon at the back of her heel. 'Grandfather cut him here.'

'He did *that* just to stop him leaving?' Lars was horrified.

Sarah and Ruth nodded together. 'And he would do that to *you*,' Sarah said. 'It is a promise to the elephants as old as the very Mount. Like the word of an Englishman, it is a promise that cannot be broken.'

Lars sat silently, thinking deeply.

'Why is it so important then?' Ryan asked.

'When I was younger I asked Father that,' Ruth replied. 'With his floppy foot, Mr Fotheringay knew he could never leave here on his own, so he became married to our mother and begat us. He told Sarah and me about the ways of *his* People, how some of them would steal the ivories of elephants to exchange them for money. The elephants here had always feared that men would come and steal their ivories from the Mount, so my People, who loved the gentle elephants, agreed to stop all strangers from leaving here, if any ever came. And so it has always been that way,' she added.

While listening to Ruth, Ryan had also been watching the heads of two frogs amongst the lily-pads on the far side of the small pool. Both frogs, which were about a foot apart, submerged together, then rose again with hardly a ripple.

He looked harder, then suddenly leaped to his feet, shouting, 'Holy cow – there's a croc in the pool!' He rushed over to a startled Ruth, who was still dangling her feet in the water, and pulled her backwards.

Lars and Sarah scrambled back from the edge and were staring across the pool.

'Are you sure?' Lars asked.

'Sure I'm sure. It was over there,' he said, taking his arms from around Ruth to point to where there was now only a jacanda bird stepping daintily from one lily-pad to another. The *frogs* had gone. He daringly put his arms around Ruth's body again, enjoying the smooth feel of her skin and, much to his delight, she nestled back against him.

As they walked back up to the shelter to tell De/ne about the crocodile, Ryan was holding Ruth's hand, but Lars, who was walking ahead with Sarah, was keeping himself and his thoughts to himself.

Tembo Chief Guardian announced to his fellows that he was going back to being called Tembo Three Eyes. 'No more of that *guardian* nonsense for me,' he said. He was angry with Tembo Carefree – what a stupid name – and was feeling as he had when that old fool M'zee had humiliated him on the mountain when he had done nothing but eat a few bananas.

Bananas! He had seen the humans were growing bananas in a moist, fertile area across the stream, and he wanted some. He wanted bananas more than he had ever wanted anything. Even more than he had wanted to joyn with a female when the mustdo had been on him. He was going to have bananas!

'Follow me,' he commanded and set off towards the plantation.

When he realised he was alone, he just snorted and carried on wading across the stream and walked openly to where the succulent bunches hung between wide green leaves.

Two Eyes and One Eye had dropped back when they saw where Three Eyes was heading. They were already ashamed of their behaviour, especially after Tembo Carefree had compared them to heaps of dung, which had hurt them like a hornet's sting on the back of an ear.

They stood uneasily, each occasionally snatching at a tuft of grass and stuffing it into their mouth as they watched their long-time companion stride away towards the bananas. They saw him splash through the stream, pull down and swallow several small bunches without even chewing on them, then with another larger bunch clutched in his trunk he strode back to the water's edge.

'What should we do, One Eye?' Two Eyes asked as Three Eyes put down the bunch and lowered his trunk to drink, but before his friend could answer they heard a muffled snort and saw Three Eyes straining back from the bank with his trunk outstretched. The tip was out of their sight below the water. In a single movement they charged into the water towards him.

A water-biter had sunk its teeth into the end of Three Eyes' trunk and was hurling and twisting its huge body around in the water, trying to bite and rip it off. Three Eyes was trumping in pain as his fellow tembos splashed into the stream but by the time they'd reached him the water-biter had gone and Three Eyes was standing, shaking, on the bank, blood pouring from the bitten-off end of his trunk.

'Get me away from here,' he pleaded, his old bravado gone.

Two Eyes and One Eye took him back across the stream, looking carefully to left and right in case the water-biter came back. Then, with one of them on either side of their injured companion to hide his bleeding trunk from the tembo families grazing near the Mount, they crossed the grassland, passed Rafiki, who was standing guard, and entered the gorge.

De/ne listened intently as Sarah and Ruth told him about the crocodile, the girls speaking rapidly in Bushmantaal while Lars and Ryan stood close behind them. How had one of those hated creatures got past the guardians and into the Place of Peace? Whatever had happened, it was here now and he must deal with it, while still making sure that none of the men had any opportunity to leave the crater. He went to the highest shelf in the shelter and searched through the horn containers to find the one containing the most powerful of his poisons. He handled it with extreme care, knowing that the slightest trace in his mouth or on any cut or scratch on his skin would mean an inevitable and very painful death. He would rather use one of his more gentle poisons which killed painlessly but they would not be strong enough to kill a fully-grown crocodile.

Killing it within the Place of Peace would break the ancient agreement with the elephants that no animal was ever to be killed there – but was a crocodile an animal? Mr Fotheringay had called them 'reptiles' and had talked about them in a very different tone of voice to one he used when speaking about elephants, antelopes and such other creatures. Should he ask the elephants? No! They could be in as much danger as the humans and he would need to act at once for the sake of them all.

He took his bark quiver down from the peg above his bed and selected several of his best arrows. With Lars and Ryan watching him, he spelled out the dreadful power of the poison as he coated each arrow-head with the black, gummy substance, using a thin stick which he burned immediately after he'd finished.

'I leave my granddaughters in your care,' he said, looking first at Ryan, then at Lars, and they stood with the girls watching as he walked slowly down the path towards the stream, as tense and silent as a cat stalking a bird.

Downstream of the bridge, the elephants were keeping well away from the water's edge and there was none of the joyous splashing and playing that had been so common before. De/ne took an arrow from the wooden quiver, placed it in his bow and walked slowly along between the elephants and the water, pausing frequently to study the opposite bank. He was glad to feel the sun was hot on the bare skin of his back. Crocodiles often basked half out of the water when the sun was high.

When he reached the gorge, he spoke briefly to Kidogo who was on guard, and asked if she or the other guardians had seen the water-biter, hoping it might have decided to leave the crater. When she told him neither she nor the others had seen it, she also told him that the three young tembulls had left the Place of Peace earlier without saying a 'fare well', and that she had smelled blood on the path and thought one of them must have been injured.

De/ne thought about this as he walked back up to the log bridge. Perhaps the crocodile had attacked the elephant. He went on upstream, bow at the ready.

A family of tembas and their youngsters were grazing near where Kidogo was guarding the gorge entrance. The Tembella came up to Kidogo, saluted her with a slight raising of her trunk, and said, 'It is time we were leaving here.'

Kidogo had been expecting this, as all the tembulls who had come to the Place of Peace carrying tusks had already left, and she knew that for most tembas their way of life was to wander the bush, along well-known pathways, grazing and browsing as they went. Very few would be able to accept a life of staying in one place, no matter how peaceful or beautiful it was, but Kidogo told the Tembella that she herself felt she never wanted to leave the Place of Peace.

'One of my daughters, who has yet to joyn with a tembull, feels as you do, Kidogo, and has asked to stay here,' said the Tembella. 'I am sure she would share the duties of a 'guardian.' She stood back waiting for Kidogo's reaction.

'She would be most welcome. Much as I love my friend Rafiki, I would be pleased to have other females here. Which is she?'

The Tembella signalled and a temba of a similar age to Kidogo, but with a slender pair of tusks, came forward.

'Kidogo, this is my daughter, Temba Happy,' said the Tembella.

Kidogo touched Happy's forehead, and said, 'I have often seen you playing in the pool. You are well named, Happy, and I would be honoured if you were to stay here with us – but you must give it *much* thought. It is an important decision for a temba to leave her family.'

'*You* must have,' Temba Happy replied.

'It was not my choice,' Kidogo told her. 'But we will not speak of that now. Tomorrow, if you still feel the same, you may join me as a guardian of this sacred place.'

Above the bridge, De/ne found footprints where the crocodile had briefly left the water and a flurry of elephant and crocodile footprints splashed with dried blood that told him Kidogo had been right, one of the elephants *had* been injured. He was hoping the crocodile would have swum on upstream after the attack. The water there would be even shallower and the crocodile would be easier to see. He moved on, a step at a time, scanning the water and both banks, hoping for a glimpse of the beast before it saw him.

He was lucky. Rounding a slight bend, he saw the crocodile lying on the bank, looking just like a rotting log. Birds walked along its back, poking their beaks between its scales in search of parasites. De/ne slowly lowered himself to the ground and wriggled forward, using every bit of available cover and remaining still whenever the crocodile opened its eyes.

Eventually, De/ne was close enough, but it would be no use shooting arrows at it yet. Its skin was so thick and tough they wouldn't penetrate it, and would only alert the creature to the fact that it was being hunted. He must wait.

He lay in the grass, ignoring the flies buzzing around his head, and the ants and other insects that crawled over his body – any movement of his might be noticed. The sun was even hotter now and he was glad he'd worn his leather hat, which gave some protection to the back of his neck.

The crocodile moved its tail. De/ne tensed, afraid it was about to slip into the water and swim away, but it simply stretched each of its legs in turn, and yawned. De/ne raised his body slightly to get a clear line of flight for his arrow. It yawned again, opening its mouth in a gape. Immediately, the birds fluttered up from its back and pecked around its teeth, searching for morsels of food. The crocodile closed its eyes contentedly.

This was the moment De/ne had been waiting for. He knelt up, bow at the ready and fired an arrow across the stream straight into the open mouth. The crocodile, perhaps thinking it was a peck from a clumsy bird, shook its head, part-closed its mouth as the three birds flew out – then opened it again. De/ne's second arrow followed the first and he knew the crocodile had only a few hours to live. He turned away and walked back to the bridge.

When the injured Three Eyes had left the gorge, he stumbled along between his companions, retracing the route beside the stream they had so eagerly followed when they had first come to find the Place of Peace. His trunk had stopped bleeding but flies now clustered thickly around the end and every now and then he plunged it into the water hoping this would get rid of them but it didn't – as soon as he withdrew it they landed again. He tried blowing down his trunk but this only made the pain worse. Why had he been so stupid? A few bananas were not worth this! He would be glad when darkness came and the flies departed – the pain was bad enough without these creatures.

When the three tembos had almost reached the top of the cliff where the stream went down the hole in the ground, Two Eyes decided they should stay there for the night, as Three Eyes was groaning with every jarring footstep.

Kidogo woke next morning to find several tembo families grazing nearby. Temba Happy was amongst them and she came forward with two other young tembas.

'These are friends of mine from other families,' Temba Happy told Kidogo. 'They want to stay here with me – and with you. Our Tembellas have agreed – and we *have* all thought about it,' she added.

'If that is so, then I welcome you all,' Kidogo replied as an older temba came forward hesitantly.

'I too would like to stay,' she said. 'I have a crooked foot and it hurts me to walk far. Here, I would not be a burden to my family, here there is plenty of food and I could be as good a guardian as any other temba.'

Kidogo counted in her head. With Carefree, who had let it be known that he wanted to be called Tembo Guardian again, Rafiki, the three young tembas, the older one and herself there were seven to cover the guardian's duty. She did not count M'zee nor the two Sisters who were devoting their time to looking after him. 'How are you named?' she asked.

'I am known in my family as Temba Aunt as I have no babies of my own.'

Kidogo touched the older one's forehead and said, 'Temba Aunt, you are welcome to stay with us. You can keep we youngsters in order.'

All the Tembellas made their way to the Mount to say 'Fare well' to M'zee and the Sisters, on behalf of their families. Then, walking in single file with their Tembella leading, each family left the crater through the gorge, every one of the tembas and their babies waving to Temba Aunt, Kidogo and *her* new family as they passed. After they'd all left, the grasslands seemed very empty to Kidogo.

De/ne asked Lars and Ryan to bring the spade they had brought with them from the Land Rover and come and help him bury the crocodile that he knew would now be dead. He was more and more sure that Lars was planning to leave and he wanted to keep him in sight until he was ready to marry Sarah.

When they reached the body lying on the bank, De/ne approached carefully and poked at it with a long stick to make sure it was dead. As it made no movement, Lars paced along its length. At its head he went to lift one of its lips to look at its teeth.

'No!' De/ne shouted. 'Don't touch it! We'll bury it here,' he added as Lars stepped backwards. 'The poison I used will kill any creature that touches its mouth or tries to eat its flesh.'

Vultures were gathering even before they had dug a large enough hole in the rich soil of the crater floor to roll the body into, and the birds perched despondently on trees across the stream watching as their hoped-for meal disappeared into the ground. When the crocodile was safely buried, De/ne left them, saying he would go to the Mount and let the tembos know it was safe for them to bathe in the pool again. Lars shouldered the spade as he and Ryan trudged down to the bridge.

Ryan was thinking about what the girls had told them. He was convinced De/ne *would* actually cut the tendons of any one of them who tried to leave – just as he'd done to the girls' father. As far as he was concerned this place was Paradise, and he knew he could happily live there with Ruth for the rest of his life. He could forget the world outside, a world obsessed with progress and acquisition. A world increasingly dependant on ever-dwindling supplies of oil and gas. Why couldn't Lars feel the same? Surely his friend wouldn't risk having a tendon cut by the Bushman for the sake of getting back to all that?

From the shelter, Sarah and Ruth had seen the flesh-eating birds gliding in towards where their grandfather had gone with Lars and Ryan.

'The crocodile must be dead,' Ruth said, and the girls walked down to their washing place in the stream, took off their skirts and poured cool water over each other, using the half-gourd they had carried down with them.

Sarah kept glancing along the path, and Ruth laughed. 'Remember Bathsheba in the black book. King David wanted to marry her after he had seen her bathing. You are waiting for your Lars to come and see you!'

'I am not,' her sister replied indignantly, then she too laughed, and said, 'Well, perhaps I am. Surely, I am not so ugly that he doesn't want to be married to me?'

'If you are, then so am I – and I know that my Ryan wants to be married to me. He has told me so!'

'He has already asked you?'

'So he has.'

'You're already talking like him. I am very happy for you. Now you must help me make *my* Lars want to marry me.'

Ruth sat on the warm rocks while Sarah combed out her sister's hair and started to plait it. 'Do you remember,' said Ruth, 'that Mother used to make medicines from plants for many things?' She paused a moment before adding, 'Well, she used to use one of them whenever Father got restless and

409

wanted to leave. Of course, he knew he couldn't leave because of his floppy foot but whenever she put some of the medicine in his porridge, he didn't *want* to leave for a long time after that.'

Sarah stopped plaiting Ruth's hair and asked, 'Are you suggesting we should put some of Mother's medicine in my Lars' porridge just to make him stay? If he doesn't want to stay here for me, I don't want him here!' She snatched up her skirt, wrapped it tightly around her waist and strode up the path to the shelter.

Ruth finished plaiting her own hair, put on her skirt and went to meet the two men who were coming along the path.

'May we bathe in your pool again?' Ryan asked. 'We stink of croc.'

Ruth left them there and, while Sarah was bringing in wood for the cooking fire, she rummaged through the leather bags that her mother had always kept on the high shelf. Most of the herbs in them had crumbled to powder but she was sure she knew which one her mother had mixed in with her father's porridge. She found it, then hid the little bag in the cigar box her grandfather had given her the night he had returned home. If she *could* make Lars stay longer she knew he would want to marry Sarah and make her sister as happy as she was.

CHAPTER THIRTY-FIVE

Maggots were already cleaning up the ragged flesh of Three Eyes' trunk when Two Eyes looked at it closely in the morning light, but it was beginning to smell of rotten meat. Leaving One Eye with the injured one, Two Eyes went off to collect fresh forage and make food-wads as he had seen Kidogo and the Sisters do for M'zee. But when he returned with the food, Three Eyes just ignored it.

'The Sisters may be able to help him,' Two Eyes whispered to One Eye. 'If they can't, his trunk will rot away and he will die. We'll have to go back.'

'The old one will be angry about the bananas and the way we *viewed* Tembo Steadfast's ivory,' One Eye warned.

'I know that. Even so – it's Two Eyes' only chance.'

They squirted water from the stream into their friend's mouth and nudged him back onto the path.

'We're going back,' One Eye told him. 'To save your trunk – and your life.'

De/ne had washed himself a little away from Lars and Ryan, then left them sitting in the sun to dry themselves while he walked up to the shelter, thinking. The crocodile was dead and the Place of Peace was safe again – but that stupid white man with the yellow hair was still not wanting to marry his granddaughter D/aw/a. Perhaps he already had a wife somewhere but De/ne was sure that he hadn't – there must have some other reason.

The elephant families were leaving the crater and he

sensed their restlessness and their need to travel on. Was Lars like those elephants? Did he have the same strong impulse to keep moving from place to place? Perhaps the girls were not attractive to white men – but that couldn't be true. Ruth had told him only this morning that Ryan had asked her to marry him. So at least one part of his plan *was* going as he had hoped. Then there were the American and the blind Maasai to consider – they just hung around the shelter as though waiting for something to happen. He wondered if he might encourage one of *them* to marry Sarah but immediately dismissed the idea. He was sure Lars was the right one for her. Somehow he must be made to know that. Perhaps if he could see how pleasant things *could* be . . .

De/ne himself was getting older. It would be good to have children here in the Place of Peace again. Children to love and cherish – children to teach how to hunt for food and find berries and wild food – children to ensure some trace of the First People continued into future generations.

At the shelter he spoke to Ruth. 'There is no reason for you to wait any time before being married to Ryan and begetting babies with him. When he comes up here you should take him to choose a home for yourselves from one of the shelters that are no longer used.'

Ruth smiled at her grandfather, then glanced a little guiltily at Sarah who had been listening.

'When the men come up, we will all go together to choose a home for us,' Ruth said and took her sister's hand in hers.

De/ne left them and walked back to meet Lars and Ryan, who stepped off the track and into the shade of a tree when they met. Watching Lars' reaction, he said to Ryan, 'My granddaughter, Lo//te, who you call Ruth, wishes to marry you and beget your children. That is my wish too. I have told

412

her that you may choose any of the other shelters to live in together.'

'Are you really sure about this, Ryan?' Lars said to his friend. 'It's only *three days* since you met!'

'It's OK by me,' Ryan replied. 'Never in all my life have I been more sure of anything.' Then speaking to De/ne in a formal voice, he said, 'I swear I will love Ruth and look after her for as long as I live – and beget lots of grand-children for you.'

Lars shook his head in disbelief and concern.

The girls were sitting on a rock outside the shelter. Ruth stood up and curtsied to Ryan, who smiled and held out his hand to her. Should he kiss her? Did she know what a kiss was? Did she know anything about how children were begat – or was it *begotten*?

Lars stood behind him, trying to be happy for his friend, while avoiding looking at Sarah.

De/ne, who had gone ahead of them, came out of the shelter taking a small woven basket from his leather bag. He gave it to Ruth. 'It is a present,' he said. 'A present for your marriage. I collected these when I went outside to look for good husbands for you both.'

Ruth peered into the bag, then tipped the contents into a hollow on the top of a rock.

Sarah and Ryan stepped forward to look. In the hollow were seeds of many kinds. Ryan recognised orange and apple pips, seeds that might be any kind of melon, pumpkin or papaya, some black-and-white ones he knew were sunflower seeds, two large mango and three avocado stones and several that might be from peaches or apricots.

'All of these should grow well here,' De/ne said. 'With a man to help you, you can dig more of the old vegetable patches.'

'You can have my spade,' Lars said, and instantly regretted it. He did not want De/ne to know that he had definitely decided to leave. He glanced at De/ne but his expression told him nothing.

Walt heard the sound of talking and came out of his tent, walked past Moses who was sitting on a rock-ledge mumbling to himself, and went to where De/ne and the others were standing around a rock, looking at something on the top of it. All Walt could see were a few dried up seeds and fruit stones.

'What are these for?' he asked.

Ryan picked up one of the avocado stones. 'Ruth and I are going to get married,' he said. 'De/ne has given us all these seeds as a wedding present. I love avocados.'

Ruth was feeling the textures of the peach and apricot pits, both obviously unfamiliar to her. Then she picked up one of the mango stones and weighed it in her hand.

'Mango,' said Ryan.

'It's so *big*,' Ruth said. 'I thought it must be the seed of the tree of the knowledge of good and evil.'

Ryan smiled, remembering the stories from the bible the nuns had taught him when he was a boy. 'Just a mango,' he said. 'You don't get turned out of the Garden of Eden for eating these. But you do get sticky fingers.'

'I don't suppose you brought any tobacco seed?' Walt asked De/ne. 'I could grow me some cigars.'

De/ne reached into his leather bag and took out a smaller one, loosened the drawstring and tipped some of the contents into his hand. Walt touched the tiny black seeds with a finger-tip. 'I know about growing these,' he said. 'One of my uncles lived on a plantation in South Carolina and I used to go down there a lot. I even learned how to roll cigars. Tell me when you're going to plant them and I'll give you a few tips.' He grinned at De/ne. 'I could do with a cigar right now – but maybe I'll have kicked the habit by the time these are ready.'

Lars had stepped back, but was listening to this conversation. It sounded as though Walt was in no hurry to leave, and Ryan was clearly obsessed with Ruth and was going to marry her whatever *he* might say. Not that he could blame him – she really was a lovely, innocent girl. So, of course, was Sarah, but even as he thought that, dark clouds came rolling into his brain and blind panic grasped at his guts. He must leave soon. Get out of this crater before he was trapped – or worse. If De/ne had once been capable of maiming the girls' father to stop *him* leaving, the little man was equally capable of cutting *his* tendon – probably while he was sleeping. He made an excuse to go into the shelter to where he and Ryan slept, and unobtrusively checked over his few belongings.

De/ne watched Lars in the same way as he observed an animal he was stalking, seeing almost as much when he looked elsewhere as he did by staring directly at it. The man was planning to leave, there was no doubt about it. Probably that night when Ryan and Ruth had gone to whichever shelter they had chosen.

The Vice President of Schwiner Enterprises Inc. addressed the reconvened board. 'Gentlemen. As you will recall, we agreed to e-mail Mr Burns in Tanzania instructing him to spare no cost in locating Walt. I have to report that the news from there is not good.

'Mr Burns has replied as follows: *"Received your message today. Regret there is no possibility of arranging a search for Mr Schwiner. The economy of Tanzania is in a state of collapse due to lack of oil. Power stations are operating at reduced capacity and we have been warned that electricity will soon be rationed and, if no tankers arrive at Dar es Salaam soon to supply the power stations, it will cease altogether. If this happens I will not be able to contact you again in any way.*

Food here in the city is scarce and many Africans are already leaving to return to their tribal lands where they can grow vegetables. My own plans to leave Arusha have been frustrated by lack of diesel oil and I cannot see what the future holds for ex-pats like myself.

I regret I cannot provide any more information re. Mr Schwiner but here it is virtually 'every man for himself'. Regards, John Burns."

'Not good news, gentlemen. Does anyone have any suggestions?'

'We've got a tanker going east near Singapore. We could divert that to Dar es Salaam.'

'I don't know if that'd work, but I'll look into it. I'd hate to have to face Walt when he gets back if we haven't explored *every* possibility.'

Two Eyes and One Eye heard a murmur of tembotalk ahead of them as they took Three Eyes along the path by the stream. They stopped and stood to one side as several families of tembas with their babies passed by with scarcely a glance of acknowledgement. One Tembella stopped as she came level with Three Eyes and passed dung in an obvious expression of disapproval before she moved on.

It was evening by the time they got back to where the stream flowed out of the gorge. Tembo Three Eyes was in great pain and exhausted, so they decided to rest there and go up into the crater the following morning.

Kidogo had left Rafiki to guard the upper entrance and gone with her new family of guardians to see M'zee. As she neared the Mount, she passed Tembo Boy and Temba Girl grazing together and they raised trunks in salutation as her little group passed.

Kidogo led the way through the narrow passage and into the inner paved circle. M'zee was leaning comfortably against the hollow tembo-tree with his eyes closed. It was clear to Kidogo that he would soon step-over, and she knew how much she would miss his Love and his many kindnesses.

The Sisters were standing close by, ready to perform whatever service M'zee might need. The whole area around him was clean and free from dung, which Kidogo suspected was also thanks to the two tembas, who she noticed were themselves beginning to show their age. Tembo Guardian was on the upper wall, assiduously tweaking seedlings from the crevices between the stones and flicking them over the side.

Temba Comfort touched M'zee's side gently and said, 'Your Shadow is here.'

Kidogo stepped forward and raised her trunk to the old one's forehead. 'I am not your Shadow now,' she said. 'But I regarded it as an honour when I was. If you ask – I will gladly be your Shadow again.'

'Thank you,' he replied. 'It was an honour for me too, Kidogo, but I will step-over very soon and Mana is saying he has one more thing that I must do, but he will not tell me what it is.'

Kidogo waited to see if M'zee was going to say any more before she introduced Temba Aunt and her new family of guardians but he had closed his eyes again. She quietly stepped backwards and, with her new companions, left the Mount to go back to where Rafiki was standing guard by the gorge entrance. As they walked, the tembas who had accompanied her spread out to graze the lush grasses.

CHAPTER THIRTY-SIX

Ryan and Ruth, holding hands, had gone to choose which of the several empty shelters they would make their home, while Sarah and Lars followed behind more soberly. Lars' mind was elsewhere, planning how to get away before De/ne cut one of his tendons and he was trapped into a relationship with Sarah. Elephants guarded the way out of the crater through the gorge, and Lars had noticed how much more alert *they* were since the crocodile had somehow got past them.

Although he had no ropes, he was a skilled climber and was sure he could find some way up the cliffs surrounding the crater and down the other side. From there he could trek cross-country to the Serengeti and find a warden to take him out. Ryan would be OK here. All his friend had ever wanted was a place in the country with a so-called 'colleen' of his own, and now he had that. As for Walt and Moses, they were not his responsibility. He scanned the cliff towards the peak, looking for a possible route up as he walked. Sarah followed silently behind him, carrying a brush made from twigs.

When Ryan and Ruth had chosen a shelter that would catch the morning sun but be shaded from the heat later in the day, the two women swept out the dust and leaves gathered over several decades of disuse, while the men walked back to collect the couple's bedding and Ryan's gear.

'You don't have to go through with this,' Lars told his friend. 'We can sneak away. I'm pretty sure there must be a way out over the cliffs.'

Ryan turned and faced Lars. 'Listen to me, will you? I love that girl, this place is a paradise – Shangri-La – a Garden of Eden. There's nothing more I could be wanting. Like you, I've got no close family back home. And I can't understand you not falling for Sarah. Is it a bit of prejudice you've carried with you from South Africa? A native woman and all that.'

Lars was taken aback by his friend's charge. 'No. It's not that! I hated apartheid. I'm just not *ready*.' Dark clouds were sweeping into his brain again and numbing his thoughts. 'I'm just not *ready* to settle down. It wouldn't be fair to Sarah.'

'I told you before, you're being a prat about this. How old are you? Think about that! If you're not ready now, you never will be.'

Lars opened his mouth to reply, but Ryan went on. 'Now, if you're my friend, I want you be happy *for me* today. It's my wedding day, it is, even if we haven't had a stag night or even a wedding ceremony. Still, as they say, when in Rome . . .'

'OK. If it's what you *really* want, I *am* pleased for you.' Lars smiled and held out his hand. 'I'll be thinking of you tonight.'

'You be minding your own business then. That's for me and the lovely Ruth.'

As the sun dipped below the far peak of the crater rim, Ruth was ladling soup from a cast-iron cooking pot and passing the filled half-gourds around in the firelight. She had sprinkled some of her mother's 'calm him down' medicine into the bowl she had planned to give to Lars, but as soon as she had filled that bowl a jovial Walt took it from her hands and passed it to Moses.

There was no more powder in the bag and she had been just a little concerned about whether or not it had been the

419

right one. Her mother had kept several different medicines in similar bags. Perhaps it was just as well – if it was the wrong one she would rather the blind man swallowed it than the man she wanted to marry her sister.

When they had finished eating, De/ne made a short speech welcoming Ryan into his family and saying he was sure he would soon be welcoming Lars too. Then, to everyone's surprise, he produced a large gourd of banana beer he must have brewed secretly for the occasion. Lars drank sparingly and was pleased to see De/ne drinking heavily from the gourd – hopefully it would make him less alert in the night.

When the meal was over and Lars had watched Ryan and Ruth walk away from the fireside towards their new home, he went to the space he had shared with Ryan for the past few nights. As the light was fading he lay down, his Bergen backpack near his head. The words THE VIKING on the pack stood out in the half-light. Yes, that was him, he was a Viking – a rover. The settled life was not for him!

When he heard De/ne go into his own area, lie down, and start snoring, he got to his feet, quietly packed his few belonging into the Bergen and tiptoed away.

Kidogo and Rafiki were at the top of the gorge with Temba Happy, Temba Aunt and the other two tembas who had chosen to stay, instructing them in the duties of a guardian.

'One or two of us must *always* be on watch here or in the cave down in the gorge. We must *always* be on the alert for anything unusual. The entrance must *never* be left unguarded. Tembos and humans of the First People may come and go freely – but no other humans can ever be allowed in. And those who are here now, the ones called *Lars, Ryan, Walt* and *Moses,* must not be allowed to leave.'

'What about the two females – Sarah and Ruth – are they of the First People?' Rafiki asked.

'I think they are,' Kidogo answered, 'but I will make sure by asking Tembo Guardian the morning.'

'What about other creatures?' Temba Aunt asked.

'Guardian has told me that very few of them have ever tried to come up the gorge. Lions, leopards, hyenas and water-biters must definitely be turned back. It is a part of our promise to the humans that we will protect them. Temba Aunt and Temba Happy, will you be guardians through this night? Tembo Rafiki and myself will take over in the morning. Remember, at least one of you must always be at the entrance, and *alert*.'

Lars was glad of the moonlight as he sneaked away from the shelter, treading as lightly as he could with the Bergen on his back. He crossed the tree-trunk bridge and walked up the stream bank, past where they had buried the body of the crocodile. He was following a well-worn track and was expecting it to fade out as he got farther from the bridge but it continued alongside the stream, even when this turned into a series of small waterfalls as the ground started to rise sharply towards the cliffs surrounding the crater. When he came to where the springs bubbled up out of the ground as they had done at the foot of the escarpment, he drank deeply and filled his water bottle to the brim. How long would it be before he found drinking water on the other side of the volcano wall?

The path didn't even finish at the spring as he'd assumed it would, but continued upwards following ledges on the rock face and twisting and turning to pass around boulders and projecting trees. In one place he had to scramble up a steep slope of smooth rock using tiny foot- and hand-holds that someone must have cut there in the past. Several times, when the moon slipped behind clouds, he lost the way but each time, when the moon reappeared, he backtracked and found the path again. Even so, it was much easier than he had expected and he reached the crater rim about three hours after leaving the shelter.

Lars rested there, resisting the temptation to drink any of his water but he did bite a mouthful of biltong off one of a few sticks he had brought with him. He chewed on this until the meat was soft and sweet in his mouth and no longer felt and tasted like old leather. Then he searched for the path he was now convinced must lead down the other side and on towards freedom. But the only *onward* path turned along the narrow rim towards its highest point. He followed this, watching for where it must surely turn downhill but, after an hour of slow progress, he realised he was close to the top. Perhaps the path would lead down from there.

He reached the summit, sat on a conveniently placed rock, sipped a little water and bit off another mouthful of biltong. The moon was close to the far horizon which meant it would be totally dark before he could hope to find the downward path, so he took his sleeping bag out of the Bergen, got into it and lay down, using the pack as a pillow.

He lay awake for some time, watching the brilliant stars above his head and thinking of Ryan and Ruth in their new home. He wondered what Sarah would think when she discovered he had gone. The black clouds came rolling into his mind again and he shivered.

Lars woke as the first light of morning crept across the crater rim and he could hear a dawn-dove start to call far down in the trees lining the walls. He lay, snug in his sleeping bag, listening to the gentle '***Dee-daadaa, dee-daadaa,***' before he sat up.

De/ne was sitting on a rock watching him, his hunting bow across his lap with a black-tipped arrow notched onto the bowstring.

Another dawn-dove woke Tembo Two Eyes where the stream came out of the gorge. He nudged Three Eyes awake, and said, 'We must get you to the Sisters so they can make you well again.'

Three Eyes groaned as he moved his shortened trunk and winced when he tried to flex it, but didn't move his body.

One Eye pushed him from behind, putting his shoulder to Three Eyes' rear, while One Eye guided him towards the gorge entrance that yawned darkly ahead.

Ryan turned over on the sweet-smelling bed of dry grass and felt the warmth of Ruth's body against his under the un-zipped sleeping bag which covered them like a duvet. Lars was a fool, and he thought of his friend lying alone while Sarah, who was just as lovely as his own Ruth, also lay alone nearby.

Ruth had not known much about *begetting*, as she so charmingly called it, but had been happy to learn and now she lay asleep beside him. Ryan felt himself to be the luckiest man in the whole world.

Walt had heard Moses crying out in the night and moving about restlessly. He was sure that at some time he had also heard vomiting.

When he woke and crawled out of his tent there was no sign of the Maasai man. He walked stiffly across to the glowing embers of the fire where tiny wisps of white smoke rose from the ends of the charred logs. Neither Lars nor De/ne were in their sleeping places, which surprised him. He'd have expected the Bushman at least to be fast asleep after the amount of beer he had drunk the night before. Ryan and Ruth would be in their new home, and he didn't like to peep into the recess where Sarah would have slept on her own.

He knelt and blew at the ashes, moving half-burnt sticks together until he had a little blaze going. He couldn't recall when he had ever felt so relaxed. His remaining heart tablets remained unused in his pocket and his business world was far away, with *other* people having to make the decisions. Here, there could be no phone calls from his ex-wives or their attorneys, with evermore outrageous demands. Here, he didn't have to prove anything about himself to anyone. He was not going to rush back to all that, and anyway he had promised to teach De/ne to grow tobacco and roll his own cigars.

Sarah must have heard him moving about for she came out from her sleeping place, wearing the short skirt that suited her so well and with a skin-cloak around her shoulders. Her eyes were red and he guessed she had been crying. Walt smiled and she half-smiled back at him, at the same time trying to see if Lars was in his sleeping place.

'He's not there, Honey,' he said. 'He's probably gone for his *morning walk*.' The euphemism made more sense here than '*gone to the bathroom*'.

Lars was terrified. He knew from his time as a guide in Botswana how deadly the Bushmen's poisoned arrows were. Ryan was right, he was a fool. How on earth could he possibly have hoped to get away from one of the most expert trackers in the whole of Africa?

The sun was rising behind De/ne's back, outlining the little man in a kind of all-round halo, so bright that Lars couldn't see his face to read his thoughts. Wouldn't be much good even if I could, he thought ruefully. The Bushman was an expert at hiding his emotions. He wouldn't like to try and beat him at poker – and here the little fellow held all the aces.

Kidogo and Rafiki heard Temba Aunt trump a challenge down the gorge as they came to take over the morning watch from her and Temba Happy.

424

'We have come back to see if the Sisters can heal Three Eyes' trunk.' It was Two Eyes' voice that echoed through the gorge in answer to the challenge.

The tembulls stepped out of the gloom and Kidogo walked forward to examine Three Eyes' injured trunk-tip.

'Is this what the water-biter did?' she asked although she knew the answer. Flies were buzzing around the unhealed flesh and white baby-flies wriggled in the raw hollows of the nostrils. The smell of rotting meat dragged her back to the time she had stood helplessly beside her dead mother so long before, but she pushed that thought away and turned to Temba Aunt. 'Will you and Temba Happy go with these tembulls to the Sisters at the Mount? They all look exhausted and may need your help. Rafiki and I will take over the guard duty.'

De/ne was angry with this arrogant young man who had rejected his granddaughter and run away, leaving her and his friend behind. He deserved to be shot with the arrow and left to die in prolonged agony, but *that* wouldn't get a husband for D/aw/a. He had definitely rejected Walt and Moses as possible mates for her. *This* was the man who would father the best grandchildren for him, even if he had to be crippled to ensure he couldn't run off again. But not here! If the deed had to be done, it was best done at the shelter.

As Lars started to wriggle out of his sleeping bag De/ne raised the bow.

Lars froze, and said slowly, 'Wait, *please*. Wait!' But he didn't know what to say next. It would be unmanly to plead for his life as he had seen hostages made to do in terrorist videos. He'd rather die than do that. An apology seemed both inadequate and inappropriate.

De/ne seemed in no hurry and stood up, turned his back on Lars and stared down into the crater, still holding the bow.

'Is *this* not enough for you?' he asked, half turning. 'Here you have peace and a good woman who wants to be a wife to you and to have your children. Food is plentiful, if you are prepared to dig the ground and plant the seeds. Here, there is good water, and elephants to guard us from dangers. I cannot read the words in the black book their father gave to D/aw/a and Lo//te – Sarah and Ruth – but they believe this to be the place that is called the Garden of Eden.'

He faced Lars and leaned the bow against a rock, wrapped the arrowhead carefully in a strip of bark-cloth which he'd taken from his ever-present bag, and looked the other way over the surrounding land. 'Out there are bad people – people who have forgotten how to love one another. I saw many of them when I went to Arusha. Then I thought perhaps it was just in *that* city where people were like that but, since I have been home, I have come up here several times to listen to the radio-thing, which a man gave to me in exchange for money. Now, I know that people in the rest of the world are even worse, and I wonder how it is that Mantis does not destroy them as the black book says *your* God did, by flooding all the land with water.'

Lars tried to defend his people. 'They're not all bad—' he started to say, but De/ne ignored him, took the little radio out of his bag and switched it on.

'Listen for yourself,' he commanded.

Tembas Aunt and Happy accompanied the three tembulls across the open grassland towards the Mount, keeping upwind of Three Eyes. Halfway there, Temba Happy stumbled on a huge tusk lying in the grass. Recognising it as one of Tembo Steadfast's, she lifted it with her trunk and was surprised to find that it weighed much less than it had when she had taken a turn at carrying it on their journey to the Place of Peace. She remarked on this and Temba Aunt

426

took it from her. 'You're right,' she said. 'It feels empty – like a hollow tree. I will take it to the Mount.'

As they drew near, Two Eyes took the tusk from her. Perhaps its return would please the old one – but he feared it wouldn't.

Up on the crater rim, Lars was standing beside De/ne, looking outwards at the vastness of Africa, hearing the news reports on the radio, and wondering why he wanted to be out there – rather than snug and safe in the crater. Perhaps he *was* a fool.

De/ne's keen eyes observed five elephants walking from the gorge entrance towards the Mount and he could just make out that one was carrying a large tusk. None of the five were the small, tuskless female who had been so active in leading the herds to the crater. He scanned the grasslands and spotted her and the one-tusked male, who was almost always at her side, guarding the gorge entrance. The previous day he had seen most of the families leaving the crater but there were still several elephants in and around the Mount, although he couldn't be sure which they were. The big old Bull *must* be there – he only had a few days at most, to live.

The radio, on the ground near his feet, was reporting the World News, especially the growing oil crisis seriously affecting many of the poorer countries. The sound coming from the radio was less strong than it had been when the man did the deal with him in Arusha. Perhaps, he thought, like the elephant in the crater below, it too was near the end of its life.

M'zee's legs were weaker than ever, and he was glad of the support given by the tembo-tree he was leaning against. Sometimes he was sure the tree was talking to him, urging him to stay alive just a little longer. At times he thought the tree was telling him something he would soon have to do – but the suggestion was so outrageous he was certain it must be only in his own hazy imagination. Even the food-wads, so lovingly prepared by the Sisters, lay untouched at his feet. He felt too tired to pick them up, but it didn't matter now if he didn't eat. Tembos Boy and Girl were there too. They helped the Sisters with keeping the Mount clean and in gathering food for him but otherwise just grazed nearby as though waiting for some action from him.

Tembos were coming into the Mount – he could hear Tembo Guardian greeting them – but his neck was so stiff he could hardly turn to see who they were. He closed his eyes – the morning sun was bright now and hurt them.

He heard Tembo Guardian saying to him, 'M'zee, Tembo Three Eyes' companions have returned the tusk of your friend, Steadfast, which was missing from here.'

M'zee opened his eyes and blinked. There was a foul smell of decay wafting around and three tembulls stood in a row before him, one holding a free tusk he immediately recognised as that of his long-dead friend. He reached out to take it, expecting to feel the familiar weight of the stored Love and experience held within it – but the ivory was curiously light. Was another of his senses fading? He put the tusk down between his feet and tried to read it but there was nothing there – some human or tembo must have robbed it of its stored treasure. Energy surged through him and he trumped at the three tembulls. 'What has happened to this ivory?'

Two Eyes tried to explain about the *viewing* and how they had thought, at the time, that it was more fun than reading but M'zee had heard enough. Angrily, he tossed the tusk into the dark opening of the fire-pit, then turned and reached into the hollow of the tree. He drew out Steadfast's other tusk and threw that into the pit after the first. Then, finding even more unexpected inner strength, he turned again, fumbled inside the tree, pulled out Tembella Grace's slender tusks and tossed these after Steadfast's into the gaping pit. 'I will not risk *these* being defiled by walking dung-heaps like you three,' he roared.

The other Tembos backed away, awed by the savage energy and anger the huge old Tembull was displaying as he strode towards them, his trunk swinging wildly from side to side. But then, M'zee stopped. A low growling sound was coming from the fire-pit. They all swung round in time to see a brilliant flame flare up out of the hole, bend sideways as though seeking the tembo-tree, flicker into the hollow trunk, and retreat back down the hole from which it had come.

No tembo moved.

M'zee felt all the remaining energy drain from his body. As flames and smoke poured out of the hollows of the tree behind him, the old Tembull dropped to the ground. He tried to remember if any tusks were still in there . . . he could picture two huge ones . . . even bigger than Steadfast's.

He waved his trunk feebly at the burning tree. 'The tusks of Tembo Jay—' was all he could gasp as an eddy of smoke caught at his throat.

Three Eyes stepped forward, thrust his injured trunk into the burning hollow, screamed with pain but somehow drew out the two sacred tusks one by one and laid them on the ground near M'zee, his eyes streaming tears and his breathing harsh.

M'zee reached up his trunk from where he lay and touched Three Eyes' forehead. 'That was well done,' he wheezed.

Moses had not slept at all. His head had been full of snakes and he had been violently sick in the night. Before dawn he

429

had felt his way down the path to where Walt had taken him a couple of times to wash himself in the bathing pools. Here, he splashed water on his face to cleanse the vomit from around his mouth, then stripped off his clothes and splashed more water over his body before lying full length on the rock and feeling the cool air move over his body. He woke when the warmth of the sun touched him, sat up, looked around, and realised with mounting joy that his sight was clearing.

'Praise the Lord,' he called out loudly but there was no one to hear. It didn't matter. 'Praise be to God,' he shouted, feeling as light-headed as if he had over-indulged in banana beer, although he had drunk only one small gourdful the evening before.

Now he could hear a voice in his head talking to him as quietly and as insistently as his conscience had done when he was a boy at the Mission. He remembered Mr Jackson telling him about his namesake, Moses, hearing the voice of God coming from a burning, fiery bush. He looked across the crater floor and saw for the first time the stone structure which must have been what the Bushman and the elephants called the Mount. The tree in the centre of it was on fire.

Moses knew what he must do.

With the heat from the burning tree scorching his skin, M'zee struggled to his feet but his legs gave way again and he slumped down onto his side. As Tembo Boy hurried over to see if he needed help, a naked Moses ran up the ramp shouting, 'I am the voice of God. Hear me and obey.'

'What is that man saying?' M'zee asked Tembo Boy who was spraying water from his own throat reserve over the old one's dry skin. It was cool and pleasant. 'You understand the talk of humans.'

'He is saying he is the mouthpiece of Mana and that we tembos must do what he says.'

Moses was shouting again, and Tembo Boy translated for M'zee.

'Now he is saying that *Mana needs all the Love that is stored here in our ivory to change the way the world lives – and we must put it all into the fire-pit*.'

'That's interesting,' M'zee murmured, 'that's what the tembo-tree has been trying to tell me.'

Kidogo, guarding the gorge, smelled smoke and saw it was coming from the Mount. Worried about M'zee, she called out to Rafiki who had left her side briefly to graze – but he was too far away and there was no answer – and now the smoke was rolling across the grassland, hiding him and the Mount from view. Should she abandon her duty and run to the Mount – or must she, as she had told the new guardians only the evening before – *never* leave the entrance unguarded?

She called again into the smoke using low~sound.

'*Rafiki come ~ Rafiki come*.'

Rafiki had seen the flame rise above the walls of the Mount and smelled the smoke before Kidogo had. He knew she would want to know what was happening there, and hurried off to find out so he could come back and tell her.

He heard her calling but went on across the grassland until the walls of the Mount appeared through the smoke ahead of him. He followed the man he knew was called Moses through the narrow passageway and peered around trying to take it all in. Tembo M'zee was lying on his side, looking very ill. Tembo Boy was standing by him obviously wanting to help. Temba Girl was also there, with the two Sisters. Temba Aunt, Temba Happy and the two other new guardians were standing in a group with Tembo Guardian. The tembo-tree was now little more than a blackened stump from which wisps of smoke were rising. The man, Moses, was now up on top of the wall shouting, but Rafiki didn't try to understand what he was saying. He had seen enough – Kidogo would want to be here herself. He turned and ran back across the grassland to relieve her.

De/ne was following the drama being played out below, glad that the smoke had now virtually cleared. He put the matter of a husband for his granddaughter out of his mind and sat on a rock watching intently. He had seen Moses, naked, striding towards the Mount and knew that no *blind* man could walk that way. That was interesting!

The one-tusked male had hurried to where the tuskless female waited, pacing backwards and forwards impatiently. Then it was obvious he was telling her something. She then touched his forehead and left him there to guard the gorge entrance while she hurried off towards the Mount.

Trying to make sense of what Boy had told him the man on the wall had said, M'zee repeated it in his mind. *Mana needs all the Love that is stored here in our ivory to change the way the world lives – and we must put it all into the fire-pit.*

The man on the wall had stopped shouting and had moved somewhere out of his sight, and M'zee could now hear *Tembo Lonely's* voice in his head, reminding him of the whale's prophecy.

When a stone mount ~ breathes fire and smoke
Mana will ask ~ a Gift of Love.
Tembos give this ~ though it hurts them . . .

A stone mount or a stone *Mount*? Aha! So the mount was *not* the Holy Mountain that had breathed fire and smoke – but *this Mount* which had just done the same thing.

Mana will ask ~ a Gift of Love.

The man on the wall had said, *Mana needs the Love that is stored here in the ivory to change the way the world lives.*

And what had the whale's prophecy said next?

432

Tembos *give this ~ though it hurts them . . .*

M'zee knew what he had to do – but he wished his Shadow was there to talk to about it. Supposing he was wrong? He was old and sick and would very soon step-over, so, at least if *he* had got it wrong, only *he* could be blamed. But if he was wrong and had involved Kidogo, he knew she would suffer for it all her life. No, it had to be *his* decision, his alone.

'Tell Tembo Guardian to come to me,' he commanded Tembo Boy, and was secretly pleased to hear the old authority back in his voice.

'You are to prevent my Shadow, the blessèd Temba Kidogo, from coming into the Mount while we carry out the command of Mana,' he told Guardian. 'She must not come in here until I say otherwise. Is that clear? . . . Yes? . . . Now, send Tembo Three Eyes to me before you go.'

Three Eyes was standing well back, with the Sisters examining his trunk where he had thrust it into the fire to save the tusks of Tembo Jay. He'd known at the time it was the right thing, the only thing he could have done, but even so he was now regretting it. The pain had changed from an insistent dull hurt to violent burning agony . . . but the Sisters were congratulating him.

'It will heal now,' Sister Comfort was saying. 'That was a valiant thing you did.'

Sister Kindness added, 'And it has saved your life. Only fire could thoroughly cleanse such a wound.'

'M'zee says for you to go to him,' Tembo Guardian told Three Eyes on his way out of the Mount. '*Now*!'

Three Eyes wondered what the old one wanted him for. With his trunk so painful there was nothing useful he could do for him, and M'zee would still be angry with him for *viewing* his old friend's ivory, *and* for taking those wretched

433

bananas! He recalled the old one once saying to him, *'Tembo Three Eyes – I sense you are intelligent and have the qualities that would make a fine leader . . .'* but that was far in the past.

Suppressing his pain, Three Eyes went to M'zee.

'I have come,' he said quietly.

M'zee lay still, looking up at the sad face of the young tembull who had suffered so much. He thought of the foolish things he himself had done when he had been young and how his mother had always found it in her heart to forgive him. She would say, *'You must try and do what Tembo Jay would have done.'* He was sure Tembo Jay would have forgiven this young tembull, so he said, 'Let us put the past behind us. *You must try and do what Tembo Jay would have done.* I want you to take charge of all these tembos here. There is something that must be done – and you are to organise it.'

CHAPTER THIRTY-SEVEN

Sarah had made mealie porridge and Walt ate his sweetened with a scoop of wild honey before wandering about outside the shelter area, wondering where everyone else was. Sarah had little to say and was busying herself brushing dust out of the shelter, so he sat on a rock and whittled at a piece of wood with his clasp knife, something he'd not done since he was a boy. It was undemanding, yet strangely satisfying.

When he stood up to stretch his legs, he noticed smoke coming from the Mount and assumed that De/ne or Lars must have lit a fire there for some reason he couldn't even guess at.

He was about to suggest that he and Sarah stroll along to see Ryan and Ruth, but then thought, *no!* They would be cooking their own breakfast and would probably not welcome visitors on their first morning together.

Kidogo reached the Mount only to find Tembo Guardian standing in the entrance. 'I cannot let you pass,' he told the young temba, respectfully.

'I *must* go in,' she panted, out of breath from her run across the grassland. 'Tembo M'zee may need me.'

'It was Tembo M'zee who ordered me not to let you pass,' Guardian replied.

'You must have heard him wrongly,' said Kidogo, trying to push past the tembull whose huge body was filling the narrow passage. 'Make way for me, *please*! Let me pass.'

'I cannot,' he replied. 'My orders were quite clear. I must *not* let you pass until M'zee tells me otherwise.'

Kidogo made one more attempt to push past him, then gave up and circled round the Mount looking for another way in, although she already knew there wasn't one.

Her dear M'zee must have been burnt by the fire that had caused all the smoke – although there was less of that now – and *that* would be why Tembo Guardian would not let her pass. There must be something she could do? If M'zee had been burnt, rain would ease his pain *and* help put out the last of the fire. If only there were other tembos outside the Mount who could linque with her. She made another circuit of the Mount and again pleaded with an unyielding Tembo Guardian to let her pass.

On the far side of the Mount, nearest to where the rim of the crater rose to a peak, she pressed her head to the smooth stones of the wall and called out, 'Rain – wet and cool – rain – bringing life to the land. Rain, rain, rain.'

She called again and again, but no rain came and she was sure her will was just not enough on its own. She stayed where she was, exhausted, her head pressed against the warm, dry stones of the wall. 'Rain, rain, rain . . .'

Inside the Mount the tembos, under the direction of Three Eyes, were taking tusks out of the caves, carrying them past M'zee, who was still lying on his side with his eyes closed, and dropping them one by one into the fire-pit. From deep down in it they could hear a rumble and a hiss as each tusk was sacrificed. But the tembos, in trying to avoid the smouldering remains of the tembo-tree and M'zee's gaunt body, were tangling with each other and in danger of falling into the pit themselves.

Watching this disorganised activity from the wall above, Moses recalled how his own people brought water up from deep wells for their cattle in times of drought. The man at the bottom of the well would fill the skin bucket and pass it up to the man above, who would pass it on and up a chain of men to the surface. If men could do this, so could elephants. He came down from the wall and went over to where the one with the burnt trunk was urging the others on.

Seeing how intently De/ne was staring into the crater, Lars felt easier about moving around on the rim. He came and stood by the Bushman and asked, 'What's happening down there?' From trying to put the crater and its inhabitants behind him, he now felt involved – and concerned.

'There is *much* happening,' the little man replied without looking up. 'The Maasai man, Moses, can see again and has gone to the Mount where fire has come out of the ground and burned up the old tree. Now he is on the wall behaving like my father used to do during a trance-dance. The elephants inside the Mount are very active but I cannot see just what they are doing, and the little female with no tusks has been trying to get inside the Mount but the Guardian elephant would not let her pass through the gap in the walls and now she is just standing with her head against the wall.'

'Should we go down and see if there's anything *we* should be doing?' Lars asked.

'No. It is a *shauri tembo* – an affair of elephants. We must allow them to do what they have to do. We can only watch.'

The Vice President had called a breakfast meeting with the Finance Director, although it was earlier in the day than either of them usually came into the office.

While his PA organised coffee and toast, he said, 'I've spoken by radio to the captain of our tanker, *The Spirit of the Age*, which is sailing through the Straits of Malacca towards Singapore. He says he *can* turn the vessel about, head back and cross the Indian Ocean to Tanzania but it will take several days to reach there, so I've told him carry on eastwards for the moment. Now I'm waiting for a call from the

American chargé d'affaires in Dar es Salaam. He's trying to find out how long it would take, after any tanker arrives, to get the refinery back on line. I also asked him about mounting a search for Walter when fuel *is* available but I think that's a lost cause. Walt's probably dead, and it would cost a fortune to turn that tanker around. I don't think the shareholders would approve. You take your coffee black, don't you?'

Three Eyes was waving what was left of his trunk, oblivious to the pain. M'zee had forgiven him for his stupidity and had trusted him enough to give him a leading role in something that needed doing, although he did not understand the reasons. It was enough that the old one trusted him again. *'You must try and do what you think Tembo Jay would do,'* M'zee had said. Could it be that simple? Is *this* what Tembo Jay would do?

The tall dark-skinned man who had been shouting from the top of the wall was now standing near him, getting in the way of the tembos carrying the tusks to the fire-pit. He was about to trump angrily at him to get out of the way, but the words of the old one came back to him again. *'You must try and do what you think Tembo Jay would do.'*

From what Three Eyes had read in his great tusks, Tembo Jay would have quietly asked the man what he wanted.

'What do you want of me?' Three Eyes asked clumsily, his speech restricted by him not having the end of his trunk, but the man clearly did not understand tembotalk anyway.

Instead, the man was making signs with his arms, pointing at the tusks that were being carried past him to the fire-pit, and trying to indicate that the tembos could pass them from one to another.

Three Eyes immediately grasped what he meant, and called a halt to the tembos' activity. He then directed them to form a line and pass the tusks from one to another as the man had suggested. It worked well and considerably speeded up the movement of the tusks from the caves to the fire-pit. He raised his trunk to touch the man's forehead in a gesture of thanks but his trunk no longer reached as far as it used to do.

Clouds had formed around the crater rim and rain was beginning to fall on Lars and De/ne, obscuring their view.

'We go down,' De/ne said tersely, moving towards the track along the rim.

'You've left your radio,' said Lars, and only then realised it had been silent for some time.

'It has died,' De/ne replied. 'And I am glad. I never liked what it was telling me. We will be happier here without it.'

A cold wind was blowing squalls of rain across the rim as they made their way along the track and down the steep path into the crater. Lars found himself wishing he was back in the shelter near a warm fire, and hurried after De/ne.

When the last of the caves were empty and all the free tusks had been dropped into the fire-pit, M'zee called to Three Eyes, who came and stood before him, once more aware of how much his trunk was hurting, although the rain felt pleasantly cool on its burnt flesh.

From where he lay, still on his side, M'zee reached up to touch the centre of the young tembull's forehead, and for the second time that day he said, 'That was well done, Tembo Three Eyes.'

M'zee lifted his head and looked around at the exhausted tembos who were standing near the walls with their trunks hanging limply.

'Tembo Three Eyes, will you send my Shadow to me?' he asked in a low voice. 'It is time for me to say *fare well.*'

Tembo Guardian left his post to find Kidogo, expecting her to have gone back to be with her friend after he had turned her away several times.

At the entrance to the gorge he found Rafiki in a state of agitation, pacing restlessly about but always keeping close to the dark opening in the cliff.

'Is the Blesséd One not here?' Guardian asked. 'Tembo M'zee wishes to say *fare well* before he steps-over.'

'I don't know where my Kidogo is, she didn't come back.'

'She was not *in* the Mount when I left it,' Guardian told him. 'I will stand guard here. You go and find Kidogo and take her to M'zee.' He had intended to add, 'Go now,' but Rafiki was already running through the rain towards the Mount, looking to left and right for any sign of his friend.

Kidogo, standing with her head pressed against the far wall of the Mount, heard him calling her but didn't move until he touched her wet back.

'Rafiki, Rafiki,' was all she could say.

'Come with me,' he said. 'M'zee is asking for you.'

She hurried after him around the walls and up the ramp, knowing she would soon be seeing the old Tembull she loved for the last time. But she was unprepared for what she did see. The ancient tembo-tree had burned to the ground, and raindrops were making little hissing sounds as they fell into the hot embers where it had once stood. Standing around the inside walls of the Mount were the other tembos who she had come to know and love. Several of them were leaning against the stone walls, obviously exhausted. She saw the empty caves and did not have to ask about the stored ivory – somehow, she knew where it had gone. On the far side, .beyond the embers of the tree, M'zee lay on his side.

Kidogo knelt beside him, touching his trunk with hers. His was already cold but his eyes were open and looking at her affectionately.

'It had to be done,' he whispered. 'Remember what Tembo Lonely told us?

'When a stone Mount ~ breathes fire and smoke
Mana will ask ~ a Gift of Love.
Tembos *give this ~ though it hurts them . . .'*

'Well, *this* is the *stone Mount* and we have made our Gift of Love. We have done what we had to do.'

Kidogo waited, but it was clear that the dying tembo had nothing more to say.

'That wasn't the end of the prophecy,' she said to him. 'There was more.

'Only the Love ~ of Tembo Jay
Can save the world ~ from human greed.'

And Kidogo then asked him gently, 'Where are the tusks of Tembo Jay?'

'I'm lying on them, and it's very painful!'

'They have to go with the others,' Kidogo told him. *'Only the Love ~ of Tembo Jay—'*

'I knew you would say that,' M'zee said, struggling to stand up.

Tembo Boy rushed to help him.

Moses had left the Mount, cold, wet and exhausted. Like Lars, he was thinking of the warmth of the fire he was sure Sarah would have built up for them at the shelter. When he reached the pool where he had washed himself earlier, he dressed in his rain-sodden clothes and walked on up the track.

Walt found he had whittled a chess king without realising what he was doing, and called over to Sarah, 'Do you play chess?'

441

'My father, Mr Fotheringay, told me about the game but he didn't have the things he needed to show me how to play it.'

'I'll make a set and teach you,' Walt said. 'Hello! Here's Moses.'

Moses walked straight to the fire and held out his hands to warm them. 'I can see again,' he declared. 'I was liken unto Saul struck blind on the road to Damascus – but now, like him, I can see again.'

The rain had stopped when De/ne and Lars reached the log bridge.

'You go on and get dry by the fire,' De/ne said. 'I would like to know what the elephants have done.'

De/ne crossed the grassland, walked up the ramp and into the circular space within the stone walls. Other than a small piece of charred root projecting from a gap in the paving, the tree had gone, leaving a circle of wet ash, and he could see that all the caves were empty. Tired-looking elephants stood around the walls and, on the far side, the elephant he knew was called Boy was helping the old bull to get up. The *shauri tembo* was still happening and he must not interfere. A flurry of rain made him step back into one of the caves – he could watch from there.

Rafiki had come to stand near Kidogo as M'zee finally got to his feet and stood there unsteadily in the lightly falling rain. Kidogo picked up one of the huge tusks of Tembo Jay, the ivory glistening with beaded raindrops, and looked at M'zee.

'You know what you have to do,' he said.

She carried the tusk to the edge of the fire-pit and as she dropped it in was almost overwhelmed by a huge sense of loss. All the stored Love of the greatest tembo who had ever

442

lived was going down the hole, to be lost from them forever.

Tembos give this ~ though it hurts them . . .

She brushed her eyes with her trunk as Rafiki picked up the other sacred tusk and stepped forward. As he did so, Kidogo heard a voice she had not heard before. It was sweet and gentle.

'Stop,' she called to Rafiki. 'Wait!'

He paused on the edge of the fire-pit, looked down into it and moved his trunk to hold the tusk more securely. Once more the wet ivory touched against his single tusk. This time, he and all the other tembos heard the voice. It was singing.

'Be kind, be gentle, and be fair
Find Joy and turn it into Love
Create enough for all to share.
When life is more than you can bear
Seek Joy and turn it into Love
Be kind, be gentle, and be fair.

When others mock – brace up and dare
They do not know the Joy of Love
Create enough for all to share.
Don't be afraid – show that you care
Teach how to turn that Joy to Love
Be kind, be gentle, and be fair.

If no one listens – don't despair
Just practise turning Joy to Love
Create enough for all to share.
The simple truth will soon be clear
*That **all** we need is Joy and Love*
Create enough for all to share
Be kind, be gentle, and be fair.'

443

Into the utter stillness and sense of wellbeing that had filled the Mount, Kidogo eventually spoke in a voice all the tembos could hear.

'Remember that song,' she said. 'And now—' She raised her trunk, and Rafiki let the second huge tusk slide over the edge of the pit.

In the silence that followed, M'zee lumbered forward.

'I come,' he said in a hollow voice. 'I come gladly, for I have heard the lost *Song of Tembo Jay* . . .'

Kidogo reached out her trunk to touch him as he passed, but the Light of Life had already left his eyes. He stepped blindly over the edge of the fire-pit and disappeared.

Moments later, a single white flame rose high into the air, flickered, and died away.

A deep sigh came from the fire-pit and the ground trembled and shook.

De/ne saw the flame and felt the ground shake under his feet, and the stones of the walls move and grind against one another. Several of the elephants trumped in alarm and he could hear the voice of the tuskless female calming them. It was time for him to go.

While sitting by the fire in the shelter, Moses had sensed the song and taken his gourd outside, where he placed it on the ground, knelt, and put his ear to it.

'Hush,' he said, holding up his hand, but he heard just the end of the song.

'Be kind, be gentle, and be fair.'

He repeated the words to himself. *'Be kind, be gentle, and be fair.'* That was all that needed to be known.

'Be kind, be gentle, and be fair.' That was a better guide for life than everything he had been taught, either as a

Maasai boy or at the Christian mission. He must go and tell this to anyone who would listen.

'*Be kind, be gentle, and be fair.*' Just that! Three simple commandments in one – '*Be kind, be gentle, and be fair.*'

CHAPTER THIRTY-EIGHT

After De/ne had left him at the bridge, Lars hesitated there, shivering in his wet clothes as he watched the little man walk so surely towards the Mount. It was quite clear what *he* wanted from life – great-grandchildren. If only Lars could be as sure of what he wanted for himself! At the top of the path that wound up through the plantation was a lovely young woman who wanted to have *his* babies. His friend, Ryan would also be there, having made his choice.

But it had been easy for Ryan, he didn't have Viking blood in his veins. Perhaps *he* didn't always want to know what was over the next ridge, what was behind the distant hill. The idea of having to stay in this one place – however peaceful and beautiful it was – horrified Lars. It would be like being in a trap or a cage, knowing one could never leave. The black clouds swept into his mind again. But then, he tried to convince himself, even Vikings settled down eventually when they found a good place to farm. And many of them had married local women.

Lars looked down at the pool below the bridge, at the purple water-lily flowers and the long-legged jacanda birds stepping from one leaf to another. A fish rose, making circular ripples that spread across the surface, and from across the crater a dove called insistently to its mate. The Joy of Life, which he'd last experienced on the walk up Kilimanjaro, flooded through him, but almost instantly was chased off again by the black clouds of doubt. He walked slowly up the path, past the cultivated area where the mealie shoots had just emerged from the ground, but he didn't see them. Before he came within sight of the shelter he slumped down on a rock. He had to find a way to escape from here! What would he say to Ryan? How could he face Sarah? Suppose De/ne did cut his tendons to prevent him leaving. . . . The little man was quite capable of doing it. He'd done it to the girls' father.

De/ne had slipped unseen from the Mount and crossed the grasslands to the bridge, pleased with the progress of at least a part of his plans. His youngest daughter Lo//te was married to Ryan and they would in time surely have children for him to love. But getting Lars to choose D/aw/a was still proving difficult. Even after the yellow-haired man had been reminded by the now-dead radio of how different the world was outside, he hadn't shown any eagerness to stay. Whereas, the no-longer-blind Maasai man and the man from America seemed in no hurry to leave. The American had even said he would stay and show him how to grow tobacco and make cigars. They could be good company for each other.

If the Maasai man wanted to leave, he would have to cut his foot—But, *no*! Without any tusks in the Mount, there was no longer any ivory to protect. The Maasai man could go now if he wanted.

De/ne paused by the mealie plot. The rain and the sunshine of the last few days had germinated the seeds, and tiny green shoots had already thrust up through the warm soil, promising a rich harvest of fat cobs within four or five moons. He was reminded of something Mr Fotheringay had taught him from the black book. Most of what he'd read out to them in the flickering firelight so long ago hadn't made much sense to De/ne but these words had stayed in his mind.

'To everything there is a season – A time to be born and a time to die – A time to plant and a time to pluck up that which is planted – A seed time and harvest – and day and night shall not cease while the Earth remaineth.'

De/ne wasn't sure if he'd got the words quite right but what they said was true. He bent and touched one of the little shoots.

Mantis was sitting upright on the highest twig of a small bush by the path. De/ne raised his hand in salute as he passed. 'Make it good for my D/aw/a,' he prayed, and Mantis' head turned to watch him as he walked on. As he rounded a bend, De/ne came upon Lars, sitting dejectedly on a rock with his back towards him.

'It is done,' De/ne said. 'All the tusks are now deep in the fires below the ground.'

Startled out of his own thoughts, Lars swung round. 'What? How? Why?' he asked.

'That is a *shauri tembo,* an affair of the elephants, not of us. And you may leave this place now, if that is still your wish. The secret we have guarded here does not need to be kept any longer – but I would ask that you do not speak of this place to others when you are gone.' There was sadness in the Bushman's voice, and Lars knew De/ne was letting go of a vital part of his hopes for the future of his family, and his People.

The full import of what had just been said finally struck him. He could leave at any time. He could leave! The clouds vanished from Lars' mind and he suddenly knew he *didn't want to go* – now that he could!

He hardly noticed the flurry of rain as he started up the track towards the shelter.

Sarah was at the top of the path, and curtsied as he approached with her grandfather following close behind. Lars held out his hand to her.

448

'Come and dry yourself by the fire,' she said, taking his hand in hers.

As Ryan and Ruth came to greet them, the ground trembled just as it had done on Kilimanjaro when Ryan and Lars had fled down the upper slopes. Birds and insects stopped calling, but resumed again a few seconds later when the sun broke out brilliantly and the earth became still again.

Kidogo felt the ground shake as she left the Mount with Rafiki at her side, both of them totally exhausted. It brought back to her memories of racing down Holy Mountain with dear old M'zee, each carrying one of the sacred tusks of Tembo Jay, and she felt sad at her double loss. But it had clearly been the will of Mana and she had played her part as well as she had been able – she could have done no more.

Together, they went to tell Tembo Guardian what had happened at the Mount. 'Do we still need to guard the entrance?' she asked, when she had told him about the great sacrifice that had been made and the rediscovery of the lost *Song of Tembo Jay*.

'We must,' he told her. 'More ivory will be brought here and, also, we still need to protect the humans and ourselves from lions and water-biters. To live without fear demands a little sacrifice from us all. I will once more be Tembo Guardian.'

A freshly animated Moses announced he was leaving the crater.

'I must go out into the highways and byways to tell people of the *Song of Tembo Jay*. It is a simple song but says all that is needed. *Be kind, be gentle, and be fair.* It is a song the whole world should hear.' He looked at De/ne. 'The secret of this place is safe with me,' he added.

449

Temba Girl was grazing fitfully by the Mount, when Tembo Boy came near. She gulped down the mouthful of grass she'd been chewing, and said, 'There is something I must tell you, Boy. Please do not be angry with me.'

'I think I know,' said Boy. You are carrying a baby in your belly – the baby of Tembo Lusty.'

'How did you know?' she asked.

'I saw you joyn with him one night near the river before the old one sent him away.'

'You do not mind?'

'Why should I? He was a fine tembull, although his thoughts were only of one thing. That is the way with most tembulls – especially when the mustdo is upon us. I am pleased for you.'

'Do you think that by now Jayne is carrying Doug's baby in *her* belly?'

'I have often wondered. Shall we go back and find out?'

Walt's PA brought an e-mail into his office, where the Vice President was trying out the Chief Executive's chair for size and comfort.

'Here's another,' she said. 'This one's from Kuwait. It says much the same thing.'

Several hours earlier, an earth tremor had passed unnoticed in the skyscraper HQ of Schwiner Enterprises Inc. in New York. Such buildings are designed to absorb such natural events and this one had only registered 3.4 on the Richter scale in the upstate geological station.

The Vice President took the paper and read it. Similar reports had been coming in from Schwiner Enterprises' various oil exploration and pumping stations for the last hour. This one read:

Following a small earthquake at 08.35 local time, all
pumps on this site ceased to flow. What samples we

*could extract from the well-heads were of the con-
sistency of jello, and were inert. Will advise further
when these have been analysed.*

The Vice President put the e-mail on the pile and shuffled
through the papers looking for the one from Alaska that had
arrived a short time before. The scary passage in that one
read:

*Early results from the laboratory indicate a tiny
change in the molecular structure of the sample but
enough to prevent it from flowing readily and igniting
in any of our tests. This seemed to have come about
at the same time as a small earth tremor occurred
here. These events may be connected.*

The Vice President fumbled for the button under Walt's
desk.

'Honey. When those slimeballs in the media get hold of
this story, all hell is going to be let loose. Will you ask all
the directors who are in the building to come up to the
boardroom?'

What could he tell them? The whole financial structure of
Schwiner Enterprises was based on oil and gas. Perhaps the
insurance would pay out – the annual premiums the corpora-
tion paid *them* were enormous. But *no*, those S-O-B's would
claim it was an Act of God. What a meaningless phrase.

Moses was striding along the path by the stream, having just
left the *Valley of the Shadow of Death* and was glad to be out
in the sunshine again. In the leather bag Ruth had made for
him there were some berries, some biltong and the stoppered
gourd that had once held *saroi* and was now full of water. He
knew he could find more food on the way.

In his head he kept hearing, '*Be kind, be gentle, and be*

fair.' And he kept repeating these words as he walked along. Truly the scales had fallen from his eyes! Here, was a wonderfully simple way of life. No more complicated and clashing beliefs, no more fear and pain, no more having to repeat things he could not really accept, no more lies – just '*Be kind, be gentle, and be fair.*'

A sound made him turn. Two elephants, who he immediately recognised as Boy and Girl, were close behind him and he stepped back to let them pass. Involuntarily, as Boy drew level with him, Moses raised his thumb in the hitchhiker's sign. Without pausing in his stride, the elephant swept him up with his trunk and sat him on his back.

The Vice President stood at the head of the boardroom table.

'Gentlemen,' he said. 'We have a problem.'

De/ne had walked down to the bridge, pausing as he passed the mealie plot. The new shoots of corn had already doubled in height since the day before, and he had half expected to see Mantis near the bright green plants but the insect was not there. Nor could De/ne see him on any of the bushes near the bridge.

He walked out over the plain, the grassland shimmering in the sunshine and the taller grasses waving in the breeze. He was enjoying the comforting feeling of knowing his plans had all worked out and that there would soon be children playing around the rock shelters again and splashing joyously in the bathing pools.

There were no elephants at the Mount as De/ne went through the entrance and prowled about the open space, peering into the empty caves. Dry ash from the burned-up tree blew about the paved area, forming little grey drifts in the sheltered corners. Then he saw Mantis. A root of the baobab tree had survived the fire and was already sending up a shoot of fresh new foliage. One day a new tree would fill the space left by the burned one.

Mantis sat upright on this shoot looking up at him with its large eyes.

'I thank you,' De/ne said as the mantis spread its wings and flew up and over the stone wall. De/ne looked briefly down the hole in the paving, gagged on the sulphurous fumes and climbed up onto the wall to breathe the purer air. Over towards the gorge entrance the two elephants he knew as Tembo Rafiki, with his single tusk ,and the tuskless female called Temba Kidogo. Beyond them, other elephants grazed the lush grasses. All was well there.

Kidogo was grazing without thinking about what she was doing. There was an ache at the base of her trunk but she put that down to having pressed so hard against the stone wall of the Mount when she was beseeching Mana to send rain – the pain would be gone in a few days. Her mind was busy on other things. She was beginning to feel the joyneed stirring within her and was glad that Tembo Lusty was not in the crater to bother her. If she *was* to joyn with any tembo she was going to make sure it was Rafiki, who had always been a true friend to her. Bearing his babies would be a Joy!

She remembered that human males and females paired up and stayed together for their whole lives. Their families were not just groups of females, which excluded males, as seemed to be the custom with Tembokind. Perhaps she could start a new tradition here in the crater where all the others appeared to hang on her every word.

Here, she felt none of the nagging fear that had so dominated her life since her mother had been killed. Here, was hope, companionship, and Joy in Life.

Rafiki stopped sweeping swathes of long grass into his mouth and looked around the crater. Tembo Guardian and

Temba Aunt were standing guard together at the entrance to the gorge and, close by them, the Sisters were feeding Three Eyes. Beyond them, Two Eyes and One Eye were grazing with the other tembas who had chosen to stay in the Place of Peace – Tembas Happy, Sweetness, and Light. How he loved these names, and this place, and his dear friend, Kidogo. Joy filled him, and finding one of her favourite plants, Rafiki plucked it with his trunk and walked over to put it into her mouth.

Kidogo raised her trunk to thank Rafiki for the little gift he was bringing her, but to her surprise he dropped the sprig. As he walked slowly towards her, he kept tilting his head from side to side apparently studying her face. Seeing the joy and love in his every movement, Kidogo murmured to herself, 'What's he looking at?'

Rafiki stopped in front of her, took her trunk-tip in his and guided it, first to her left cheek and then to her right.

On each side of her face Kidogo could feel the smooth round bud of an emerging tusk.

EPILOGUE

Did Mana fully realise the profound effect it would have on the 'civilised' world when he inspired the elephants to make their Sacrifice of Love? Dependent for so long on fossil fuels, especially oil and gas, few people had any idea how to cope with the new reality, least of all those in government.

One individual, a man in his late sixties, is jolted out of his louche life in London and decides to head west to the farm where he spent his childhood, at Chesilbury on the coast of Dorset. He records his experiences in a journal, which makes fascinating reading, as he learns to live off the land and reluctantly collects a 'family' of orphans, including an elephant, all of whom depend on his wit and resourcefulness for their very survival.

Michael Tod is currently researching and writing the first book in his new trilogy, *Chesilbury – Going Home*. He plans to follow this with *Chesilbury – Digging In* and *Chesilbury – Going Back*.